"**W**ho is your master, spy?" she hissed. "Who sent you to look upon my king's army?"

The man only gasped for breath, then attacked. He drew his knife and whirled his mace, rushing forward with a wordless cry. Exhausted as the man was, the charge was more of a lurch, which Stalker sidestepped with ease, thrusting her spearpoint into his thigh as he passed. She jerked the point free and thrust it into the back of the other thigh and the man dropped to his knees with a cry of pain. As he flung his arms out to break his fall she seized his rawhide-wrapped mace and cut its wrist thong with her knife. Before he could even think of a defense, she struck him on the back of his head, just above where the neck joined the skull. The spy collapsed bonelessly.

Smiling, Stalker set to work . . .

JOHN MADDOX ROBERTS
THE
POISONED LANDS

A TOM DOHERTY ASSOCIATES BOOK
NEW YORK

THE POISONED LANDS

A Tor Book
Published by Tom Doherty Associates, Inc.
49 West 24th Street
New York, N.Y. 10010

Cover art by Ken Kelly

ISBN: 0-812-50631-6

First edition: February 1992

Printed in the United States of America

0 9 8 7 6 5 4 3 2 1

THE POISONED LANDS

ONE

The spies lay motionless, belly-down on a crag of rock overlooking endless miles of desolation. Each was covered by a blanket mottled in gray and brown, so that they were all but invisible from just a few yards away. Only the snouts of their telescopes poked from beneath the blankets, each lens shaded by a piece of leather against the chance of casting a reflection. The rising sun was behind them, but these men took no chances. They had taken this position during the hours of darkness and had remained motionless since first light. Soon the heat beneath the blankets would be terrible but exposure meant certain death, and the scene before them was worth a day of discomfort.

"This is it in truth!" said one, his voice little more than a whisper, for there was always a chance of a roving sentry passing near. "It can be no other!"

"I am sure of it," said the cooler voice. "But calm yourself. The time for excitement is when we claim our reward."

The sight before them was enthralling only to one who could interpret its significance. In the distance a camp sprawled on the desert floor, close against the raised lip of an ancient crater. Many such craters pocked this vast desolation, but only this one was a center of human activity. Indeed, the desert was nearly void of humanity except for scattered nomads and this one, strange operation.

From the camp, files of men climbed the crater rim and descended into the depression beyond. Those in the returning files trudged under weighty loads, which they deposited somewhere in the camp. Columns of smoke rose from within the crater, but these were not volcanic in origin. Along the rim mounted sentries paced, the morning sun casting reflections from their lance points. Even with telescopes, the distance was too great to discern details of dress or equipage.

All day long the two men lay motionless, their attention sharpening at each new activity below them. The rise on which they lay was not high enough to see within the crater but they had a good view of the camp. When the sun passed zenith they put away the telescopes lest their position be betrayed by a reflection. The heat grew terrible but they endured it, sucking occasionally at their water skins.

When darkness fell, they cast off the blankets and lay gasping gratefully in the relative coolness. Moving stiffly, they rose and began to fold their blankets, packing up their telescopes, water skins and other sparse gear. Before the darkness was complete, one took a reading from a small compass. He closed the compact instrument's cover and returned it to a pocket in his outer robe.

"Look, Haffle," said the other man.

Where before only columns of smoke had been visible, they now saw a ruddy glow and ascending sparks.

"A smelting operation," said Haffle. "there can be no question of it." With his hood thrown back, he was revealed as a lean man with close-cropped black hair and a stubble of beard. The other man was of different race, short and stout, his scalp shaven on the left side. The hair on the right side was gathered into a single plait and dyed blue. Haffle picked up his spear and made to leave the crag but the other lingered.

"Ingist, we've no time to waste. Come along, we have to find our beasts before daylight."

"It's hard to believe, isn't it?" Ingist said, staring at the glow as if hypnotized. "We've found it, after men have failed all these years."

"Finding it is one thing," Haffle said. "Living to report it and collect our reward from the queen is another, so let's be away."

Reluctantly, Ingist picked up his own spear and trudged after his companion. Except for the short spears, which doubled as walking staffs, the men carried daggers at their belts but no other arms. To all appearances, they were traveling traders like hundreds of others who roamed the village-dotted farmlands along the borders of the southern kingdoms, following the small rivers and skirting the trackless waste of the desert. Popular legend filled the desert with mysteries and marvels, but these two had found little in their many expeditions except rock, sand, heat and thirst. Until this day.

They had followed hints and rumors, interrogated men who claimed to have seen this marvel, offered bribes and had even consulted seers and fortune-tellers to find this site. In the end they had found an injured workman, desperate for money to buy medicine. He claimed that he had worked for a season at the mine, and had not been fooled by the circuitous route he and the other workers had trodden. He had managed to shift his blindfold from time to time, and spot certain landmarks. The crater was not in the deep desert at all, he told them, but rather was located near the cultivated lands at the northern border of Canyon territory.

They had killed the man to prevent his telling others, and

had followed his directions to the crater that was so like the many others, except for this one unique quality. As they trudged toward the place where they had left the rest of their little caravan and their desert-traveling humpers, their hearts thrilled to the knowledge they now held. They had found the world's greatest treasure, the secret for which their queen would reward them beyond any man's wildest dreams.

They had found the steel mine of King Hael.

The heat in the crater was stifling, so that the warriors were hard put to keep their masks of imperturbability from slipping. They did not want to appear weak before the workmen, but this place tested the hardiest. In the heat they had discarded their customary skin clothing and rode in knee-length cloth breeches. Head scarves and light mantles protected them from the fierce sun. If they were lightly clothed, they were heavily armed. Each man had a great bow and a quiver bristling with arrows. Each bore a long sword of steel, and their lance points were likewise of steel. The tips of their arrows and javelins were of cheaper bronze. Their shields were of differing designs, as were the men themselves, for they were not all of a single race. They were united in their mounted way of life, despising inferior people who walked on the earth like animals.

"Three more days," said a long-haired youth to his companion. "Three more days and we can leave this furnace. I cannot tell you how sick I am of soot and smoke and the reek of these sweaty slaves."

"Not to mention the sun and the rationed water," said the other, who was slightly the younger of the two. They shared a close resemblance, both tall young men with copper-colored hair and pale blue eyes. Their high cheekbones distinguished them from the others, and each had an easy, natural grace that set them apart.

"Where will you go when the season's operation breaks up?" asked the elder, kneeing his mount up the concave side of the crater, hoping to catch some breeze up on the rim.

"Back to the grasslands and the hills, where else?" said the younger.

"Not I. I am going along with the labor escort. I want to see some of the southern towns before I return home."

"But Father has told us . . ."

"Are we boys that we must obey his every wish?" said the elder. "We are both free warriors and we need no father's permission to go where we will."

"He is more than our father, as if I need to remind you. He is also our king." They paused atop the low ridge, out of the smoke and clamor.

"And as such he has never forbidden free warriors to go where they will in peacetime, as long as they don't take military service with a foreign king without his permission. I just want to travel a little and see some new sights. To tell you the truth, I am almost as weary of grass and livestock as I am of this desert."

The other looked doubtful. "I don't know. He was reluctant just to have us both away from home on this mission. It worries him that he might lose both of us."

His brother smiled wryly. "Kairn, he cherishes the hope that one of us will someday succeed him, but you and I know that is not to be. The council of chiefs will pick some-one else. Father is the great spirit-man, the unifier of plain and hill. What are we? Just warriors like any others. We lack the spirit-force that made him like a god to the tribes. I am not prepared to spend my life near home, indulging his fond hopes for my future."

Kairn was silent. He lacked his elder brother's easy self-assertion and the thought of disobeying their father troubled him. The scene below them was busy, but the clamor of the previous weeks had ceased and the sound of sledge, pick and wedge no longer assaulted the ears. The workers were cleaning up the site and the last of the freed metal was being melted in the furnaces to free it of the last bits of concrete matrix. The molten steel was then cast into ingots for easy transportation. Prodigious effort was expended each year to bring fuel, supplies and laborers to this site, but steel was so valuable that King Hael bore the expense gladly.

Around the rim of the crater, mounted men patrolled constantly. Workers were not allowed to ascend to the rim save where the path notched its edge. They were allowed only in the crater and the camp. Any who were caught trying to get to high ground to spot landmarks were assumed to be spies and punished accordingly.

"Well, what do you say?" urged the elder brother.

"Don't press me, Ansa. This will take some thought. We have three days yet."

"During which time you will decide to remain a dutiful son, no doubt. Well, you may do as you like. I am riding south as soon as the season ends."

Kairn was thoughtful as they rode back to their tent at the end of the day. It vexed him to admit that he lacked an adventurous spirit. He was almost eighteen, and had been a warrior for more than two years. Perhaps it took more than fine weapons and a cabo to ride to make a warrior. He patted the beast's neck and it tossed its handsome, four-horned head proudly. All around him exhausted workers trudged toward their pallets. These were short, dark men, strongly built but without the fierce poise of the mounted warriors.

Kairn shuddered at the thought of leading such a life, toiling on the land or at some other equally ignoble labor instead of riding free across the endless plain. Surely, he thought, he would die before living like that. These were the stolid peasants of the southern lands, for whom his desert was just a hotter, drier place to work. They endured the hardship in return for generous pay, half of which would be claimed by their sovereigns. They deserved no better, he supposed. Men so spiritless that they would not fight should be grateful for any crumbs dropped to them from the tables of their betters.

He curried his cabo and turned it loose in the circular compound walled with piled rock. With a happy snort it trotted to the watering trough. Every drop was laboriously brought from the nearest river in wagon-mounted casks. The animals got as much as they needed. Men had to make do with less. There were more than three hundred of the creatures in the pen, each animal's horns painted with the distinctive colors and patterns favored by its rider.

Under the shade of the open-sided tent, the temperature was just bearable. The half-dozen warriors within made space for Kairn, but they paid him no special deference. The riders did not understand royalty as it was practiced in more settled nations. He was passed a water skin and he took a handful of dried food from a communal bowl. As he munched the tasteless mixture of pounded dried meat, fruit and parched grain, he thought of the cities of the south.

He had never seen them, but he had heard his father's stories of the fabulous lands to the west and south. Older warriors who had fought in the king's wide-ranging campaigns had described the sumptuous cities, their temples and public buildings, their strange entertainments and their women who (in the warrior's stories) always seemed to prefer virile nomads to their effete, civilized menfolk. He felt the tug of attraction, a curiosity to see those places, but he also loved the boundless plain. He wanted to see the exotic cities, but maybe next year would be soon enough, or the year after.

Not so his elder brother. Ansa talked of little else than travel in foreign lands. He had ridden on a few caravan escorts to the borders of Omia to the west and the Canyon territory to the south, and this had whetted his appetite for more. For the last two years he had fretted to be away, but their father had sent few missions in that direction recently, being preoccupied with the east.

No, he would return home at the end of this season. It would be good to be away from this place.

The laborers sang as they left the crater behind. They wore tunics or kilts that had once been white and most wore head scarves or conical hats of woven straw. The hornlike soles of their feet seemed to be immune to the heat of the desert floor, and their teeth flashed white in their dark faces.

Ansa turned for the last time and waved. From the rim of the crater, his brother waved back. Then Ansa set his face to the south and sternly suppressed any further sentimental gestures. He cursed his younger brother's timidity and lack of enterprise. Ansa longed to roam free, but he would have liked company. The brothers had been close all their lives, especially these last few years, when their father had grown so preoccupied with the easterners and their fire-weapons.

But they were boys no longer, he reminded himself. And had King Hael not begun his career in this very fashion? Early in his life Ansa had wearied of the story of how his father had come across the mountains with the first trade caravan from Neva, owning a spear, a knife, a longsword and a single cabo. Now he was a king. But then, his father was a great visionary, a man touched by the spirits.

In any case, Ansa had no ambitions to be a king. He just wanted to sample life away from his familiar world of hills and grasslands. As a boy he had been impatient and argumentative, unlike his younger brother. He had pushed himself to excel in the warrior arts and had suffered agonies of frustration at each slightest failure. A fall at wrestling, which Kairn could laugh off, would cause Ansa to sulk for days. He was long past such childish moods, but he yearned to test himself and he saw no sense in waiting.

He fretted at the slow pace of the march. Not only did they have to travel at the pace of walking men, but the route was tortuous, with many circlings and switchbacks. At intervals the workers were blindfolded or made to march after dark. He knew that it was necessary to keep the men from understanding where they had been, thus keeping secret the location of the crater, but it was galling to spend ten days on a march that could have been accomplished in two.

Ansa could have wept with joy on their final day in the desert. The breeze carried the scent of water and growing things. All up and down the file of mounted guards the cabos made their strange, rumbling sound of happy anticipation. Ansa reined in his mount as it tried to break into a run. He patted its neck and leaned toward its ear.

"Easy, my pet. We're still miles from the river. No sense running now. We'll be there before nightfall." He felt like running himself.

They camped that night near the first river of the Canyon territory. It was a small stream, but after the desert it was a blessing and they had to watch the cabos carefully lest they drink too much and founder. The workers were scarcely less thirsty and they rushed down the muddy bank to sprawl on their bellies, sucking up the now-murky liquid in prolonged draughts. The warriors showed more self-control, first allowing their mounts to drink, then wading upstream to clearer water before leaning from their saddles to dip from the stream with wooden bowls.

The natives who inhabited nearby villages had long grown accustomed to these visitations, and soon traders appeared with such goods as they knew these visitors craved. Fresh foods and strong drink were in high demand. The village women were ill-favored by nomad standards, but some were not so discriminating and they found many eager customers among the workmen, who were happy to spend their pay before the tax-gatherers took it.

Ansa sat at the fire with some other warriors, eating and drinking and talking endlessly, after the immemorial fashion of off-duty warriors. The tender meat of fat domestic animals was a great luxury to them, after weeks of tough game or dried rations. The king periodically issued stern injunctions against overindulgence in wine and beer, which were scarce in their homeland, although more common now that they traded so widely. His subjects agreed that these were wise rules and proceeded to ignore them every chance they got.

"We'll stay here for ten days," said Bulas, an older Matwa warrior who was in command of the mission. "The cabos can eat and drink and fatten up in that time."

"So can we," said a younger man, his voice unsteady with drink.

"I won't be returning with you," Ansa said.

Bulas peered at him through the smoke. "What do you mean?"

Ansa took another swallow of the pleasantly bitter beer. "I mean to stay here and push south. I'll rejoin you at the crater next year or the year after."

"That would be unwise," Bulas said. "You may be taken prisoner and tortured to reveal the site of the steel mine."

Ansa shrugged. "I'll claim to be from one of the southeastern peoples, a Ramdi or Ensata. Foreigners will never know the difference. Even if they've been on missions to our territory, my brother and I don't much resemble the Amsi or Matwa."

"How will you be able to bear it?" asked an Amsi his own age. "To be alone in a foreign land, without kinsman or tribesman is terrible. If you are sick or wounded, who will guard you? If you die, who will perform the rites?"

"I'll take my chances," Ansa said. "You accomplish nothing if you take no risks." Then, after a pause, "I confess, though, that I would as soon not travel alone. Will any of you accompany me?" He looked from one to another, but their expressions were doubtful. He had not expected otherwise. The tribesmen were profoundly conservative. His father's merging of the peoples had been shock enough to last a generation, and they were reluctant to face any further innovations. They loved to roam widely, but only in large, strong groups. In the end, he found no volunteers.

A few days later he rode from the campsite. His mount had regained its sleekness and spirit and was eager for travel. He bade his companions farewell with a light heart, but as soon as he was beyond sight of them, he felt his stomach tighten with trepidation. Until now, he had put up a brave show, but the reality of what he was doing gave him pause. He was now alone in a way he had never experienced before. He shook himself and thrust the mood aside. He had chosen his path and he would pursue it, come what may.

By midday his dread was gone and he found himself singing an old Amsi traveling song. As he passed people working in the fields flanking the road, they glanced up but paid him no special note. He wore short boots and baggy trousers of light cloth girdled by a broad leather belt. He wore a shirt and a light cloak against the still fierce sun, and his ornaments he had acquired as gifts or from traders over the years. No one could have named his nation by his appearance and he was just another anonymous traveler, as he had intended.

Even his steel weapons would not identify him as one of King Hael's subjects. The lively trade in steel meant that weapons of the precious metal were no longer as rare as they had been. His steel longsword, still a rarity outside Hael's dominions, would not be apparent unless he had to draw it, at which time he would not be worrying about revealing his nationality.

He followed the river as it wound through the cultivated land, and occasionally he crossed oddly straight streams branching from the river. At first he thought these were natural but soon he realized that they were irrigation ditches. The land was so arid that only by tapping water from the river could agriculture be sustained. He knew that somewhere to the south this tributary would join the great River Kol.

This was Canyon land, but the local farmers were a peasant people related to the laborers he had escorted from the pit. The true Canyon dwellers formed an aristocracy, very mysterious and credited by most people with great powers of sorcery. He had never seen any of these strange folk, for they never traveled far from their own land and always traded through intermediaries. Of all the foreign peoples he had heard of, these intrigued him the most. It was not because of their sumptuous cities, for their land was poor in material goods. It was because of their rumored powers and their sheer strangeness. It was said that their skins were blue, their hair white, and their eyes a veritable rainbow of colors. They were not particularly warlike, but no army had ever managed to advance against them, though many had tried. All such invasions turned back, generals and soldiers alike swearing they had been defeated by sorcery.

He was curious to meet these people, of whom his father had spoken frequently. He did not travel in expectation of meeting hostility. Most people reacted to a lone traveler with curiosity or disdain but seldom with mindless aggression. Isolated people usually wanted contact from outside, as long as it represented no danger, and cosmopolitan people took strangers in their midst as a matter of course. It was large, heavily armed groups entering their territory that alarmed most people.

He longed to take some game with his bow, but he was unsure whether some local landlord might object. The thought of going back on preserved rations irked him, but he knew he had best proceed cautiously. The first night, he camped by the little river and watched the black-scarred face of the moon rise over the low mountain range to the east. Through his mind went the chant of apology to the moon that his father recited most evenings at moonrise, but he did not voice it aloud. Men had wounded the moon long ago, in the days of the fiery spears. Those had been times of great and terrible sorcery, and men had been struck down for their presumption. Each people had a different tradition concerning how this had come about, but all agreed that men had brought the terrible times upon themselves, bringing an end to what had been a golden age of wealth and plenty.

The night grew chill as the heat of the day dissipated into the cloudless air, but he did not bother to build a fire. The stars were brilliant, the fixed stars and the wanderers and the ones that rose and sped across the sky and set at odd intervals. It was held by some that these latter were manmade, that in the days before the fiery spears people had actually lived on these tiny islands in the sky. Of all the old legends he found this one the most difficult to credit, but if men had truly been able to assault the moon with fiery spears, perhaps they had been able to build villages in the sky as well. The world was full of mysteries and he knew he would not solve this one. After a last check to make sure all was well with his cabo, he rolled into his blankets and slept.

His dreams were troubled, with vague, menacing faces, flashes of lurid fire and boundless, roiling waters. He woke once sweating, then slept again. By morning he remembered little of his night-visions, but he was uneasy as he rose and saddled his animal.

By his fourth day of lone travel, he was in high, forested land. There was little cultivation, but peasants grazed flocks of a sort of dwarf curlhorn, and wild game abounded. It was a place of astonishing beauty, its craggy hills and gullies revealing brilliant colors laid on in wide, horizontal streaks. The day before, there had been a brief but intense rain, and this day the ground was a carpet of riotous wildflowers that had appeared as if by magic. The sky was a blue even deeper than usual, and the clouds formed towers and ramparts of the purest white. It was a setting to put song in a man's heart and in his voice, so he sang as he rode, a wandering-lay of his mother's people, far more melodious than the Amsi chants.

As his surefooted cabo picked its way daintily along a trail with a high rock on one side and a precipitous gorge on the other, Ansa realized that he was singing a duet. Shocked, he stopped in midnote. The other voice continued for another two notes, then trailed off. The only direction that made sense was up, so he craned his neck and saw a vague shape on the rock above him. With the sun behind it he could make out no details.

"Who are you?" he demanded, chagrined that he had come so near another human being without noticing. He soothed his vanity with the thought that this was unfamiliar terrain.

"Oh, don't stop singing, please! It's such a pretty song."

The muscles of his back unclenched and his hand dropped away from his spearshaft. It was a feminine voice, youthful but beautifully modulated.

"You still haven't told me who you are," he reiterated.

"Why should I?" she said. "This is my land, not yours." Her accent was strange, but he had no trouble understanding her.

"You are right." He smiled, but the effect was marred by the way he was forced to squint. "I'm Ansa, from the northern plains. But you have me at a disadvantage. I can't see you up there."

"We can remedy that. Ride on another hundred paces, until you are off the path and in a little meadow. I'll join you there. Don't try to ride farther without me." Then the shape was gone.

He rode on, and a few minutes later the path ascended slightly, leaving the cliffside and entering the level, grassy meadow the woman had described. He halted and let his cabo graze the soft, luxuriant grass. His expert eye told him that nothing had grazed this place in quite some time. There were marks of many animals, but most of them were browsers or predators.

A few minutes later the woman joined him. She, too, was mounted, but not on a cabo. His own animal shied and made hoarse grunts of dislike as the other beast approached. It was a humper, a superlatively ugly beast, foul-smelling, ill-tempered and graceless, but strong and tremendously enduring. They were far better adapted for desert travel than cabos.

The rider was swathed in a gray robe, her head covered by its hood and her face veiled. She halted a pace from Ansa and lowered her hood and veil. Her face was long and fine-boned, as beautiful as he had been led to expect, but he found that the reality was far more striking than even his expectations. Her skin was a delicate shade of blue, her eyes had violet irises, rimmed with emerald. Her hair was white, not the white of great age but rather an almost metallic silver-white. The hands with which she pushed back the hood were thin and elegant, the fingers impossibly long.

"I am Fyana, of Alta and the Canyon." Her wide, full-lipped mouth formed a smile, and he smiled in return. "I had watch duty on this trail this morning, but I don't think I need to raise an alarm for you."

"No, I assure you I'm not that dangerous. But, do your people usually entrust a sentry-post to a single woman?"

"I have more resources to call on than you might think," she said. "Besides, that little path is not much of an invasion route."

"I can vouch for the truth of that," Ansa said. "But then, why keep watch over it at all?"

"We don't like to be surprised, even by friendly visitors," Fyana told him. This was valuable information, although she might not think so. The Canyoners were not all-seeing, as some people thought. He wanted very much to know their limitations.

"We see few plainsmen this far south," she said, "and never wandering alone. Have you lost your way?"

"Not at all. I was bored at home and wished to see new lands. My—king doesn't discourage foreign travel, as long as his warriors do not take warlike service with other kings. All my life I have heard of the southern lands, and of the Canyon. I resolved to visit some of these places before war or old age put an end to all travel for me."

"Here comes my relief." Fyana pointed to the other end of the little meadow. Another rider came into sight, this one mounted on a cabo. As the rider drew near, Ansa saw that it was a young man. His hair was darker than Fyana's, and his eyes were yellow, but the resemblance was otherwise so great that they might have been twins. The voluminous robe he wore left only head and hands exposed. It was by his bearing that Ansa knew him to be a man rather than a woman. He balanced a long lance in a stirrup socket as he drew rein a few paces from them.

"Who is this?" he asked, eyeing Ansa from head to foot.

"A visitor from the north," she informed him. He showed none of her open friendliness. "He is no threat."

"Best he were not." He rode past them, to take up his sentry-post.

Inwardly, Ansa fumed. At home, he would have called the youth out for such insolence. Here, he knew, he had no such right. "Is he so hospitable to everyone?" he asked.

"Pay him no heed," she advised. "That is Elessi. He is a new-made warrior, and wants everyone to know how fierce he is."

"You have that sort here, too? Then I'll give the matter no more thought. Junior warriors new to their arms can be a nuisance, but they always attack from the front, else how are they to build a reputation? Now, will you guide me to your village? Or had you further business out here in the wilderness?"

"Nothing of importance. Just follow me." She turned

the humper and set off at a stately, racking gait. Ansa's cabo, full of suspicion, followed the larger animal at a distance Ansa could not force it to reduce, no matter how hard he tried.

A ride of less than an hour brought them to a small valley, its floor patterned with tilled fields, neatly bordered by low stone walls. Lovingly tended orchards ranked their trees on sloping ground, some fruiting, others in full blossom. Ansa had a low opinion of agriculture, but he could not deny the beauty of the scene. The air was fragrant as well, a welcome change from the dry sterility of the desert.

At the far end of the valley, he could see a cluster of buildings erected up the sides of the narrowing gorge, whence issued a small but swift-flowing stream. The structures blended naturally with the canyon, but the walls were white, and the roofs of baked red tile. It was far more attractive than the mud-walled villages he was used to.

They passed a few outlying farmhouses. Apparently, there were some who were willing to trade the safety of town walls for the convenience of living near their fields. Then Ansa noticed that the village had no surrounding wall. For whatever reason, these people were extremely confident in their safety from attack.

Diminutive livestock scattered before them as they rode into the dusty streets of the village; tiny, domestic quil, poultry and a fat, bipedal lizard raised for its meat. All were scavengers and they helped to keep the village clean. Villagers regarded the newcomer with curiosity, but he saw no hostility in their looks.

"I will take you first to the Elder," Fyana said. "It's customary. She will grant you the freedom of the village and then you may come or go as you like."

"That suits me well," Ansa said. He found that he liked this; being in a strange land, among alien people. Most of his tribesmen would have found the situation discomfiting, but Ansa had always known he was different in this.

They halted before a small house, one no different from the others. Its doorway was flanked with two statues. In stylized form they represented a man and a woman. Fyana's humper knelt and she slid from her saddle. She made a perfunctory bow to each image, then went inside. Ansa dismounted and stood looking about him. There was no place to tether his cabo except to one of the statues, and he felt that it would be unwise to do that, so he held his reins and stood awkwardly, waiting for something to happen.

A few minutes later, Fyana reemerged from the house, followed by a taller woman who wore a striped robe. She placed her fingertips together and bowed slightly.

"Welcome, warrior. I am Ulla, Elder of this village. Will you come inside? Imasa will see to your cabo." At these words, a boy appeared at Ansa's elbow. Ansa regarded him doubtfully.

"Thank you, but this is a spirited beast. Perhaps an experienced rider . . ."

She smiled. "Imasa is an excellent cabo handler. Have no fear."

He placed the reins in the boy's hand and the cabo was led away, docile as one of the fat little quil in the streets. Ansa shrugged and followed the two women into the cool, dim interior of the house. The furnishings were sparse, but the floor and walls were covered with rich carpets. There were no windows, but light entered through skylights of thick glass. At Ulla's gesture, the three seated themselves on embroidered pads placed around a low table of carved and inlaid wood. The other two said nothing, so Ansa held his silence as well.

A young girl appeared from a rear room bearing a tray that held a steaming pitcher and cups. Fyana poured the hot liquid into cups. Ansa took one and sipped at it, watching the others closely. He was familiar with this sort of welcoming ritual, but each people possessed local customs and he did not want to give offense. The drink was a fragrant herb infusion. When he set the emptied cup on the table the women seemed satisfied that the ceremony was complete and Ulla called for more substantial refreshments.

Ansa studied the woman. Fyana had called her an Elder, but she appeared to be little older than Fyana herself. Like everything else, it seemed age was difficult to discern among these people. She had the same silver hair and blue-tinged skin, but her eyes were pale gray.

"Fyana tells me that you have left your native plains to see the world, from a spirit of adventure."

"I grew restless at home," he concurred.

"And how is the king, your father?"

He blinked and bit back a denial, knowing it would be futile. "So it is true, then, that you have magical powers?"

She laughed musically. "No need for magic. I met your father some years ago, at a trade fair. His physiognomy is quite distinctive, and you resemble him. I knew that he has sons about your age. Hence, you must be one of them. Have no fear. King Hael has been a good friend to us, and if you wish to travel incognito, we will not reveal your secret. South of here, you are unlikely to meet anyone who knows what your father looks like."

"That is a relief. In answer to your question, he does well, indeed, although I have seen little of him lately. He travels much in the east, in recent years." He left unspoken the thought that had gnawed at him for years; that his father was *obsessed* with the east, with the fire-weapons and other strange crafts of the easterners. His life had become an endless quest to maintain his military edge over his old enemy, Gasam the Shasinn.

"Yes, he has not been seen with the trade missions in some time," Ulla said.

"Do not think, because of that, he values the Canyon less," Ansa said, seeing a chance to exercise a little diplomacy on his father's behalf. "He counts you among his most valued friends."

"The Canyon lies between the plains and the southern kingdoms," she pointed out. Then, softening, "But, I know that King Hael would be our friend even if we weren't a buffer between him and his enemies."

"But Sono and Gran aren't his enemies," Ansa pointed out.

"They soon may be," Ulla said. "Gasam has taken Chiwa, and he will not be satisfied with that land alone. Surely he will try to take the other southern nations soon." She regarded him with some concern. "Perhaps this would not be a good time for you to be wandering in those lands. Stay here with us. There is much to see in the Canyon territory."

"And I wish in time to see it all," he said. "But my heart is set on seeing the great cities before Gasam destroys them all. Besides," he said, an idea forming in his mind, "if the situation in those lands is precarious, all the more reason for one loyal to my father to observe and report to him."

"That is true," the Elder said. "But there is no hurry. Tarry a while here with us."

He looked from her to Fyana. This, at least, was an easy decision to make. "That I shall."

TWO

King Gasam sat on the terrace of his palace in the city of Hima. He had chosen this beautiful mountain resort as his capital because it was so beautiful, and because he had utterly destroyed the old capital in his conquest of Chiwa. In the broad plaza that stretched before his terrace, a contingent of the native slave-troops drilled. The company he now watched was drawn from the wild jungle tribes of the southern hills, men clad in colorful skins, heavily tattooed, armed with flint-tipped spears and hide shields. He liked their looks and spirit. The peasant-conscripts drawn from the nearby villages were obedient and militarily valuable, but they were not true warriors and they filled him with contempt. He had made a practice of forming as many units as possible from the most ferocious warrior peoples in his broad dominions. War, after all, was not simply a process aimed solely at success. It was an enterprise to be enjoyed, savored for its beauty as well as its excitement.

He breathed deep of the incense smoke wafting from the braziers set atop the stone rail. Behind him stood his queen, kneading the heavy muscles of his shoulders and neck. He sighed with contentment, then winced as something plucked at his hair.

"Another one!" Queen Larissa said triumphantly, holding a long, gray hair before his eyes.

"My queen," he said, patiently, "how often have I told you that a few gray hairs are no disgrace when one has achieved elder's years? I am not yet forty years of age, and decrepitude is still many years away."

"Nonetheless," she maintained, "our people look up to us as idols of perfection. We cannot appear to be less."

He sighed. "You still do not understand the beauty of absolute power. The greatest satisfaction is in knowing that, even when you are old, ugly and diseased, people *still* must crawl before you and worship you as a god."

"You will see," she said, unanswerably. The queen walked to the railing and looked out over the city, where smoke rose from the high temples. The king had allowed the human sacrifices to continue, as long as none of his truly valuable human livestock was wasted and he was among the gods thus worshipped. He admired his queen's graceful beauty, although he deplored what he considered to be her obsessive concern with her appearance. This morning she wore a wrap of scarlet silk from armpits to knees. Just a few years before, she seldom bothered to wear clothing, considering her dazzling beauty to be raiment enough. Now she fretted over the tiniest evidence of sagging or wrinkling, imperfections invisible to him and, he was sure, to anybody else. She was still the most beautiful woman he had ever seen.

"I received another letter from Queen Shazad," she informed him.

"Ah. How fares our esteemed neighbor of the north?" The formidable queen of Neva had provided him with a long and amusing struggle for domination of the coastal nations. Her naval reforms and diplomatic maneuvers had kept him confined to the south for years.

"Sublimely polite, as always," Larissa said. "She calls me 'sister queen' and gushes on as if we were the oldest and best of friends."

"In a way you are," Gasam said. "Enemies make the most interesting of friends. Yours has been a complicated relationship. She was once your slave, after all."

"I no longer remind her of that. It was a circumstance of war, and she never thought herself a slave, only a prisoner." The queen rested her elbow on the railing, cupped her chin in a palm and stared into the distance. "She was such a lovely creature. I wish I could have kept her."

"So do I," Gasam said, ruefully. "Between them, that woman and my wretched foster-brother, Hael, have prevented me from ruling the world by now."

"Perhaps," the queen said, still dreamily abstracted. "But the world has turned out to be a far larger place than we had imagined, when we started out."

"True," Gasam said. "And, if I had it all in my hands by now, what would I do with the rest of my life?" He grinned at his queen. Leaning forward thus, she presented him with a bottom as beautifully rounded as it had been when she was a girl on their home island, although he could never convince her of it. He rose and stood beside her, wrapping a long arm around her waist.

"What else did she say?"

Larissa frowned in thought. "That her cousin, the new king of Omia, is as foolish as the old king, that black silk gowns sewn with pink pearls are the fashion this year, that her army is now being equipped with steel weapons."

"Just like her to slip that in," Gasam said. He twisted his fingers in her ash-blond hair, relishing its silky feel. "Where is he getting it, Larissa? How does a chieftain over grassland nomads like Hael lay his hands on so much of the

most precious metal in the world?'' It was a question that
had plagued him for years.

"My spies have narrowed it to the southern quarter of
the desert, on the fringes of the Poisoned Lands and to the
north of Canyon territory.''

"Still a vast area, and waterless. Without the exact location, even the best-mounted military expedition could end
in catastrophe. I dare not risk such a thing. My men follow
me fanatically, but their enthusiasm would melt if my reputation for invincibility were to suffer.''

"It is good that you remember that, my love,'' said the
queen, straightening. "Leave the delusions of godhood for
your tame poets to rave about. It has been courage coupled
with craft and cunning that have brought you thus far.'' She
looked out over the beautiful city, its surrounding farmlands
and the smoking mountain in the distance. "And you have
come far, indeed.''

All this had once been the great kingdom of Chiwa. Some
years before, Gasam had sailed hither as a roving pirate-
king, the man who had unified the northern islands of the
Stormlands and looked to extend his conquests to the mainland. He had taken a few southern islands and had entered
into an alliance with the king of Chiwa to overrun some of
that monarch's petty rivals in the islands and on the mainland to the southeast. Then, pleased with Gasam's service,
he had employed the island warriors to put down rebellion
in his own provinces. Before long, Gasam had warriors all
over the kingdom and had no further use for the king, whom
he disposed of. There had been some necessary bloodletting among the former aristocracy, but the people had given
him little trouble. They were accustomed to tyrants.

It was a beautiful and colorful land, although he did not
like the tropical climate of the lowlands. That was another
reason for establishing his capital in the mountains. Here
the air was mild and clear, the flowers grew in rich profusion, and his warriors and their livestock stayed healthy.

These days, he only went coastward to make naval forays. His ambitions now lay to the east. The rich, indolent jungle kingdoms of Sono and Gran beckoned. It would mean tropical campaigning, which he did not relish, but he intended to conquer the world before he should die, and these kingdoms were near.

The king stood and the bodyguard ranked behind his chair snapped to attention. These were tall, golden warriors of the Shasinn elite. They bore beautiful spears of bronze edged and tipped with steel and their long shields were black. They were vain of their looks and wore numerous ornaments. They were equally vain of their courage and scorned armor.

"Come with me," he said to his queen. "I want to show you something." His arm about her shoulders and hers around his rocklike waist, they entered the palace.

The walls of the great throne room were covered with brilliantly colored murals in the garish Chiwan style. Native priests in elaborate feather headdresses bowed as the royal couple entered. Slaves of many races busied themselves with their assigned tasks or stood decoratively. Some were chosen solely for beauty and served no other purpose than to grace the court and provide a pleasing setting for the king and queen. Gasam dismissed all but the bodyguard and the others filed out, bowing.

When they were gone, he turned his attention to the floor. It was covered with mosaic, an intricate map depicting the world as it was known. The stylized art of the Chiwans was not up to this task, so Gasam had imported a team of Nevan artisans and cartographers to accomplish it. The king paced along his own domains, which were figured in black. These comprised a wide crescent beginning with the northernmost islands of the western sea, proceeding southward and then curving to the east onto the mainland, devouring the old kingdom of Chiwa and a number of its smaller subject kingdoms. The black tide ceased at a mountain range figured in crystal. East of the mountains stretched the river valley kingdom of Sono and beyond that the high plateau of Gran. Gasam paced to the line of crystal and stopped.

"My warriors have been idle all year and that is not good. Lands remain unconquered and that is not proper. I propose to correct these things. My scouting teams have completed their reconnaissance of this mountain chain. There are three passes," he indicated their locations with a toe, "that offer good conditions for a marching army. I shall lead my army to a new conquest. I send out the summons today."

The queen studied the map. "Through the mountains? Would a naval invasion not be less hazardous as well as speedier?"

"I intend to send a naval force, mainly Chiwan soldiers, to seize the ports. But the south coast is pestilential, with many diseases we have never encountered. I would lose more warriors to sickness than to battle."

He returned his attention to the mountains. "Anyway, an arduous, hard-marching campaign will be good for my men. Nothing is worse for them than a long peace, and a quick, easy war is not much better. All of these passes have been used for centuries for purposes of trade as well as war. They are well marked and my scouts know all the towns, watering holes and resources along the way. No single pass is capacious enough for my entire army. I shall march through all three. I shall take the northern force. Two of my best generals will take the other two. I will march through the pass and sweep all before me until I reach the great river. There I shall turn south and link up with the other two forces. Whatever Sonoan forces lie between us we shall crack like nuts in a vise. Once united, we'll cross the river and march on the capital."

"An ambitious plan," the queen said. "But, to divide your forces thus, is that wise?"

"It may not be wise, but it is audacious," the king said. "No man has ever done such a thing before. The armies will maintain contact by mounted messengers.'' The king maintained an expert corps mounted on the swiftest animals, small, enduring men drawn from the subject peoples.

"How long a campaign do you propose?'' Larissa asked. She knew better than to suggest that he might fail.

"One season. We march as soon as the rains let up, in about twenty days. I intend to be seated on the throne of Sono before they start again, with you seated beside me.'' He smiled and she came into his arms. "As soon as I have Sono pacified, I shall march on Gran, and then the south will be mine.''

"And after that?'' she asked.

He pointed to the great map. "Then it will be time to look northward. A march northward on a broad front will envelop the Canyon and that will bring us to the edge of the great desert. Somewhere in there, we will find Hael's steel mine. A desert war will take careful preparation, but the prize is the greatest in the world. With that source of steel in my hands, the rest of the world will fall into them as well.''

"Ah, my love, you dream greatly,'' the queen said. "Unlike other men, you make your dreams come true. But . . .'' For the first time, uncertainty entered her voice.

"What is it?''

"The Canyon. There is said to be great magic there. No army has ever conquered it.''

"What of that?'' said the king with a contemptuous snort. "In our home islands, the first thing I did was crush the spirit-speakers, and what good did their curses and maledictions do them? Sorcery is nothing but mummery to gull the foolish. It is deeds that rule the world. Desert villagers with no army to speak of will grind beneath my heel as readily as any others, however loudly they chant their spells.''

"Yes, you are right, my lord. You always are. But let me send my spies thither, to find out what they may.''

He shrugged. "Why not. All knowledge is valuable and the area is poorly mapped. The spies are yours as always, my queen, but heed me in this: Send well-traveled, experienced men, such as will not be fooled by conjurer's tricks and do not believe every foolish thing they hear. I want absolutely reliable information. They are to make a clear distinction between what they see with their own eyes and what they merely hear."

"Most of my spies are just such men," the queen said. "But I shall give them special instructions. Have my intelligence reports ever failed you?"

"Never, little queen," he admitted readily. "It is just that, in this case, we will be dealing with a place and a people where men are already predisposed to believe fantastic things."

"I shall take that into account, my lord." It was for this quality that she most admired her husband. Courage, intelligence, ambition and ruthlessness had helped, but it was this great clarity of thought that set him apart from other men. This quality of mind had transformed him from a humble warrior-herdsman in the islands to an all-powerful conqueror for whom glittering thrones were playthings.

"See to it."

In a receiving room adjacent to her quarters, the queen met with her intelligence officers. This activity was hers alone. The planning and execution of campaigns was the sole province of the king. He knew that accurate intelligence was utterly vital but he had no taste for the work. She had, and his trust in his queen was without reservation.

She sat at the head of a long table. Down its length sat a dozen men, most of them traveling merchants of the sort who could fare anywhere without arousing suspicion. Two were Palana, members of a wandering, stateless people who made their way in the world as small traders and entertainers. The two Palana wore gold rings through pierced ears and noses. The ear and nose rings were connected by thin chains from which hung tiny bells.

"My servants," the queen began, "my lord the king desires of you certain intelligence, such as you have provided so satisfactorily in the past." She looked from one man to another, and each bowed in token of her utter authority.

"The nations of Sono and Gran," she continued, "have been well reconnoitered and my lord is well pleased with your service in these places. Now he wishes to know about the lands lying to the north of there, the Canyon and the desert waste beyond, the so-called Poisoned Lands."

"My lady," said one, a man with a forked beard dyed green, "traders frequent those lands, but usually they attend the seasonal fairs. The populations are sparse, and an unusually large number of traders, prying into unaccustomed parts of the land, might arouse suspicion."

"I have thought of this," Larissa said. "If asked, you need merely say that you are looking for steel, that King Gasam greatly desires more of the metal and has offered premium prices for it. That is sufficient reason to send traders scouring the land for new sources. It is both sensible and legitimate."

"What, precisely, is it that you want, my queen?" asked a gray-bearded man with a sharp nose. He was richly dressed in the robes of a master merchant.

"First of all, the usual intelligence necessary to an army: the exact location of every last village, populations, water sources, grazing land, cultivation and so forth. Any other resources of interest such as minerals, livestock, hunting areas or people with special skills. Seasonal oddities that might help or hinder a marching army, when the grass is high enough for grazing, streams with a tendency to flood, that sort of thing. And I need maps, accurate maps."

"This we can do as a matter of course," the gray-bearded man said.

"My queen," said one of the Palana, his bells jingling softly, "the Canyoners . . ."

"What about them?" she said sharply.

"Well, they are said to possess magic." He glanced at the others nervously. "Powerful magic."

"I do not believe this," she said, only half-truthfully. She did not fully share her husband's scepticism. "However, if they possess such magic, I want to know about it." She gazed around her scornfully, noting their expressions of apprehension. "Oh, come now, gentlemen, do you really think that powerful sorcerers would waste baleful spells on mere traveling merchants? Surely men such as you, who brave all sorts of peril in pursuit of markets cannot have such childish fears." Satisfied that they looked suitably abashed, she turned to the graybeard. "Master Hildas, has there been any report from the men who went in search of the steel mine?"

"Most have returned with little information of value. The desert is vast and hostile. Two have not yet reported in, Ingist and Haffle. They swore that they would not return without the information you seek."

"Would that all my servants were so determined," she said. "I remember those two, brave and resourceful men. Perhaps they may yet come through. How long have they been away?"

"Just over two years, my queen," Hildas said. "The last dispatch I received from them, almost a year ago, reported that they had contacted a very strange tribe of desert-dwellers who ride on flightless birds, like killer birds but domesticated."

"Bird riders!" the queen mused. "The world is full of wonders. If they are not dead, perhaps we shall hear from them soon. As for the rest of you, prepare yourselves for this mission. Glory to our king!"

"Glory to our king!" they chorused.

* * *

"Glory to our king!" The shout echoed through the valley, wrenched from the throats of the thousands who stood rank upon rank in their units, ready to be inspected.

The king and his highest officers stood atop a stone platform dominating one end of the huge parade ground, a grandiose paved plaza constructed by some long-forgotten king. Rows of statues lined the edges of the paving, each twice man-height and depicting a squat, crouching deity with an animalistic face. The king raised his glittering spear, and the army came forward by units for his inspection.

Gasam saluted each unit as it passed the reviewing stand. He loved this ceremony. Never did he feel the sense of his own power so keenly as when he reviewed his troops. They were grouped as to race and armament for efficient handling.

First came his pets, the women warriors drawn from the most primitive jungle tribes of coast and mountain. Raised from childhood to serve first the king of Chiwa and now King Gasam, they could overwhelm an enemy by the mere ferocity of their appearance. Tattooed and scarified, they wore garish plugs through lip and ear, and ornaments dangled from their pierced nipples. Their feathers and animal pelts were savage, but their weapons—short spears, chopping swords and hatchets—were the best Gasam could procure for them. They were merciless in battle.

The next units were far more drab in appearance. These were peasant levies, useful for protracted fighting where high casualties could be expected. They were eminently expendable. They had hide or wicker shields and most had padded armor. The officers wore armor of laced bamboo splints lacquered in various colors. Their weapons were spears tipped with flint or bronze and most carried stone-headed maces.

A contingent from the southern coast marched by. These men wore their black hair tied in topknots, and long mustaches drooped beneath their chins. Each man carried a bow taller than himself and a quiver of arrows as long as a man's arm. They wore white kilts but no armor, and carried only long knives in their belts for close-in fighting.

With a critical eye, Gasam watched the next unit canter past. These were mounted troops, cabo-riders drawn from the Chiwan uplands. He had wanted to build a strong mounted force, but had come to distrust both the quality of the men and the effectiveness of mounted warriors. He had seen with his own eyes how devastating were Hael's mounted archers, but his own riders were not born in the saddle like Hael's and he could not duplicate their remarkable bows. He did not intend to depend heavily on these riders in the coming campaign. The jungle climate was said to be unhealthy for the beasts.

After the companies of subject peoples came the backbone of his army: the islanders. These were from a number of tribes, all of them matchlessly warlike. The softness and decadence of the mainland civilizations had never touched them. He trusted implicitly in their warrior qualities.

Last of all came his pride and joy: the Shasinn. These were the people of his birth. Tall men, slender but powerful, with bronzen skin and hair ranging in color from almost white to deep gold. They were inordinately handsome and quite aware of the fact. Their beautifully crafted bronze spears and long black shields were recognized everywhere. Gasam had put an end to tribal warfare in the islands, and now he had Shasinn in greater numbers than he had ever dared hope. There were senior warriors who had served him for years and junior warriors fresh from the islands, their hair dressed in the innumerable tiny plaits of that class.

Gasam was miserly with the lives of these warriors. In battle, they formed his reserve, to be committed only in an emergency or when an opportunity came to finish the fight with a sudden, powerful thrust. They, in turn, worshipped him with a fervor the mainlanders reserved for their gods.

In the islands of his youth, these men had guarded the

tribe's cattle and raided other tribes for theirs. They had been grouped into warrior fraternities and had been forbidden to marry until they achieved senior warrior status, usually in their late twenties. Gasam had changed all that. He had abolished the fraternities and had given his people slaves to do the herding. Now all the warriors devoted themselves solely to war. He encouraged them to marry young and breed as many children as possible to increase his strength. He could never have enough Shasinn.

"They are ready, my king," said a scar-faced Shasinn officer who stood by his side.

"They are, indeed," said the king, with deep satisfaction. "We march tomorrow. Luo, you will take your force through the middle pass. Urlik, yours is the southern pass." Urlik was a chief of the Asasa, an island people who resembled the Shasinn except for their dark hair and eyes.

"As my king commands," said the Asasa. "How will you divide the army?"

"Each of you shall have a regiment of Shasinn; I will take the rest. Luo's force and mine will each have a small squadron of the mounted troops. They will be little use in the fighting, but they may prove valuable for reconnaissance. Urlik, you will take the rest. The terrain to the south is more favorable for their employment."

Urlik nodded. "Good. I have some ideas for their employment and this campaign will be just the place to try them out."

"Excellent," the king said. "Give me a full report if your ideas work out." Gasam encouraged his officers to try out new innovations. Having invented his own war-making system, he had no military tradition to hinder him.

By units they divided the army. Nearly half of the army would be under Gasam's direct command. The other two commanders would have the rest. Their task was to ravage the land before them until they reached the river, and then hold position there. They were strictly enjoined to avoid

open battle and to retreat to the north if necessary to avoid
it. Major fighting would commence only when the armies
were reunited. The partition of the army went smoothly.
The three commanders had worked closely together for
many years and Gasam heeded the counsel of the other two.
His subcommanders were equally competent.

There was no morale problem. The warriors were eager
for the campaign, the peasant levies resigned. Victory would
mean loot and a chance for advancement, and none doubted
that Gasam would be victorious. Death in battle or on the
march was a risk, but refusal or desertion made it an utter
certainty. War was just another hazard of lives already hard
and uncertain.

Gasam's army marched with minimal impedimenta. They
would live off the land to the greatest extent possible. The
soldiers were expected to fabricate their own shelters as
needed. Even Gasam took no tent with him. Pack animals
were few and wagons were nonexistent.

The king left the parade ground well pleased with his
preparations. That evening, he held counsel with the queen.

"Surely you will take me with you, my lord!" Larissa
said. "I have been at your side since your conquests began,
and I wish to stay with you now."

"Not this time, little queen," he said. "Before, we were
in our islands, or ravaging the coasts, where you could stay
aboard our ships until I established a base. This march will
be long and arduous, and although I know you do not shrink
from hardship, I would not wish to inflict this upon you."

"But I will miss all the fighting!" She had always enjoyed the blood and excitement of battle, seeing her husband reduce his enemies to corpses or to terrified, fleeing
remnants.

"Ah, you have the heart of a warrior, my queen." He
held her close, stroking her ashen hair. "But I need you to
hold the throne here for me. I no longer lead a rootless war

band. I rule a kingdom and I can trust no one else to hold it for me while I am away on campaign.''

She was somewhat placated. ''Will my power be absolute in your absence?''

''You shall be as a goddess to our subjects. Life and death, freedom, imprisonment or slavery, yours to inflict or withhold at will. Conduct diplomatic relations at your pleasure. The treasury is yours. Undertake those building projects you always speak of. Make a royal progress through the new domains so that your subjects may properly abase themselves before you.''

''Very well, my love.'' She was truly sorry to miss the campaign, but this promised to be even more rewarding. She knew that the king was happy to rid himself of these responsibilities. Like most warriors, he had a broad streak of laziness in his character. Boundlessly energetic in any activity having to do with war, he had little patience or aptitude for the everyday management of his kingdom. She, on the other hand, enjoyed that sort of work.

''I knew you would be pleased with the prospect. Here, see what I have had made for you.'' He snapped his fingers and a slave entered the room bearing a long parcel of rich brocade. He took it from the slave and placed it in his queen's hands. Smiling, she slipped back the heavy cloth sheath to expose a miniature spear made entirely of steel. It was fashioned in the shape of a Shasinn spear with a long, wasp-waisted head and a fluted butt-spike. It was a model of the king's own famous weapon.

''This is your scepter of power. Let other kings have their crowns and jewelled staffs and thrones. We know the real symbol of power, do we not?''

She hugged him fiercely. ''With this, I will rule your people as sternly as you, my love,'' she vowed. ''And bring back plenty of treasure from this war. Some of my projects will be costly.''

Laughing, the king enfolded her in his arms.

THREE

"All my life I have heard of the Canyon," Ansa said. "Now I am in Canyon territory, yet I see no such feature." He was out hunting with Fyana, who rode beside him on a small, well-behaved cabo. This was a great relief to him, for he detested the ugly, foul-smelling and ill-tempered humpers.

"What did you expect to see?" she asked.

He shrugged. "I've seen canyons before. I have been told that this one is bigger."

"It is that," she affirmed. "It is the biggest canyon in the world. A canyon as big as a kingdom."

"*Is* it a kingdom?" Ansa asked. She favored him with that smug, secret smile he had come to associate with the Canyoners and which he greatly disliked.

"Of a sort. It isn't a kingdom as other nations know such things. There is the Canyon proper, and the high arid lane around it, which we call the Painted Lands. Then there is the lower land to the west, near the big lake, which the

Nevans call the Zone. Last, there is the desert to the north. Collectively, these are known to foreigners as the Promised Lands.''

''But does all this constitute a *kingdom*?'' he persisted.

''Well, there is a man in the Zone who calls himself a king, and we of the Canyon acknowledge a certain fealty to him. At least that simplifies many of our dealings with foreign lands.''

He sensed that she was baiting him, but he could think of no clever, witty response. ''I have never known of a land with so many names,'' he said. ''Why the Zone? Why the Poisoned Lands?''

''Those are very ancient names, from the time of the fiery spears, the great catastrophe. We do not use them.''

''I had hoped to learn something of this land,'' Ansa fumed. ''It seems that you wish to hinder me in this.''

''To truly know this or any land, you must live in it a long time, and learn the ways of its people.'' She scanned the brushy hillside and held a finger to her lips to silence him. He wondered if she meant that she wanted him to stay. He was sorely tempted, but then he had barely commenced his travels and he was not yet ready to stop. Still, there was no real rush.

''Sss . . .'' she hissed at him, pointing to her right. He saw a fat, young curlhorn browsing on a bush a hundred paces away. The creature's upper lip was drawn out into a long, prehensile point which it wrapped around twigs, methodically stripping the leaves and thrusting them, bundled, into its mouth.

Ansa took an arrow from his quiver and nocked it. Slowly he raised the bow and pulled the string back to full draw, taking a sight on the spotted flank just behind the shoulder. The string thrummed faintly as he released it and the arrow sped on its swift, silent arc. It sank to the feathers in the animal's flank and Ansa knew the satisfaction of making a perfect heart shot. The curlhorn started in surprise, whirled and made two long leaps before collapsing abruptly. Its feet quivered for a moment, then it was still.

"Well shot!" Fyana said. "You did not exaggerate when you described plainsman archery."

"That was not a great distance for a still target," he said, modestly. "Let's collect this one. There will be more. Curl-horn never wander very far alone."

"We'll put on a feast for the whole village," Fyana said.

"Fyana, will you guide me to the Canyon? I want to see it."

She rode to the dead animal and dismounted. She took a colored stick from her pouch and with it drew a ritual sign on the creature's brow. Then she looked up at Ansa.

"Yes. I will take you there."

They had ridden from the village just that morning, but already the air felt different. At first he thought it was cold, but he knew that could not be. They had been climbing most of the day, but not enough to effect a notable drop in temperature. He felt that the air was somehow charged with a power he could not see or truly feel, but that touched a seldom-used sense. He shook his head, unable to put it into words. He decided that a great many spirits must live here.

The trees were of a sort new to him, rough-barked with twisted limbs bearing fragrant, dark-green needles. The ground was thickly carpeted with fallen, yellow needles of years past, and every step of their cabos sent up a fresh wave of the clean scent. The land they had ridden through all day had been brightly colored but the animals were few. There were no herds and small, scattered family groups seemed to be the norm.

Except for the sounds they made themselves, the land was wrapped in a great silence. In other places, the quiet might have seemed to him sinister or portentous, but here it just seemed restful.

"My father would love this place," he said, as the sun gave long shadows to the trees.

"Why is that?" she wanted to know.

"He loves two things above all: spirits and a quiet place to meditate. This place has both."

"You think there are spirits here?"

"Aren't there?" he said, surprised. "I am no spirit-man like my father, but even I can feel the power in this place."

"There is that," she said. "My people don't speak of spirits, but maybe we mean the same thing."

He found this confusing, but he had given up on getting a straight, simple answer from her. They rode on until the light was so dim that he could see no more than a hundred paces ahead. He would have stopped earlier, but his pride would not let him demand a halt. When he could barely see her ahead of him, he decided he had had enough.

"It is foolish to ride in the dark. You must be lost."

She looked back and he saw her teeth flash white in the gloom. "Oh, I know this way well. We will go just a little farther and stop for the night."

Sorry that he had spoken, he held his peace. In some obscure way, he felt belittled. They rode on for a few more minutes, then she stopped and dismounted. They tethered their cabos to trees and unloaded their saddles and gear. Ansa rubbed his animal down and then began to care for Fyana's mount. As he did he noticed an orange glow. She had started a fire.

"I didn't hear you strike a light."

She looked up from the flames. "There are other ways to start a fire."

He began to rub down the beast more roughly than necessary. More tricks. The animals seen to, he walked to the fire and sat wearily on the thin stack of his blankets. She handed him a skin and he drank deeply. It was watered wine mixed with herbs and it went down well after the long, dry ride.

"Why do you speak in riddles, when you speak at all?" he asked her.

"I am not riddling, or trying to confuse you," she said. "But there are many things that are not easily answered. How do you explain how you shoot to one who has never seen a bow or an arrow? How would you explain the difference between shooting at a still target and one that moves?"

He thought for a while. "I would demonstrate."

"You could do that, if you had your bow handy. Even if you got the idea across, the one to whom you demonstrated could not take up your bow and use it as well as you, could he?"

"No," he admitted. "I began shooting as a child, but I was near manhood before I reached full proficiency." He tossed a stick into the fire and it sent up a shower of sparks.

"And archery is a manual skill, requiring a few simple tools. How much more difficult to express something which employs only the mind and is entwined with a whole way of life?"

"I had not thought of it that way. I would appreciate it, though, if from now on you would say something of the sort, instead of just smiling to yourself as if you possessed some secret knowledge which the ignorant outlander has no hope of comprehending."

He thought she looked abashed. "I am sorry. Hereafter I will do my best to explain things. I fear that I may not be successful."

"Just so the effort is made," he said. "Now, how far is it to the Canyon?"

"Nor far. In fact, I recommend that you do not wander around in the dark tonight. You might fall into it."

"Still having fun with me," he muttered as he spread out his blankets. He thrust his lance into the ground by its butt-spike and arranged his sword and knife over his saddle, where they would be ready to his grasp should an unpleasant surprise interrupt his sleep.

For a while he lay awake, his head resting on his hands, his fingers interlaced. There was a mild, cool breeze, but the trees overhead resounded to the slightest movement of the air, giving forth a sighing sound that was extraordinarily restful. He closed his eyes and decided that, whatever she said to the contrary, this place was full of spirits.

He awoke in the gray light of dawn. Immediately, without making a movement, he took stock of his surroundings. There seemed to be no threat, but he sat up slowly. The cabos dozed with their heads down. On the other side of the fire, Fyana was still bundled in her blankets, with just the top of her blond head showing.

Silently, he rose and picked up his weapons belt. He walked away from the campsite as quietly as if he were stalking prey. When he was well out of sight, he set his weapons on the ground and prepared to relieve himself. He was just out of the trees and in the dim light the land before him looked decidedly odd. Opening his trousers, he blinked to clear his vision, but the vista before him remained strange. Then he decided that this uncanny place was affecting his hearing as well, because his activity was not rewarded with the customary patter of water falling upon dry evergreen needles. He looked down and his heart shot up into his throat and pounded there as he saw that his stream arched past his toes and down into an abyss at least a thousand feet deep. He stood on the lip of the most horrendous drop-off he had ever encountered in his life. Raising his eyes, he saw the reason for his confusion. The Canyon was a feature of such immensity that a mind unprepared for it had no grasp of its scale. It was a gash in the earth so vast that mountains were minor elevations within its bowl.

As the light grew, the Canyon's colors began to emerge, some subtle, others dazzling. Time, wind and water had carved the rock of the Canyon into shapes he would not have thought possible outside of dreams. The tortured yet beautiful wonderland stretched as far as he could see. His shock and momentary terror dissipated as a sense of exultation struck deep into him. As jolting as the experience had been, he was glad that he had discovered the place in this fashion, instead of it coming before him a bit at a time as he rode, with Fyana telling him what to expect.

"Isn't it beautiful?" It was her voice behind him. Hastily, he closed his trousers and turned.

"A mild word. Last night I thought you were gulling me again, saying that I might fall in in the dark. I almost did."

She joined him at the dizzying brink and pointed down. "Look. Do you see that thin silver ribbon winding around the base of that hill?"

"I see it, just barely. Is that a small river?" He was still troubled by the scale.

"That is the River Kol."

"It can't be!" he exclaimed. "Then again, that is a foolish thing to say. This canyon holds mountains. But how can a mighty river look so small? How deep is it?"

"More than a mile at this point. This is one of the deepest spots."

"Truly? A mile doesn't seem so great on level ground. It is different to see it straight down. How long and how wide is it?"

She pointed straight ahead. "More than twenty miles from one side to the other." She spread her arms wide. "At least two hundred miles from end to end."

He sat on the rim, letting his feet dangle in the emptiness. "I think I could stay here for a year and never tire of looking upon this."

"It's not even full light yet. Wait until you see it then. The view, especially the colors, change from hour to hour. The very shapes of the rocks and hills seem to alter with the passing day."

"I am glad that I came to see this. I would have missed something glorious otherwise." Below him, huge ledges sprouted brush thickets and even small forests. Animals grazed and browsed among the growths, insectlike in the distance.

"Where do we go from here?" he asked, tearing his gaze away reluctantly.

"About five miles to the east there is a trail that descends to the floor of the Canyon. It will take most of the day to reach the bottom."

"I am surprised that it can be done in one day."

They returned to the campsite and retrieved their belongings and their mounts. Fyana led them to a rock-lined pond fed by a tiny stream and they let the animals drink. Then they mounted and rode east along the rim of the Canyon.

"I've seen no sign of people," Ansa noted.

"This place is so vast that sometimes I think all the people in the world could be crowded into one of its gorges and you wouldn't be able to see them from most spots on the rim," she answered. "There are many towns, but they blend in with the terrain. Some are even dug into the walls. There are fields down along the river, but most of the people live by herding."

The path proved to be well-beaten but narrow, with heart-stopping drop-offs along much of its length. It zigzagged down the canyonside, with switchbacks every few hundred yards. At intervals it opened onto one of the broad ledges and on these they would rest. Throughout the descent, Fyana entertained him with explanations of what they saw and a recitation of the Canyon's wonders.

"Plants grow here that grow nowhere else," she said. "There are medicinal plants, plants that induce visions, plants to weave into cloth and others with which to dye the cloth. The growth on these ledges differs greatly from one level to another as we descend."

They came to a ledge where strange animals browsed on the branches, lifting heads crowned with palmate horns to gaze at the intruders. The creatures had short bodies and slender legs tipped with clawed feet. Their hides were splotched tan and russet, the colors of the nearby cliff walls.

"Those are climbers," Fyana explained. "They are always found near this level, never up on the rim or down in the bottom. They can climb on slopes too steep for any other animal. That is what they use the claws for."

"They seem fearless. Does no one hunt them?"

"Animals are never hunted in the Canyon. Here they are . . . different. It is not just that they look different from other beasts, although no animal native to the Canyon is quite like any other outside it. Many of them have powers, and there is a tradition that great misfortune befalls one who kills them, and that deadly sickness follows eating their flesh. At any rate, there is plenty of game outside the Canyon, so nobody risks hunting these beasts."

Ansa pondered this. "When my father speaks of animals, he often mentions their spirit-force. It is something that few people can feel, save spirit-speakers. But he says that the spirit-force was far stronger in the islands of his birth. There it was so palpable that the beasts could actually be ranked according to the force they made evident. The little, burrowing creatures had almost none. The big cats and the longnecks had a great deal."

"We have longnecks in this territory," she said. "They are rare, but they wreak havoc among our herds."

"In the islands there is a giant breed, many times the size of the ones we know. He says that their spirit-force is so great that a whole body of ritual law and tabu surrounds them. He killed one once, single-handed. That had never been done before in all the history and legends of his people."

"So he became a great hero?" she asked.

"No, he became an exile. The beast was so sacred that there could be no excuse for killing one, even to save your own life, or the life of a tribesman." He shrugged. "That is what my father says, at any rate. Something about this place put me in mind of my father's old stories, of which I tired while still very young.''

''Why does the Canyon make you think of his stories?'' she prodded, gently.

Ansa struggled to articulate his thoughts. He was not used to analyzing his feelings, but there was something about this uncanny place, with its great beauty and its air of brooding mystery, that turned his thoughts in the direction of supernatural matters.

''I think,'' he said at last, ''that it has something to do with the Time of Catastrophe, and the hard ages just after. Everyone has legends about those times. The stories differ widely, but all agree that men brought some terrible disaster upon themselves, and that in the time of tribulation that followed most men and animals died, and those that survived were all changed in some fashion. Spirits came back into the world at that time, according to many.'' He paused.

''I have heard many tales of this sort. Go on, please,'' she prodded.

''I think that much of the world has emerged from those times. Spirit-power is important mainly to eccentric old men or visionaries like my father. In the lands of the great cities, so I hear, the spirits are ignored entirely. Instead they have what they call religion, in which a class of professional priests act as intermediaries between the gods and men, and perform all the rituals.''

He scanned the Canyon on all sides. ''I think that there are some parts of the world where the time of tribulation lingers. In my father's islands, and here in the Canyon, there is still strong magic. Here men and animals and the land itself have an . . . an affinity for one another.''

''You may well be right,'' she said, looking upon him with a more sympathetic interest than she had previously shown. ''These are deep thoughts for an independent young warrior. But then, you are your father's son.''

''There have been times when I wished I was not,'' he

said. They were near the canyon floor now, and he saw a pack of very strange creatures climbing in a stand of stunted trees and scrambling about on the ground beneath them. He thought at first that they were deformed men, small and hairy. Then he saw their vestigial tails and their long, befanged muzzles. At the approach of the riders the creatures ceased their play to chatter and hoot at the intruders. Their motions seemed so human that Ansa could not determine their nature.

"Are they men?" he asked.

"No. These are called hanumas. They are the most manlike of creatures, but they have no power of speech. They can be dangerous if you get too close or threaten them, but they will not trouble you otherwise."

"In the coastal areas, I hear there is a creature called man-of-the-trees, but they are said to be tiny. These are half the size of a large man." He laughed as the strange beasts made gestures intended to be threatening but which succeeded only in looking comical.

"They are pests and great raiders of crops and stores, but we tolerate them. Even at their worst, they are entertaining. The infants are especially fun to watch."

He saw what she meant. The fearless little creatures scampered about among the feet of their elders, tussling and playing in total disregard of the adults' alarm. With their snouts as yet unformed, the young had faces that were uncannily human, with bright, round eyes and tiny noses. Their faces were hairless and had a pinkish color.

As they rode past, the hanumas ceased their unfriendly demonstrations, but watched warily. Ansa was astonished by the intelligence in their dark eyes. They might not be men, he thought, but they were close.

The valley floor had appeared to be flat when seen from the rim, but it was rugged when they got there, scored with deep gullies, rocky and hard. The cabos had to pick their way warily among the stones and the innumerable burrows of the underground dwellers. Once, a tiny nosehorn poked its head out of its hole and studied them, the tiny eyes unblinking behind the short, forked horn that sprouted from its diminutive snout. Ansa pointed at it.

"A nosehorn! You said that the Canyon animals were unlike those outside. I've seen this fellow's like everywhere I have traveled."

"They look similar," she maintained, "but these climb out of their burrows each day at sunset and the whole colony of them sing in unison. Do the ones you have seen do that?"

"No," he admitted. "They just dig holes and mind their own business. The only sound I have ever heard them make is the cry that tells the others that a predator is near."

"These do that, too. And they are just as much a pest as the ordinary kind. They are just Canyon nosehorns, that is all."

As they neared the river the land flattened into a narrow floodplain. Here the soil was far richer, supporting an abundant growth of thorny brush, stunted trees and colorful, flowering plants. All of the vegetation swarmed with bird and animal life, as if most of the Canyon's life concentrated near the water. Here and there he saw fields that had once been cultivated. They were outlined by low, irregular walls of piled stone. He asked Fyana about these.

"Fields are usually farmed for a year or two, then left fallow for three or four. These have been out of cultivation for at least three years."

Ansa surveyed the enclosed fields disdainfully. "I have never understood how people could spend their days grubbing in the dirt and then call it a life." He sensed that she might resent this and added: "But then, you said the Canyoners live mainly by herding. That is a far better life."

"They will doubtless rejoice to hear of your good opinion," she said dryly.

"I didn't mean it that . . ." He cut off abruptly. "What is that?"

They had been riding in a roughly northerly direction along the river and had come to a narrow strip of floodplain with the river on one side and on the other a cliff of red sandstone that bellied out dramatically far above their heads. He pointed at a deep indentation in the cliff where irregular mud structures clustered like the nests of giant, cliff-dwelling birds.

"That is the village of Redstone."

"Village! You mean people live in such a place?" But now he could see them, ghostly forms in reddish robes moving among the bizarre houses, some of them tending little herds of small beasts. At the foot of the cliff were some pens for livestock and an apparatus for dipping water from a stone-lined pool. The pool was connected to the river by a channel, also lined with cut stone.

Smoke drifted up from stubby chimneys and the smell was clean in the still air. His stomach rumbled and he remembered that he had not eaten since that morning, when they had breakfasted on trail rations.

The quiet of the place was strange. From somewhere out of sight came the honking bellows of ill-tempered humpers, but that was all. Ansa had always thought of villages as noisy places. They certainly were when he and his friends rode into them. He had spent months amid the clamor of the steel pit and was unused to so many people making so little noise. As they drew nearer the village, he saw that even the children played quietly.

"How should I behave?" Ansa asked as they reached the outskirts of the village.

"As a plainsman," she said, "I suppose there is little you can do to temper your arrogance. Just carry yourself as you did in my village and you will probably cause little offense."

Ansa had always thought his manners to be excellent, and it nettled him to hear that she thought him overbearing. Did she expect humility? He had borne himself as he thought a plainsman should, when traveling among inferior people. What else would be more fitting?

A tall, stately form approached them as they reached the watering-pool. As Ansa had found disconcertingly common among these people, sex was not immediately apparent. The hood was raised with its veil drawn across the face against the omnipresent dust, revealing only a pair of amazing eyes, the exact color of new-minted gold coins. Ansa heard a sharp intake of breath and saw Fyana make an obeisance, the first such gesture he had seen from her, or from any Canyon dweller, for that matter.

"Lady Bel!" Fyana said, "I had not expected to find you here."

The woman responded to the obeisance by placing a long-fingered hand against Fyana's forehead.

"I came to meet you here. I was expecting you."

How could she be expecting us? Ansa wondered. Did they have the power to read the future? Did they have extraordinarily swift and clever spies? Or was this just more mummery to make him believe their sorcerous claims? He suspected the latter.

The woman turned her golden eyes upon him. "Welcome, Ansa, son of Hael. Welcome to Redstone." A small group of villagers had ranged themselves behind Lady Bel.

"I thank you, my lady. It seems that my attempts to conceal my paternity have little effect here."

He could see nothing of her save her eyes, but they smiled. "You have no need to use subterfuge with us. Where are you going, though, it will be very necessary, indeed."

"How do you know where I am going?" Ansa asked. To cover his confusion, he led his cabo to the pool and let it drink.

"We needn't speak while standing out here," Lady Bel said. "It is inhospitable behavior at the very least." She turned to one of the villagers behind her. "Elder Yama, perhaps we could retire to the lodge with our guests."

The man bowed. "Of a certainty." He turned to Ansa. "Allow me to extend the welcome of my village to our distinguished guest from the north."

The formality of these people began to infect him. "On behalf of my father and my people, I accept gladly."

Lady Bel introduced the others, all Elders or important personages of the village. It still seemed strange to him that mere villagers could have the style and bearing of nobles. That city-dwellers considered his own people to be nomadic savages was, to him, only proof of their ignorance.

Boys took charge of their animals and they retired to the lodge, which was a mud structure a good deal larger than the others, with a single, long room with conical fireplaces at each end. Ansa thought that mud was an ugly and impoverished building material, but he was forced to admit that the interiors of the mud houses were wonderfully cool and comfortable in the fierce desert country. The company ranged themselves down the length of the room in two facing lines and sat on the floor. At one end of the double file sat Lady Bel. At her gesture, Ansa and Fyana sat at her right and left hands, facing one another.

"First," said Lady Bel, "you two must eat and refresh yourselves. We shall talk later."

Ansa knew better than to protest that they had done no more than engage in a leisurely, sight-seeing ride for the last two days. Hospitality demanded that they be treated as if they had ridden hard for a year and arrived at the village as if at death's door. They sat making small talk while they were served with food and drink.

Lady Bel lowered her hood and veil, revealing a face Ansa could not quite define as elderly. Her facial skin was as smooth and unlined as Fyana's, but it lay thin against the fine, aristocratic bones, the veins showing as a darker blue tracery against the pale blue of her Canyon features. Her hands were likewise youthful-seeming, without the gnarling and distended veins Ansa associated with great age. Nonetheless, he was certain that this was a very old woman.

When the demands of hospitality were satisfied, they were given cups of an herb infusion lightly mixed with a heavy wine. It was customary to breathe the steam for a few moments before ceremoniously sipping at the hot liquid.

"You have come at a crucial time," Lady Bel began. "For some time now, the focus of important events has been far from the Canyon, the desert and the plains. Your father has busied himself to the east, establishing trade and military relations with the peoples of those lands. Gasam had conquered and consolidated Chiwa and some nearby kingdoms and islands. This balance and relative quiet is changing now. Gasam is on the march again, this time to the southeast. He is crossing into Sono. He will not stop there. In time he will take Gran as well and after that he will move north."

"Gasam!" This was news, indeed. He had been a boy when his father's lifelong enemy had last threatened the people of the plains. Chiwa was a remote kingdom, and Hael had hoped that Gasam would somehow die in his wars there. It now seemed that he had not.

Ansa felt a rush of excitement. Others might consider these developments to be alarming, but for a young warrior the only opportunity for honor and advancement lay in warfare.

"Do not be so eager," said Lady Bel, as if she could read his thoughts. "In the first place, it will be some time before that madman turns his armies northward. But, more importantly, it will be absolutely necessary that we have accurate information as to his doings and intentions."

"It seems to me," Ansa said, "that you already have such information."

"We have our agents in other lands, watching out for our interests. They have ways of contacting us with little delay.

But this will grow more difficult now that Gasam is on the move. There will be great confusion for a while. Someone fully trusted by King Hael should be there to observe.'' She gazed at him steadily.

''You mean that I should go there, into the midst of Gasam's invasion, alone?'' He had been seeking adventure, but nothing quite this drastic.

''No,'' Lady Bel shook her head. ''Not alone. With her.'' Now she nodded toward Fyana. ''Someone *we* fully trust should go as well.''

''What! To go alone would be suicidal. To go burdened with a woman would be''—he found that he had left himself short of dreadful prospects—''well, worse than suicidal.''

'' 'Burdened,' '' Fyana said. ''We shall see who is to be the burden on this mission.''

''Why do you both speak as if I have already agreed to this madness?''

''Lady Bel has said that I shall go,'' Fyana told him, ''and so it shall be.''

''And you will go,'' Lady Bel added, ''because it will be a feat worthy of a great warrior. For the king's very son to go within the grasp of his hereditary enemy is a thing to be sung of. At last you shall have done something to match your father's warrior feats.''

He knew that they were manipulating him through his warrior pride, but it was none the less persuasive for his knowledge of the fact. If he agreed to this, and if by some miracle he should survive the experience, none could ever doubt his worth. Although he had no wish to succeed his father as king, this would earn him a high place as a warleader, perhaps even as a counselor. It galled him to know that these Canyoners were cornering him, making it difficult for him to avoid the task without appearing to them, and, far more importantly, to himself, as a coward. Especially since Fyana showed not the slightest apprehension at going on a mission that would probably mean her death, or worse, at the hands of Gasam or his equally fearsome queen.

"The mission would be a worthy one," he said, reluctantly.

"More than that," said Lady Bel, "it is necessary."

"Very well," he said, knowing that this was probably his doom. "I will go."

FOUR

It was good to be leading his army again. Gasam could have ridden, but he despised traveling on an animal's back while his army went on foot. He had always led his warriors as a warrior, and now he strode at the head of the army, his long, muscular legs setting a fast pace. Back in the islands, his Shasinn had customarily gone raiding at a fast trot, to give an enemy the least possible time to prepare. On a march as long and hilly as this one, such a pace was not practical, and none of his mainland troops were runners like the Shasinn. Still, he had no intention of moving at the snail-like crawl of the lumbering civilized armies. He could still have his army before the gates of a capital city before they knew that he had crossed their borders.

Even so, he fully understood the importance of mounted scouts and he kept them ranging far ahead, sending one of their number back frequently to deliver reports of what lay in the army's route of march.

An observer would not have taken him for a king. Except

for his extravagant spear, which was entirely made of steel except for a short, wooden hand-grip, he was unadorned. He wore none of the paint and jewelry so loved by the other Shasinn. His belt and loincloth were of plain red leather and he was unshod. Behind him a bearer carried his shield, a long, oval construction of hide stretched over a wicker frame, painted black. It was identical to those of his Shasinn warriors. But behind him came the rhythmic slap of thousands of bare feet, and every one of them marched at his command, to do his bidding.

These pleasant thoughts went through his mind as the army reached the foot of the mountains. Somewhere up there he would pass the end of his own domains and enter enemy territory. He corrected himself. He was the rightful ruler of the world, but violence was necessary to force some people to acknowledge the fact. This was good because he enjoyed violence. The physical domination of his fellow men made life worthwhile for Gasam. When people succumbed to him without bloodshed, he felt cheated.

He had sent word ahead so that when they camped for the night there were plentiful provisions heaped up for them, the produce of the local farms. There were many beasts ready-slaughtered and ready for the cooking fires, but he had given strict orders that there was to be no strong drink for the warriors. That was for *after* a victory.

The army made camp, which was primarily a matter of stacking weapons and building fires. After the final unit, the Last Man entered the camp, and the men fell silent as he passed. He always marched a few hundred paces behind the host. A hulking native of the southern jungle peninsula, he carried a glaive slanting over his shoulder. It bore a broad, cleaverlike blade mounted on a short haft. It was the Last Man's duty to behead any member of the army who fell out on the march. He also carried a large mesh bag to carry the heads for display in each night's camp. It was still early in the march, and he had thus far collected no heads, but that would change before much longer.

A group of junior warriors gathered brush and withies and with these simple materials they constructed an island-style shelter for their king. There were no villages nearby, and Gasam preferred this familiar structure to commandeering some peasant's foul-smelling hut.

As night fell his senior officers gathered around the fire before his hut. They were a varied lot, with the features, dress and weapons of a dozen races. These were men who had profited well from their master's conquests, and their ornaments were rich, even on campaign. Firelight winked from jewelled swordhilts and golden neck-chains. Some wore paints, others were tattooed. Tunics, shirts, leggings and capes were of fine fabrics or leathers. None wore footgear, for Gasam believed that men were swifter and more agile when barefoot. Those who had been accustomed to going shod had suffered greatly during their early days in Gasam's service, but they had hardened or died. To disobey Gasam meant an appointment with the Last Man.

The king sat on the ground, nibbling daintily at a skewer studded with balls of finely ground meat. Like all Shasinn, he was abstemious with food, somewhat less so with drink. The others joined him and soldiers or local villagers brought them baskets of provisions. Gasam allowed no slaves to be brought on the march for these menial duties.

"Tomorrow we begin our mountain crossing," Gasam said. "We may meet with resistance as we cross. Our scouts have reported that they've found the remains of fires, abandoned villages and such along our route. These may be outlaws or hunters but it is possible that they will resent intrusion. I doubt that they have any loyalty to the king of Sono. They are too few to threaten such a host, but we may have some harassment. Be sure your men are aware of this."

"How long a crossing are we to expect, my king?" asked a man who wore a long robe, with his hair tied in a topknot.

He fingered the jewelled handle of his belted dagger as he spoke. Even the hard-bitten captains of Gasam's army were nervous when addressing their king directly.

"No more than three days. These are not great mountains and the path is a good one. On the other side we will be in rolling hill country, and there we must be ready for battle at any moment. I do not expect to meet organized resistance early in our campaign, but nothing is certain in war save my ultimate victory. We could meet an army returning from a skirmish in the north, or one under a rebellious satrap. We must be ready for anything. The greatest peril for an army on the move is to be caught in marching order by an enemy who is already formed for battle. As soon as we reach the other side, we will drill daily in taking up battle order to meet a threat from any direction. You all know what to do. See that you do it smartly."

"We will, my king!" they chorused.

"From the foot of the mountains, it is six days fast march to the river. There is a small town there called Marn. We will sack that place and provision ourselves, then we swing south and march to meet the force led by General Luo."

An officer of levies shifted where he sat, his armor of laced bamboo creaking softly. "My king, will we be marching through heavy jungle?"

"The hills are forested, the flatter land as we approach the river is largely cultivated. We should encounter no true jungle on the early stages of the march. As we make our way south, we will meet with the heavy growth. Red Knife."

"Yes, my king?" said the woman thus named. She was heavily carved with ornamental scars, and rank with the animal fat smeared on her body. The men seated to either side of her had edged away surreptitiously.

"Wherever we encounter heavy growth, I want your women working the bush to both flanks. The main army will travel the roads, preceded by the riders. Your women are accustomed to jungle fighting. Archers can work their way close to the army, shoot their arrows and be away in a heartbeat. You are to flush them out and kill them. Be watching for spies. I want none to escape ahead of us and bear word of our coming. Select your best runners to chase these down and kill them.''

"It shall be done, my king!'' She grinned ferociously, displaying teeth filed to points and reinforced with sharp bronze caps. Gasam's fighting women made even his hardest warriors uneasy.

"We march at first light,'' the king said.

Two days later, Gasam stood on the crest of the final mountain line, looking down upon the rolling, green land beyond. Most armies would have taken many days to accomplish this crossing, but Gasam pressed his men vigorously. Each evening, the Last Man entered camp with a full sack.

There had been no difficulty from the sparse inhabitants of the mountains, who had faded back into the brush when the great host came in sight. There was little likelihood that any had run ahead to give warning of their coming. The riders would have intercepted any such.

The riders themselves would be mistaken for the mounted bandits that infested the southern lands, so Gasam did not worry that their appearance would imply a following army to any Sonoans who might see them.

The terrain he scanned did not look at all difficult. The hills were low and rounded, cleared here and there for small farms. Within sight were three small villages, each consisting of no more than a dozen thatched huts from which smoke curled lazily. He knew that his army would make swift progress through this country, and that it would not march hungry.

The descent was rapid. The men were relieved now that the most arduous part of the march was over and the action about to begin. They were accustomed to hardship, but any true warrior preferred the hazards of battle to the fatigue of a long march over steep ground.

Wan Pegra, commander of Marn's small royal garrison, made his way slowly from his comfortable quarters at the base of the town's wall. He had just breakfasted heavily and he lurched a bit as he climbed the stair to the sentry-walk that encircled the inner side of the wall. At the top he belched, giving himself a second taste of the fierily-spiced jungle fowl that had perished for the sake of his appetite that morning.

Pegra wore a feather-plumed, gilt leather helmet, suitable for ceremonial parades but not for combat. His quilted armor lacked protective stuffing, rendering it light and cool. His duties required that he be in uniform, but he saw no reason why he should endure discomfort in their discharge.

Following his invariable routine, he turned left when he reached the walk, to stride along the wall that fronted along the river. Atop the river gate, the sentry on guard stood to attention at his commander's approach. This man wore the full panoply of the Sonoan infantry. His helmet was of thick leather overlaid with horn and strapped with bronze. His padded cuirass was more than an inch thick, its once-brilliant dyes now faded. He carried a bronze-tipped spear in one hand and a stone-headed war hammer thonged to his belt. His curved, rectangular shield of hide-faced wicker leaned against the battlement.

Pegra examined the sentry's face-paint closely, making sure that the outlines were sharp and clear, and that no color blended sloppily into any other. It was well known among the men of the garrison that if a stinging insect landed on one's face, one just had to put up with it. Pegra had been known to have men flogged mercilessly for being on guard with smeared face-paint.

The commander made his way around the wall from one sentry-post to another. Along the river wall no one had anything to report. There was never anything to report on the river. The main duty of the sentries on the river wall was to keep an eye on Pegra's luxuriously appointed riverboat. As he walked the wall, he thought pleasantly of the fishing trip he planned for the coming afternoon. He would take his cronies and some professional ladies of the town. These last were in no way comparable with their sisters of the capital, but they were acceptable for this provincial hellhole. He would take along his two pretty new concubines. They were twins, no more than fifteen years old. In the midst of these musings he came to the post above the road gate. The sentry there was staring toward the western hills.

"What do you see?" Pegra demanded.

"Riders to the west, sir," the man said. "I think there are some peasants running this way before them."

"Bandits, eh? They grow bold, to ride so near in daylight." He took his telescope from its belt case. The fine Nevan instrument was as much a mark of his rank as his gilt dress helmet. He fitted it to his eye and adjusted the focus. An early heat-haze made the picture wavery, but he could see that the riders were indeed herding some fleeing peasants before them. Even as he watched, a rider speared a running man through the back. The other riders sought to emulate him, pursuing the terrorized farmers across the cultivated fields. Pegra lowered the telescope.

"This is a strange sport," he muttered. Something here was not right.

Ordinarily, bandits struck outlying villages, usually at night, and were gone to their lairs in the hills by daylight. They killed peasants often, or captured them for sale to slavers, but they did not chase them for sport, certainly not under the very noses of a royal garrison.

"Sound the gong," Pegra ordered. "We'll have the cabo troop out after these rogues." He raised the glass again in time to see the last of the fleeing peasants skewered by a rider, whose exultant whoops he could now hear clearly.

They were scarcely a bowshot away from the walls of the town.

Next to Pegra the alarm gong began to reverberate. Then the beating of the great bronzen disk ceased. "Commander!" said the sentry in a strangled voice.

"What is it?" He turned and saw the guard pointing up the road, beyond the now-circling riders. With a sinking feeling, Wan Pegra raised the glass again, looking past the mounted men. Over a low rise in the road came a column of men. The column was four files wide, and as they came into view the files split, two going to the right, two to the left. They came on endlessly, splitting and resplitting until a great army faced the town, rank upon rank of them, every man holding before him a tall, black shield. All of this happened so quickly that the garrison was still scrambling up the steps to the battlement when the black tide advanced.

"Gasam!" Pegra said, almost choking. "It's that madman who conquered Chiwa! Where did he come from?"

"From Chiwa, is my guess," said the sentry, with very little deference in his voice. "And I wish we had a real soldier in command just now."

Somehow, Wan Pegra took no offense at the man's tone. He was unable to feel anything except blinding terror. He tried to think of a quick, safe way to surrender. Even in his agitated state, though, he knew that to be futile. Gasam would accept the surrender of ordinary soldiers, to swell the ranks of his own army. Seldom did he allow officers to take service under him. Commanders, never. They would always be put to death. If they were captured after a fight they were executed swiftly to show the futility of resistance. If they surrendered without a fight they died slowly to demonstrate the consequences of weakness and cowardice.

To cover his fear and gain time to plan an escape, he shouted blustering orders to his officers and men. They ignored him, knowing their work well enough. Bows were strung, sheaves of arrows and bundles of javelins were brought up from the arsenal, along with crates of round, smooth stones for the slingers.

While all this bustle went on, Pegra slipped below, ostensibly to don his field harness. No one watched him go, since every man had his own concerns just then. As his concubines cowered wide-eyed in a corner, he dashed through his quarters, stuffing his most valuable and portable possessions into a sack. He threw off his dress helmet and cuirass and donned a nondescript tunic.

With the sack over his shoulder, he raced to the river gate. He was ignored, as everyone in the town had rushed to the road side to gawk at their oncoming doom. Panting with fright, he shoved the locking bar aside and tugged the gate open. He dashed through the gate, not bothering to reclose it. The town was no longer his concern. Almost tumbling down the riverbank, he ran out along the wooden wharf and threw the sack into his riverboat, leaping in after it, cutting the mooring line with his dagger in his haste.

As the boat began to drift downstream with the current, he breathed more easily. Already, he could hear screams coming from the town. In all probability, no one would be spared. Relaxing a little now, he started to devise a story that would stand up at court. He would tell how he had conducted the defense of Marn until his last man fell, of how, barely escaping with his life, he had contrived to board this boat—no, he dived into the river, arrows and javelins splashing all around him, and found this boat drifting, boarded it and hurled his defiance at the thousands of howling savages on the shore, as he made his way south along the river, to bring his king this terrible news and render further heroic service. . . .

The boat rounded a sandbar to the south of the town and his bowels liquified as he saw the line of mounted men, their cabos belly-deep in the water, grinning and shaking their long, cruel spears in anticipation of this excellent sport. Pegra would have dived overboard and tried to swim for it, but he could not swim. As they closed in he fell to his knees, clasped his hands before him and tried begging for his life, but that did not work either.

Gasam watched the town burn with some satisfaction. It was larger than he had expected, so there would be good provision for his army, which was beginning to get hungry. He had not asked for surrender in his usual fashion, because he wanted his newer troops to be blooded now, while it was safest. The small garrison had fought stoutly, despite the futility of the odds. This pleased him, for it allowed his least experienced men to think they had been in a fight, and it meant that, later in the campaign he could expect to acquire some high-quality soldiers when enemy regiments sensibly surrendered on his terms.

He had achieved complete surprise, as he had expected. More importantly, the garrison here had been commanded by a fool, just some court appointee. This was the sign of a foolish, overconfident king, who gave idiots with high connections commands considered undesirable. That meant that Luo and Urlik would probably encounter commanders similarly ineffectual. Only after the army was reunited and marching on the capital would the king of Sono understand that his very throne was in danger and send forth a competent commander, if indeed he had such a man in his employ. This was shaping up into a wonderful campaign.

Stalker padded through the dense jungle growth as silently as a ghost. For the last few days the army had been passing through jungle country, and the women were out as flankers, charged with killing guerillas and spies. Stalker greatly enjoyed this duty. Like her sisters, she had chafed at the necessary but arduous marching. That was a tedious business, with no opportunities for glory or bloodshed.

It had been so different in the king's earlier campaigns, when they had traveled by ship from one island to another, overrunning each and subduing or slaughtering its inhabitants. Then, the elite corps of the women warriors had lounged on deck, renewing their paint or dressing each others' hair, while the sailors saw to their transportation. When it came time to fight, which was to say, to justify their existence, they seized their weapons and attacked whomever the king told them to.

The later campaigns on land had been similarly enjoyable, for the distance had not been great, and there had been much fighting with relatively little marching.

Now she was happy and content, performing with consummate skill a duty the men in the army could not have done half so well. Even the Shasinn, wonderful warriors that they were, were not at home in the jungle like Stalker and her sisters. None had sight or hearing so keen, none could move so lightly on their feet, or avoid brushing the dense growth with such fluid grace.

Stalker would have been esteemed a comely woman in civilized lands had it not been for her outlandish and bizarre ornamentation. Her tawny hair, clubbed behind her neck, was threaded through hollowed out human fingerbones. Her cheeks were laced with parallel scars, and further scars, carved in stripes and spirals, decorated her breasts, belly, thighs, buttocks and upper arms. They had been incised with a ritual flint knife and the wounds rubbed with a mixture of pumice, fat and soot to cause the flesh to heal in raised welts of a deep blue color. Besides these she bore many less symmetrical but equally honorable scars earned in battle, training and hunting. Her full lips were further everted by a small lip plug of jade and the pointed bronze caps that reinforced her teeth. Gold hoops dangled from her ears, the septum of her nose, and her pierced nipples.

That morning, she had painted her body in jungle colors laid on in broad streaks. Only her clear gray eyes shone through the mask of brown, green and black. She wore only a belt supporting a sheathed knife and she carried her favorite weapon: a short spear with a slender, six-inch point of razor-edged steel. Of all Gasam's army, only the women warriors were fully equipped with steel weapons. She did not like swords or axes, preferring the elegant precision of her little spear.

As she prowled the jungle with the soundless deadliness of a hunting cat, she thought of her latest lover. He was a Shasinn junior warrior, and his sinewy, powerful body and tireless youthful virility perfectly matched her savage appetites. He found her barbaric bodily adornments exciting, and his hands would endlessly trace her ropy scars while they coupled like animals. He impaled her with his flesh as he impaled enemies with his spear and their sensuous struggles were nearly as violent as battles. For him, she was willing to scrub off her customary coat of animal fat and anoint her body with the fragrant fistnut oil so loved by the Shasinn.

Thoughts of her lover disappeared as she caught a hint of movement ahead of her. She paused, holding still as a statue until she saw the movement again. It was a patch of coppery skin just visible through a tiny gap in the brush fifty paces ahead. It flashed into view, vanished, and came back again a few feet farther to the left. She knew that it was a man, that by his color he was not a member of the army, and that he was working his way closer to the army.

Her pulse quickened and warmth flooded her lower belly. This was an enemy and she would kill. Slowly and deliberately, she worked her way forward and to her right. She wanted to be directly behind the man before she commenced closing the distance between them. This was her special skill. She had earned her name with this art and hers was the patience of a stalking animal. Once behind him, she immediately cut his trail. Her prey probably passed for a skilled woodsman in these parts, but to her his trail was as clear as if he had tramped through leading a crippled nusk. A torn leaf, a fallen twig pushed out of alignment, a small pebble overturned to show its wet underside, the sharp scent of a crushed jungle herb, these were to her as the landmarks on a map. Once she found a partial print of a sandaled foot. She suppressed a snort of contempt. To her, footwear in the jungle was as absurd as court robes in battle.

As she drew near, her mouth opened, allowing her to breathe deeply without making a sound. Then she came to a clearing and saw her prey clearly. He was a short, strongly built man with skin the color of tarnished bronze, and coarse, black hair. He wore a loincloth of supple leather that had ornamented flaps dangling to the knees front and back, and a necklace of polished stones. She saw a short dagger at his waist and a stone-headed mace, stitched over with rawhide, thonged to his wrist. His sandals were molded closely to his feet.

Slowly, looking from side to side, the man reached out and parted the fronds just before him. Not far away she could hear the marching army, and she knew that this was a vantage point chosen by the man to spy on it. As he stood in utter stillness Stalker worked her way closer. She could see a muscle working at the corner of his jaw, as if he were speaking, but he made no sound. From this she deduced that he was counting silently. Her suspicion was confirmed by the movement of his left hand, as the tips of his fingers and thumb ticked against one another in a formalized enumerating ritual. Was this a trained spy, or just a peasant who knew how to count livestock? She suspected the former. Few save trained spies combined the skills of warrior, hunter and herdsman.

She could have hurled her spear into his broad back, but she wanted to see how close she could get before he detected her presence. A cautious step at a time, she closed the distance. She considered an amusing way to apprise him of her presence and his doom. Perhaps an ear-splitting war cry, or a gentle tap on his shoulder with her spear-point. Even as these things things ran through her mind, something

made the muscles of his back tighten. Slowly, he turned his
head to the left. She froze, but as she knew that she was
within his field of vision, she gave him a hideous, bronze-
toothed grin. He whirled, his eyes gone wide with shock
and terror at what must have seemed to him a jungle demon
sprung to life ten feet behind him.

He wasted little time despite his shock. With a swift
bound she would not have credited, he dashed away to his
left and the jungle closed behind him. Stalker plunged into
the bush after him. As she ran she smiled. This was the
part she liked best; the chase. The slow stalk was enthralling, but the swift pursuit of the doomed quarry carried an
erotic charge that made every nerve in her body blaze with
vibrant life.

Now she had no need of the hunter's arts of reading signs.
She could hear him ahead of her and occasionally catch
glimpses of his sweaty hide as he tried to put distance between them. He was a powerful runner, but she knew she
was better. Soon he would slow, both from fatigue and because he would think he had lost her. She deliberately kept
her distance in these early stages, so that he would not see
her behind him should he look over his shoulder.

Her long legs propelled her over the ground and her body
flexed from side to side with serpentine fluidity, avoiding
growth so dense that most normal humans would have
needed to chop their way through it. Always she watched
for traps. If her prey were truly skilled, he would have
seeded his planned route of escape with snares, deadfalls
and pits.

When she could tell from the sounds ahead of her that
the man was staggering, she slowed and calmed her breathing. The sweat dripped from her body in streams but her
movements were as deft and sure as ever. When she knew
that he had slowed to a walk, Stalker began to circle. This
was going to be intensely gratifying.

A few minutes later, the spy walked into a little clearing

where the afternoon sun streamed down through an opening in the green canopy. His sweaty chest worked like a bellows and he looked behind him as he began to cross the open space. Turning back, his eyes bulged in disbelief to see Stalker emerge into the clearing directly in front of him.

"Who is your master, spy?" she hissed. "Who sent you to look upon my king's army?"

The man only gasped for breath, then attacked. He drew his knife and whirled his mace, rushing forward with a wordless cry. Exhausted as the man was, the charge was more of a lurch, which Stalker sidestepped with ease, thrusting her spear-point into his thigh as he passed. She jerked the point free and thrust it into the back of the other thigh and the man dropped to his knees with a cry of pain. As he flung his arms out to break his fall she seized his rawhide-wrapped mace and cut its wrist-thong with her knife. Before he could even think of a defense, she struck him on the back of his head, just above where the neck joined the skull. The spy collapsed bonelessly. Smiling, Stalker set to work.

When the man woke, groaning, his eyes unfocussed and his stomach nauseous, he was staked to the ground, his loincloth gone. His eyes straightened and filled with terror as realization of his predicament struck with full force. Stalker stood grinning above him, and the man knew himself to be in the power of something supernaturally evil.

"Now, spy," she said, "who do you serve?"

"I . . . do . . . not . . . ." His words were halting and strangely accented, but she could understand him.

"Do not what?" she asked.

"Not talk to you," he said, his chin firming, knowing he was going to die. His face grew puzzled as she walked to him and stepped across his legs, straddling him. Then she sank to her knees.

"Oh, yes, you'll talk, my little spy." She drew her knife with one hand. With the other she grasped his penis and testicles, drawing them up tight as she laid the keen edge of her knife against their root. "You'll tell me what my king wishes to know. No man defies my king."

The man began to scream, then to talk.

"He was just a scout for a regional commander to the south," Stalker said, displaying her bloody trophies to Gasam. "Some river boatmen caught sight of the fires of Marn burning and turned back down the river. The commander thought it only important enough to send a scout on foot. His garrison is only about three times the size of the one at Marn, but he does have a team of mounted messengers. With these he may be able to send word of our coming to the south and thence to the capital."

"Excellent, Stalker," Gasam commended her. "Again, you have proven to be my best scout and hunter. See if you can catch me another one on tomorrow's march."

Smiling, the woman departed to gloat among her sisters. Gasam congratulated himself once more on his wisdom and foresight in acquiring these unconventional warriors. He had asked for them specifically back in the days when he had allied himself with the king of Chiwa, whom the women had previously served. Led for once by a true warrior-king, they had happily transferred their allegiance. His more conventional followers found them horrifying, but that was why he liked them so much.

"Those mounted messengers could cause us trouble, my king," said Raba, one of his Shasinn senior commanders. He was a much-scarred veteran from Gasam's earliest days of conquest.

"I shall detach a small force, including some of the archers. They shall run ahead and take up position on the road to the south of the town and deal with any messengers sent south. If some get through . . ." He shrugged. "They should only run into Luo's force. Surely they have reached the river by now. If not, Urlik's riders will catch them for sure.''

"They might swim the river," Raba pointed out.

"It is possible, but even if they reach the capital, they will not be in time to do King Mana any good. It would be amusing to arrive before his capital unannounced, but there are advantages to giving him some warning. He will concentrate his forces to defend the capital, where we can deal with them all at once. Otherwise his regional lords might break away with their personal forces. Then we will have to deal with them one by one, a tedious business.''

Raba tossed another stick into the fire and took the wine jug passed by a fellow officer. Now that there had been a little blooding, discipline was slightly relaxed. In any case, officers were allowed more license than the common warriors. He took a long swallow of the tart wine and pondered his king's words.

"Are you sure that he will give battle before his capital, my king?'' Raba asked.

"Assuredly. It is a peculiarity of these mainland kings that they will always defend the capital rather than fight on ground of their own choosing. It is a great weakness in them. They are very attached to their fine cities and think that if an enemy takes the capital, the war is lost. That is why it is important to drive deep into an enemy country before the king has a chance to assemble his forces. Given a chance, they will mobilize and march to keep you outside the borders. Once you menace the capital, they can think of nothing save defending it.''

"Incredible,'' said a senior officer of the Squall Island Shasinn. His hair was dressed in the triple braids of that tribe. "Why don't they just *give* us their kingdoms, rather than make war so foolishly?'' The others gathered at the king's shelter laughed.

"It suited them well enough as long as they fought only among themselves,'' Gasam pointed out. "Faced with an enemy who cares nothing for their customs, they can only act in the way with which they are familiar. That is why we must attack swiftly and win a quick, decisive victory. Because they are not wholly stupid and they can learn from their errors. Young commanders will take over when we have killed the old fools. Speed is everything in a war of conquest.''

FIVE

Queen Larissa had à blinding headache. It was the third in a month, and this both annoyed and frightened her. All her life, she had enjoyed extraordinary health, never knowing sickness, recovering swiftly from injury. These devastating but decentralized pains caused her an unwelcome sense of frailty, a feeling of mortality to which she had thought herself immune. Irritably, she called for one of her women to massage her shoulders and neck. Sometimes that helped.

"Will you go out to oversee the new bridge, mistress?" the woman asked.

"If this headache will abate," she said. This was one of her new projects. The capital was built on both sides of the river, yet for centuries the kings of Chiwa had been content to use primitive ferries to connect the two banks. It surpassed her powers of imagination to come up with a reason why they would build vast temples and tombs of imperishable stone, yet depend on a ferry system worthy of a mud village.

The great bridge was just one of the projects she had set in motion. She had seen the great engineering works of Neva, and she wanted her kingdom to be in no way inferior to Shazad's. A new port with separate merchant and naval basins was under construction, complete with covered ship houses. The capital would soon have a fully roofed market, with spacious warehouses around its perimeter, and she had ordered others built in all the principal cities. Those cities would be connected by roads paved with cut stone.

The old kingdom of Chiwa had consisted of royalty, nobility and priesthood existing in great magnificence atop a foundation of tremendous squalor. Larissa intended that her land would be wholly magnificent. Her husband needed a huge warrior class for his conquests. Peasants and slaves might be necessary for the everyday work of empire, but there was no reason why they should have to offend the eyes of their betters.

"Shall I send for the litter?" the slavewoman asked. Larissa had never liked to use any form of land transportation save her own feet, but Chiwans were accustomed to obeying masters who rode on the shoulders of their countrymen, and in recent months she had found it a pleasant sensation. There was something fitting, after all, in being borne along by the musclepower of subject peoples. Slaves deserved their fates, and should be kept aware of the fact. Like the Chiwan lords and ladies before her, she had selected a team matched for size, skill and beauty.

"Yes, have them standing by." Already, the pain was lessening. The woman had been one of her earliest acquisitions on the mainland. This was one of many skills which Larissa now found to be indispensable. More and more, she depended on her slaves. She had too much to do every hour of the day.

It was a fine day for an excursion, she had to admit. The

gentle rocking of her litter was soothing and the high clouds caused the sun to glare less fiercely than usual. The streets of the city had been swept clean, by her order. Beautiful as the city was, she had been appalled by its stench when she and her husband had entered it as conquerors. The filth of humans and animals, combined with the reek of sacrifice from the many temples, had turned the air into a strangling fog despite the tons of incense burned everywhere.

It was a very ancient city, much built over, many of its buildings constructed of stone scavenged from even older structures. There were statues of kings whose names were long forgotten, of gods no longer worshipped. Mansions of the wealthy abutted great blocks of slums and on the out-skirts of the city the mud huts of peasants were surrounded by beautifully laid out, lovingly tended gardens, fields and orchards.

At the bridge site, the usual gawkers prostrated them-selves as they saw their queen borne among them. The royal overseer and the foreign engineers bowed with greater dig-nity as the litter was lowered to the pavement.

"Welcome my queen," said the overseer, once a Chiwan guild master. "You are just in time. Today, we put the key-stone of the first span in place."

"That is what I came to see," she told him. The engi-neers began to speak of the mysteries of their craft, of weights and materials and stresses. She listened with half an ear, knowing that she could not understand anything so abstruse, but content that these men knew their business. She had hired their services from Queen Shazad of Neva. Her sister monarch was always happy to engage in trade and peaceful projects, but she drew the line at cooperation on military matters.

The bridge scarcely looked like a bridge as yet. Pilings had been sunk at intervals and several abutments were com-pleted, but the soon-to-be-finished span was so encased in wooden frames and scaffolding that little of the beautiful stone was visible. Lashed to the span's abutments was a huge raft topped by a massive crane, operated by a tremendous wheel in which clambering slaves furnished lifting power. From the crane's lifting arm dangled the massive, wedge-shaped keystone that would complete the span and make its arch a freestanding unit. Workmen handled ropes to keep the great stone centered as, an inch at a time, it was lowered.

There was a general holding of breath as the stone descended the last few inches. A foreman shouted and made dramatic gestures which the workmen ignored, concentrating instead on their delicate steering task. The fit of the stone was so precise that, once in place, there could be little wedging or fine adjustment.

The stone settled and the workmen set up a cheer, which was taken up by the watchers on the riverbank. The engineers and the overseer let out a long-held breath. The overseer turned to the queen, mopping a nervous sweat from his brow.

"Perfect, my queen. Now the scaffolding and the frames come down. By this time tomorrow, you will be able to appreciate the span in all its beauty."

"Well done, all of you," she proclaimed, loud enough for the workers on the bridge to hear. "Finish the other spans as well, and your queen will reward you richly." The cheer was raised anew. Men were easily recompensed, she thought, even for such prodigious labor as this.

She returned to the palace in a much better frame of mind. The pain in her head was gone, and she had a feeling of real accomplishment. The bridge had been her idea. She had declared that the bridge should be, and now she could see it coming into being, day by day. Her husband enjoyed glory and power. She liked to see tangible results. Glory and battles and reputations could be forgotten, like the forgotten kings whose images she saw everywhere around her. Her bridge, her harbors and markets and roads would last for centuries. She could look on her works and know that her power meant something.

One thing she had vowed: She would build no temples. There were already too many of them and, splendid though they might be, they were useless. She did not like priests and she liked their gods even less. Some of the temples of this kingdom were awe-inspiring, but magnificence for its own sake disgusted her. She still felt some lingering respect for the spirits of her ancestral islands, but she had violated most of their tabus so she preferred not to think of them.

As she entered the palace, she saw two men rise from the bench upon which they had been sitting. This was the entrance hall where she usually received petitioners and she was about to tell them to come back another time when something about their appearance stopped her. She knew she had seen them somewhere before.

The men came forward, bowing. A Shasinn junior warrior who had been lounging against a wall sauntered forward to stand by his queen, his spear held casually in one hand. Had she nodded to him in a particular way, the youth would have spitted both men in half a heartbeat. His studied languor disguised the lightning killing reflexes of the Shasinn.

"Who are you?" she asked as the men thrust back their hoods, revealing a man with short, black hair and beard, and one with a half-shaven head, the remaining hair dyed blue.

"I am Haffle," said the black-bearded one, "and this is Ingist. We are . . ."

"I know who you are." Now she remembered them. An excited tingle began inside her. For these two to approach her like this could only mean one thing. "Come with me. Say nothing until I bid you."

Wordlessly, they followed her into the palace proper, the young warrior at their backs. She led them to a broad courtyard where a table was quickly furnished with food and wine by the palace slaves. She dismissed the slaves, and the young warrior took his place against a wall, just out of hearing distance. It looked trusting, but Gasam picked all the palace guards personally. At the first hostile motion, the boy could launch his spear at one man, snatch the throwing-stick from his belt and hurl it to brain the other. The ball-headed stick would be whizzing through the air before the spear split its victim's spine.

Playing the generous hostess, she filled three cups and gave one to each man. As she sipped at hers, she studied them. They were nervous, keyed up and elated. For the sake of form, they sipped at their wine and picked at the food before them, but she could tell that their stomachs were paralyzed by excitement.

"You have not reported to Master Hildas?" she asked, naming her chief of intelligence. She saw their eyes widen slightly, knowing that they had staked their fortunes on this gamble.

"My queen," said the one named Haffle, "so vital is the intelligence we bring you that we decided it must be heard only by yourself or the king. When we reached this land, we found that the king had already embarked on a war of conquest. Having no desire to tramp through a war-torn country in search of the king, we decided to come straight to the palace and report directly to you."

"That was wise," she said. "If you have brought me what I think you have, no one could ever question your bravery. I will see that Hildas gives you no trouble. He is busy with a new task in any case. Now, tell me."

"My queen," said the blue-haired one, "we have found the steel mine of King Hael!"

She let out a sigh of pure, sensuous pleasure. "Go on," she all but whispered.

In one hand the queen clutched her miniature steel spear, the emblem of her power as regent in her husband's absence. In the other, she held the most precious object in the world: a map, scrolled and encased in a watertight tube of lacquered leather.

She had been sitting thus for hours, her face clenched in a frown. Her slavewomen trod lightly, frightened at the change that had come upon their mistress. Never before had she behaved thus. They had thought they knew her many moods, but this one was new. Larissa was a dangerous woman when she was upset.

They need not have worried. Their behavior was the last thing in her thoughts. The queen was afflicted by an unfamiliar sensation: indecision. Ordinarily, she behaved as naturally and instinctively as an animal. This situation was unprecedented. Gasam had been specific in his instructions: She was to stay here and govern in his stead. Yet, she had to get this map and this report to him, wherever he might be. And there was no one, absolutely no one, she could trust to do this for her.

For much of the night, she sat unmoving. The slaves brought candles and lamps. Food was placed before her but she left it untouched.

As the gray light of dawn flowed over the terrace outside, she rose. The decision was not that hard, after all, she thought. The work of the country would carry on without her. The civil side of affairs would be competently handled by her own, hand-picked staff. Authority would be enforced by the royal garrisons left behind when her husband marched. They were scarcely needed. The terror of Gasam's name was sufficient to quell any thought of disorder.

"Prepare my bath," she ordered, "and summon General Pendu." The slaves rushed to do her bidding. An hour later, a tall, hard-faced Shasinn warrior entered her antechamber. The years of hard campaigning had etched deep lines beside his mouth and around his eyes, furrowing his brow. His dark-bronze hair was heavily grayed, but his body might have been cast from molten metal and his stride was that of the junior warrior he had been when he and Gasam had been boys in the same warrior fraternity.

"Yes, my queen?" he said, without preamble.

"Pendu, something extraordinary has happened. I must go at once and join my husband."

"What? But the king has . . ."

"I know quite well what the king's instructions were," she snapped. "This is something unforeseen. I have information that I must deliver to him personally. And I must act quickly. I shall take my personal bodyguard, since they have all been trained to ride. The rest of the Shasinn I leave here with you."

"My queen!" Pendu protested. "The king left me here because he would not leave you here unprotected. If this is so important, take me with you. Never before has the king gone on campaign without me."

"Pendu," she said, gently, "he needs a Shasinn presence here to remind this great herd of human livestock to behave themselves. We are not roving pirates and raiders anymore, but the rulers of an empire. He chose you and your regiment because, besides himself, you and Luo and Raba are all that is left of the old fraternity. The rest are all dead." She did not mention Hael, who was worse than dead. "You three are the only ones he trusts, so it had to be one of you. Next war, you will be by his side, I promise. Now, go and see that my men are mounted. Have remounts and supplies assembled. I will need horses for two other men as well. I will take no slaves with me."

"The other two," Pendu said, "they would not by any chance be those two spies who arrived yesterday, would they?" A look of comprehension crossed his scarred features.

"Don't be thinking, Pendu," she chided. "My husband and I will do the thinking. Just do my bidding and keep order here. And, Pendu," she added, "be ready to receive unexpected marching orders from the king."

His face flamed with pleasure. "Yes, my queen!"

"Go now," she ordered. The man turned and left without bowing. Such royal niceties were not practiced among the Shasinn. Besides, he had known her since childhood and anything more than the respect due a chieftainess would have felt awkward for both of them. She would have liked to tell him of the steel mine, but she knew he suspected, and she had resolved to keep it secret. She trusted absolutely the loyalty of Gasam's fraternity brothers, but they were just warriors with no extraordinary mental gifts. The less known of this matter, the better.

Larissa did not enjoy riding, but she felt elation as she mounted the fine cabo held for her by a guard. This was action. She was going to make a desperate ride to join her husband in the middle of a foreign war. She had forgotten how much she loved living like this.

Around her were fifty young warriors, all of them eager for the ride. The two spies were there as well, considerably less eager, but willing to do their duty. She had promised them rewards beyond even their fevered imaginings, but all was contingent upon the steel mine being captured by Gasam. The map was wonderful, but she also wanted guides who could give the army mile-by-mile advice.

They rode from the city without fanfare. As far as the population was concerned, she was just going on another of her frequent inspections.

Although she was not fond of the practice, Larissa rode well. All Shasinn had an affinity for animals, and she knew she made a splendid picture, riding with her long, ashen hair streaming. She refused to wear the sort of riding trousers favored by mainland women, so she wore a warrior loincloth and a voluminous cloak that shrouded her almost to the ankles. She had not ridden hard in many months, and she knew the sort of pain she was in for. She had had her saddle and her stirrup leathers heavily padded as a precaution, but the help would be marginal. She was accustomed to hardship, though, and her body was resilient enough to recover and toughen in a few days. Besides, her attitude toward pain was not that of most people.

She had not felt this alive in years. The greatest secret in the world was sheathed at her belt. Pointing the way with her little spear, she rode with the wind in her teeth, laughing.

SIX

The two riders, man and woman, crossed into the kingdom of Gran by way of a rickety bridge across a slow-moving river, its banks densely overgrown with tangled, tropical growth. Everywhere they looked were signs of swarming life. The air buzzed and screeched with the calls of birds and reptiles, the wing-noises of insects, the cries of small animals hunting, mating and dying. In the distance, they sometimes heard the bellows of far larger animals, and were thankful that the great beasts were not close enough for them to see.

Ansa reined his cabo midway across the bridge. In the murky, sluggish depths below, something was disturbing the surface. Abruptly, a long form broke the surface, churning it to froth with its scaly sides and thrashing tail. He had an impression of a long, pointed snout, bristling with teeth and gripping something silvery that writhed and struggled. Then the killer slid beneath the water, leaving only a swirling eddy behind, where fallen leaves danced in circles before calming and resuming their leisurely, current-borne voyage to some faraway sea.

"What was it?" he asked, aghast.

"Something big and mean," she answered. "Be thankful that it prefers the river to the land."

The journey from the Canyon had not been lengthy as Ansa, accustomed to the wide plain, judged such things. But the change in terrain had been dramatic. South of the Canyon the land dropped sharply, and each day's travel had brought them into a zone of climate and flora distinct from that of the day before. Most notable with the drop in altitude was the increase in humidity. Before they had been traveling long, they entered land where rainfall was everyday instead of seasonal. They had to cross streams and small rivers each day, sometimes more than one each day. Avoiding swamps became commonplace. Biting insects were first an annoyance, then a plague. Fyana brought out an ointment that gave some relief but smelled so disgusting that Ansa would almost have preferred the bugs.

For the last two days they had been passing through true jungle, the first such Ansa had ever seen in his life. Even more astonishing than the dense flora was the sheer, overwhelming presence of *life* everywhere. On the plains he had been accustomed to seeing great herds of livestock and of wild game. At the time of great migrations, it was not unusual to see many thousands of animals rumbling across the grasslands in a mass. But then it was relatively large animals, all of a type.

In these lands, he could take in a score of life-forms in a single glance. Besides the pestiferous insects, there were birds, bats and reptiles in the air and in the trees, mammals of all sorts, including man-of-the-trees in many varieties. Cats seemed to be the predominant predators.

Here nature seemed inclined toward whimsical experiment, and many creatures departed from their accustomed niches. In his home plains Ansa was accustomed to flightless birds, and in the great desert to the north of the steel mine he had seen land-roving bats that hunted in packs. But here he saw bats that swam. A spidery-limbed reptile hung by its tail in the branches to catch flying creatures as they passed by. He saw a type of man-of-the-trees that could glide from tree to tree by means of a broad membrane that stretched between its arms and its hind legs. Its tail was a flat paddle used in maneuvering.

"Well, you wanted to see strange sights," Fyana said as he continued to stare at the spot where the river monster had disappeared.

"Most of the jungle life we've seen is small," he noted. "The rivers are different. I think I'll forego swimming in these parts."

"Wise decision." She pointed toward the southern end of the bridge. "I think we are about to meet Granian authority."

There was a small building of mud and wood at the end of the bridge, and a man emerged from it as their mounts clumped from the bridge's log surface onto the hard-packed dirt beyond. He was a stout, almost fat figure wearing a loincloth so elaborate that it almost constituted a kilt depending from a cummerbund so broad that it reached up to the official's drooping paps. His face was shaded by a hat of woven straw with a wide brim, and a crown worked into a number of bulbous shapes, one atop the other.

The face thus shaded was brown and egg-shaped. The nose was very long and broad, above a wide mouth with no visible lips. His eyes were crossed, apparently by design as an amber bead dangled from the front of his hat brim to form a focal point. He held a tablet and stylus and had the air of officialdom everywhere.

"Your names, please?" he said without preamble. He spoke a dialect of Southern with an accent so strong that Ansa had to concentrate to understand the words. They gave their names.

"Your business?" He scribbled in his tablet.

"I am a dealer in Canyon medicines," Fyana said, patting the bales borne by the humper she led. "This warrior is my escort." They had agreed upon this story. It was plausible, since such medicine merchants were quite common, and a woman traveling alone could be expected to hire an escort. Canyon medicines were in high demand everywhere. Best of all, it would provide them with a means of livelihood while they sought out information concerning Gasam's doings.

"Very good," said the official. "If you will open your packs, I will verify their contents. There is no import duty on Canyon medicines."

They wrestled the packs to the ground and revealed their contents: packets of powders and dried herbs, stoppered flasks of fluids, bundles of stalks, leaves and fronds. The official nodded wisely, as if he knew what he was looking at.

"All seems to be in order," he said at last. "Which is to say, I would know if you tried to bring in contraband." He made out passes for them, written with a peculiar violet ink on paper made of a veiny, pressed leaf. "These you must show to any royal official on demand," he said. "They give your names, occupations and business along with the place and date of your entry into the country."

Fyana looked closely at her pass. "It is difficult to make out the writing," she said. The background color of the pressed leaf was dark and the violet marks were only a little darker.

"All government officials are used to it and will have no trouble," he said, happy to be speaking of the mysteries of his profession. "What is more important is that royal ink is impossible to duplicate." He turned his head and gave a low whistle. A small animal appeared from the interior of the customs house and circled his feet, rubbing itself against his ankles. It was furry, with short legs and a long, very bushy tail. Its narrow, pointed snout terminated in a rubbery ball of nose, which twitched continually. The man stopped and held out one of the passes. The little beast sniffed at it and made a buzzing, contented sound.

"Had it been altered or tampered with in any way, he would have let me know in no uncertain terms. For which reason, you would be well advised to wrap these carefully, so that neither sweat nor other contamination sullies them." He handed the passes to them. "Obey the laws, comport yourselves decorously and," he raised an admonitory finger, "do not seek to introduce the worship of foreign gods. Observe these simple rules, and your stay in our country cannot fail to be pleasant and beneficial."

Repacked and on their way into the country, they passed through a village whose inhabitants wore variations of the official's garb. As jaded occupants of a border town, they paid little attention to the newcomers. Ansa noted that their headgear was simpler and more utilitarian than that of the official, but still of a shape bizarre to his eye.

"Is it always like that, crossing a border?" he asked Fyana.

"So I've heard," she said. "Although I understand they can be far more unpleasant."

They left the village and rode past its fields and the jungle closed in again. The road was of plain dirt, but it was fairly broad and quite well marked. From time to time they passed stone posts carved with the Granian script. At less regular intervals, they saw images of gods set into niches in roadside shrines, where insects buzzed over the remains of food offerings. The gods were of both sexes and varied in dress, activity and in the enigmatic objects which they brandished.

Late in the afternoon, they came upon a sizable band of travelers setting up a camp for the evening. It was plain that the site was frequently used. It was near a clear stream and had semipermanent fire pits lined with riverbottom stone.

Tents were being pitched and fires kindled. A bearded man, obviously not a native, smiled at them as they rode in.

"Welcome! Stay the night with us, friends. There is security in numbers and we grow bored with each other's company."

"Gladly," Fyana said. By their looks, most of the travelers were small merchants, along with a few mountebanks.

"Is there danger here?" Ansa asked. "Such as causes people to seek safety in numbers?" He dismounted and stretched his legs. The clean smell of smoke perfumed the heavy air.

"Bandits, such as plague every land. But they will not molest a band this size, especially if we have a warrior among us." He bowed. "I am Samis, a merchant of Neva. You, madame, need hardly identify yourself as to nation. And you, young sir, have the look of the grasslands about you. I take it that you are one of King Hael's subjects?"

"That I am. Ansa, a warrior of the Ramdi. This is Lady Fyana, a trader in medicines." It was unusual for a mere trader to use a title of nobility, but all nations recognized that Canyoners were not as other people.

"I am honored, my lady," Samis said. "I hope you will favor us this evening with some of the legendary skills of your nation."

"That may be," she said. "It is not like a manual skill, which may be called upon at will."

"Of course, I understand," said the merchant. "But, come and sit by my fire. My servants will unload your animals and set up your tents." He clapped his hands and four young men, little more than boys, came running. At his rapid commands, they took charge of the two cabos and the humper. A place was made for them by a large fire and they sat. It pleased Ansa to see the deference paid to Fyana, although he could find no true reason for his satisfaction. He had no illusion that this all but courtly honor was being paid him. Warriors were respected or feared, but that was the extent of it.

"What did he mean?" Ansa asked, inspecting his lance-point for rust.

"You'll see. It's something we Canyoners can do. Well, sometimes we can do it."

He studied the other travelers. He saw no countrymen, nor did he expect to. There were no other Canyoners. The band contained representatives of a half-score of nations and there were a few Palana, who had no nation. Several were native Granians, the rest Nevans, Chiwans, Sonoans and people of no land he could recognize.

Even before the cook-fires were fairly burning, Fyana did some business. A number of the traders were bound for parts where medicines were scarce and they bought stocks of the sort they knew would be in demand. With portable scales they weighed out currency and scraps of trade metal. Ansa even had several offers for his fine steel weapons, which he rebuffed with poor grace. He had a warrior's dislike of commerce, although his father had tried repeatedly to teach him of the importance of trade. The idea of trading away his precious weapons for mere money disgusted him.

After a congenial dinner, the travelers traded stories and information. Casually, Ansa asked about disturbances to the west.

"A merchant recently arrived from Sono," Samis told him, "said that there is some sort of disturbance there. King Mana has been calling up his army, apparently to meet an invasion from the west. It is all very unclear at the moment. Were you aware of this?"

"A rumor from the desert," Ansa equivocated. "I am interested, because I am a warrior and my services may be in demand there."

"If war it is," said the merchant, "that is one I would avoid. The only credible threat from the west is King Gasam, and where he marches only devastation is left."

Ansa was about to retort that Gasam's reputation was based on the islander's own myth-making rather than fact, but he held his tongue. A personal grudge against the king might appear suspicious.

"It might not be a bad thing," said one of the Palana, idly juggling three stuffed leather balls. "One great king here in the south, instead of several small ones. There are too many borders to cross, too many officials to deal with."

"You can say that," a Sonoan said. "You Palana have no land. Most of us are content with rulers of our own kind. From what I have heard, this Gasam is nothing but a bandit or pirate who has made himself great by toppling weak and foolish kings." Most of the others seemed to agree with this assessment.

"He will not have an easy time of it in Sono," the man continued. "King Mana is a warrior, and his army is great."

"Mana's greatness is in his monuments," Samis muttered to Ansa under his breath. "His army may prove equally insubstantial."

Ansa digested this information and resolved to spend some time in conversation with the merchant, who seemed to be remarkably well informed.

A nusk handler approached Fyana, complaining of a pain in his jaw. She peered into his mouth and felt the swelling along his jaw, at which he flinched.

"This is a simple toothache," she said. "Nothing mysterious about it. Next town we come to, find a tooth-drawer. Failing that, a smith with a pair of pliers. That tooth must come out if you would save the rest."

"But that will be painful," he said. The others laughed and he glared at their lack of sympathy.

"If it's done swiftly the pain will be gone soon. And it will be as nothing compared to what will happen if you do not have it attended to."

Others came to her to have ailments diagnosed. To Ansa's astonishment, Fyana would place her fingertips against their foreheads for a while, then tell them what was wrong internally. She could not read all of them, but was able to prescribe medicines for more than half. Later, Ansa asked her about this.

"You had not told me you were a healer."

"I am not," she said. "True healers are very rare, even among us. But many of us have the ability to read disorders within the body. It doesn't always work. We can't detect the presence of internal parasites, for instance, although we can read the damage they do. Sometimes it is very sad. You saw that man who came to me with a bellyache?"

"I did."

"He has a growth in his stomach that will surely kill him within the year, but what point in telling him? There is nothing to be done, so I told him of some painkillers that can help. That is all you can do, in a case like that."

"This sounds more like a burden than a gift," he said.

"That it is."

The next morning they continued their journey. Most of the travelers were headed for the capital, a city named Kwila. At the slow pace of the little caravan, they were still some twenty days from that city, but they elected to stay with the group. As part of such an assemblage, they were fairly anonymous. Time did not seem to be a crucial element in their rather loose plans, so they saw no reason not to amble along in leisurely fashion, enjoying an excursion into an exotic and interesting land.

Ansa's sense of time was attuned to seasons rather than any formalized concept of scheduling. As long as he reached his destination eventually, he had no urge to rush things. There was much to see in this strange land. The people seemed much occupied with rituals, their every action accompanied by a multiplicity of gestures that seemed strange to Ansa. They constantly recited formulas, prayers and invocations. They were fond of amulets, talismans of various sorts, and incense. Many swung clay censers as they walked, and a few even wore tiny incense burners atop their hats.

Once, he asked Samis about all these religious observations.

"I cannot say," the merchant told him, "that the rewards they receive from the supernatural world are in any way commensurate with the time and energy they spend on their devotions. I know little about their beliefs, and they are close-mouthed about them. From what I have learned, they have a great profusion of gods, demons and spirits of one sort and another. All of these must be worshipped or placated in some fashion. It seems a great tedium to me, but it suits them well."

"My own people are respectful of the spirits," Ansa told him, "but our beliefs and practices are simple compared to this. Is it true, as I have heard, that they practice human sacrifice?"

Samis looked about, as if to see whether any Granians were in earshot. "Yes, it is true," he said, in a low voice, "but they allow no outsider to witness these rituals. I would not inquire too closely, if I were you. There are always tales of strangers who suddenly disappear just at the time that these sacrifices are called for."

"These people might be chancy to dwell among," Ansa said.

The merchant waved a hand dismissively. "Rumors, only rumors. I have no personal knowledge of such disappearances. People allow themselves to be overly alarmed by these unlikely perils, when there are simpler but far greater dangers around them every day."

Ansa ducked as a bat swooped by in pursuit of a tiny bird. The bat's span of leathery wings was as wide as his arm was long. Both creatures disappeared instantly in the dense growth that flanked the narrow road. In places, the trees interlaced branches overhead, so that they seemed to be making their way through a gloomy, green tunnel.

From all directions came the cries, calls, whoops, bellows and other sounds of the jungle fauna. In the limited visibility of the jungle, it seemed, noise was at a premium. Those creatures that attracted mates or warned off enemies with displays were colored brilliantly and were often of grotesque shape. Once, Ansa was startled by what he took for the snarling mask of a longneck in a bush nearby. Unexpectedly, the "face" flickered away and Ansa saw that it was the deceptive pattern on the back of a winged reptile.

There were carnivorous plants large enough to capture small animals and birds, along with the inevitable rumors of others in the deep jungle that could eat men. Even lacking this unlikely form of vegetation, there were plenty of hazardous plants. In the unceasing struggle for survival with such abundant competition, many of the plants had developed unusual defenses and strategies for reproduction. There were stinging plants and itching plants. There were plants with exudations so poisonous that one had to be careful when gathering firewood, for they could generate choking, stinging smoke when burned. There was a plant that could fire barbed, dart-shaped seeds into the skin of a passing creature from a distance of several feet.

All this made for wary traveling. Ansa quickly learned that the greatest beauty could hide the deadliest peril. There were huge, beautiful blossoms that exhaled a soporific fragrance that could bring about death. The decaying victim enriched the soil around the plant's roots.

They passed a village where peasants toiled in their fields, stooped to the endless task of pulling the weeds that sprang up so pestiferously in this fertile clime.

"I've seen farmers and villagers and traders," Ansa said, "and a royal official or two, but I've yet to see any warriors. Are these people so unused to war?"

"Far from it," Samis told him. "The armies are concentrated in forts at strategic parts of the country, mostly near the borders and guarding important waterways. The peasants are a dull and placid lot as you have seen, so there is no need for numerous garrisons to keep them in line.

"The rulers of this land," the merchant continued, warming to his subject, "are a warrior aristocracy. They subdued Sono several generations ago. The armies are not recruited from among the old native class, although a large part of the civil service are."

"How do they fight?" Ansa asked. "Are they riders? Archers? Spearmen?"

"They employ some missile troops, but the backbone of the army consists of highly disciplined regiments of heavy infantry armed with spears and axes."

Ansa looked around him. "That seems a poor choice for fighting in this jungle."

"They seldom fight in the jungle. No one does, really. The highlands are far more open as well as more healthy. That is where most fighting takes place, when the southern kings contend for power. There is also much contention over mountain passes and the more important cities."

"All my life I've heard of the great cities of the south," Ansa said, slapping at an insect that was probing his neck for blood. "So far, I've seen nothing but mud villages."

"Once again," Samis said, "this low, jungle country is not conducive to great settlements. When we are farther south, on more open ground, you will see the great cities built on the broad fields and waterways. Already we are climbing. By tomorrow, you will begin to see the difference."

"That can't happen soon enough for me," Ansa rejoined. His mount started and skittered sideways a few steps, and he had to wrestle it back under control. "Or for him either. These insects are driving the poor beast mad. No wonder the southerners make little use of mounted troops."

"Very true," said Samis. "This is not a good place for delicate, high-strung beasts. Nusks and humpers are better, with their thick hair and thick hides and even thicker intelligence. But this is not bad. Past the highlands, the land descends once more to the coast. The coastal swamps are so deadly that your cabo would not last ten days there, and you might not last much longer, although the Canyon lady's medicines might keep you hale for a while."

"I shall remember that, and avoid the coast if at all possible." Dying of some loathsome disease did not fit in with his ideas of the adventurer's life. He spoke of these matters with Fyana that evening.

"I know a good many medicines," she told him. "In the Canyon, we know how to treat many diseases. But nobody really knows what *causes* some sicknesses. Bad water brings sickness, so does the bite of some insects, but that is just . . . transmission, not the disease itself. With medicine, we treat sickness as injury. All we can do is repair the damage, or at least lessen it."

"Some here talk as if you Canyoners can cure anything," he said.

"That is because people *want* to believe it. That is why there are so many frauds. People are so desperate for cure that they will believe anything."

"That is disappointing," he said. "As a warrior, I can expect frequent wounds."

"Wounds are simple to deal with, at least," she assured him. "Broken bones can be set, gashes stitched up. All this is very painful, but a warrior can endure pain."

"Naturally," he said stoutly.

"Of course," she pointed out, "it might make more sense to avoid such injuries in the first place."

"Where is the honor in that?" he asked.

She sighed and ran a hand across her face, as if wiping away a bad memory. "Sometimes I wonder why we bother with healing and doctoring, when men make such efforts to harm themselves and others."

This seemed a perversely female attitude to Ansa, but he was not inclined to argue the point with her.

SEVEN

The great, black-shielded army swept southward at its swiftest marching speed. Even so, King Gasam chafed, longing for the days when his army had been made up entirely of Shasinn. *They* would have made this journey at a run. Eight days before, he had linked up with Luo's force and now they plunged southward down the river to catch a hastily assembled royal force between this army and Urlik's.

Even as they marched, Gasam knew that word of the invasion was speeding to the capital. There was no help for it at this date, and it was a small matter if their surprise was not total. Even if King Mana sought aid from the king of Sono or his smaller neighbors to the southeast, they could not possibly send reinforcements in time to do him any good. King Gasam's campaigns were always quick, savage and merciless. Before those other kings knew what had happened, they would have a new neighbor on their borders, a very unfriendly neighbor, indeed.

Gasam laughed as he thought of these things. He loved war, loved all its planning and preparations, loved its action and excitement, the bloodshed and the mastery of other men. To be king in his capital and see his subjects fall on their faces in his presence was pleasant, as was receiving the trembling honors rendered by foreign representatives. But none of these things carried the deeply satisfying thrill of active conquest.

The only thing missing, he thought as he marched at the head of his army, sweat streaming down his chest and his steel spear flashing in the bright sunlight, was that he did not have his queen by his side this time. This was the first conquest she had not shared with him.

From the very first, when he was nothing more than a junior warrior with grandiose dreams and she the unwed daughter of a chief, they had shared everything. In those days he had advanced his plans through subterfuge and treachery, and she had aided him in every way. She had no warrior scruples about such tactics, and she admired him for his cleverness as much as for his bravery. In later years, when he conquered by leadership and naked force, she had been equally at home with those qualities.

These were the burdens of kingship, he thought. It was a wonderful thing to have the world grovel at his feet, but the station carried responsibilities he could have done without. Having conquered nations, those lands became his responsibility. He had to care for their prosperity, where before he had only desired their destruction. Once, it had seemed to him that the task before him was simple. He would destroy his enemies, raze their cities and farms and turn all of his conquered lands into pasture. To his people, the only life worthy of a warrior people was the herding of livestock. This plan had proven to be impracticable. The institutions of civilized nations were more enduring than he had imagined. The small warrior bands of his youth were not adequate to his ambitions. Great armies, in turn, required ships, provisioning, arming and all the other resources that could only be provided by a civilization based on agriculture and possessing administrative centers and networks of roads.

This, in turn, meant that he bore all the rest of the baggage of civilization: scribes, clerks, functionaries, administrators, diplomats, merchants and so forth. These galled him in a way that craftsmen did not. Craftsmen were not the equal of warriors, but even Gasam was forced to admit that without them he could not have useful things like telescopes and fine weapons. But worst of all he hated the priests. Back on his home islands, it had been the spirit-speakers who had resisted his rise to power. When his take-over was complete, he had wiped them out.

Now he longed to do the same to the priests who infested all his cities. To him they were worthless parasites, like the bloated ticks it had been his duty to pull from the hides of the tribe's kagga when he was a boy. He longed to annihilate the whole breed of them. And yet, somehow, they had made themselves indispensable. By some strange magic, they had made themselves an unassailable place in the civilized societies, with their temples, their gods and their endless rituals.

Gasam had found to his wonder that he could brutally oppress his conquered people and they would meekly submit. But let him threaten their priests and they would rebel. What value they found in the fat, layabout priests he could not imagine. They lived off the produce of the peasants and the offerings of the townsmen and gave, as far as Gasam could see, absolutely nothing in return. It was further evidence to him that all people save warriors were abysmally stupid and deserved to be slaves.

Fortunately for him, Larissa actually enjoyed the day-to-day work of administering his broad conquests. She liked to build and to see their subjects working for the greater glory of their king and queen. She was splendid at diplomacy and loved to carry on royal correspondence with rival monarchs. She had even learned to read so that she could make sure her scribes copied her words accurately. She even had facility at manipulating priests, an activity upon which Queen Shazad of Neva had given her much useful advice.

Still, the priests were like a canker gnawing at him. It was as if there were a hole in his conquests, making them incomplete. One day, he would do something about these human ticks. It might have to wait until he had conquered the whole world, but as sure as that was an inevitability, just as sure was the fate of the priests.

He thrust these disagreeable thoughts from him. It was a beautiful day, the sort of day that was meant for battle. Behind him he could hear his men, smell their sweat, feel their bloodlust. The two little fights behind them had whetted their appetite for blood. They had been easy, cheap fights which had cost him little and gained him much in spirit, as if the spirits of his men fattened on those of slain enemies. He felt this to be true, that with each enemy killed, the warrior's strength was increased. He, Gasam, devoured whole nations, and therefore he was the strongest man in the world.

More important for his present purpose, the small battles had given his younger and more inexperienced warriors an easy introduction to battle. Having had these trifling bloodlettings, they would be the better prepared for true battle, when it came.

This he expected to be very soon. They would be linking up with Urlik by the next day at the latest, and somewhere between the two was an army led by the royal commander of forces west of the river. He had no idea how large the force would be, save that it was not a major part of the national army and his own force would surely outnumber it, if he could combine forces with Urlik. He expected no more than a stiff fight. He had often defeated forces many times his own numbers. After all, he was a warrior king and leader of warriors. All others were livestock.

His breath caught in his throat as he saw a scout galloping down the road toward him. The land had opened in the last few days. They were marching through a territory of open fields and low hills. The higher elevations were thickly forested, but there was no true jungle. It was good terrain for battle, and he was sure that battle was just what this hurrying messenger portended. The man reined in, whirled and dismounted. Leading his cabo by its reins, he began to trot beside Gasam. The king would not halt or even slow a march just to receive a report.

"My king, the Sonoan army is before us, no more than five miles down this road!"

"Their numbers?" he snapped.

"About seven of our regiments, light and heavy infantry, about half and half." The man panted his report, having ridden hard.

"More than I expected," Gasam said. "No matter."

"No matter, indeed, my king. Their backs are to us!" The man grinned despite his exhaustion.

"What!" cried Gasam, incredulous.

"General Urlik harasses him from in front. Their general has them drawn up in battle formation, facing away from us. General Urlik makes great demonstration with his riders and archers, but he has not attacked, as you have commanded him."

Gasam laughed aloud. "I could almost believe in those gods the priests prate on about! This was my plan, but even I never dreamed it could fall out so well. Scout, is your beast good for another hard ride?"

"My mount and I are ready for anything my king commands, though it kill both of us."

The king laughed again. "Good man. Ride to General Urlik. Go around the enemy army and use the terrain to keep from his sight as much as possible. Tell Urlik to continue as he is doing now. Within two hours, I will fall upon the enemy from behind. At that moment, he is to attack.

Tell him he is to flank them on the left, but to leave their river flank open. When the panic begins, they will flee into the river, where it will be easy to pick them off.''

"It shall be done, my king!" The scout mounted and galloped away.

Long ago, Gasam had learned the unwisdom of completely encircling an enemy. Thus surrounded, men fought stoutly, with desperation. But an open route of escape preyed upon the minds of frightened men as a magic spell. They would break and run even from a battle which they might still win.

"The enemy lies before us!" the king shouted. Far behind him, warriors called the news to those beyond hearing. A deep rumble began, not a cheer but a growl from deep in the chest, like the sound of a hunting beast. "Be swift!" he called out. "We will fall upon them like a pouncing night-cat and devour them! Follow me!"

With that, Gasam broke into a trot. Behind him, the whole army shifted gait. A low chant began, with a grunting bark each time the men's left feet struck the dirt of the road. Gasam longed to break into a run, but he needed to give the messenger time to reach Urlik. Besides, he wanted his men fresh for the battle. Had his army consisted entirely of Shasinn, he would have run anyway, but he had to avoid wearing out the lesser peoples.

His blood sang as he trotted at the head of his army. It was for this that he was born, that he had been raised up above other men. His excitement swelled with the prospect of the great killing to come. He felt that his famous spear of steel drew him forward, vibrating in its urgency to drink the blood of his enemies.

An hour at this pace brought them to a sharp bend in the road. At the bend the road ascended a low rise, and there he found four of his scouts. These had remained to keep an eye on things while their comrade had ridden back to apprise the king of what awaited. Gasam raised his spear to halt the army and every man came to a stop on the same pace.

"My king," said the leader of the scouts, "go to the lip of that rise, and you will see the enemy army laid out before you."

"Excellent," the king said. "Have they seen you?"

"No. They are so busy with what lies before them that they have not even posted a rear guard. General Urlik is giving them such a show that they must think our whole army lies before them. It is my guess that he has fooled them into thinking that we circled them in the night and linked forces with Urlik from the west."

"It couldn't be better!" Gasam said, trotting up the road to see. A hundred paces farther, the road crested, then descended a long, gentle slope. A half-mile down the slope, in a broad valley, was a sight to gladden his heart: rank upon rank of disciplined, well-armed troops, all of them facing the other way. How any commander could bring such a fine army to a good battlefield in excellent order, and neglect to post observers on the road to their north escaped him. Behind him, Luo and his other unit commanders had run up, but they stayed below. He waved for them to come join him and they ranged themselves beside him, staring in amazement at the sight below.

"They could see us," Gasam said, "but they won't even turn to look." Beyond the enemy army, they saw a great cloud of dust, undoubtedly Urlik's force raising pandemonium to keep the Sonoans distracted.

"This is beyond belief!" said a shaven-headed islander. He twirled a short axe in restless circles, his wrist as supple as a lizard's neck.

"What you see before you," the king said, "is what happens when an army has fine organization at the lower levels, excellent small-unit leaders, and fools in overall command. These are good soldiers prepared for a hard fight, but they have been utterly failed by their commanders." His captains all nodded in agreement at this analysis.

"Well," Gasam snapped, "this is very intriguing, but now it is time to fight. You all know what to do. We have done this many times before. I will have the crescent formation. You are to give the center extra depth, using the southern subject troops. These men look like they could prove stubborn, even taken by surprise. Get into formation quickly, but quietly. There is to be no chanting, no beating of shields. I want to preserve the element of surprise until the last possible moment. When formation is complete, I will order the advance. It is possible that we may be fully in formation before they see us." He eyed the heavy growth to either side of the road where the army now waited. "It is a pity we can't form up on the reverse slope and come over the crest in battle order, but it cannot be helped. Get to work."

His commanders ran back to their units. Quietly, their bare feet making only a faint shuffle, the men began filing over the crest, each man holding his weapons well away from his shield so as to make no clatter. With his spear, Gasam indicated where he wished to station each unit. In the center he stationed the best of his subject infantry, equipped with large shields fitted with neck-straps and extra-long spears. This last was an innovation he had devised to give extra strength to the native infantry, whose battle efficacy he doubted. When all was ready, he raised his spear and brought it forward and down, pointed at the enemy. Since this battlefield offered him no distinct point of vantage, he placed himself at the forefront, something he had not done for many years. It was a sensation he had missed.

Miraculously, the Sonoans had not yet seen them. Then he saw a few men glance over their shoulders. Moments later, all the rear ranks were looking back, their eyes wide with shock. He knew then that there was no further need for silence. In a loud voice he began an ancient Shasinn battle-chant. Instantly, the rest of the army took up the chant, stamping their feet in time and beating their spear-butts against the backs of their shields. He knew that the sight to the enemy must be truly horrifying, as the huge crescent of barbarians closed in from behind, their spears flashing in the brilliant sunlight, their ornaments of waving fur and nodding feathers, their pitiless black shields.

Nonetheless, amid a snarling of trumpets and shrilling pipes, the Sonoan army began to reverse its order in disciplined fashion. Officers hurried to this new front, their coppery faces suddenly pale as they understood that they had spent the morning staring at a ruse, that the real army had taken them unawares.

Inexorably on came the black-shielded warriors. Gasam did not halt to make speeches, to demand surrender or parley. He had come here to kill his enemies and that was what he would do. From the rear ranks of his crescent, arrows began to shower upon the Sonoans. This caused him to remember that, exposed as he was, he would be the prime target of archers in the enemy ranks. He slackened his pace slightly, to let his army close upon him. His long, Shasinn shield would be proof against arrows, but there was no sense being killed for a heroic gesture.

With a roar, the armies collided. Gasam found himself faced by a hard-faced Sonoan soldier who was a bit slow raising his shield. The Shasinn spear darted into the man's neck and out again with the flickering speed of a lizard's tongue. The falling man was replaced by another and Gasam traded a few thrusts and blocks with him, reveling in his own skill and the enemy soldier's stolid competence. Soon he was surrounded by equally stolid Chiwan infantry, blunt-faced men who did a workman's job with shield and short-sword and axe. A pair of them quickly enveloped him with their shields, protecting him from any further threat from the Sonoans. Through his blood-haze, he heard the growl of a Chiwan underofficer in his ear.

"Get you to the rear, my king. This is our job up here."

Gasam stepped back, letting the black-shielded ranks close before him, stepping backward between their files and holding his own shield high to protect himself from arrows, javelins and other missiles. Soon the last rank reformed itself before him and he was in the rear, seeing the struggling mass of men before him and hearing the indescribable sounds of two armies locked in death-grip.

Gasam shook himself and tried to clear his mind. He had been indulging himself shamelessly, behaving like a junior warrior on his first bloodletting. This would not do. He had a battle to direct. More than that, he had a campaign to conduct and an empire to rule. It was time to resume his place as king, as conqueror.

He ran around the right end of his army, to the place where his force and Urlik's struggled to envelop and crush the enemy's flank. With the confusion of fronts, it was now impossible to style that flank right or left. The important fact was that this was the landward flank, while the other flank abutted the river.

The din of screaming, struggling men and the clatter of their arms was indescribable. Above the swaying mass of footmen he could see a few mounted enemy officers, their shouts unheard, pointing and trying to direct a battle, but Gasam knew how futile were their efforts. The maneuvering was over and they had no reserves to commit. Now there was nothing but the grinding attrition of a static battle.

He found Urlik mounted on a cabo, leaning forward, hands braced on the pommel of his saddle and a broad smile on his face.

"Another fine battle, my king!" he shouted when Gasam drew near.

"So it seems, but I can see nothing of importance." The two men clasped hands and Urlik bawled for several of his mounted men to come forward and make a platform. Two of the strongest placed themselves stirrup to stirrup and held a shield between them. Gasam scrambled onto the shield which the two men, grunting with the effort, lifted above their heads and held at arm's length. From this wobbly point of vantage Gasam surveyed the battle.

The Sonoans, hemmed by enemies on three sides, were edging toward the river. Their ranks were now packed so tight that the men could not use their weapons effectively and there was no way to avoid treading on the fallen. The swaying, cursing mass no longer constituted a fighting force and Gasam marveled that they had not broken already.

He had not been atop his shaky tower for long when the inevitable disintegration began. A half-dozen men threw down their shields and weapons and dashed to the river, where they cast themselves into the water and began swimming frantically for the farther shore. Others saw and did likewise. With a speed that was startling, the entire army seemed to collapse as men who, only moments before, had been struggling to strike a blow at their enemies, were fighting just as hard to push past or climb over their comrades, desperate to get to the escape represented by the river.

Gasam shouted a command and the officers of archers withdrew their men from the main battle and ranged them along the riverbank, from which convenient location they began to send arrows in upon the swimming men.

On the land, the true killing had commenced. As long as soldiers kept their formation, casualties were minimal and they could defend themselves well against even the most spirited and skilled of warriors. When the formation broke and they dropped their weapons and presented their undefended backs to the enemy, killing them became a matter of mere physical effort.

The Sonoans were being slaughtered in droves and Gasam's army had ceased to take casualties. In place of their warrior fortitude many were overwhelmed by a mad bloodlust. Some sought to thrust their spears or swords through as many fleeing backs as possible. Others hacked and stabbed at fallen bodies, mutilating them until they were no longer recognizable as the bodies of men.

In the river, the panic was so great that many more were drowning than were perishing by Gasam's arrows. Men made mindless by terror climbed on the shoulders of men who had minutes before been as brothers to them. From escaping the battle, their frantic desire had narrowed to achieving just one more breath.

Gasam descended from his shield platform. There was nothing more of any importance to see. Slaughters were all alike. The stench of blood and spilled entrails were as perfume to his nostrils. He acknowledged congratulatory hails from his officers. They had detached themselves from the battle, since the mechanical business of killing unresisting beasts called for no leadership.

"How many do you think will escape?" Gasam asked a Chiwan captain who had been directing archers on the bank.

"No more than three or four score, my king," said the officer, dismounting from his cabo. The king did not like to look up when he spoke with subordinates.

"That is good. There is to be no pursuit on the other side of the river. We need enough escapees to spread word of the defeat. Without them, the king will insist that it never happened."

"The men are becoming disordered, my king," said Luo, a man who disliked any breakdown of discipline.

"Let them have their way," Gasam ordered, "so long as they don't fight among themselves. All of them have had a longer march than they have been accustomed to, and they've fought a good battle here. There is no credible enemy for many days' march, so we are in no danger. Let them celebrate." His captains nodded acknowledgment, although Luo watched the frenzied butchery with distaste.

To his surprise, Gasam realized that he was tired. Never before had he felt tired after a battle, however strenuous it had been. The long march, the running and fighting, all had drained his strength. Perhaps, he thought, Larissa was right. Perhaps his age was catching up with him.

"Come to my camp, my king," said Urlik. "You are not needed here, and there we can relax. You've lost flesh since we parted and you need to restore yourself."

"An excellent idea," Gasam said. Together, the two men walked from the battlefield, Urlik leading his cabo by its reins.

Only a quarter-mile from the scene of the fighting, Gasam was astonished to see an elaborate camp complete with tents and temporary island-style shelters. Everywhere he looked there were piles of provisions, jars of wine and grain liquors, heaps of forage for the animals. Captives tended the needs of the warriors and cared for the wounded men who had been brought in from the battle.

"I did not know you would be marching through such a rich district!" Gasam said, delighted. Urlik motioned to a well-cushioned chair before the largest shelter and the king sat, accepting a cup proffered by a slavewoman.

"No richer than what you marched through," said Urlik. "You remember when I said that I had a new employment for the mounted men?"

"I remember."

"Well, this is it. Forget about their uses in fighting, which is small, or scouting, which is only a little better. What they are really good for is foraging! Once we were in enemy territory, I sent them out, not in little detachments, but in *strong* force, each detachment with fifty or a hundred riders, with one task: round up provisions for the army and its animals." The islander propped a foot on a barrel and leaned toward his king. "How many times have we starved in fat country? And why? Because the peasants and the villagers know we are coming and they hide all their best produce. With the riders going before and ranging wide on the flanks, they catch the peasants unaware and herd them along with their livestock back into our arms. We've lived fat through this whole march. I wouldn't let the men carry enough to slow them down, naturally, but they could look forward to good eating at each night's camp. When we reached the river, I had this camp built and we gathered all the wealth of the district here. Do you know why I did this?''

"Because you like easy living?" said the king.

Urlik grinned. "Doesn't every man? No, it was to give me an excuse for making a stand here. The Sonoans saw how much we had to protect and they never suspected that I was holding them here as a ruse. They assumed that only the whole army could accumulate so much plunder.''

"That is what I would have thought in their place,'' Gasam said. "Before, only when we've taken a city have we ended up with so much provisioning.'' He leaned back and took a long drink, the wine refreshing to his dry throat.

"What is our next move?" Urlik asked.

"We will abide here a few days. The men and the animals are sore-footed and in need of a little rest. Tonight the men can celebrate. Tomorrow they can recover from the celebration. The day after, we reorganize the army. We'll need to find a good river crossing.''

"I am told that there is a good bridge about two days' march to the south,'' Urlik told him.

"Tomorrow, send some riders to locate it.'' He thought a while. "I'll send a detachment of my Chiwan soldiers to guard it. It's just possible that some commander on the other side of the river might get word of the battle in time to destroy it.''

"Best to be sure,'' Urlik agreed. He noticed that the king had an uncharacteristically melancholy expression. "What ails you, my king?''

"I wish Larissa could have come with us,'' he said, waving a hand toward the ghastly scene by the river. "She is missing all this.''

"We all feel the queen's absence,'' Urlik said. He had

never known a man and woman as devoted to one another as Gasam and Larissa. They were not as other people.

That night, the revelry in the camp was uproarious. Besides the feasting and drinking and the use of the local village women rounded up by Urlik's foragers, there were other amusements. Among Gasam's followers there were those who delighted in torture, others whose religions required human sacrifice in thanks for a victory. For these, there were plenty of prisoners upon whom they could practice their arts.

Gasam had long made it his custom to reward his men thus after a battle, but he laid down some stern restrictions. There was to be no brawling. If fights broke out, all who fought were to be executed instantly. Also, while the men might perform whatever religious rites pleased them, there was to be no attempt to practice magic, divination or fortune-telling. These things he considered to be bad for morale and subversive of his own authority.

Past midnight, the fires still burned high and the sounds of revelry were still nightmarish in the still, humid air. Luo approached the seated king, his face wearing a distraught expression. Gasam lolled in his chair, his eyes red and heavy-lidded. He had gorged and guzzled as heavily as any, and even his heroic capacity had been tested.

"My king," Luo began, hesitantly, "something awful is going on, down there among the trees. It's your southerners, including the women." He pointed to a copse in the low ground a few hundred paces from them. The flickering light of a fire was just visible between the tree trunks.

Gasam frowned. "Are they fighting?"

"Far worse. They took some of the prisoners down there."

"What of that? Let them have their fun. I gave orders that there were to be no live prisoners by morning."

"It isn't just that," Luo said, his distaste plain. "They are . . . well, they're *eating* them!"

Gasam was intrigued rather than appalled. "Truly? I'd always heard the rumors, but I never really believed them. It must be part of some ritual. After all, it's not as if we lack the more common sorts of meat."

"You are not going to do anything about it?" Luo said.

"Why should I interfere? They are violating no order of mine. Besides, rumor travels even faster than my armies. This simple practice will spread the terror of my name, and make my enemies tremble even more than they do. My enemies and prisoners are as livestock, so why should they not be consumed as such? Leave them to their own feast, Luo."

The warrior departed, clearly unhappy. Gasam knew that his Shasinn disliked the license he allowed some of the warriors of lesser races. They were jealous of the favor he showed to the women warriors. He did not care if they were displeased, so long as they obeyed. Heavily, he lurched to his feet and began to walk toward the copse from which were coming such strange sounds. This was something he wished to see for himself.

EIGHT

As the merchant Samis had promised, the Sonoan highlands were far more pleasant than the jungled low country they had trudged through. Here the foliage was thinner, and had been yet further thinned by extensive cultivation. The population was far denser as well, and the rolling hills were covered with gemlike fields, lovingly tilled and tended by farmers. Every few miles was a village or a sizable town, and they began to see some of the fabled temples of the land.

These structures came in a number of forms, but height seemed always to be a major consideration. Some were pyramidal constructions of rectangular or even triangular boxes of diminishing size. Others were conical towers with stairways or ramps wound spirally around them. Smoke ascended from the crest of each and they saw frequent processions going to and from the huge, enigmatic edifices.

This, Ansa felt, was more like it. He had come to see exotic, civilized lands, and that what he saw now. Here the road was actually paved, its surface set with finely cut stone, slightly humped in the center to drain water, with raised curbs along the sides. So well ordered was this part of the country that, every few miles, they found permanent campgrounds where they could pass the night without having to crowd into some village or squat on a protesting or profiteering farmer's land.

Once, they passed a military camp where Ansa paused to watch several hundred soldiers drilling in tight formations. The soldiers' armor was of padding and laced bamboo splints, that of the officers consisting of leather studded or splinted with bronze. Officers also had bronze helmets with elaborate feather plumes.

Their lockstep movements were strange to his eyes, accustomed as he was to the mounted archery of his own people. All this maneuvering by ranks looked gross and awkward. It was difficult for him to imagine how such tactics could be effective on an open field. At commands transmitted by trumpet and flute, they wheeled, changed front, raised and lowered their spears, brought their shields across to form a portable wall before each rank, halted and even stepped backward. A front rank would kneel behind their shields and the two ranks behind thrust their spears forward to present a spiky, forbidding hedge to any attacker. Another time, they raised their shields overhead to form a solid roof.

This was fascinating, but it looked to Ansa like a profoundly boring way to soldier. The sheer repitition of the endless drill looked mind-numbing. But then, he reflected, that might be precisely the point. His father and others who had campaigned in the settled lands had told him that only one will, that of the leader, had any significance in such fighting. It still looked boring.

"We will reach the capital by tomorrow," he said to Fyana.

"I know that," she said. She had a downcast look, which seemed odd to him. He was excited at the prospect.

"You don't seem to relish the idea."

"No, I don't. This is all alien to me. I find it disturbing, and I expect the great city to be worse."

"It is no less alien to me," he pointed out. "But I am fascinated by all I see, just *because* it is new and unlike anything I have known before."

"You come of an unsettled, wandering people," she said. "We Canyoners are not like that. We rarely travel far from home. I think we are so attuned to our land that we languish away from it." She paused. "I am glad that I have you to accompany me. You are better at this sort of activity than I."

This was a new side to his strange companion. She had heretofore seemed so poised, self-assured almost to the point of arrogance, as had seemed true of all Canyoners. Now, separated from her land and her kind, she was more human. She seemed, indeed, to be an insecure young woman, little more than a girl.

"It will pass," he told her. "It takes time to grow used to something entirely new. You have never before been separated from your people. In time this constant changing of surroundings will seem natural, and you will think your former life dull by comparison."

"I am not sure of that," she said, then smiled. "But thank you for reassuring me. I don't mean to be a gloomy traveling companion."

"Just remember that I am here to protect you," he assured her. "This way, nothing bad can happen."

"I shall remember," she said, still smiling.

Despite his growing sense of his own cosmopolitanism, his first sight of the capital the next day came as a shock. This settlement, which bore, in Granian, the remarkably unoriginal title of Great City, stood on a great plain surrounded by mountains, some of them producing thin plumes of smoke.

The rising sun was still behind the city as they approached it, and at first Ansa thought he was looking at an oddly shaped hill. Only as they drew nearer did he understand that he was looking at the work of human hands. The massive city wall was not sheer, but it was high, slanting back from its base to a parapet seventy or eighty feet above the surrounding plain. The wall was not well cared for and it sprouted shrubs and even small trees, adding to the illusion that it was a hill.

Above the parapet he could see jumbled masses of buildings, apparently erected up the slopes of a natural or else a man-made hill. He could make out few details, but the most prominent structures seemed to be yet more of the towering temples peculiar to this land. At the very center, one of the conical, spirally wound temples formed a peak, larger by far than any other building and exceeded in massiveness only by the great city wall itself.

As they had neared the city, the road upon which they traveled had joined or been joined by many others, until now it bore a voluminous traffic, from caravans far larger than theirs to the solitary carts of farmers, some of these last drawn by the farmers themselves.

Some of the beasts of burden he saw were unlike any he knew, although most appeared to be variant breeds of two familiar animals: nusks and humpers. They came in a multitude of sizes and bizarre conformations, and with every possible variant of hair and horns. He did not see many cabos, although he was relieved to note that those he did see were almost identical to his own. The cabo, it seemed, was one animal which had produced few variant breeds.

With the strange, alien place looming over him, Ansa felt much of his earlier confidence draining away. The massive, brooding presence of the walls intimidated him, and he was sure that the people who built and lived in such a place must be very different from any people he had known. What sort of cave-dwellers could live in structures like that?

His first close look at the wall did not lessen his apprehension. The base stones flanking the gate were tremendous, each, he estimated, at least ten feet high and forty feet long, extending an unknown depth within the wall. He could not comprehend the sheer labor of cutting such stones, much less of dragging them to this place and setting them into the wall. He pointed them out to Fyana, who rode beside him.

"Surely," he said, "only sorcery could accomplish such a thing."

She shook her head, as mystified as he. "I cannot imagine it otherwise. This must be the work of giants."

The gate itself was of thick wood, strapped with bronze. Just past it the roadway ascended like a ramp, ending at a huge market square full of livestock pens and vendors' stalls. The periphery of the square was lined with the warehouses and shops of more substantial merchants.

They had taken their leave of the other caravaneers. Although they were foreigners in this place, the people in the market stepped quickly from their path and showed a reflexive deference. Apparently, people riding cabos meant aristocracy to the citizens. Once, a group of native riders passed them and Ansa had his first sight of the warrior overlords Samis had mentioned.

The riders were as dark as the other Granians, but their features were narrower, with hooked noses and thin lips. Their black hair was curly rather than straight, and they did not wear the voluminous loincloths of the lower-class natives. Instead, they wore close-fitting trousers and shirts and short, leather vests heavily embroidered with colored thread. They wore weapons: long, narrow swords with decorated handles. All wore heavy jewelry of silver and gold. They stared at him arrogantly, and he stared back. He was unaccustomed to lowering his eyes before any man and saw no reason to do so here.

"We need to find a place to stay," Fyana reminded him.

"How do we go about it?" he wondered.

"I suggest we ask," she said. "In a city like this, with throngs of visitors passing through all the time, there must be plenty of inns."

He looked around doubtfully. "Maybe we should camp outside the walls."

"You are just looking for an excuse because you are uncomfortable in these surroundings. Well, so am I, but we shall stay anyway. This is the best location for learning things, and we will have plenty of funds, so start asking."

Unable to argue with her, he did as she directed. There were many inns near the market, but these were crowded, squalid and verminous. Their search took them up the stony hill that formed the core upon which the city was built. By noon they found a hostelry for more prosperous travelers. Here they boarded their animals and took a suite of spacious rooms that fronted on a balcony overlooking a broad vista of the city and the plain beyond. The rooms were clean, furnished with hangings, low tables and cushions. After a brief survey, Ansa seated himself on a cushion on the balcony as a woman belonging to the inn laid out a meal for them, and decided that he might be able to grow accustomed to this.

"Now," Fyana said as she joined him, "isn't this better than another night encamped on the ground?" She tore a strip from a flat loaf and dipped it in a pot of honey.

Ansa selected a skewer of smoked lizard meat. "It seems bearable so far. What do we do now?"

"I will let it be known in the city that I have medicines to sell. Some of these are very rare and expensive. That should attract people from the highest families, perhaps the court. By talking with them, we may learn the situation here, what they plan to do about Gasam."

"Why do you think these exalted ones will talk with two wanderers who have just come from the desert?"

"People always talk to those they think can cure them." She frowned into her cup. "I admit it isn't much of a plan, but it's all I have for now."

He shrugged. "It's worth a few days. If we turn up nothing here, we can travel west, toward Sono. At the border, we're sure to pick up some information."

She looked at him. "You are not really enthusiastic about this mission, are you? It's just an excuse to travel and see new things."

"I think that what we do will have little effect. My father and Gasam were born to destroy each other, and that is how it will fall out, someday. I've seen only a little of the southerners, but what I have seen gives me little confidence that they can beat Gasam. They could even join him without a fight."

"Then, wouldn't you want to know about that?"

"Yes. It could be valuable. Tell me." He learned forward. "Just what would you Canyoners do if Gasam were to march north? With or without the southerners?"

"No one has ever invaded us with success," she asserted.

"But you've never been invaded by anyone like Gasam. What I saw of your land tells me that your people are few and widely scattered, even combined with the Zone. Everything we can learn here will be of little help when Gasam attacks."

"Knowledge is always helpful," she said, then she smiled. "And, it can be enjoyable to gather. Now stop talking and let's eat. This is the first decent meal we've had in days."

He could not argue with that and so they fell to. Later, replete, he left the inn to wander the streets of the city while she attended to feminine things.

It was an unusual sensation, he found. In villages, he had

never been far from the open country, which was usually visible in any given direction. Here, he could climb a ridge of city, and on the other side descend into a little valley that was also city. There was a temple next to their inn. It had three tall pillars on its roof, each topped by a statue of a bat-winged creature, possibly a deity. He fixed this in his memory to serve as a landmark because he knew he would quickly be lost in this unfamiliar landscape.

Never before had he encountered people in such numbers, packed together in such tight proximity. Most of the streets were actually narrow alleys in which he had to turn sideways to pass another walker. The streets were also steep, occasionally turning into stairs. Except for the occasional markets, there seemed to be no separation of living and commerce districts. The ground floors of many buildings were shops or storehouses, their upper stories divided into living quarters. Everywhere, balconies overhung the streets, turning them into veritable tunnels. People leaned on the balcony railings and gossiped with neighbors across the street or contemplated the scenes below.

Despite the all-stone nature of the city, there was no lack of vegetation. Most of the balconies sported planting boxes and these were lovingly tended, with flowers growing in great profusion. Hanging plants were also favored, and from some buildings actual curtains of greenery descended to brush the heads of pedestrians below. In some places, Ansa found himself treading on a thin carpet of leaves and flower petals. He was grateful for this. It softened the hard edges of the city.

He noticed that people were studying him furtively. The population here was accustomed to foreigners, but not to his type. It occurred to him that perhaps he should have left his weapons at the inn. He had left his lance and bow there, but he had belted on sword and dagger without thinking. Now he noticed that nobody here was armed except the nobles and a few natives who were attired as soldiers. He decided to stay as he was until challenged. He was, after all, a warrior, and warriors were armed by definition.

He could not go far without passing one or more temples. Some of these were true buildings with dark interiors from which drifted incense smoke and the sounds of wailing music and rhythmic chants. Others were towers of solid masonry, with shrines and altars atop them. He was curious about these, but he dared not enter or climb one without invitation. He had heard that civilized people could take their religion very seriously, and might fiercely resent the intrusion of an unbeliever.

The markets were another oddity. The big one just within the gate had sold a profusion of goods, whatever happened to come in by caravan on any given day. The smaller markets scattered throughout the city were different. Each seemed to be devoted to a different commodity. There were many food markets, some selling flesh, others reeking of fish. The latter even had water tanks from which live fish were sold. There were separate markets for fruit and for greens. An aromatic baker's market was near a pungent spice market.

He could tell from the din of hammers on metal when he neared the smith's quarter of the city. Here he found jeweler's markets where he saw much to attract him but nothing he could afford. He had never seen such a profusion of gold and silver, or so great an abundance of pearls, jewels, colored stones and coral. He noticed that many of those examining the wares in this market were women of the aristocracy. These were tall, stately creatures dressed in diaphanous layers of sheerest cloth. Their hair was dressed in elaborate arrangements of curls and their faces were masks of cosmetics. He decided that many of them would be very beautiful with the paint washed off. Some seemed similarly interested in him, bringing upon him the stone-eyed stares of their hulking bodyguards. These attendants were of yet another race, pale-skinned, bald-headed men whose mountainous bellies did not detract from a sense of great physical strength.

A few streets away, he found a more congenial market. This one sold weapons. Here he found a fine selection of swords and daggers, most of them still made of bronze or of bronze with steel edges, but there were a few all-steel weapons, evidence that his father's steel mine was having its effect here. Once, only kings or great nobles could afford weapons of steel.

He admired the artistry of the bronze weapons. Steel had a brutal efficiency, but bronze presented far greater scope for decoration and could be cast into a multitude of shapes. The lustrous red-gold color of the metal was sensually pleasing in a way that the silvery gray of steel could never match.

Some shops featured entire cuirasses and helmets of bronze, armor fit for the most exalted of officers. Ansa could never see the sense in wearing such encumbrances in battle, but he could not deny that it was impressive. He saw no bows like his own, but he found some tall bows built up of split bamboo and lashed with sinew. He took up several and tried the draw, finding them to be nearly as powerful as his own bow, although far too long for use from the saddle. Their arrows were also of bamboo, cleverly constructed from long splints to make them perfectly cylindrical. Their heads were of many forms and materials for various purposes, from round, wooden knobs for bird hunting to compact bronze points for war. There were even bulbous, hollow heads variously pierced for delivering signals by whistling, humming or hooting as they flew through the air.

On one table, he found weapons of stone. Even among his own people, stone hatchets and war-hammers were not uncommon. Since few of the plainsmen bothered with armor these weapons were as effective as the equivalents made of far more costly metal. But the southerners made far greater use of stone, and some of these weapons were quite beautiful. He was especially taken with a stone axe, its double-bladed head crafted from a strange green stone, lovingly polished until it shone like jade. Its slender shaft was made of a tough, flexible wood, completely covered by a sheathing of rawhide thread braided intricately into decorative designs. The rawhide continued over the narrow part of the axe where the handle passed through the pierced head. The whole was as solid as if made from pure stone, save that the rawhide-covered handle retained its slight whippiness, magnifying the force of a blow. When he held it loosely by his side, the head just brushed the ground. This Ansa considered to be the ideal length for a weapon designed to be swung at arm's length.

The price was low, but he bargained the vendor even lower, stressing the obsolescence of stone weapons, their low status compared to bronze and steel, the absence of gold and jewels or other decoration beyond the braiding.

He walked from the market well pleased. There was nothing like acquiring a new weapon to put him in an excellent frame of mind. He slid the handle through his belt on the side opposite his sword. The small, compact axe head was not uncomfortable in that position. Its narrow edges were not truly sharp, as the weapon was more of a club or hammer in the form of an axe than a true chopping weapon. He decided that in the future he would wear his traveling cloak to cover his profusion of armament. That was a compromise he could live with.

Having no particular destination, his steps took him upward. As he ascended, the construction grew less crowded and jumbled and he passed stately mansions set behind high walls surrounding formal gardens. This, he was certain, was where the aristocracy lived. Guards stationed atop the estate walls eyed him suspiciously, but none sought to hinder him. The streets were wider here, and they were not thronged like those below. He saw tradesmen carrying their wares to the great houses for the benefit of those who had no taste for rubbing elbows with the lower classes.

"Warrior!" Ansa knew he was the only such person in the vicinity so he looked upward toward the source of the voice. He saw a woman leaning over a terrace wall, long curls as thick as a child's arm framing a face covered with the masklike makeup of a high-caste woman. She leaned with her elbows atop a balustrade, her forearms encased in innumerable bracelets of gold and silver.

"Yes?"

"Do you speak Granian?" she asked.

"If you do not speak too quickly."

"Where are you from?" She spoke bluntly and directly, and he wondered if that was because she thought she was speaking to an inferior.

"I am from the plains beyond the desert to the north."

"Is that not the realm of Hael, the Steel King?"

This was the first time he had heard that title. "Yes. My name is Ansa, a warrior of the . . . Ramdi." He had to pause for a moment to remember which tribe he had decided to claim.

"Warrior Amsi, would you come into my house? I wish to speak with you."

"Gladly," he said. This was odd, but among his people one did not refuse an invitation to another's house or tent without giving severe offense. Even so, he reminded himself that he must comport himself with circumspection. His people might be unsophisticated compared to these, but he was perfectly aware of the dangers presented by jealous husbands.

A gate in the estate wall opened, and a wizened old slave admitted him. Immediately within stood one of the huge, cold-eyed men who seemed to exist in this city solely as bodyguards for noble ladies. He stepped inside. It was almost like entering the city gate, for the door opened on a stair which they ascended to the level of a broad terrace heavily planted with high shrubs and flowering plants. Just beyond was a house almost obscured by plantings, but the bodyguard conducted him to an open pave next to the balustrade, where marble benches faced a breathtaking vista of the descending levels of the city and the wide, rolling farmlands beyond. In the distance, smoking mountains ringed the plateau upon which the city stood. The woman stood at the rail and turned at his approach.

"Welcome, warrior Ansa," she said with a slight bow and a gracious gesture of her left hand. She smiled, and with a shock he thought that the woman was toothless. Then he saw that her teeth were lacquered black. It was a bizarre touch, but no more so than the rest of her cosmetics. Her eyes were strongly outlined in black, the rest of her face painted dead white except for odd highlights. Her eyebrows had been covered with white and redrawn midway up her forehead. Round, red spots marked her prominent cheekbones. Below her eyes flowed a delicate line of blue-painted tears. Her lips were scarlet and, when she blinked, her eyelids flashed yellow.

He touched a spot above his heart with the fingertips of his right hand. "I am the protector of your home," he said. He meant this. By the customs of his people, he was bound to protect this house as long as he was enjoying its hospitality.

She bowed a little deeper. "Your life is the first concern of this house. Your happiness is its second." She noticed the wideness of his eyes, scanning the vista beyond her. "I sometimes forget how stunning is this view. This is your first visit to Great City?"

"It is. The beauty of my own land is such that I had thought the rest of the world had nothing to compare. I see now that I was wrong. And this point of view is magnificent. I climbed the streets all day to look out thus from the heights. I never thought that such a view was to be seen, even from the peak."

"I would not brag," she said, "but even within this city, the view from this terrace is esteemed the finest."

"I can believe that," Ansa said. "Looking to the north, it almost seems as if I could see to my homeland."

"Well," she said, "the view is not quite that good, but it is better than most."

Having exhausted this topic, Ansa waited to hear why she had invited him here. He did not know local customs and feared that he might give offense by asking directly.

"Please come and accept the hospitality of my home," she said.

"Gladly." He followed her through the formal plantings toward the house. Her elaborate gown floated about her as she walked. Individually, the layers were all but transparent. In their multiple layers they achieved opacity. Her many ornaments rattled and jingled to her every movement. The heavy makeup made her age difficult to judge, but the hands were unwrinkled and she had the walk of a young woman. The bodyguard fell in behind him.

The air was heavily perfumed by the flowers that seemed to be these peoples' passion. In the city, he had actually seen a market that sold nothing but flowers. The house she led him to was huge by his own standards, but of modest size compared to some of the mansions he had seen as he ascended the hill.

The elderly slave opened the front door which, to Ansa's astonishment, slid aside on rollers. They passed within and he was further astonished by the abundant and strangely colored light. Looking around him he saw that the windows were covered by panes of colored glass and that further light was admitted by glass-covered skylights. Glass was still a rarity in his homeland, although his father's houses had glass windows, laboriously imported overland from Neva.

The walls were painted in repetitious designs, either abstract or depicting flowering vines. Incense burned in decorated braziers, apparently to perfume the air rather than for ritual purposes. As she led him through the hall, the woman studied him.

"You are . . . well armed for a man on an afternoon stroll in the city."

"As a warrior, I am accustomed to go armed. I haven't been unarmed since childhood."

"Excellent," she said, for no reason he could fathom. She led him to a smaller room, one wall of which was made entirely of blue-tinted glass panes. At her gesture, he sat in a thickly padded chair. He was unaccustomed to chairs, but found this one remarkably comfortable. She sat at a similar chair. Between them was a table which servitors quickly set with various wines and plates of small pastries. He was not in the least hungry, but he sensed that she would not get down to serious talk until he at least made a show of partaking. He selected a small pastry roll and bit through the crisp, flaky crust into a filling of highly spiced meat. It was delicious and he wished he had the appetite to appreciate it properly. He sipped at a goblet of delicate, pink wine and held his silence.

"You have excellent manners for a . . ." She hesitated.

"For a barbarian?" he finished for her.

"Well, I would not have put it that way." He could not tell if she was blushing, but the tone of her voice suggested it. "Are you a prince of your people?"

"I am of high birth," he said, cautiously. He did not want his identity revealed, but he saw no harm in letting the woman know he was not her social inferior.

"I thought so. Tell me, did you not arrive in the city this morning accompanied by a very young lady from the Canyon?"

He was proud that he betrayed no shock. "Were you there, or is this magic, or does news just travel fast in this city?"

She laughed, covering her face with a kerchief as she did so. "The latter. We are awfully jaded here, and of all foreigners, Canyoners are the rarest. Even plainsmen like yourself are seen more often. I have met a number of King Hael's emissaries, but I have seen only two Canyoners in my life, and both of those were elderly men, although quite beautiful in their way.''

"They are a handsome people," he agreed. "Am I to assume that it is Lady Fyana who is the true object of your interest?"

"Oh, I was anxious to meet both of you! But, to be sure, I have a particular reason for wishing to consult with a person from the Canyon. I would have sought her out had I not happened to see you passing by below my terrace. Do you think she would consent to come visit me? Or is she otherwise engaged here in the city?"

"I am sure she would be pleased to accept." He felt a certain relief. He was still thinking of the hulking bodyguard and jealous husbands. This woman might be a good source of information. If she had met his father's emissaries she must be connected with the court in some fashion. "Whom shall tell her extends this invitation?"

She covered her face again, apparently a sign of chagrin. "Oh, please forgive me! My manners have fled with the intensity of my fascination! I am Lady Yasha H'Aptli." The second name contained a guttural sound that was not in his native language.

"When would you wish us to call upon you?" he asked, making sure she understood that he would be with Fyana when she came.

"I am sure the lady must wish to rest today, after such a journey. If she feels rested by tomorrow evening at dusk I would be most honored to entertain her here. And she needn't trudge all the way up this hill. I have stables for your mounts." She spoke to a slave and the girl rushed off, to return minutes later with a small box. This the lady presented to Ansa.

"Please accept these guest-gifts. It is the custom here."

He took the box, which was of substantial value by itself: a beautifully crafted construction of exotic woods and ivory. Whatever it contained was heavy. He took his leave, and a slave conducted him to the gate.

He was unused to walking long distances, and his feet pained him as he walked back to the inn. He was grateful that it was downhill. It had been a long, strange day. He looked forward to telling Fyana all about it.

NINE

The queen had come to enjoy the sensation of riding. By the third day she dispensed with the extra padding of her saddle. By the eighth, she discarded the saddle itself. She found it an indescribably sensual feeling clutching the powerful beast between her thighs, feeling its heaving ribs, the warm hide and the great muscles sliding smoothly against her flesh. The smooth knobs of its spine massaged her intimately.

Riding and living in the open country was a joyous experience after the confinement of the city, and from time to time, when the pleasurable sensations were overwhelming, she had to remind herself sternly that she was on a mission of utmost seriousness. Still, the land was beautiful. She felt a kinship with the riotous vegetation and the abundance of animal life. She laughed like a young girl at the antics of the little man-of-the-trees that scampered everywhere in a multitude of species, some with gorgeous, flowing fur, others all but bald with shiny red backsides.

The hunting was so fine that they did not have to dip into their preserved rations. This was to the good, because they would soon be entering land that her husband's armies had passed through like a horde of devouring insects.

Each evening, as they sat at their campfires, Larissa quizzed the two spies about their find. She wanted to know about each of their expeditions in search of the mine, what lands they had traveled through, the nature of the people, everything that might possibly be of value. They were like sponges of information that she was determined to wring dry. The men knew their profession and answered every question patiently, going over each sequence of actions again and again until she was satisfied that she had everything of importance committed to memory.

One evening she walked from the fires into the dark forest beyond the light, ostensibly to answer a call of nature but in truth to be by herself for a while. It might be foolish, for she knew nothing of the night-roaming predators of these mountain forests, but she doubted that there was anything in this place as horrific as the huge longnecks of her island home.

Thinking of longnecks made her think of Hael. He had saved her from a longneck, many years ago. Hael had loved to wander alone in the forest, as she was doing now. He said that the spirits spoke to him there. She shook Hael from her thoughts. Absurdly, she had never gotten over the guilt of her betrayal of him.

She heard no spirits, but the soil of the forest floor felt good beneath her bare feet. The rich, natural smells were soothing. She enjoyed being queen in a great city, but she knew she would never feel truly comfortable there. She had grown up on an island of primitive tribesmen and had spent too many wild, exciting years at Gasam's side, raiding among the islands and on the mainland, years of battle and bloodshed and continuous movement. She was now un-suited to a settled life, however much she might throw herself into her building projects, her diplomatic and espionage activities.

Somewhere off to her right she heard a low grumbling sound. Her scalp tightened and her skin tingled all over. Her nipples hardened. She tried to pierce the darkness to her right. Was it a predator waiting to pounce? She wondered if she could hold it off with her little spear long enough for her men to come to her aid. She thought of it out there, something huge and hairy, vaguely man-shaped. She imagined its claws tearing into her flesh, being borne down beneath its weight, feeling its teeth, the feral smell of it as her blood gushed. The thought was weirdly pleasurable and her thighs trembled.

She waited a while, but there were no more sounds. She turned and walked back to the comforting light of the fires.

When they descended from the mountains the signs of the army's passing were everywhere. They passed ruined villages and wasted, hungry-looking people. All who saw them ran away, or else prostrated themselves in a frenzy of fear and worship. Her husband was good at breaking people. She felt no compassion for the wretches they passed on their journey. Slaves deserved slavery. The weak deserved to be dominated by the strong. Defeat was the natural lot of the weak, the decadent, the foolish. If people did not wish to be slaves, they could always choose death.

Now they had to make use of their rations or else send out hunting and foraging parties well away from the army's path. Larissa disliked doing that because it slowed them, but fresh provisions were necessary from time to time. Luckily, there was no shortage of grazing for the cabos. The army had not taken many animals with it, so the land was not overgrazed.

They reached the river to find a blackened ghost town, devoid of humanity but swarming with scavengers fighting over the heaps of bones, some of them with scraps of flesh still clinging to them.

"This place could not have presented much of a fight," said Bada, the commander of her guard. "It's too small, the wall was too weak."

"It would have been a useful blooding for the young men." She looked behind her and saw the envious looks on the faces of her guards. Like Pendu, they resented it viciously that they had been excluded from this bloodletting.

She smiled at them. "Don't worry, my lord will have plenty of killing for you to do in the days to come." They grinned in embarrassment, worshipping her and fearful that they had been caught thinking disloyal thoughts.

The trail of devastation led them southward, along the river. They found the signs of another fight, this one a small battle in an open field, at the place where Gasam's force had made contact with Luo's.

"Just as the king planned," she said. "He trapped this district's royal force between his men and Luo's." Her guards poked among the bones and the broken weapons, trying to estimate the size of the enemy force.

"The king never miscalculates in warfare," said Bada. "All his enemies are destined to fall before him."

"That is true," she said. "Come on, perhaps we'll catch up with him before the next fight."

But it did not fall out thus. Farther south, they found the remains of a much larger slaughter. This, she knew, had to be the place where the three-part army had finally reunited and the Sonoans had been caught between Urlik's delaying force and Gasam's army smashing down from the north.

"At least we are gaining on them," Bada said, wrinkling his nose. The bodies were much fresher here, and the scavengers burrowed within them, searching for entrails. Heaps of dead lay where they had fallen, bloating in the heat. Her two spies looked decidedly ill. They were hard men, but this was a rich sight and smell even for those with experience of war. The youngest of her guards tried to show a properly warriorlike indifference to mass killing, but they were not convincing.

Larissa herself had little taste for the scene. She had a liking for blood, but only if it was fresh.

"My queen," said a warrior, "I think you should come and see this."

She followed the young man to a copse of trees where a small group of her guards stood around the remains of a fire, pointing and speaking among themselves in low voices. She dismounted, as did Bada and the two spies. Here, too, there were bones, but the ends of them were blackened. A smoke-dried human limb was still suspended over the ashes by a wooden skewer.

"The people here must be starving indeed," said Haffle, "to be raiding a battlefield for such food."

Larissa saw a glint on the ground and prodded at it with her toe. It was a thin, silver ring set with a teardrop-shaped garnet. This was the sort of ornament the women warriors wore through their pierced nipples. She smiled to herself.

"No," she said, "I think the king's pet women fighters are living up to the worst of their reputation." Even Bada looked shocked.

"Come, now," she said, "we do far worse to living people, why be so squeamish about what was done to these after they died?"

Bada had to nerve himself up to disagree with his queen. "It is not natural, my queen!" he insisted.

"Is it not? Many of you thought that it was not natural for women to be warriors, either. Yet, they proved their ferocity in many battles. Is it so strange that they should have a taste for man-meat? So long as they serve my husband with fanatic loyalty, they can gnaw on live prisoners with those metal teeth of theirs, for all I care."

"As my queen says," Bada acquiesced. "Nothing takes the place of loyalty."

Fascinated, she stared at the signs of the awful feast. She

wondered if Gasam had attended this orgy. This was something new and stirring in a deep, fundamental way. Unlike her men, she felt no horror. She never questioned the rightness of anything that gave her excitement or pleasure. Perhaps, she thought, after some future battle, she would drop in on the women's victory feast.

Late the next day they crossed a bridge that spanned the river. They knew that the king and his army must not be far ahead, now. The signs of devastation were ever fresher. Villages still sent up plumes of thin smoke from their ashes. The survivors still looked as much dazed as fearful.

That night they camped on the other side of the river, enduring a frightful storm of warm rain accompanied by shattering thunder and lightning. Their homeland was known for its violent storms, though, and they made little of it. This meant that the rainy season was beginning early this year, and it would be a wet campaign.

"Uncomfortable for the men," Bada said, "but not bad for the campaign." The junior warriors leaned forward, ignoring the water that poured down their faces, to hear war-teaching from a more experienced warrior. "Our king's army is not so dependent on animals and wagons as the southern armies. It is they who will be bogged down by this rain and its mud."

"But only a tenth of our army is Shasinn," said a junior warrior, stroking his spear through its rainproof sheath of gut. "The rest are inferior people."

"What does that matter?" said Bada, smiling. "They fear the king more than they fear the weather. They will move as fast as he wishes them to."

"That they will," said Larissa. She sat with them at the fire they had finally managed to start once the rain slacked off. The storm had blown up so suddenly that they had not bothered to construct shelters. So sodden were her clothes that she had discarded them and sat naked on her folded cloak. To the warriors, many of whom had done the same, this was natural. One did not look upon the queen as a man looked upon a woman. The spies, men of another culture, carefully looked elsewhere.

Larissa found herself enjoying even this. In recent years she had been reluctant to display herself thus, but the long ride with its attendant hardship had firmed her body, relieving it of the excess, wobbly flesh she so despised. She felt lean and hard, better than she had felt in years. Surely, now her husband would know that she was fit to accompany him in his warring.

She felt, in fact, reborn. Surely, she thought, this was a portentious beginning to a renewal of their fortunes, that, as splendid as the past had been, they perched on the brink of wonders undreamed of. She and Gasam, god and goddess, would rule the world, a world they would remake according to their own dreams and wishes.

Two days later, after a ride through a devastated countryside, they found the combined army. The land they had passed through was stripped, its only inhabitants corpses and hollow-eyed refugees. Only the wildlife seemed well pleased with the situation. Herds of branch horn and wild nusks grazed and browsed on land that had been carefully tended and farmed a few days before.

The army was encamped on a small plateau which had supported a sizable village and its fields. Here, for once, there were no signs of slaughter. The queen and her guard rode in with the sun setting behind them. The warriors in the camp shouted and waved their spears when they recognized who had arrived.

She rode past the men encamped in their regiments, knowing that the rumors must be flying fast by now. Eyes widened and jaws dropped. On the eastern side of the village, where the plateau dropped off toward a broad river flat carpeted with forest, she found a knot of high officers surrounding the king.

Larissa took a few moments to savor Gasam's expression

of perplexity before she reined her animal to a halt and dived from its back into his arms.

"Larissa!" He whirled her in several full circles as lightly as if she were a child, joyous despite his puzzlement. Then he held her away from him, his hands beneath her arms, her feet still not touching the ground. He frowned. "What is it? Did the Chiwans revolt as soon as I was gone?"

"Those kagga?" She laughed at the thought. "Livestock do not revolt. I left Pendu in charge. He'll keep good order there. My lord, I've brought you the greatest news you could hope for. I must speak to you apart from the others."

"Then come with me." He set her down and they walked to the edge of the plateau, his arm about her shoulders, hers around his waist. In the fading sunlight, she could just make out the towers of a large city in the distance.

"My love," she said in a low voice, "I have it for you! My spies had found King Hael's steel mine. And it is not nearly as distant as we had feared!" For a moment he stood like a statue, and through her arm she felt a trembling like that of a kagga that had been stunned by a blow to the brow in preparation for slaughter.

Then he leapt straight up, jerking his spear skyward. The setting sun cast bloody gleams from its mirror-polished length. He let out a shout that, she was sure, could be heard in the distant city. When he landed, he began one of the ancient victory dances of the islands. Then he jammed his spear into the ground, picked her up and whirled her again.

"The world is ours! With this, my mastery is complete!" He set her down and she saw the knot of gaping men a few dozen paces away.

"Well," she said, "so much for keeping this secret."

"What does it matter?" he said through a face-splitting grin. "I am in the midst of my assembled army and there is nothing that can stop me now!" He tugged her toward the village. "Come. We'll have a house prepared for you and tonight you can give my senior commanders a full report.''

She scanned the intact village. ''This place does not look like the others we passed through.''

''No. For the last two days we have marched at a leisurely pace, giving the villagers a chance to flee before us. The king has known of our coming for some time now. I am letting the people flock from the countryside into the capital—that is the city you can just see from here—where they will eat up its stores and spread the fear of us.''

''Will there be a siege?'' She hated sieges. They were long and dull and smelled terrible.

''That will depend on many things. I hope to avoid one. If King Mana is fool enough to fight a pitched battle before the city, I will crush him quickly. If not, there is still the possibility we can take the city by storm. I have not had a close look at the defenses yet, and my scouts are not skilled in that task.''

They entered a house that had belonged to the village headman or perhaps a priest. It was a substantial structure, built of mud and timber with a thatched roof. It had several rooms and was raised on stone pilings to avoid flooding, ground rot and the wood-burrowing insects native to the land. It had a broad porch running entirely around it.

''I am glad you left the houses whole,'' Larissa said. ''The season of heavy rains is already upon us.''

''Not just the roof,'' he said, sweeping her up in his arms. ''Let's see what serves this place for a bed.''

That evening, Gasam and Larissa stood in the house's main room, which was crowded with a score of the king's highest officers and smoky from the burning wicks of a number of lamps. None minded the smoke, as it kept off the worst of the night-flying insects. In the center of the room was a table, and on this rested Larissa's precious map.

For two hours, she had drilled them on the operations of her spies and their findings. The last hour had been devoted to the operations of Ingist and Haffle. The seasoned soldiers had stood thunderstruck at her command of every detail pertaining to the crater, its location and, most importantly, the possible routes of approach. She knew every road and trail, every village, waterhole and grain storehouse. She knew which rivers were dry in summer and which were prone to flooding.

Gasam beamed with pride at her performance. Of course, he knew that no such detailed briefing was necessary this early, and perhaps none was truly needed at all, save for himself and two or three of his top commanders. Larissa was making sure that everyone who counted knew exactly how important her work had been and her total mastery of this invaluable facet of his operations. She was also letting him know that she had every intention of coming along on this campaign. He knew better than to forbid her this.

"You see what an opportunity lies before us," Gasam said when the queen was finished. "I only wish we could break camp and march there this minute. But, I have begun the conquest of Sono and I will not stop until it is beneath my heel. And, in practical terms, it would be folly to leave while Mana has his entire army at my back. No, we must deal with him first. With this to look forward to, we can't let him draw the war out or even bargain for terms. He would just use the time to join forces with Gran, and that above all we must not allow."

"We will need the time anyway, my king," said an officer of Chiwan troops. "A desert march will be far different from this campaign. It will be difficult and arduous even if there is no fighting. We will need transport, because we'll need to take rations and other supplies with us. For the last stages, we'll even have to carry our water. No campaigning at a fast Shasinn march, my king. We will have to move at the pace of nusk-drawn wagons and we will need to take many slaves along."

"All that is true," Gasam said. "I give you the task of

planning this campaign. Work with the queen and the spies to find the best route to the crater. You are to have first call upon all supplies, animals and slaves you think will be needed.''

"I shall not fail you, my king," said the Chiwan, swelling with new importance.

"Remember that this will not be a raid. I intend to take that place and hold it forever. That may well mean building a great fort to defend it. When I have subdued Sono, requisition all the skilled stonecutters and masons you will need for such a task. The fort will have to be kept supplied. See · to it that there will be sufficient water transport.''

"It will be done," the Chiwan said.

Larissa was content. Gasam had no intention of sending her back now. The Chiwan might direct the troops and the slaves, but it would be she who was in charge of this. The planning of a whole campaign! One that required far more than simple marching and fighting. Her head whirled with plans. There would have to be the most careful planning.

An inspiration struck her. She would pry a force of warriors from her husband and take a pack of slaves for the work. She would not only plot out the route of march, she would establish ration and supply dumps along the route and stock them fully. That way, when the king finished with the southerners, he would be able to march his forces north into the desert at something close to full speed. This was a new idea. She would work out the details while Gasam attended to the tedium of the siege, if that was what it was to be.

They stood before the walls of Huato, surveying its defenses. Thus far, King Mana had declined open battle. Gasam had no intention of assaulting the city before he had a masterful knowledge of all its defenses. They took advantage of a heavy rainstorm to draw closer to the wall than usual. The king was accompanied by Larissa and his senior commanders. A squad of Chiwan soldiers carried huge shields as a portable wall should the enemy loose missiles at the royal party. So far, they had declined to waste ammunition in such a fashion.

"What do you think?" Gasam asked, addressing the group.

"Stronger than most we have encountered," said Raba. "The walls are higher and they look thicker. More defensive towers, closer together."

His islanders were stone-faced. They loved battle, but they hated this sort of warfare: mining, sapping, blockading, battering. It was all tedium and labor. Only when the ladders and the siege towers were actually against the walls for a storming could they even grow interested. The mainlanders were impassive. This was the sort of combat they were trained for. They knew that Gasam would use them for this duty, holding his island warriors in reserve for better things.

"Let's see if we can find a weak spot," Gasam said. They procceded to make their circuit of the wall and he went on conversationally. "This is what comes of destroying his early forces so utterly. Even a fool like Mana cannot deceive himself that he can best us in open battle. Instead, he trusts to his walls."

"I don't understand these people," said Urlik. "What is so bad about a quick death in battle? He knows that as long as he is in there and we are out here, we will be destroying his country."

"He knows," Larissa said, "and he doesn't care. Just because they are his subjects doesn't mean he cares for them. They are nothing to him. However many we kill, he knows the survivors will breed plenty more."

"They always do," Gasam said.

Halfway through their circuit they came to a small river that entered the city through an archway protected by a heavy double portcullis of timber and bronze. Towers pierced with multiple loops flanked the opening.

"Tempting," said a Chiwan siege engineer, "but the river is too small to float anything really heavy against it."

They crossed the river on a small footbridge. The ground on the other side sloped downward, so the wall on this side was higher. The siege experts speculated that the higher wall might be thinner, as was often the case, but the slope of the ground was not favorable for rams or other engines. Mining was a possibility, but they ruled out storming so high a wall across such steep ground.

Gasam sighed. "Well, let's see what the main gate offers us."

A royal highway ended at the main gate. The gate itself was a massive construction of timber and bronze, hinged so that the valves only swung outward. Prisoners had furnished them with a description of its interior plan: a tunnel thirty feet long furnished with double portcullises and a secondary gate at its far end. The length of the tunnel was furnished with loops in walls and ceiling for discharging missiles and pouring hot oil into the tunnel. The gate was flanked with the city's two largest, strongest defensive towers. From their peaks, royal banners hung limply in the sodden air.

Larissa wrung water from her hair. "This is looking more and more like a siege," she said.

"I fear so," said Gasam. "If Mana does not offer battle in the next few days, I must make preparations for one. When my scouts report on conditions in the country, perhaps I can detach parts of the army to go raiding elsewhere. It will give them something to do and prevent a plague. There is nothing unhealthier than a siege camp."

"Except for a city under siege," said an officer, rousing a laugh from the gloomy party.

Larissa smiled. She would broach her plan to the king as soon as he was satisfied that it would be safe to divide his forces.

TEN

Fyana held up her gift and examined it in the lamp-light: a necklace of large pearls alternating with amber beads of matching size. Pearls and amber were separated by tiny beads of gold. It dangled between her hands like a chain of solidified light.

"Magnificent!" she breathed.

Ansa wore his own gift on a wrist and turned it to catch the light from different angles. It was a massive band of silver, studded with coral and jade.

"I agree," he said. "These would not be despised as royal gifts. What can the woman possibly want? No one gives gifts like this casually, to insignificant strangers."

"We should know tomorrow. Do you think she is just mad? She might be some wealthy lunatic who does things like this on impulse."

Ansa considered the possibility. "I don't think so, although I own that I could be deceived in this. It is difficult to read a person of a different land. I could understand her words easily enough, but I am not used to this dialect so her tone meant nothing to me. And with that face-paint, she might as well have been wearing a mask.''

"But your overall impression was not that she might be unhinged?''

He shook his head. "No, she seemed lucid and no more than eccentric, something always tolerated in wealthy, important people. And she was specifically interested in you. And in you as a Canyoner, at that. You would know better than I what her motives might be.''

She put the necklace back in the beautiful wooden box. "I hope she isn't ill and expecting some miraculous cure, or wanting to contact a dead child. People sometimes think we can do things like that. And it can be dangerous to disappoint important people.''

"Then we must play her carefully. Someone with influence and contacts at court could be just what we came here to find.''

She smiled. "You're enjoying this, aren't you?''

"Yes, I am,'' he admitted. "It isn't warrior's work, but it is something close to it.''

"It can be dangerous. That should satisfy your warrior pride. How old is she?''

"Difficult to tell, but not old.''

"Any sign of men in the house?''

"I suppose you mean besides slaves. No, but then I didn't see much of the house.''

"That makes sense. The form of her surname—H'Aptli—means that she is the widow of someone named Aptli.''

"I needn't have worried about jealous husbands, then,'' he mused.

"What?''

"Never mind.'' She was looking at him sharply, something he found amusing.

The next evening, now mounted on their cabos, they called at the gate of the high mansion. Servants appeared, one of them a handler who took their mounts and led the animals farther up the street, to a wooden gate in the wall. At the top of the stairs, Yasha H'Aptli stood to greet them.

"Welcome to my home, both of you. You do this house honor."

They bowed and gave their own formula of greeting. Ansa saw that the woman was not wearing the heavy makeup of the previous day. Her face was lightly dusted with powder, with heavy cosmetics only around the eyes. The stylized tears were still there, and it occurred to him that these were a mark of widowhood. Her face looked younger than he had expected. She was no more than thirty years old.

After the inevitable appreciation of the view, curtailed by the dimming light, they retired within. As they passed through the garden, many night-blossoming plants unfolded their flowers, releasing a heady perfume. Among them fluttered flowerbats, their leathery, white wings soundless as they hovered, thrusting their elongated muzzles into the blossoms, their threadlike tongues sweeping up nectar along with unwary insects.

Inside, the house was illuminated by lamps suspended from the ceiling by chains. These burned within globes of colored glass, tingeing everything below with a soft, pastel radiance. Fyana assumed her pose of Canyoner dignity and did not appear at all overawed by the richness of the surroundings.

"For now," Lady Yasha said, "you must join me in the aquarium. Later, we shall be joined by my other guests, persons of great dignity and importance, who will dine with us."

"I had not expected to be meeting high personages other than yourself, my lady," Fyana said.

"Oh, I fear that I gossiped too freely today," said Yasha. "I let it slip that I had secured you two as my guests when I called upon friends this morning. The word reached certain high personages who expressed an eagerness to meet you. They are not such persons as I could very well refuse such a wish.''

Either this was another example of the lightning speed with which news traveled in this city, Ansa thought, or the woman was dissembling. He suspected the latter. He sensed, though, that it was a result of a reluctance to approach or express anything directly and simply. Whether it was a custom of local mores or merely a personal eccentricity, he had no idea. Nor had he any idea what an aquarium might be.

She led them into a room with an odd, not unpleasant smell of damp stone and water plants. Its center was a circular pool in which swam an array of golden and silver fish. The creatures swarmed to one side at their approach, surfacing with their mouths open like so many baby birds. On a pedestal next to the pool stood a bowl, and from this Lady Yasha took a handful of greenish pellets and cast them to the fish, which immediately went into a thrashing frenzy of feeding. She tossed more to them, cooing nonsense words all the while.

To Ansa this was a remarkable spectacle. In his experience, fish were well able to look after themselves, and that anyone should bring them to a hilltop house for purposes of feeding seemed odd in the extreme. Then he saw that Fyana was entranced by the walls. He joined her and saw to his astonishment that they were lined with windows that looked out onto underwater scenes.

At intervals of a pace or so, panels of smoothest glass were set into the walls, and beyond them swam yet more fish, these of the most amazing variety of color and conformation. Light shone through the water from some unknown source.

"This is marvelous!" Fyana said, her poise slipping to reveal girlish enthusiasm. A graceful fish swam before her, its palm-sized body propelled by huge, near-transparent fins. Another, circled with rainbow stripes, darted by. Below them crawled a nightmarish thing of tentacles and suckers, changing colors sweeping over it every few seconds.

"How is this done?" Ansa asked.

Ladÿ Yasha was clearly pleased by their awe. "Each pane of glass you see is the side of a tank. Beyond the walls are narrow rooms which form the true aquarium, this room is just the viewing area. Lamps in those rooms provide the light. Here I have fish from a score of lakes, rivers and seas. Some tanks hold salt water, others fresh." She took them around the walls, pointing out especially fanciful creatures. She assured them that hers was far from the most elaborate aquarium in the city. "Why, the royal collection has sea dragons and giant tortoises."

When curiosity was satisfied, they sat at a table set with appetizers and wines. "No fish," Ansa noted with some amusement.

"I wouldn't feel right about eating them in front of my pets," she admitted. "Although I'm not sure why. They eat each other readily enough. And there are some that would eat us if they had the chance."

"My lady," Fyana said, "I have heard before of the aquariums of this land, although I could not picture to myself what they must look like until now. And I've heard of the royal menageries, where animals of every land are kept. What I have never determined is *why*? Why do you collect living creatures?"

"A difficult question," Yasha said. "I suppose it must have begun with some peculiar noble who grew bored with amassing inanimate objects and decided to acquire the living sort. It is easy to learn to take a delight in them."

Ansa had his own thoughts, but he kept them to himself. The ruling class of this land was overprivileged, bored, decadent. They had no serious duties to occupy them, so they turned to frivolous, wasteful diversions. His father had spoken of such people, in other lands, always with contempt. He wondered if that was why he and Fyana were there, just a new diversion for wealthy, bored people, like an unfamiliar animal from a far country.

A servant entered and whispered in Lady Yasha's ear. "You must excuse me for a moment," she said. "My other guests have arrived a bit early and I must go greet them. I shall not be long."

"Isn't this place fabulous?" Fyana said in a low voice when the noblewoman was gone.

"It is . . . different," Ansa said. He confided to Fyana his suspicions, and she considered his words.

"No," she said at length, "I think not. Those gifts were too rich for a pair of entertainers to provide an evening's diversion for bored aristocrats. I can't yet imagine what is behind this, though."

"I think we'll find out soon enough."

Moments later, Lady Yasha returned with two guests, a man and a woman. The woman wore the heavy, masklike makeup Ansa had seen on Lady Yasha earlier, and the man wore a genuine mask, an artful thing of leather, tiny bones and feathers, covering his face to the upper lip. Below it, his mouth was framed by a short beard, black shot with gray.

"Lady Fyana, noble Ansa, allow me to introduce Lord Klon and Lady Hesta." The pair made elaborate formal bows. Something seemed wrong to Ansa. The names did not sound like those he had heard belonging to high-caste personages. These must be assumed, in keeping with the woman's daytime makeup and the man's mask. These people wished to conceal their identities. It was all very mysterious.

Yasha conducted them to a formal dining room where enough food had been laid out to feed fifty people instead of five. Ansa wondered whether this was genuine extravagance, or if the remains of the banquet would go to feed what must be a large household staff.

While the dinner was served, and throughout its many

courses, the clandestine couple confined their conversation to small talk. They wanted to know about the Canyon, about Fyana and Ansa's journey hither, about their impressions of the city. Ansa noted that Lady Yasha deferred to the couple indicating superior rank. He also saw that, as he had expected, their interest was in Fyana. He was paid only perfunctory courtesy. This suited him well enough. He had so far not formed a favorable opinion of the Granian ruling class, and he welcomed the opportunity ·to observe from outside, without having to weigh his words constantly, as Fyana now must.

"Lady Fyana," said Lord Klon when the platters were cleared away, "certain people of your homeland are gifted with . . . healing powers, as it were. Would you be one such?" The question coincided with their being served a powerful, fruity liqueur in tall, narrow goblets. Ansa wondered whether this was the signal that substantive conversation could begin. These people seemed to set much store by this sort of social ritual.

"I have certain gifts. I would not call myself a healer. My talents are more those of reading the human body and diagnosing its ailments. I cannot heal, but I have a knowledge of medicines and can often recommend beneficial ones."

"That will be . . ." Lady Hesta caught herself. "That is, I mean, most fascinating. How is this done, if it is permitted to ask."

"There is no secret. I must touch the sufferer on the brow, sometimes on the body over the affected part, and the source of illness or injury may be revealed to me."

"Must the person be conscious?" asked Lady Hesta.

"That is best," Fyana said. "It is all a property of mind. But sometimes I can make a diagnosis on an unconscious person. Then it can be a lengthy process, and it may not work at all. The mind is always present, even in the unconscious state, but when it is not conscious, it cannot send clear . . . signals, you would say. The impressions then are quiet confused.''

"And if one is perfectly healthy, can you attest to that?'' the masked man asked.

"Almost always,'' Fyana said.

"Would you demonstrate?'' Hesta said. "On me, for instance?''

"If you wish,'' Fyana said. Both women leaned forward and Fyana placed the tips of her slender, blue fingers against Hesta's heavily painted brow. Both women closed their eyes.

"Is there something I should concentrate on?'' Hesta asked. "My body, perhaps?''

"Not necessary,'' Fyana assured her. "Simply relax.'' For several minutes the women posed thus, while the others remained silent. Then Fyana removed her fingers and sat back, surreptitiously wiping their tips on her napkin. Hesta had five tiny smears in her makeup.

"How am I?'' the lady asked, with a touch of eagerness.

"Quite healthy. And congratulations.''

"Congratulations?'' Hesta said. "Upon what?''

"Your pregnancy. You have been so for nearly the turn of two months. Surely you knew?''

The woman's mouth dropped open. She groped for words, then regained control. "Indeed I did, but no one else!''

A smile showed beneath Lord Klon's mask. "I think this lady is exactly what we have been searching for.'' He turned to Fyana. "My lady, we act on behalf of one whose name we dare not speak just now. This person stands in need of your special services. Would you be willing to undertake a commission for this person who is, I assure you, most generous?''

"I always stand ready to aid those in need, although I do have my limits. It does not appear laborious, but the exercise of my skill can be quite exhausting.'' Ansa admired the confidence and serenity with which she spoke to these strange people.

"Then," said Lord Klon, "if it is convenient to you, a servant will call upon you tomorrow at noon to conduct you to the . . . residence."

"That will be most satisfactory. Oh, and my escort must come with me." She gestured toward Ansa.

"Ah . . . truly, this mission does not call for the expertise of a warrior. However, if you insist . . ." He let the sentence trail off.

"I am afraid that I must," she said, calmly but with steel in her voice. Again, Ansa was impressed.

"Then, tomorrow I will see you both at the . . . residence," Lord Klon said, with a slight bow.

After that, the subject was banished and small talk resumed as if everyone were following the strict forms of a ritual. Ansa managed to insert some queries concerning the neighboring kingdom to the west.

"We've had disturbing news from the border in recent days," Klon said, sounding uncomfortable. "Refugees, some of them quite highborn, have been fleeing hither with word of a war. They say it is not a civil war, but an invasion from across the mountains to the west. They say that King Gasam has descended upon the nation and even now lays siege to Huato, absurd as that sounds."

"Why absurd?" asked Ansa, to whom it sounded not at all unbelievable.

"Why, the speed of it!" Even through the mask, the man seemed rattled. "The great bulk of the man's army is on foot, and this time he did not strike from the sea, after his usual fashion. We are not sure whether to credit these stories, although why terrified refugees should fabricate a falsehood is a mystery. A reconnaissance has been sent into Sono to find out what is going on."

"I suspect that they are telling the exact truth," Ansa said.

"Perhaps, but you are from the plains, and it is well known that King Hael's mounted army moves as the wind. Here in Gran, though, we are well used to the pace of armies traveling afoot. The swiftness of this putative expedition strains credibility."

"From all I have heard," Ansa asserted, "King Gasam knows how to move a foot army nearly as speedily as others conduct a mounted force." He also strongly suspected that these people had lost touch with the realities of serious warfare. Gasam was a threat such as they had not faced in many generations, if indeed they ever had.

With many elaborate courtesies, the lord and lady took their leave. Lady Yasha conducted them to her gate, then returned to her somewhat bemused guests.

"Forgive me for asking, my lady," Fyana said, "but is this sort of intrigue really necessary just to arrange a visit to the palace?"

Lady Yasha laughed, once again covering her face. "I am sorry, one forgets how strange one's customs may seem to a person unaccustomed to them. The special circumstances of their mission are such that they keep their identities concealed for now. You understand that this is a matter of the utmost delicacy, concerning the well-being of one whose health it is forbidden to discuss as a matter of ordinary conversation?"

"I think I am beginning to understand," Fyana said. "Is this, this . . . nonrecognition, shall we say, a formal matter? I would think that anyone who knew your two guests at all would be able to recognize them despite the heavy cosmetic and the mask."

"Of course," Lady Yasha said, "but no one would ever acknowledge it. That wouldn't be proper."

"But this business about the person in the pal—" Now it was Ansa's turn to curb his tongue. "The residence, that is, is a more serious matter?"

"Oh, yes! This is a matter not of custom but of law."

"Well, we shall know by tomorrow," Fyana said.

"Just so," said Lady Yasha. "And now, my dear, if your warrior companion will excuse us for a while, I would like to consult with you on a matter that requires privacy." She broke into a tittering laugh. "Poor Hesta! The expression on her face when you announced her to be with child!"

"Perhaps I should have been more discreet," Fyana admitted. "But, among my people it is not . . ."

"Oh, think nothing of it. I'll treasure that flabbergasted look forever. Now, please come with me." Taking her hand, she led Fyana away.

Ansa, left without company and with nothing to do, wandered into the garden. To his astonishment, some of the flowers and vines glowed softly in the darkness. They had encountered none such in the jungles during their journey, so he knew they must have been brought from a far land, like the fish. The fragrance from the night-blooming flowers was overwhelming and he went to the balustrade at the edge of the garden to get some unladen air.

As he stood looking out over the spires and hulking shapes of the city, he felt the alienness of the place. There was little light save the sickly radiance cast by the quarter moon. What light shone from the city was cast by lamps, glowing through colored panes. Momentarily, he longed for his native plains but he shook off the mood. He had come to see strange things and new places.

At a sound he turned and saw the two women coming toward him. He could tell little in the subdued light from the garden lanterns and glowing plants, but Lady Yasha seemed to be wearing a relieved expression.

Amid effusive farewells, they descended to the gate. Outside, a slave held their mounts with one hand. In the other, he held a staff slanted over his shoulder. At the top of the staff was a double hook bearing a pair of lanterns.

They walked their cabos back to their inn, the slave trotting ahead of them, his lanterns bobbing, making their shadows sway. The cabos were half-asleep and walked with their heads drooping, making gentle, snoring sounds.

In their rooms, they compared notes.

"Do you think all this secrecy is as innocent as Lady Yasha said?" Ansa asked.

"I believe her. But that doesn't mean there are no complex power games being played here. Everything I have heard about the courts say that they thrive on intrigue."

"We must remain on our guard."

She covered a yawn with her hand. "But I never hoped we would get into the palace so early in our mission. I am grateful for that."

"What did Lady Yasha want?" Ansa asked.

She smiled sleepily. "A female matter. Don't pry."

Ansa went to his bedroom and cast himself down on the mattress, feeling equal parts excitement and trepidation with the morrow's prospects.

ELEVEN

The scouts were muddy, their trousers and cloaks spattered by days of hard riding. The men stood before the king's chair, tendering their report. Beside the king sat Larissa, idly twirling her little spear. Despite her seeming abstraction, her eyes would sharpen on a speaker the instant he spoke of a matter of more than passing interest.

"We encountered a strong force of riders a day this side of the Granian border, my king," said the captain of the mission. "Our guide said that these were dressed in the habit of Gran. They sheered away when we drew near. They did not flee, but they were a hundred at least, and we fewer than a score, so we did not press the matter."

"What does this signify, my lord?" Larissa asked.

"A reconnaissance," Gasam said, "sent by the king of Gran, or perhaps by a border commander, to find out what all the fuss is about. Fugitives have been pouring across the border for weeks now. Even the somnolent rulers of Gran must be waking by now.''

''Do you think they will send an army to the relief of Huato?'' she asked, not liking the idea. It might interfere with her own plans. She had broached her idea to Gasam, and he had approved, conditionally. He did not want just yet to divide his forces. The city was proving to be hard to crack, and tedious mining operations were under way.

''I wish they would,'' he said. ''I could march my army east, smash them in one battle and be back here before the livestock huddled in this city knew that I was away.''

Sometimes Larissa thought that Gasam was reckless in his self-confidence. But then, it was his ability to make extravagant dreams become reality that had won her in the first place.

''This might be the time to use diplomacy, my lord,'' she said.

''What do you suggest?'' he asked, yawning. This sort of inactive campaigning always made him bored and morose.

''We could exchange letters and representatives with the Granian court. Emphasize that you invaded Sono because of King Mana's inexcusable insolence, or because he reneged on a naval treaty, or something else of the sort. Proclaim that you have no territorial ambitions east of the present border, that your love for your brother king, Ach'na of Gran, is boundless and bottomless.''

He frowned. ''Would they believe something like that?''

''Men who are in great fear will believe anything. And, there will be wiser men who are high in the Granian court. They will see the hollowness of these words and will seek to use them to their own advantage. They will contact us secretly, promising cooperation in return for high favor when we have taken Gran.''

''You are wiser in these matters than I,'' Gasam admitted. "Write your letters and choose a diplomatic team. Do it at once."

"I shall," she said, happy to have work to do once more. "I would go myself, but they might try to keep me hostage. I think I will proprose a meeting near the border in the near future. That way, I may work on them myself, and be sure that my promises are weighted properly. I always feel in better control when I can manipulate people myself."

"At that, my queen, there is none your match in all the world."

She smiled upon him. "Also, a meeting will give the traitors among them a better chance to approach us." The scouts had drawn away while the king and queen spoke. Now she signaled for the leader of the scouts to come forward.

"Yes, my queen?"

"What constitutes the border between Sono and Gran? A river, is it not?"

"The River Kol, my queen."

She knew of that river. It lay near the northern border of Gran and played a considerable part in the plans to seize King Hael's steel mine.

"On my maps," she said, "that river runs roughly northeast to southwest, along the northern periphery of the Granian cultivated lands, just south of the Poisoned Lands."

"So I understand as well, my queen. But somewhere near the Zone, it makes a great bend and from that point it flows due south until it reaches the sea at the Gulf of Dragons."

"Is there a convenient island on that river, large enough for two royal parties to hold a meeting on neutral ground?"

"There is one such, about three days ride from here. It is where the main highway linking the capitals crosses the river. A ferry links the east bank with the island. The island lies nearer the west bank and a bridge spans the channel between island and shore." He thought for a moment.

"Villagers call the place the Isle of Sorrow, for many river craft are wrecked on its upstream rocks when fog is heavy."

"Excellent," the queen said. "My lord, with your permission I will propose a meeting between myself and the chosen representatives of Gran upon the Isle of Sorrow as soon as possible."

"Do so," he said, smiling fondly. "Lull these livestock into a sense of safety. Convince them that, once I have gobbled up Mana and his nation, I shall be satisfied. When time comes for the meeting, take an impressive guard of honor, most of them Shasinn. I want you safe. Those cowering southerners might try to play you false."

"I think they will know better, but I shall of course take a strong force, all Shasinn and other islanders." It was an attractive prospect. She would erect a royal pavilion on the island. They had captured a general's ornate tent in the baggage train of one of the armies Gasam had defeated earlier. The Granians must be shown how powerful they were, that King Gasam was so utterly in control here that he could send his queen to a diplomatic parley. She loved this sort of power game. Then something occurred to her.

"Has there been any activity or news from the north?" she asked.

"The north?" said Gasam, disingenuously. "You mean from the desert?"

"From farther north," she said, impatiently. "From the plains. From Hael."

"Not a sound," he said. "It is far too soon to anticipate any action from him. I fully expect that, long before he can mount any sort of action, I shall be fully in control of the entire south."

She thought he might be engaging in optimism, but voiced no doubts. She always left military matters to her husband. She had an uneasy feeling. She felt that, somehow, they might be facing a problem other than simply military.

* * *

King Gasam entered the mine gallery and strode down it, careful not to allow his body to brush the dank walls. From time to time dirt would sift down between the overhead planks, causing him to shudder each time it fell on him. Going underground like this filled him with dread and loathing. This was an unnatural place. He loved the open sky and the feel of natural earth beneath his feet. Even being under a roof made him uncomfortable.

"Men should not burrow beneath the earth like horndiggers," he said to his entourage. Most of them nodded and muttered agreement, too oppressed by their surroundings even to speak clearly.

"But necessary, if you want to take this city," said the officer who led them into the bowels of the earth. He was a Nevan mercenary, an officer of sappers and siege engineers. The Nevans alone excelled at this sort of warfare, which involved far more labor than fighting.

"If I could do it any other way I would."

"Your choice, my king," said the Nevan. He was a professional and his deference was purely that due to an employer. "But I've surveyed that city from every angle and if you plan to take it before pestilence breaks out in your camp, these mines are the only way you'll do it."

"Yes, yes, I understand that," said Gasam testily. He was annoyed that these surroundings could rob him of his usual serene control. "How far down are we?" The tunnel had leveled out after slanting downward for a hundred paces.

"Not deep. About ten paces below the surface."

Gasam thought of all the tons of earth over his head and forced himself to stride onward. While the royal party was on its inspection, the workers had downed tools and vacated the mine. Everywhere there were picks and shovels, hammers and spikes and the baskets used to carry the earth out of the gallery. Torches and lamps cast a smoky light and made the air close. Working in here, Gasam thought, must be truly nightmarish. To his relief the tunnel ended at a great wall of stone.

"This is the base of the city wall. You see this angle in the stone? We are at the southwest corner. A wall is always weakest at an angle like this."

Gasam did not know why this should be nor did he care. He was satisfied that the man knew his work. "What will you do next?"

"That depends upon what you wish, my king. We can drive the tunnel through and come up somewhere in the city. Then you can mount an attack through the tunnel and into the city. That I must warn you is a very chancy prospect. It is best done when you have multiple tunnels. Now that we are at the walls they may hear us. Each day risks discovery and counteraction."

Gasam did not like the idea of sending his men into such a place. To attack on such a narrow front against an unknown resistance was not his style of warfare.

"What are my alternatives?"

"From here, we can dig deeper, beneath the corner of the wall. It will be hard digging down there, but in a few days I can hollow a space sufficient to bring the corner down. As we dig, we support the angle with heavy timbers to keep it from collapsing prematurely. When the excavation is sufficiently large, we fill it with oil-soaked brush. We fire the brush and it burns the timbers, weakening the stone as it does. The timbers collapse and the angle of the wall comes crashing down, creating a breach."

"A breach large enough to force our way into the city?"

The Nevan shrugged. "If your men fight hard enough."

"Will a fire burn so far underground?" Gasam wanted to know.

"I plan to cut a series of chimney vents from the fire chamber to the surface. As the heat escapes through these, air will be sucked in through the tunnel. It will get *very* hot, hot enough to crack stone."

"Very well," Gasam said. "Commence digging your fire chamber immediately."

"As my king commands."

Gasam pondered a moment. "You mentioned counteraction. What measures might they take?"

"If they locate our mine by sound, they may dig a countermine."

"Then men could come storming through at any moment?" he asked, his fingers flexing on his spear. The thought was not unpleasant. A good fight would be better than the brooding horror of his surroundings.

"It could happen. However, if I were Mana's commander of engineers, I would drive a tunnel from the river which flows through the city straight into this one. We are well below the river level here. The water would come through with great force."

Gasam thought of a column of water blasting into the tunnel and the sweat sprang out on his brow. His bowels quaked within him. It was a uniquely unpleasant sensation, for he had seldom experienced physical fear. He forced his voice to be steady when he spoke.

"Is this likely?"

"I would hear them if they were close," the sapper assured him. "When we dig the fire chamber I will drive metal rods far into the ground beneath the city. By putting an ear to these I will know if they are driving a countermine anywhere close."

"Excellent. You have your orders, Nevan. Get to work." Gasam whirled on his heel and his followers made him a path through their midst. He led them out, forcing himself to keep a stately pace, although he wanted badly to run. He vowed to make the people in the city pay a terrible price for making him feel fear.

Larissa watched the siege operations as she composed her letter. The king had ordered a tall viewing platform to be built overlooking the south wall of the city, just beyond missile range. It was ten feet higher than the wall itself, allowing a view into the city beyond. The queen lounged on a cushioned couch as she dictated to a scribe who sat cross-legged before her. An awning protected her from sun and rain.

"To the glorious and illustrious King Ach'na of Gran from the invincible King Gasam of the Isles, conqueror of Chiwa, and from his queen, the beauteous Larissa, greeting." She turned to the scribe, a captive Sonoan. "How does that sound?"

"Why not, 'the beauteous and exquisite Larissa,' my queen?" the scribe simpered.

"That sounds even better," she said, smiling. "Change it so. Now, to continue: I, Queen Larissa, extend to the gracious sovereign of Gran my and my royal husband's warmest and fondest regards. Please accept my lord's most heartfelt assurances that only the greatest of affection lies between us, and that the present unpleasantness between us and King Mana of Sono in no way alters the affection which we feel for our brother monarch, Ach'na of Gran.

"The present state of hostility is purely the doing of the insolent and rapacious King Mana, who has behaved intolerably toward us, violating an important naval treaty and addressing us with contempt. He now suffers the rightful consequences of such flagrant treachery and discourtesy.

"If, as I am sure he has, the cowardly and craven Mana has petitioned you for military aid in this matter, I pray that you will pay him no heed. We wish ardently that only the most peaceful and serene relationship should prevail between ourselves and our beloved brother monarch, Ach'na of Gran."

She paused. "Does this sound too flattering? I do not wish to sound insincere."

"My queen," the scribe assured her, "there is no way that one can flatter a Granian monarch too heavily."

"Very well. I conclude thus: In order that all made be smooth between us, I propose a diplomatic meeting, to take place on neutral ground between us. King Gasam will be detained for some time by his military activities, but in earnest of his sincerity in this matter and as a sign of the perfect trust, as well as esteem, which he feels for his brother king, Ach'na of Gran, I, Queen Larissa, shall serve as his personal envoy. In ten days, I shall be upon the Isle of Sorrow in the River Kol. I realize that it would be too much to request your own royal presence on such short notice, but I shall be most agreeable to a meeting with whatever representatives you see fit to send, to the end that peace and cooperation shall reign forever between our kingdoms. Eagerly, I await your reply by your speediest messenger." She stopped and thought for a while. "I can think of nothing further to add. Complete it with the customary compliments, and draw up a final draft, then show it to me. I can read the formal Southern used in royal correspondence, so I will know if you have altered my words in any way."

"My queen, I would never alter your words in any way!" the scribe protested.

"See that you don't." Larissa had learned to read as a grown woman, and she lacked confidence in her penmanship. It had been a relief to her to learn that royalty were not expected to write their own letters, but employed scribes trained in the art.

She rose and walked to the front of the platform to study the scene below. The tower upon which she stood was sturdily constructed of heavy timbers, but it swayed gently in the breeze, creaking softly as it do so. Other towers were ranked by hers, these mounted on wheels. In an assault, the wheeled towers would be pushed against the walls by captives and nusks.

Leaning against the towers were long ladders which would be carried to the walls likewise and men would try to climb them to secure a foothold on the ramparts. This sort of fighting seemed suicidal to Larissa, but then, that was why Gasam would use the soldiers of inferior race for the assault. He would reserve his islanders for the wall-breach he planned to make. The open end of the mine gallery was well hidden from the walls, and the dirt was disposed of secretly. He hoped to keep the tunnel secret until the last possible moment.

She leaned on the railing and surveyed the great army that engirdled the city. The soldiers dug earthworks to foil a sally from within, although most of them would have welcomed any such action as a break in the monotony. They had dug ditches and lined them with slanting spikes of wood or bamboo and behind these had thrown up earth ramparts.

The lordly island warriors lounged far back from these labors, aloof from all such drudgery. They were growing dangerously restive. After the exertions of the march and the excitement and dangers of the battles, this static campaigning was a severe letdown. The king would have to find something for them to do, and soon.

The scribe brought her the letter and she studied it closely, having to concentrate to follow the words in the midst of the floridly decorative calligraphy. The words were as she had dictated them. She sent a slave to summon a royal messenger and a few minutes later a man in a yellow-plumed headdress tied up his cabo at the base of the tower and ascended its steps. He knelt before Larissa and held forth his message case. This was an ornate tube of bronze plated with gold.

Larissa opened the tube and thrust her rolled letter inside. The scribe applied a ball of wax over the tube's clasp and pressed it flat. Larissa applied her seal to the wax.

"You are to deliver this to King Ach'na of Gran. Go like lightning."

"As my queen commands." The man dashed down the steps and moments later the hoofbeats of his cabo were facing in the distance.

TWELVE

To reach the palace they rode uphill, past Lady Yasha's estate and around the slope to the opposite side. Beneath the hulking temple crowning the city, the palace complex sprawled messily, a clutter of large and small buildings surrounded by a twenty-foot wall. Sentries paced boredly atop the wall, uniformed as colorfully as if for a festival.

They followed their guide through an open archway into a paved courtyard. At the far end of the courtyard a road ascended to a vast building. The road was lined with towering trees that bore lush, spindle-shaped foliage. The trees were alive with exotic birds and arboreal mammals and at the base of each tree was a wide bowl full of food for the tree's inhabitants. The road was flanked by a park full of tame animals. Among them, Ansa was astonished to see a creature resembling the man-of-the-trees, but human-sized. It looked dangerous to him, but it ambled on all fours, unmolested, its, thin, vestigial tail held erect.

At the palace, the servant took charge of their mounts and gestured for them to enter the high doors. Guards beside the door paid them no flicker of attention. This surprised Ansa. He expected to be challenged since he was armed. A sharp-face, bearded man met them just within the doorway. Even before he spoke Ansa knew it was Lord Klon. He thought that even without the mask the man looked much as he had wearing it.

"Welcome to the palace of His Majesty," Klon said. "You are to consider yourselves his honored guests." There was a throat-clearing sound from a blocky, uniformed man who stood by an open door.

"I am being reminded," Klon said. "I am afraid that you must leave your weapons here in the guardroom. It is the custom, and there are no exceptions save for visiting royalty."

This was not the time to protest that his father was a king, so Ansa handed over his sword and dagger. It felt strange to be without them, but he had expected this. Kings were notorious sticklers concerning who might be allowed to bear arms in their presence.

In any case, he reminded himself, he was no longer a simple, steppe warrior. He was an important . . . what? He was reluctant to think of himself as a spy. That seemed faintly dishonorable. Spies, he had always heard, were professional skulkers who sought out secrets and sold them to whoever would pay the most for them.

Whatever his new identity might be, he knew that being deprived of his weapons made him no less a warrior and that his task called for an alert and observant mind. His father had always stressed that fighting skills were the least of a real man's accomplishments, and weapons merely tools of necessity. As a boy, he had assumed that this was just more of his father's foolishness. Now it did not seem so unreasonable.

Klon began to lead them into the palace. "The, ah, personage to whom I now guide you for consultation is . . ."

Fyana laid a hand upon his arm. "Lord Klon, forgive me, but my companion and I are from lands less sophisticated than this one. We are unused to your court customs and usages. We are most especially uncomfortable with these circumlocutions which to you, no doubt, are familiar and simple. Please do not think that because we lack court polish we are stupid or ignorant."

"My lady!" he protested. "I would never suggest . . ."

Once again, she laid the calming hand upon his arm. "Of course not. I simply wish to set some things straight between us. It is quite clear that we go to treat either the king or his heir. The sovereign's state of health and that of his heir are, naturally, legitimate subjects for state secrecy. Questions of government stability and dynastic succession may hinge upon them."

Ansa enjoyed the stupefied look on the courtier's face. He was, as always, impressed by Fyana's quick assertion of equality, if not superiority. He knew that it cost her an effort because they were now in the inner environs of the palace, a place as new to her as to him, and it was a place of marvels. On the road to the city, and since they had been here, he had heard of some of the earlier kings of Gran, many of them men of legendary eccentricity.

They passed between two pillars of clear glass. Within the pillars were swimming fish, their bodies weirdly distorted by the curvature of the glass. Golden-furred man-of-the-trees seemed to scamper about at will. Murals, mosaics and sculptures abounded everywhere he looked.

"To begin with," Fyana went on, "may I know your real name? We are in the palace now, surely there is no pressing need for secrecy."

"Ahm, ah, well, of course, you are right. I am Lord Osha Kl'an, chamberlain to His Majesty. I am sorry, but the extreme delicacy of the situation necessitates all this secrecy. That, and a certain love of mummery on our part.''

Fyana smiled. ''That is better. Now, is it the king I am to see, or his heir?''

They climbed a broad stair between tall statues of winged, beast-headed men. Beyond the landing at the top of the stair the rooms were smaller, more intimate. Apparently, these were the actual living quarters of the palace. What they had just passed through had been reception rooms and areas for public functions.

''It is the king,'' Lord Osha finally admitted. ''And the king has no heir old enough to inherit the crown.''

Fyana stopped and turned to him. ''Before I go farther, tell me something: Will I make deadly enemies if I am able to help the king? It will have no effect upon my treatment, but I wish to know.''

Osha said nothing for a while. Fyana and Ansa watched him closely.

''You will have friends who are stronger,'' he said at last.

''Very well,'' she said. ''Lead on.''

They came to a door guarded by men of yet another new race. These were short, burly men with fair hair and beards, their faces heavily tattooed. They glared suspiciously at the approaching strangers. At a word from the courtier they drew aside. The guards wore colorful, padded armor and bore fearsome polearms. Each had a four-foot wooden shaft topped by a broad, curved steel blade two feet long. A small, circular handguard separated blade from shaft. These were the first large steel weapons Ansa had seen since arriving in Gran. Their bronze caps were embossed to resemble the scaled hide of a reptile.

''Bamen,'' Lord Osha said, ''men from far northeast of here. They have formed the royal bodyguard for generations. They are savages, but their loyalty is unshakable.''

He said this with pride, but it seemed to Ansa a poor thing that a king should have to hire foreign primitives if he wanted loyal men near him. Foreigners would be less likely to be involved in the intrigues of rival nobles, naturally enough. That, too, said something about the nature of this court.

They encountered servitors and other courtiers. Even the most bejewelled and richly robed of the latter bowed deeply to Lord Osha. All were silent or conversed in low voices, and all wore mournful expressions. The women wore makeup that made the corners of their eyes and mouths appear to turn downward, with dark circles drawn beneath the eyes. They even appeared to have applied an irritant to their eyes to make them red. The impression was that they were all in a prolonged fit of weeping. Had it not been so bizarre, Ansa would have found it comical.

They stopped before a closed door heavily plated with gold. The courtier spoke a few quiet words to an elderly, bearded man who entered the room and closed the golden door behind him. A few minutes later, a handsome woman in her later thirties came out. Her skin was pale, her hair dark. Strikingly in these environs, she wore no heavy makeup. Lord Osha lowered himself to one knee before her, bowing his head.

"Your Majesty, I present the visitors of whom you have heard: Lady Fyana of the Canyon and the noble Ansa, her escort."

Fyana bowed gracefully and Ansa somewhat less so. He was unfamiliar with the practice of knee-bending and made no effort to emulate Lord Osha. The queen seemed satisfied.

"My deepest gratitude to you both for assenting to come here today," she said. Her voice was warm and infinitely gracious. It was so well done that Ansa could not tell whether it was sincere or just well practiced.

"I hope that I may be of some aid," Fyana said. "Is this the patient's chamber?"

"It is. Please come with me." The queen took Fyana's

hand and led her inside. Ansa followed closely, before anyone could have the opportunity to forbid him. He had no
intention of letting Fyana out of his sight in this strange
place.

The chamber was large, but the air was murky with incense
smoke. Hangings covered the walls, completely blocking any
windows that might have been there. A sizable crowd jammed
the room, berobed men and elaborately gowned women hovered around a bed on a dais in the chamber's center. The
lugubrious expressions on their faces did not bode well for the
chances of the bed's occupant.

The queen led them to the dais and they mounted its three
steps. In the bed lay a man whose age was difficult to guess.
His hair and beard were lank, brownish. On his face, the
skin lay thin over prominent bones. His pale blue eyes stared
upward at nothing. Lavish bedclothes covered him to the
chest. His arms lay outside the bedclothes, his hands protruding from the sleeves of his robe to lie pale and motionless atop embroidery of gold and scarlet thread. Except for
the faint rise and fall of his chest, the man made no motion
at all. Even his fingers did not twitch.

"He has been thus for ten days," the queen said.

"How did it happen?" Fyana asked. She made no move
to touch the king. Ansa studied the others in the room.
Some looked at Fyana with haughty resentment. Others had
no expression at all.

"There was a banquet. The king was just as always, in
the best of health. He had gone on a hunt that day, riding
in the forest, and none of his companions or attendants
noted anything unusual in his behavior. In the middle of the
banquet, he grew pale and told me he would retire early,
that he did not feel well. He left, but it was so unlike him
that I quickly followed. I found him lying on the floor,
unable to move or speak, as you see him now.'

"You found him?" Fyana looked up sharply. "Did none
of the servitors, none of your palace attendants see him

collapse?'' This seemed strange to Ansa as well, but he had agreed to let Fyana do all the talking here, unless he was directly addressed.

"There is a passage connecting the public rooms and the royal apartments. It allows us to pass back and forth without using the crowded hallways. That was where he lay. He has not moved or spoken since that moment. Can you help him?'' Her tone was as dignified as her demeanor, but there was pleading in her eyes.

"I will do what I can. But, please, could you have the curtains and windows opened? The air and smoke in here are enough to kill a sick man.''

"Your Majesty, I protest!'' A white-bearded man in a black robe came forward. His robe was embroidered with designs of animals and what looked like stars in silver thread. "To open the windows is to allow spirits of infection and pestilence to enter the royal chamber!''

Another came forward, this one in the clothing and headgear worn by Granian priests. "Truly, you must not do this, Your Majesty! I have established spiritual safeguards around this chamber for His Majesty's protection. If not only air but sunlight are admitted,'' he paused dramatically, "then I cannot be answerable for the terrible consequences that must inevitably follow.''

"Gentlemen,'' the queen said, "I thank you for your efforts but now I must try other measures. You may withdraw.'' She turned back toward the king but both men protested.

"This is an outrage and an insult to the High Guild of Physicians!'' said the black-robed man.

"And to the temple!'' said the priest. "Will you allow this desert savage to countermand the measures of your high clergy?''

Ansa decided that he had been silent long enough. "You men have done the king no good in ten days. Begone! Or does the command of your queen mean nothing to you?''

Throughout the chamber there were subdued gasps of horror. The physician and the priest stood as if struck by lightning, unable to believe they had been defied by a barbarian scarcely past boy's years. The queen glared at them stonily.

"Yes. Shall I summon the Bamen?"

Muttering apologies, near apoplexy from mortification and rage, the two men withdrew from the chamber, and with them went a substantial party of subordinates. Quickly, servants drew back the curtains and swung open the glass-paned windows. In minutes, the air was nearly clear and the chamber was brilliantly illuminated.

"I shall need a chair," Fyana said, "and some time alone with the king. You needn't withdraw from the room, but I should be alone here on the dais with him. I cannot say how much time will be necessary. As I told Lord Klon—I should say Lord Osha Kl'an—this can take a long time, when the patient is unconscious."

"Whatever you wish and as much time as you need. Everyone here will obey your instructions as if they were my own." A servant brought a chair and the queen herself held it as Fyana sat. She composed herself for a moment, then the blue fingers touched the king's brow.

Ansa felt a touch at his arm. The queen beckoned him to follow her. As he left the room, he saw a young boy sitting in a chair against one of the walls. He was no more than ten years old and his huge, dark eyes were stunned with grief. Yet, when they met Ansa's, the child summoned a smile. This, Ansa knew, must be a son of the king. And he felt that his defiance of the overbearing physician and priest had earned him the smile.

The queen led him to a small sitting room where the usual tokens of hospitality were laid out on a table. At her gesture, he sat and took a goblet.

"Young man, you are not easily overawed by men of

great prestige. Somehow, I do not believe that this is a matter of ignorance."

"Priests are nothing to me," he said. "My people have none such. And a physician who can show no results after ten days has no right to puff himself up. Least of all does he have a right to display insolence toward his queen."

She sighed, a sound of anger rather than of resignation. "Would that all my subjects had this wisdom. Well, have no fear. I will see to it that you and Lady Fyana come to no harm from them."

Ansa smiled faintly. "Forgive me, Your Majesty, but I am sure that, if Lady Fyana is able to save the king, she will have earned enemies of far greater merit than those two."

She favored him with a calculating look. "I see you are not unfamiliar with how courts are."

"I am wellborn," he said. "I have spent time at King Hael's court, and I think all courts are the same."

"Are you a kinsman of King Hael?"

"We are connected," he said, cautiously.

"He came to his kingdom a stranger, a wanderer from the far islands. so you must be of the family of Queen Deena?"

"She is my kinswoman," he admitted.

"A close one, I suspect. My guard captain says that you surrendered weapons of pure steel when you entered the palace, including a sizable longsword."

"I see that it is not only the royal family who use the secret passages in this palace," he said, growing angry. "Did someone go running ahead of us to report to you?"

"The least of my precautions," she said. "If you only knew how many plots surround me."

"I think I am beginning to learn. As for the steel weapons, they are no longer a rarity in my kingdom. Every warrior has them now."

She swirled wine in her goblet. She looked unutterably

weary but sat erect. "King Hael has two sons, one named Kairn, the other Ansa. If you were going to travel in disguise, you should at least have changed your name."

"Ansa is not an uncommon name among the plains people," he said, embarrassed.

"Ansa, I have met your father, and the resemblance is unmistakable. Why you wish to disown your patrimony is your own affair and I will respect your wishes in the matter, but I want things to be clear between us. I will not offer you princely honors if you do not wish them."

He drank ruefully. "Your Majesty . . ." She cut him off with a gesture.

"In private you may address me as Masila, please."

"Masila, then. I am not a prince as you know such things. My father's preeminance is as much spiritual as royal. He is king by acclamation of the assembled tribes. When he dies, it is unlikely that his place will be taken by a son. There is no tradition of an inherited kingship among us."

"I understand. Are you here, then, just as a traveler? Did you come seeking a military appointment?"

"I can see," he said, uncomfortably, "that you don't share the local fondness for indirection."

"I have no time," she said shortly.

"Then I shall be as direct. Yes, I had no more than wanderlust in mind when I rode south. As I rode, however, rumors began to reach me. There are reports that King Gasam is on the move again. I came to see whether the stories are true."

"All too true. He has invaded Sono and even now he lays siege to King Mana's capital city, Huato. My agents have interrogated refugees, who pour across the border in their thousands."

"I must learn more of this. Gasam and my father are deadly enemies and have been since childhood."

"You see, my husband's affliction could not have happened at a worse time." She spoke as calmly as ever, but there was agitation in her eyes. Ansa considered his next words for some time before he spoke.

"I wonder whether this is coincidence." He saw the narrowing of her eyes that proclaimed better than words that she had been thinking the same thing.

"About that I shall say nothing until I have heard Lady Fyana's assessment of His Majesty's condition. If he can be restored to health, all shall be well."

Ansa had severe doubts about that. What he had seen of Gran gave him no such confidence. Magnificence did not translate into military effectiveness, and he doubted that the king of these people, even in the best of health, could prove a match for the fearsome King Gasam of the Islands.

"My lady-in-waiting Amahest M'Ilva tells me that Lady Fyana favored her with a certain diagnosis when I sent her to meet with you yesterday."

"Assumed names do not conceal everything," Ansa remarked. "I trust the lady will not be excessively embarrassed?"

"That is between her and her husband." She fell into a silence which Ansa did not interrupt. He had a great many questions troubling him, but he did not want to presume upon his sketchy acquaintance with the queen, a woman already beset with too many concerns. Finally, he decided upon a neutral subject.

"The boy I saw in the king's chamber, is he your son?"

She brightened. "Our only child, Prince Gehlis." A shadow came over her face. "I think I feel as much concern for my son as for my husband."

He could well understand that. If the king should die while his son was still a minor, there might be a struggle for the succession. At best, the boy could become a pawn in a power game between regents. When a regent had enjoyed several years of control, it might be convenient to dispose of the prince as he neared majority. These were dismal thoughts, and he felt sure that the queen spoke so openly to him because she had few friends here, few persons in whom she could confide. He was a stranger, but for that very reason he was not involved in court intrigues. He was a king's son, so she was not speaking to a social inferior.

"If I may be of any assistance, you have only to ask," he assured her. "Unlike Fyana, I have no healing gifts, but I have skills of combat, as well as of discretion. Such gifts as I possess I place at your disposal."

She bowed her head graciously. "For this offer I thank you most sincerely. I know that you do not make it as a mere display of form. I think I may well call upon your skills, and that in no great time."

"You have but to command," Ansa said.

The queen picked listlessly at a plate of delicacies. "Have you any idea how long Lady Fyana will need?"

"I cannot say. I've seen her diagnose simple ailments in seconds, but those were common cases, things she had much experience with. The patients then were able to tell her what troubled them. Something outside her experience, with a patient who is not conscious . . ." He shrugged. "From what she has said, it could take many hours, perhaps more than one session. And I think she may be exhausted at the end of it."

The queen rose. "I shall see to quarters for the two of you. I will send servants to your inn to fetch your belongings and any animals you may have there."

Ansa liked the inn and did not relish the thought of moving to the vast, strange, and possibly hostile palace, but he saw no way to reject this hospitality without giving offense.

"That is most generous. May I request that Lady Fyana and I have adjoining quarters? I know that your guards are loyal, but I gave her people my word that her safety would be my responsibility."

"Of course. Now I must go. Please treat my house and my servants as your own."

He rose and bowed her out of the room. When she was gone he wondered what he should do next. Sitting in this small room, however comfortable it might be, was a dismal prospect. She had offered him the use of her servants, but he could think of nothing they could do for him. He had seen to his own needs since childhood and had never lived among servants.

He went to the king's bedchamber and looked in. Fyana sat exactly as he had last seen her, as if she and the king formed a sculptural group. Around the wall stood servants and courtiers, keeping their distance and maintaining silence. The boy was no longer in his chair and Ansa did not see him in the room.

Ansa crossed the chamber as quietly as he could and stepped into the corridor outside. Faces turned expectantly toward him, many of them painted, as if they expected him to give them some news of the king's condition. When it was plain he would not speak, they lost interest. He wanted to go outside, to be away from the oppressive walls and heavy ceilings of this place. He longed for direct sunlight and fresh air.

A short walk from the chamber brought him to a wide double door opening onto the outside. He stepped through it and found himself on a terrace overlooking a remarkable structure. From the terrace a long stairway descended into a roofless, oval enclosure surrounded by tiers of what he took to be seats. The enclosure was sunk about eight feet below the level of the lowest tier of seats. It appeared to be floored with sand. He could imagine no use for such a structure. Was it a temple?

"I see you have found our stadium," said a voice behind him. He knew the voice and turned to see the lady who had, the night before, gone by the name of Hesta.

He bowed. "If you say so, Lady Amahest M'Ilva. I have never seen such a place. What is it used for?"

Her hands spread on the flounces of her elaborate gown,

she walked toward him. This afternoon her cosmetics were far more restrained and he could see that she was a beautiful woman of about thirty, with very white skin, a good deal of which was visible. Her tight bodice ended at her nipples, leaving her shoulders and the upper surfaces of her breasts bare.

"This is a place of exhibitions. On days of the shows, there are animal performances, dancers, acrobats, magicians. There are trials of athletic skill and combats. You see here only the bare bones. When the shows are on, there are cushions and hangings, flowers, bright awnings and fountains to cool the air. There are night shows by torchlight."

"Combats?" he said.

"Yes. Masters of arms come to show their skills or to challenge each other. It can be very beautiful, almost like a dance."

"They fight to the death?"

"Usually just until one surrenders or can no longer go on fighting. Occasionally, a master who deems himself to be greatly insulted will insist upon a death-fight. Of course, losers sometimes die of their wounds. You are interested in combats?" She smiled strangely.

He shrugged. "I am a warrior. This is something I've never encountered, although like everyone I've watched when two warriors decide to fight a duel. That happens at almost every gathering. The king permits it because otherwise they would just ambush each other in secret, and that would lead to blood feuds."

"Your people sound very—how shall I say it?—very *vital*." She stood close and he could smell her perfume. It was subtle, something he would not have expected here, where all sensations seemed to be overpowering.

"We are accustomed to a hard life," he said.

"You've not had a hard life here. Barely in the city and welcomed in the highest houses. Already you have had a

private audience with Her Majesty. Many people of high
station are here for years without being granted that favor."

"Her Majesty is most kind," Ansa said. "But Lady Fyana and I represent hope at a time of great distress for her.
I do not harbor the illusion that I have been exalted in her
court."

She nodded. "You are very wise in this. I am glad of it.
Allow me to speak as a friend. Royal favor is as dangerous
a thing as royal disfavor. It can be more dangerous, for
while a sovereign's disfavor gives you one powerful enemy,
favor can net you many less powerful ones."

"I am aware of that. Yet I could not have acted otherwise
than I have done."

"An estimable attitude, the attitude of a noble youth. If
I may make a suggestion, you might be well advised to play
the part of a simple barbarian here; brave and true, but
lacking in sophistication. The great ones here at court will
perceive little threat in you if you behave thus."

He inclined his head. "I will keep that in mind. If I may
ask a question, just who represents the greatest threat? There
are those here who will be sorely disappointed if the king
should recover."

She lowered her eyes. "Here you presume too much.
Suffice it that you know to be on your guard. You need not
concern yourself with identities."

"Then I will not press the matter. Again, I thank you for
your candor."

"Enough of such solemnity," she said. "Please regard
me as your friend while you are here."

"That I shall," he said, with severe inward reservation.
In this place, he would need more than a simple assertion
of friendship before he bestowed his trust on anyone. In the
meantime, Lady Amahest seemed determined to be pleasant company. She took him on a tour of the stadium, ex-
plaining its appointments and decorations. Its arena wall
was surmounted by a series of grotesque statues, some of

them depicting animals, others representing deformed humans. She related to him an involved legend in which the beasts and the dwarfish humans participated in a war between gods.

She told him of the building of the amphitheater by a king three centuries before, a man with a passion for blood sport but too indolent to leave the palace for their enjoyment. He had beasts of the chase brought to his arena where he could pretend to hunt them and where he could set prisoners to fight one another for his amusement. The entertainments were no longer so bloody, she assured him. Bloodshed was now a spice, rather than the very purpose of the entertainments.

During her recitation, she found frequent cause to take him by the hand or arm to point out items of interest. She stood closer to him than seemed absolutely necessary, and early on found an excuse to tell him that her husband, an elderly man, was off governing a province on the southeastern border with the small kingdom of Missa, a swampy place she could not endure.

He was simultaneously amused and alarmed. She was a beautiful woman, but this was a complication he did not need in an already precarious situation.

"Let me show you the chambers beneath," she said. "Some are for the animals and some for the entertainers to prepare themselves. But there are others whose purpose no one knows. They are very dark and mysterious." She took his hand and tugged, "Come."

"Perhaps another time. I have been away too long. I think I should go back and see how matters stand between Lady Fyana and the king."

Her look darkened. "She said herself that this might take a very long time. There is no need for you to hurry back."

He had no idea how dangerous this woman might prove to be. He had no wish to insult her, yet he could not discount the possibility that she was deliberately keeping him away from the king's chamber.

"I am sorry, but I am sworn to the lady's service."

"So you are. Perhaps I should not have been so quick to suggest that you play the part of the simple barbarian. Very well, go to her. But remember that we have not finished our tour of this place."

He bowed. "Rest assured, I shall not forget." Relieved, he made his way back to the king's bedchamber, where everything seemed unchanged. He crossed to the small receiving room where he had spoken with the queen. It, too, seemed unchanged except that servants had restored the small depletions in the refreshments. It had been some time since he had eaten substantially, so he helped himself to the viands. He rose and bowed when the queen entered. She gestured for him to resume his seat.

"A court is a strange place at a time like this," she said. "Nobody knows what to do. On ordinary days, every action of every person is regulated by the king's schedule. Now they are stymied. Adherence to routine is impossible, but they have no guide for their actions. The court is not centered on the king's actions, but neither is it in mourning. They cannot act until this matter is resolved. One way or the other." Idly, the queen tapped something on the table and Ansa saw that it was an ornate bronze tube. He recognized it; a messenger's case. It bore a thick waxen seal, as yet unbroken.

"You have received a royal communication?"

"Yes, and I am reluctant to open it. I am afflicted with my court's inability to act. It is from King Gasam, and I fear what it has to communicate."

Ansa felt a chill creep up his spine. A message from Gasam! Was it a challenge? Or was it just more of Gasam's suave lies? It could not have arrived at a more portentious time.

"Yet you must read it soon," he said.

"I know. But I will do that in the presence of the king's closest advisers." She continued to tap the metal tube on the table. "I wish you to be there too."

"I appreciate the honor," Ansa said, "but your high officers will resent it."

"Let them resent," she said. "I care not. But you are new here. You can see things with fresh eyes."

"And what would you wish me to see?"

"The faces of those high officers. I would like your impressions of what they look like when they first hear Gasam's words, before they have had time to reflect and to compose themselves. Gasam is engaged in a war of conquest on our border. I think this," she gave the table an especially forceful tap, "is some sort of ultimatum. Some will already contemplate abandoning the throne, going over to Gasam."

"Surely they can have little to gain by that," Ansa said.

"Perhaps, but in some men treachery is bred bone-deep. They can no more restrain themselves from double-dealing than they can stop breathing air. I would value your opinion upon them."

"I am at your service. When do you propose to do this?"

"Barring a sudden change in the king's condition, tonight. All the counselors have been assembled here for days, so it will be no problem to summon a meeting." She broke off when the door opened and Fyana entered.

Ansa was alarmed by her appearance, which was wan and haggard. Two serving women supported her on either side. The queen snatched a chair back from the table and the women helped Fyana into it. The queen dismissed the women and poured wine into a goblet. Then she reseated herself and watched with concern as Fyana fumbled in her belt pouch like a very old woman. With trembling fingers she withdrew a tiny vial and unstoppered it. She allowed six drops to fall into her goblet, then she returned the vial to her pouch. With both hands, she raised the cup and drank.

A few minutes passed, during which time all three remained silent. Fyana drank several times, and the color began to return to her face. Finally, she was able to hold her cup with one hand and return it to the table without trembling.

"This will pass soon," Fyana said in a hoarse voice. "When the treatment is this deep, the healer comes to partially share the affliction of the patient."

"Please refresh yourself," said the queen. "Speak when you feel strong enough."

Ansa refilled her cup and set a plate before her. Slowly, as if she feared the abundance of viands would make her ill, Fyana ate some tiny pastries and skewers of grilled fish. Soon she was eating ravenously, as if her body had been starved of sustenance for days. At last she sat back, replete. She looked tired but otherwise well.

"I hope you will forgive my strange behavior, Your Majesty."

The queen waved a hand dismissively. "My physicians and priests behave far more strangely and they accomplish nothing. Can you tell me anything of the king's condition?"

"I will need more sessions with him," Fyana said. Seeing the queen's downcast expression, she added quickly, "I can tell you this: The king was poisoned."

"I suspected as much. But everything the king eats or drinks is tasted. How was it administered?"

"That I have not yet determined."

"A minor consideration now," the queen said. "How serious is it? Can he be restored to health?"

"I must make some tests, but I think that the effects of the poison can be reversed. It is a paralyzing agent and the king is robbed of all ability to move of his own volition. Otherwise, his health is excellent. That is why he is still alive. Had he not been exceptionally strong and healthy, the poison would have paralyzed the faculties that regulate breathing and he would have suffocated. A much stronger dose of the poison would have stopped his heart and he would have died instantly, at the banquet.''

The queen closed her eyes and shuddered. ''I will have revenge for this, but that is for later. What may be done now?''

''I must begin a course of medicine treatments and tests. Some of the items I need are among our belongings at the inn . . .''

''They are already here at the palace,'' the queen interrupted.

''Very good. Other things I will have to find among the apothecaries here. May I have writing materials?''

The queen clapped her hands and a serving woman appeared. At the queen's order she left and returned minutes later bearing a tray upon which rested a stack of paper, pots of colored inks, and a rack of pens and brushes. Ignoring the pens, Fyana took a brush and began drawing lines of mysterious symbols. Finished, she blew on the wet ink, then handed it to the queen.

''Have this sent to the apothecaries. In a city this large, we should be able to locate all these items.''

''I will have copies made and send them to all the apothecaries at once. That should save time.'' She summoned a secretary and gave the necessary instructions.

''Is there any more you can tell me now?''

''Nothing until I have been able to test some medicines.''

''What else will you need? Ask anything.''

''I will need assistants.''

''Regard my physicians and their servants as your personal slaves,'' the queen said.

''I am sorry, Your Majesty, but I do not trust your physicians and therefore I cannot trust their servants.''

The queen did not protest. ''Who, then?''

''I want you best animal doctor, the one who tends the

beasts of the royal stables. Have him bring his assistants, or a couple of strong stablemen if he has no apprentices or servants."

Now the queen was truly shocked. "A cabo-doctor! Surely this cannot be true! I cannot allow such base persons to attend to my husband!"

"Your Majesty," Fyana said, "right now what I need is someone skilled in the messy but necessary art of getting medication into an inert body. In such a condition, a man's body is little different from a cabo's, and a king's no different from any other man's. You may, of course, wish to dismiss all unnecessary persons from the king's chamber. It is not a dignified procedure."

The queen was stony-faced. "It shall be as you say."

"I can do nothing more until tomorrow, by which time I hope all the medicines I need shall have been located and brought here. May I take my leave of you? I truly need rest."

"Of course. I have put a suite of rooms at your disposal, and that of Prince Ansa."

Fyana looked at Ansa and smiled wanly. "That deception didn't last long."

"You'll find that little gets past Queen Masila."

The queen led them back through the royal bedchamber and into the great hall beyond. Immediately outside the door rested a litter. At its corners stood four stalwart bearers, their arms folded. At the sight, Fyana almost laughed.

"Your Majesty, I am tired. I am not an invalid. I think I can make it to my quarters under my own power."

"I will not have it," said Masila. "As of this moment, I treasure your health second only to my husband's. Just now, I think the two are one and the same. Rest now. My people are to obey your instructions as if they were my own." She turned to Ansa. "I will send for you this evening, as we discussed earlier." The assembly in the hall bowed deeply as their queen returned to the bedchamber.

Embarrassed, Fyana climbed into the carrying-chair. The slaves stooped and raised the litter to their shoulders. Grinning, Ansa walked alongside. Courtiers bowed as they passed. Word of this extraordinary royal favor had spread through the palace like lightning. The slaves set the litter down before a door flanked by a pair of the brutish-looking Bamen.

"I have never been carried by men before," Fyana said as she dismounted. "It is the oddest sensation." She did not look as if the sensation had been unpleasant.

The suite they entered was little inferior to the king's in size, appointments or staff. A dozen servants awaited them, in the charge of a supervisor, a woman who carried a small, ceremonial whip. She immediately took charge of Fyana and led her to a bath somewhere in the rear of the suite. Ansa found his own room and walked out onto its balcony. A pair of Bamen guards stood there as well. It appeared that the queen was not confident of their safety even within her own palace. He would have felt more secure with his own weapons.

With that thought he glanced at the diminutive pile of his belongings that stood near the bed. From a bag protruded a hide-wrapped handle. Seizing this, he withdrew the stone-headed war axe he had bought two days before. He whipped it through the air, producing a satisfying hiss and instantly feeling far better.

He found that a bath adjoined his own chamber and decided to try it out. He dismissed the overeager attendants, feeling that this was something he could manage for himself. It still seemed odd to him that these people seemed to need help to accomplish the simplest and most basic of actions. He decided that it must make them feel more important. From what he had seen, they might well stand in need of such reassurance.

Scrubbed and lathered, he relaxed in the lavish marble tub and pondered his situation. It was a strange sensation, being in a setting of incredible luxury but in as much danger as if on a battlefield. Here there was absolutely no one he could trust, although the queen seemed to come close.

Dried, powdered and dressed in clean clothes, he lounged in his chamber until he heard Fyana call his name. He found her in her own chamber relaxing on her bed, her back propped by a pile of immense cushions over which a pair of serving women fussed like two artists arranging a sculpture.

"Please leave us for a while," she said, and the two bowed themselves out of the room. She turned to Ansa. "Now, tell me all about your doings while I was occupied with the king."

He sat on a corner of the huge bed and told her of his talk with the queen, and of his tour of the stadium, including Lady Amahest's none too subtle attempts at seduction. He was gratified to see Fyana's eyes narrow and nostrils flare.

"That slut! And a married woman, too!" She fumed for a minute. "I suppose you conceive yourself to be irresistible now?"

He laughed for the first time that day. "I would very much like to. She is a beautiful woman." He enjoyed her expression for a while. "But, even I am not that conceited. These are people who do little without some advantage in mind. I think she may well have been put up to this, in hope of learning more about us or gaining some sort of influence."

"Or access. Well, as long as you understand this."

"Seriously, though, I have my apprehensions about this. Whatever her motives for flinging herself at me, I could earn a deadly enemy by rejecting her out of hand. There are sayings about a woman scorned."

"No problem," she assured him. "You are a simple barbarian, are you not? Just let her know that among your people it is an abomination for a man to lie with a woman who is pregnant. You were there when I told her of her condition. That will give her a pride-sparing excuse to leave you alone. Don't look so unhappy at the prospect. She won't be the last to offer you access to her body.'' Her eyes narrowed again. ''Two months. I wonder how long her husband has been away.''

''That,'' Ansa said, echoing what the queen had said, ''is between her and her husband.'' He went on to tell her of his later visit with the queen and of her apprehension over the missive from King Gasam.

''I can understand that she is unsettled. I would be too, at the thought of dealing with that man. This must be the sort of thing the king and his advisers have dealt with before. Now she has this, as well as her husband's health to deal with. It does astonish me that she wants you present when she reads the letter to her husband's counselors.''

''I think she suspects some of them to be behind the king's condition. Maybe she just wants to have one actual friend present.''

''She does not strike me as someone who is all that quick to bestow her trust,'' Fyana said.

''I think she is like those sick people you spoke of once,'' Ansa countered. ''When they are desperate, they will believe anyone who offers them hope. I think that we represent hope to this queen.''

Fyana mumbled agreement, but her lids drooped lower and within a few seconds she was asleep, sagging back against her pile of cushions. Quietly, Ansa rose and tiptoed from the room. He found the two serving women they had dismissed and told them to tend to Fyana but on no account to wake her. They went into the bedchamber with the attitude of experts who have just been told their work by an amateur. Ansa went to his own chamber to rest. Now there was nothing to do but await the queen's summons.

THIRTEEN

A servant touched his shoulder and Ansa realized that he had been asleep. This surprised him, for he was accustomed to going for two days or more without sleep. He remembered the wine he had drunk that afternoon and decided that it had had more effect than he realized.

"Sir, the queen sends for you," the servant told him.

"What hour is it?" Ansa asked.

"The second hour after sunset."

It was not late, but he felt better for the brief sleep. He rose and another servant held a basin for him as he splashed his face and then took a towel from yet another. In a large mirror he examined his clothing and decided he would pass in polite company.

Outside the door to the suite an elderly man in royal livery bowed to him. "If you will follow me, sir." Ansa did so and a few minutes later he was bowed into a room not far from the chamber where the king lay unmoving. The room was not large by the standards of this place, about twenty paces long by ten broad. At one end was a low dais upon which stood a heavy chair of rich, dark wood. A long table stretched the length of the room and around it stood a gathering of men, most of them middle-aged to elderly, and all richly dressed. They looked startled when he entered.

Their faces were familiar. He had seen them that day in the king's bedchamber or standing immediately without. Lord Osha Kl'an was among them and he nodded to Ansa and walked to his side.

"I take it that Her Majesty has requested your presence?"

"She has," Ansa answered.

"Might I ask why?" He did not seem resentful, merely curious. But Ansa knew better than to make judgments from the mere expressions of these people, to whom personal control was of paramount importance.

"She seems to have reasons sufficient to herself."

"Of a certainty. Allow me to introduce my colleagues." The courtier presented and named each. The unfamiliar names flew past him, but the titles were easier to retain: Minister of War, Minister of the Treasury, Minister of Diplomacy, Lord of the Sea, Master of the Merchant Fleet, Senior Counselor, a few others. Osha Kl'an himself was Mayor of the Palace.

The courtiers bowed toward the throne when the queen entered from behind a hanging to the rear of the dais. She was formally dressed in a black gown sewn with pearls and gored with panels of a shiny, white fabric. On her brow rested a restrained tiara of gold and jewels covered by a sheer veil which descended to frame her face.

Ansa understood that this was a formal government function. He further guessed that the queen was determined to impress her majesty and power upon men accustomed to deferring to her husband at times like this. The queen seated herself upon the throne.

"Gentlemen, please be seated." There was a rustling and scraping as the ministers settled themselves. Ansa noted that once they were seated, there were no chairs left. He wondered what to do when the queen addressed him.

"Noble Ansa, please sit here." She gestured to a low chair to the left of the throne. He had not noticed it before. He strode to the dais and sat. The queen did not look at him and neither did the counselors. He decided that she wished him to be an invisible presence. That suited him. He began to fix faces in his memory, so that he would be able to remember them later.

"My lords," the queen said, "this afternoon, a messenger delivered this to me." She held up the bronze tube. "It is from King Gasam, who even now besieges the capital city of King Mana. As you can see, the seal is yet unbroken. I did not wish to open it until you were all assembled to favor me with your advice." Ansa could read nothing from their faces. They seemed politely attentive, nothing more. In their heavy robes, their chains and jewels, they were as weighty and dignified as mountains.

She tore loose the waxen seal and tossed it onto the table. Ansa saw the simple device stamped upon it: a pair of crossed spears. He knew the form of the spears. His father had one like them, and always carried it. It was the Shasinn spear and it was clear that Gasam felt no need for a more elaborate device. The spears expressed his character and history clearly.

The queen unrolled the paper and began to read. The recitation was short, and Ansa did not have time to thoroughly read the expressions of this many men. The Minister of War looked angered, the treasury official was impassive, the master diplomat looked deeply interested. The queen finished and rerolled the letter.

"There can be no question who composed this," she

said. "I have received many letters from Queen Larissa, and her tone is unmistakable. The calligraphy is that of a skilled Sonoan scribe, probably a captive. I think we can determine that Queen Larissa is, indeed, with her husband at the siege of Huato. Lord Ulfas, you seem agitated."

The Minister of War touched his breast and bowed. "Your Majesty, this is drivel. You know well that I am no admirer of King Mana of Sono, but I know full well that he was never foolish enough to offer Gasam an excuse to invade his nation. This royal pirate wench merely prevaricates. They attacked Sono without provocation and they will do the same here as soon as they have consolidated their gains there. Have nothing to do with this proposal. Answer it with a defiance and let us assemble the army to march to the relief of Huato."

Ansa had no doubt that the man meant what he said. On the faces of the others, he saw no eagerness for war. The Minister of Diplomacy indicated a desire to speak.

"Lord Floris, share your thoughts with us," said the queen.

"While I agree with our estimable Lord Ulfas that the motives of King Gasam and his queen are questionable, I think that, barring formal hostilities, there is always room for diplomacy and negotiation. What harm can come of sending an embassy to speak with this queen and request that she make clear her intentions? Surely, if Queen Larissa herself is to be present, there can be little likelihood of treachery. Gasam would scarcely expose his queen to danger in such a fashion."

"How would we know it was Larissa?" said the naval chief. "Has any here seen this woman?"

"She is said to be surpassingly beautiful," said the queen.

There was a snort from the Minister of the Treasury, a fat, bejewelled man with a sensual face. "Your pardon, Majesty, but I have many such in my own household."

"This is no problem," said the diplomat smoothly.

"Members of my staff have been on embassies to Chiwa since the islanders conquered that land. They know Queen Larissa by sight."

The Senior Counselor rose and his queen nodded for him to speak.

"Of the qualities and intentions of these—these adventurers I cannot speak. They must be treated as hostile until proven otherwise by their own words or actions. What concerns me more is the condition of our king. It is not fitting that we take warlike action while he lies unable to move or speak. Therefore, I counsel that we accept this invitation to parley upon the Isle of Sorrow. If nothing else, it will buy us time. While our respected Minister of War," he bowed slightly toward Lord Ulfas, "has shown his customary zeal in conducting warlike preparations, I do believe that they are still far from complete, and that it will be some time before we can contemplate offensive actions in a foreign land." The Senior Counselor resumed his seat.

"Lord Ulfas," the queen asked, "how do our preparations stand?"

He shifted uncomfortably. "When the first rumors of this invasion reached us, His Majesty ordered the district lords to summon their forces, as a precaution. Only a few days after that, the king was stricken and action has been delayed. The district lords gather their men, but we have been years without a war and mobilization exercises have been few. The majority should have assembled at the district forts by now. If you will give me the order, my queen, I will send messengers ordering that the entire host be brought to a place of assembly."

The Senior Counselor cleared his throat. "There is no precedent for taking such a step without the order of the king."

"Never before has such an emergency arisen when the king of Gran was incapacitated," the queen said. "Before his affliction, the king ordered a regional summoning of the royal host. I am certain that, upon proof of the danger to the nation, he would have continued the process of mobilization and ordered a summoning of the host. Therefore, acting as regent, I order that this step be taken. Assemble the host at the Field of War within sight of the city walls.''

"At once, Your Majesty," said Ulfas.

"A moment," said the senior diplomat. "I yield to none in my respect and loyalty toward Your Majesty, but no action has been taken to name you regent. I remind you that the council here assembled is not empowered to do this. Only a full parliament of the lords of the realm can decide this.''

"Lord Floris," the queen said. "When last I looked, your duties were those of foreign affairs, not the inner ordering of the realm. As a member of the council you have a right to voice an opinion upon any matter of business that comes before it, but please remember your realm of competence." She raised her voice to address the table. "Will we dither here while a conquering army of foreigners nears our border? I, for one, have the fullest expectation of the king's recovery. It would be well that he finds his kingdom still in existence when he is ready to resume his throne. Is there anyone here who does not wish for that happy outcome to this ordeal?'' There was a shocked silence until the Senior Counselor spoke.

"Your Majesty, there is no need to question the loyalty of your advisers. Of course, we all cherish the strongest hopes for His Majesty's fullest recovery.''

With a tiny gesture, Lord Osha indicated a desire to speak.

"We will hear from the Mayor of the Palace."

"Your Majesty, my lords, there is no need for this unseemly bickering at a time when we may well face a deadly danger to the realm. Since there is some question as to the exact nature of Her Majesty's authority in this, am I wrong in believing that all of us here would accept the decision of the parliament of lords?'' There were grumbles of assent.

''And need I point out,'' he went on, ''that if the war host is assembled, with each district lord leading his own troops, then we will have just such a parliament assembled?'' Low, reluctant voices agreed that this was so.

''Then,'' he concluded, ''I propose that, in view of an unprecedented emergency, the queen and council issue a summoning to a combined war-hosting, to be followed by a special parliament where the exact legalities of the matter may be determined.''

''It's a lot of rigamarole just to get the army together,'' Ulfas grumbled, ''but I'll vote aye to that.''

''As long as all is done according to law and custom,'' said the Senior Counselor, blandly.

''Let us all hope that these precautions are rendered unnecessary by the king's speedy recovery,'' said the queen.

Lord Floris, Ansa thought, looked like a man who had lost a few points but was still in the game.

''With that settled, Your Majesty,'' he said, ''there still remains the question of the embassy. As Lord Ulfas has said, the mobilization for war shall take longer than one might wish, and as Lord Impimis has pointed out,'' here he bowed toward the Senior Counselor, ''a parley, if nothing else, is a convenient way to buy time.''

''Yes, I agree,'' the queen said. ''Let us have plenty of talk, so long as we believe nothing they say that sounds conciliatory. I believe that we can trust only Gasam's threats, which he always makes good. How shall our embassy be composed?''

''This is an extraordinary matter, Your Majesty. Therefore, I will personally lead the embassy and parley directly with the barbarian queen.''

The Senior Counselor rose. ''I believe that I, too, should go, with Your Majesty's permission.''

"This is not usual," the queen said. "In a time of crisis, the place of high counselors is near the throne."

"That is *usually* the case," said Lord Floris. "but you see, Your Majesty, King Gasam is sending his queen to negotiate. It is, of course, unthinkable that you should attend personally, but it would not be fitting to send a mission composed of officials of second rank. At the very least, Lord Impimis and I should head our delegation."

"I am reluctant to diminish the council even for a few days, but I suppose at this juncture it would be unwise to give even the appearance of offense. Very well. Prepare your missions and render me a list of names of those you plan to take. And this above all." She held up an admonishing finger. "Under no circumstance is any hint of the king's condition to be released. If anyone tells the barbarians of this, I will have heads."

She looked from one to another of the councilmen, but no one seemed to have anything to add. "Very well. I shall send a letter to King Gasam accepting the offer of a parley on the Isle of Sorrow, at the specified time. All of you are to exercise your duties in the expectation that war may break out at any time. You may go now."

The men rose, bowed, and filed from the room. Ansa watched them go, then he looked at the queen. Below her veil, he could see sweat beading her forehead. The tone of the council had been fairly sedate, but he knew that it had been a power play, which she had fought to a draw.

"Ansa," she said. "In the room behind this you will find a beaker of wine and some cups. Would you be so good as to bring me some?"

Ansa found the wine and poured her a generous goblet. She drank half and sat back with a sigh. "Well. That could have turned out worse. I feared a palace coup and I think there would have been one save that they are uncertain of the king's future, especially now that Lady Fyana is treating him."

"Might some ambitious lord not simply kill the king and try to seize power in the confusion?"

"No, they fear a rampage by the Bamen. That is one reason why the royal family have always kept a bodyguard of those savages. Should the king die untimely, they would massacre everyone they thought might be jealous of his power. I am sure the members of the council would be the first to lose their heads. Now, tell me what you thought."

"Most of them did not speak and carefully guarded their expressions. I think you can trust Ulfas, the Minister of War. He seems like a loyal man. The Senior Counselor—Impimis, is it? I would watch him closely. As for Lord Floris, your best course would be to execute him at once. The man is a traitor. He is not going on this embassy to add dignity to the mission. He plans to treat with Gasam and betray you. Impimis may well have the same plan."

"I think you may be right, but I cannot take action against Floris just now. His family is one of the most important and has many supporters. Control of the many districts is chancy at the best of times, with each lord looking out for his own advantage. At a time like this, when royal power is shaky and foreign relations in turmoil, many of our subjects and vassals need little excuse to look for a chance to aggrandize themselves."

"Then you must send off this diplomatic mission on the assumption that you will be betrayed."

"I would have no confidence in Gasam's promises in any case," she said.

"Was this typical of royal council meetings?" Ansa asked.

"I am still new to this. When the king was healthy, he never had me sit in on one of these, but I think this was a fair example." She laughed ruefully. "I don't suppose that your people would be so long-winded at a council."

"Oh, our chiefs love to hear themselves talk. They like to thrash out matters endlessly. We are only recently a kingdom, you know. My father rules a dozen peoples, all of them formerly at war with one another. But they can move with speed and unanimity if an outsider threatens. I would hope that there would not be so much inner strife and advantage-seeking when a time like this descends upon our kingdom.''

"I hope not. Soon enough, we may have to send to King Hael for aid. Not that it would be in time to do us any good," she added. "Gasam moves so *fast*!"

"Our armies can be swift as well," Ansa said. He waited for a moment, thinking. Then, "Masila, I would like to accompany your diplomatic mission."

She was startled. "Whatever for?"

"I came to learn as much as I could about Gasam and his intentions. This would be an opportunity to see his queen close up. There is nothing for me to do here, while Fyana treats the king. At the Isle of Sorrow, I could be accomplishing something."

"But you are a foreigner. There is no official capacity I could assign to you. You would not be granted the official safe-conduct guaranteed to royal ambassadors."

"Within Gasam's power anyone's safety is purely a matter of his whim. Still, it would be good to have some sort of official standing. What about this? Give me a letter stating that I am a representative from the chieftainship of Ramdi. They are a people who dwell in the southeast of my father's domain. They acknowledge him as their overlord in matters of war but are otherwise independent."

"And what would be your excuse for accompanying my embassy?"

"First because it is a chance to extend my chief's greetings to another people, but principally because I have heard of the legendary beauty of Queen Larissa and wished to look upon it with my own eyes."

At this she almost summoned a smile. "The witch might believe it at that. All kings and queens are vain as a matter of form and tradition. Gasam and Larissa seem to take flattery seriously."

"Then I shall go. The danger is slight. After all, their very purpose in this meeting is to lull you into a sense of security. Therefore, they will almost certainly treat your representatives with more than mere courtesy."

"Your mind works well," she said. "I think that, with age and experience behind you, your people could do far worse than choose you to succeed your father."

Ansa had not been thinking along these lines and was alarmed. "Please, Your Majesty, make no such suggestion! I set out from my home to get away from all such concerns and have some fun. The last thing I want is to be a king, or even a prince."

"You will find that one's own wishes are of little account in matters of destiny. And for one bent upon enjoying life, you pick strange amusements. Walking openly into an enemy camp, for one."

"As long as it is only my own life I'm risking, yes. That is what adventure is all about."

"I see. Well, if you are bent upon this course, I will not deter you. You shall have your letter. Whether Queen Larissa will choose to honor it is out of my hands."

"I thank you. I wish to send a letter to my father apprising him of matters across the border. Could you spare a messenger to deliver it? It is a long ride, and you won't see your messenger again any time soon."

"Certainly. I have plenty of messengers. They spend too much of their time living on the royal bounty with too little to do. But, you must not mention the king's condition in your letter. It might fall into the wrong hands."

"Agreed."

FOURTEEN

"**Y**ou are going *where*?" Fyana was furious and aghast. "You cannot be serious!"

"But I am. Is this not why we came here? How better may I learn of the situation with Gasam than by going into his very camp? Well," he amended, "not exactly into his camp, but into Queen Larissa's camp. I think I can learn a lot there. This city and its palace are interesting and amusing, but this opportunity takes precedence."

"But we were supposed to travel together!" she protested.

"However, you are now committed to the treatment of King Ach'na. There is nothing for me to do here while you tend to him. This embassy is only for a few days, and then I will be back." He patted her hand soothingly, but she just glared at him.

"I don't like it. There are too many things that can happen. You could be recognized and taken prisoner."

"Who would recognize me? I have never seen Gasam or

Larissa. I was a child the last time I was in my father's house when a Sonoan embassy was there."

"Queen Masila saw the resemblance between you and your father."

He shrugged. "Because I am the only other person of that blood she has ever seen. I favor my mother's people far more than my father's. To the purebred Shasinn, I will not resemble them in any way."

"You just want an excuse to run off by yourself and play the adventurer."

"And why do I need an excuse? If I have a duty to perform, I will carry it out in the manner I find most fitting. How does it occur that I must have your permission, or even your approval?"

She tried to be indignant, but tears welled up in her eyes. "It's just—it's just, oh, I just don't want you to leave me alone here."

His anger deflated, he sat on the bed and put his arms around her. She rested her head on his chest as he stroked her silvery hair.

"Forgive me, Fyana. I am behaving like a heedless boy, chasing after my own excitement and forgetting that I leave you here in a situation of great danger. But still I cannot pass up this opportunity to see the enemy at close hand."

She sighed. "You are not to do anything foolish, like try to abduct Larissa or strike down Gasam with your own hand."

"Tempting as that sounds, I am not an utter fool. Besides, any such attempt would give them a genuine excuse to invade this land, and that would be a poor way to repay Queen Masila's trust."

"Just so that is understood." She had calmed, but he did not want to let her go just yet. They had been cautious and distant with one another, two young persons of different race and culture attracted despite themselves. She was warm and slight in his arms. She smelled like desert herbs and female musk.

"Since I will be away, the queen has agreed to double your Bamen guard. They are fanatically loyal and will guard your life as they would the king's."

"How comforting. If the king dies, I will be the first they kill."

He had not thought of that. "In his condition, it will be difficult to know just when he is dead, if it should come to that. If he should die, say he is asleep and get away from here as quickly as you can."

"And I was worrying about you," she said. Then she tilted her face up and his mouth was on hers. Their tongues touched and she fell back against the cushions. He pressed her down and her body pushed back against his. Their spontaneous, unplanned actions grew urgent as they were seized by mutual passion. They opened each other's garments. He felt hard young breasts against his palms. The lamps had burned out and in the dim moonlight her blue body was dusky, centered with a triangle of startling white.

Her long-fingered, slender hands explored him as he took her nipples into his mouth, tongued her navel and kissed the white mound between her thighs. Then he was kissing her mouth again and her legs parted beneath him. Her hand guided him and he slid into unbelievable, delicious warmth. Her body felt slight and frail beneath him, but she moved with passion and power, the upward thrusts of her hips lifting him as her arms clung and her breath flowed warmly along the side of his face.

Above the pounding of blood in his ears he could hear her gasps and cries, never quite forming words. With a final, almost savage plunge he went rigid, shuddering as his seed jetted from his body and she screamed his name.

For a long time they lay entwined as their breath quieted, he still firmly within her. They held each other without speaking, content with their closeness.

"I did not expect this," she whispered, "but I am glad that it happened. Now I am sure you will come back to me."

"Could you have doubted it?" he said.

"Yes."

"Well, surely now you cannot doubt that I would carve my way through all of Gasam's hosts to get back to you."

"Just keep yourself safe and return." She circled his neck with her arms and nestled her face against his neck. In minutes, she was asleep.

Ansa resumed his weapons at the palace gate. He would only be walking through the city, but he felt undressed without them. With sword and dagger belted on, and his stone war-hammer thonged to his belt, he felt complete once more.

He had only wanted to get out of the palace for a while. Fyana was closeted with the king again, surrounded by pots and bags, vials and canisters of every medicine imaginable. A cabo-doctor and a brace of burly stablemen stood by to assist her, to the stupefied scandalization of the whole court.

He would be leaving with the embassy in two days, and he told the queen that he needed to replenish his travel kit, which was, indeed, much in need of renewal. She had told him to take what he wanted from the palace but he had pointed out that rough conditions in the field could not be met by palace materials. She had thereupon pressed a heavy pouch of golden aurics upon him and bade him furnish himself with the best.

His first stop was the district of bowyers and fletchers. From his belt he took a single arrow and ordered twoscore copies to be ready by the next evening, by the queen's order. The master arrowsmith assured him that his shop would drop all other work to meet the order.

In the clothier's quarter he replaced his stained, ragged travel cloak with a fine cloak of quil hair, which was both light and warm. He had been informed that the evenings would be dank and chilly for the rest of the season. He was very pleased with the cloak, which was dyed deep red. It would serve as both garment and blanket and was guaranteed to shed water like the fur of the diving bat.

His stirrups had abraded his riding boots almost through at the ankle, so he indulged himself with an exceptionally fine pair of new boots, these of the latest Nevan design. He reminded himself that he would be calling upon the world's deadliest queen, and that he should be properly dressed for the occasion.

He saw people wandering into what appeared to be a large park and entered it out of curiosity. It turned out to be a royal menagerie which was not a part of the palace grounds and on this day was open to the public. He gawked at animals so outlandish that he would not have believed in them had he heard them described by a stranger. He was amused when he saw others gawking at animals of the northern plains and hills that were as ordinary to him as his clothes.

He finished the day in a wineshop located in a quarter dedicated to entertainment. Sounds of strange music drifted from every doorway and mountebanks performed in the streets. In the shop where he ate a refreshingly unpretentious dinner, a trio of women danced lasciviously among the tables. At another time he might have found them enticing, but now he was interested in no woman except Fyana.

When the servers began lighting lamps, he knew it was time to return to the palace. Pleasantly full of food and wine, but not foundering, he went outside. From long habit, he stepped to one side of the doorway, his back against the wall, while he waited for his eyes to adjust to the gloom. When he could see with some clarity, he set out toward the palace. The entertainment quarter was thronged and noisy even at night, but as soon as he left its confines the streets were empty and silent.

He enjoyed the moonlight and the cooling air. Apparently, even these hot southern lands had a season that was less sultry. He had been walking for several minutes when he thought he heard sounds behind him. He turned but saw nothing. He shrugged and went on. In open country, he could easily keep track of his surroundings. In this alien place he was uncertain.

A few streets further on, he heard the furtive sounds again. This time he did not slow or turn. At the next side street he entered as if suspecting nothing, then he sprinted quietly to a deep-shadowed doorway and stepped into the gloom. He set his bundle of purchases by his feet and readied his weapons. The narrow street was not a good place to use his longsword, but he made sure that it was loose in its sheath. He took the stone axe from his belt and gripped it in his right hand as he drew his dagger with his left. The foot-long blade was single-edged, slightly curved and razor keen. His fingers flexed on its bone handle as he awaited his stalkers. In an odd fashion he welcomed this. His heart pounded in his ears and his throat felt constricted, but these were good feelings, the feelings of battle. This was far better than the uncertainty and ambiguities of the last few days. Here in the street he could meet enemies who openly sought his blood.

Two men appeared at the entrance to the side street. They wore nondescript clothes, and metal glinted in their hands. One had a shortsword, the other a shortsword and a club. They halted when they realized that their prey had disappeared. Cautiously, they widened the distance between them by a pace before they began to stalk down the street. These were experienced predators.

He knew that his best course would be to attack the instant they were in range, not allowing them time to organize a coordinated attack. But he wanted to know who had sent them.

It was unlikely that they would fail to detect him as they passed and he did not want to be cornered in the doorway. When they were within ten feet, he stepped into the street.

"Who sent you two?" he demanded. "What do you . . ." Instantly, he knew he had made a serious error. They were not interested in talk. The one with the club feinted toward his head, at the same time aiming a gutting blow with his shortsword. The other thrust at his side.

Ansa sprang back and whipped the stone axe against the hand that held the club. There was a sound of splintering wood and bone and the attacker cursed. His companion, missing his first thrust, followed it up with a backhanded slash. Instead of springing back to avoid this, Ansa stepped in and cut with his dagger, slashing the man's forearm to the bone. The sword clattered to the pavement as Ansa brought the axe across in a short, backhanded chop. It crunched into the man's temple and he dropped atop his own sword.

The remaining attacker, recovered from the pain and shock of his smashed fingers, renewed his own attack, aiming swift cuts at Ansa's head, keeping him on the defensive. Ansa retreated, feinted high with the axe, then brought it whistling down against the man's knee. The assassin grunted and tried to shift his weight to his good leg, but in so doing he let his sword-arm swing wide and in that instant Ansa darted in and thrust his dagger into the man's belly, ripping upward. He stepped back as his foe began to collapse and gave him a hard blow to the head with his axe, just to make certain.

Breathing hard and tingling with excitement, Ansa studied his handiwork. Both men were irrefutably dead, and he was going to get no answers from them. The fight had been short and had made little noise. Nobody looked out from the nearby houses to investigate. Satisfied that he was unobserved, he cleaned his weapons on the clothes of the dead men, picked up his belongings and went back to the wider street to resume his trek to the palace.

Who were they? It was possible that they had been mere thieves. He had been highly visible all day, spending freely. Somehow, that did not seem likely. There had been something military in the silent swiftness with which they had attacked. He was sure that his death had been their aim.

He walked back to the palace, surrendered his weapons and returned to his quarters. Fyana was not there and a slave told him that she was still with the king. He pondered his next move. Should he report the attack? If so, to whom? Whoever had sent the murderers after him, it had to be someone here in the palace. He decided he would tell the queen privily, and no one else except Fyana.

Fyana returned late, looking unutterably weary. "He is beginning to respond," she told Ansa. "I am isolating the effects of the poison and we were able to get some nourishment into him."

"Will he recover?" he asked.

"I cannot say, but I have more hope now. It will be a few days before he can sit up and talk. Beyond that, I have no idea just now. He blinks and the muscles of his face show some movement now. The queen acts as if he is almost healed. I hate to rouse her hopes so."

When she was rested a bit, Ansa told her of the attack.

"This is an evil place!" she said. "But why this? Is it because we try to aid the king, or because you are going on the embassy, or both?"

"I've wondered myself. It seems that we can't do much without angering some of the powerful of this land. All the more reason for me to keep an eye on what they do when they meet with Larissa. And you must keep these guards close by you, annoying as they are. Be careful what you eat, too. We know that somebody here is skilled in using poisons."

"And I am far more skilled in detecting them. You needn't worry for me on that account. I am far more worried about you. Next time they may send ten instead of two."

"I'll feel safer away from here," he said.

"But I will mourn while you are away." She came into his arms and he held her, feeling the fatigue that weighted her body.

The diplomatic mission left on a foggy morning, exiting the palace enclosure through the main gate and descending the hill by the city's major boulevard. The populace blinked and gaped in astonishment as the glittering procession of noblemen, their servants and their guards passed by. There had been no public proclamation of the meeting, but rumors of war in the west were already making the rounds of the city.

Amid the gaud and pomp, it was unlikely that anyone took special note of a single, unostentatious rider who rode with solemn face in the rear of the procession, distinguished only by his foreign features and a large, powerful bow cased at his saddle.

Ansa was sad to be leaving, but only because he was leaving Fyana behind. Otherwise, this would have been one of the most exciting moments of his young life. He was riding incognito to meet with his hereditary enemy, the sort of adventure he had dreamed of when he was a boy. Now, concern for a woman stole the excitement from the moment. He wondered if real life always intruded thus in the world of a hero.

Outside the city walls, they picked up their honor guard of the king's own escort, an elite unit with barracks near the Field of War. These men had splendid uniforms and bronze armor, and were mounted on fine cabos that were themselves colorfully caparisoned. With all assembled and orders of march distributed, they set forth on the western road.

Ansa, constituting a virtual embassy of his own, had no particular place in the procession, a fact which suited him well. The lordly ministers saw fit to ignore him as an outlander of no account. He wondered whether one of them had hired his would-be killers. Having this suspicion, he knew that he would not be able to sleep easy for the duration of this mission.

He took advantage of his pariah status to ride among the guardsmen and converse with them. They spoke freely of their profession, taking great pride in their skills as riders and spearmen. He learned that they fought as heavy lancers and were accustomed to riding down footmen with relative ease, or else engaging other aristocratic riders.

When Ansa explained the properties of his powerful bow, they showed tolerant amusement. Their shields and armor, they said, were proof against any such weapon. It was clear that it had been years since they had seen any real action. He was impressed by their esprit, but he knew that it took more than aristocratic elan to win battles against such warriors as Gasam led. He hoped that the infantry of Gran were more promising.

Making camp proved to be an elaborate process, for the high nobles and their retinues required large pavilions furnished with every luxury. Ansa was not as contemptuous of this as he might have been, for he knew that making a splendid visual impression was an important part of such an embassy. Great displays of wealth signified the power and majesty of their sovereign.

He asked guardsmen whether their leaders actually went to war thus lumbered, but they assured him that, while their tents and furnishings were by no means austere, they knew better than to campaign with this sort of ostentation.

The land ascended as they rode west, into a higher terrain that was less heavily forested. As predicted, the nights were cool and damp, with heavy fog in the hills they traversed. The pace of the march was ponderous, so Ansa took the opportunity to ride into the forests to hunt. Game was plentiful and his quarry made him welcome at whatever fire he chose to share in the evenings.

As they neared the river, the road grew choked with refugees fleeing Sono. The border posts had been swamped by the sheer volume of traffic and some had swum the river rather than bother with the formalities. During their halts Ansa and others questioned the fleeing Sonoans. They heard stories of terror, of rapine and devastation on a fearsome scale. The invaders seized land, livestock and crops, raped at will and took able-bodied men for slave labor at their siege works. The slavers who followed all armies like carrion bats had come in to lead women and children away roped together neck-to-neck in long, tearful processions.

All this was common enough, the sort of thing that took place in every war. What was disturbing was the incredible speed with which Gasam had accomplished the subjection of a good part of Sono. He now seemed to have the run of the country while its king sat impotently in his capital, bottled up and besieged by Gasam.

While he had no conversation with them, Ansa had little difficulty in reading the expressions of the great lords. Most of them were grim-faced. It was plain that Gasam, in the person of his queen, would be negotiating from a position of great and undoubted strength. Floris, the Minister of Diplomacy, and Imprimis, the Senior Counselor, had serene faces. Whether this was because they had superior control or because they felt they had little to fear from the ascendancy of the islanders he could not say with certainty.

FIFTEEN

They came to a broad, cultivated hillside sloping gently to the river. At first, the River Kol was an astonishing sight. When he had last seen it flowing through the arid country far to the north, it had been a great river. Here, it was huge. Many tributaries spilled their water into it as it passed through the rainy, jungled lands of the south. Wide though it was, it was not deep and its current was placid save when it was swollen by floods.

The Isle of Sorrow formed an elongated oval in its stream, its northern half a low, wooded hill, the rest a flat expanse of grass. Even from a distance, they could see that colorful tents had been erected on the flat land, and many animals grazed the grass. There was a twinkling glitter as of the sun's light glancing from many weapons. Before they began their descent to the river, Lord Floris called a halt and addressed the diplomatic mission and the guards separately. Ansa listened to both speeches.

"My lords and other gentlemen of the diplomatic corps,"

he began, "the woman we are about to meet is a blood-stained savage who pretends to royal station. However laughable this may be, it is incumbent upon us to behave as if she were in truth what she claims to be. Behave with all the solemnity and courtesy that you are accustomed to show toward true royalty. We are not aware of the pirate's intentions toward Gran, and that is what our mission is to discern. At the moment relations are not belligerent and we wish that they should remain so. If the behavior of the queen or her minions seems uncouth or provoking, you are to remember that they are barbarians, unacquainted with civilized standards of behavior. Take no offense, or at least display no umbrage. Insults may always be requited later, at a time more propitious for us."

He rode to the assembled servants and guards and addressed them.

"Men, we go among savages, but we are a mission of peace and you are to remember that. Those barbarians over there are not part of a civilized army such as you are accustomed to, but instead form part of a polyglot horde, the scum and scourings of many nations overrun by the pirate chief Gasam. Among these the island warriors called Shasinn are renowned throughout the world for their arrogance and pride. You are to put up with any insolence and not allow yourselves to be provoked into fighting. If King Gasam's representatives do not like the way the talks are going, they may set their men to insulting you, trying to provoke you into drawing your weapons. That way they can say that *we* disrupted the talks. That is an old trick and that is why we always employ elite soldiers for our escort instead of ordinary troops. You are well-bred men who are firmly disciplined and know how to keep your tempers. Now, remember what I have said and show these savages that you know how to comport yourselves as civilized soldiers."

Thus prepared, they made their way down the slope with full pomp, preceded by standard-bearers, every man dressed in his best finery. Military musicians played on flute, trumpet and drum. It was an amusing spectacle, and Ansa wondered whether it would occasion awe or mirth among the barbarians. He suspected the latter.

A short ride brought them to the border station, where the small group of nervous officials prostrated themselves before the royal party. With the invaders holding the island, refugees no longer tried to cross at this point. Tied up to a broad wharf made of stout timbers was a huge raft, capacious enough to accommodate the entire diplomatic party, minus its military escort. Ansa boarded the raft with the rest of the party and watched with interest as nusks turned a great capstan, winching the raft across to the island on long cables. The cables sagged almost to the surface of the river and Ansa assumed that river traffic must pass on the other side of the island, which was said to be connected with the far bank by a bridge.

At the island landing they were greeted by a man dressed in long, gray robes and tall headgear shaped like a truncated cone.

"Welcome, gentlemen. Her Majesty bade me conduct you to her presence. Please follow me." They rode off the raft and made their way up a gentle, grassy slope to the flat land. A hundred paces from the bank stood a large tent, resplendent with streaming banners. Beside him, Ansa heard a member of the diplomatic party speaking to a companion in a low voice.

"A Sonoan noble. Some of them are changing sides already."

Ansa was more interested in the warriors who stood everywhere, watching the newcomers with curiosity and amusement. He knew instantly that these were Shasinn. They looked so much like his father that the resemblance was startling. All of them had the same bronze-colored hair, golden skin and blue eyes. The wide cheekbones, broad brow and tapering chin were the same, as was the extraordinary fluid grace of body and movement.

Mere arrogance was not the word for the attitude they exuded almost palpably. Without speaking a word they conveyed a calm assurance of superiority that made the pomp of the royal diplomats seem mean and shabby. Their spears, of a form he knew so well, were like scepters in their hands. They were enemies, but he felt a surge of pride in the knowledge that his veins bore the blood of these men.

At the entrance to the great tent, a single figure stood beneath its outstretched awning. Hardened courtiers, accustomed to maintaining impassive faces, allowed their jaws to drop, almost audibly.

Queen Larissa was as beautiful as the legends had said, but even the legends were poor preparation for the sight. Despite himself, Ansa felt himself lost in admiration. Now he understood why his mother glowered every time this woman's name was mentioned. Her hair was almost as white as Fyana's and her face was of an almost inhuman perfection. She wore a cape of shimmery golden material and very little else save jewelry. She held a miniature Shasinn spear, made entirely of steel.

Let these Granian fools say what they will, Ansa thought, this is what a queen should look like. He knew that she was within a year or two of his father's age, but this hardly seemed credible. She looked little older than himself. Perhaps, he thought, this was another way in which the Shasinn were different.

"Welcome, gentlemen," Larissa said. "I extend the greetings of my husband, King Gasam of the Islands, of Chiwa, and now of Sono. Please dismount and enter. What poor hospitality I can offer in these straitened circumstances is yours without stint. Let us make ourselves comfortable before we settle down to serious talk."

Caught offguard by her informality, the diplomats covered

their confusion as they hastily dismounted and summoned their gift-bearers.

The walls of the great tent had been half raised for ventilation, but it was floored with lavish tapestries and hangings. The queen crossed these on bare, bejewelled feet and sat, or rather sprawled, on an overstuffed hassock. Incredibly, she accomplished this without loss of dignity.

"Now," she said, "be so good as to name yourselves. And please sit down. We are all friends here, are we not?"

Ansa, standing in the rear of the assemblage, was amused at their discomfiture. She would not allow them their overblown dignity, but she did not display the naive ignorance of the barbarian. She was so poised and confident that it was they who appeared awkward.

Floris, seeking to regain ascendancy, introduced himself and the highest officials of the embassy. He then brought forth the royal gifts; treasures selected from King Ach'na's palace. There were perfumes, jewels, fabrics and works of art. Larissa admired each present and praised her fellow monarch's generosity.

"Since we are on a military campaign," she said, "I have nothing so magnificent to send back to King Ach'na and Queen Masila. But, have no fear. As soon as we take Huato, I will send them the pick of the treasures we take there."

"Ah, um, most generous, Your Majesty," said Lord Imprimis in a strangled voice.

She scanned the assemblage, smiling. "Now, please be seated and let my slaves serve you some . . ." She stopped and her face registered something that was almost alarm. She was looking straight at Ansa. "But, who is this noble youth? We have not yet been introduced."

Lord Floris looked back. "Oh, this man is not an official member of our delegation, Your . . ." but she was not listening.

Ansa strode forward and bowed. "My name is Ansa,

Your Majesty. I am a son of the High Chieftain of Ramdi.''
He took his letter of introduction from his tunic and handed
it to her. ''I was visiting the court of King Ach'na when
your invitation to a conference arrived. I could not miss this
opportunity to extend the greetings of my chief to your royal
husband and yourself. The king was good enough to attach
me to this mission.''

''That is very enterprising of you.'' She searched his face
as if seeking something there.

''It was a subterfuge,'' he said.

''What do you mean?'' Casually, she touched a bloodred
stone that nestled between her breasts. It was a signal. The
guards behind her stiffened ever so slightly.

''I just wanted an excuse to see with my own eyes the
most beautiful woman on earth.''

She smiled radiantly and patted the cushion beside her.
''Oh, you and I are going to get along very well. Come, sit
by me.'' While the others seated themselves and were served
by the slaves she turned to Ansa. ''Ramdi, you say? I have
seen the name on maps. It is to the southeast of King Hael's
domains, is it not?''

''That is correct. It is a land of plains to the west, of hills
to the east, all the way to the great river.''

''Are you subjects of King Hael?'' she asked.

''Our chief is a member of Hael's association. It is an
alliance of mutual support in war if one of us is invaded,
and it involves trade agreements. We do not acknowledge
Hael as our sovereign.''

''I see. Is this true of many of his subjects?''

''It varies. We were among the last to join him. As his
allies, we have a favored trade status. That means that even
a common warrior can afford fine steel weapons and a bow
from his bowyery.''

''Ah, yes, that famous steel mine of his,'' she murmured.
''A wonderful monopoly for a king to have. Have you ever
seen it?''

He shook his head. "Only the Amsi and Matwa are sent on those expeditions. King Hael is not anxious to part with that secret."

"We must talk more later. But, I see that I am neglecting my other guess." She turned to Floris. "My lord, I am having a banquet prepared, although it will be a poor one, under the circumstances. We can commence serious talks tomorrow. For now, allow me to assure you that King Gasam, my husband, has none but the friendliest and most benevolent feelings toward his brother king, Ach'na of Gran. It is our fondest wish that peace and brotherhood shall always prevail between us. These unpleasant events here in Sono are entirely the fault of King Mana, who treacherously reneged on our naval treaty and then offered intolerable insult to our nation and to us, personally. I urge you to set your minds at ease concerning future relations between our nations." She smiled radiantly.

Lord Floris rose and bowed deeply. He launched into a practiced speech, full of warm sentiments and fulsome promises of eternal peace and harmony. Larissa listened with a smile which was intended to be friendly but which was just short of laughter. She lacked the court schooling that banished all sincerely felt emotion from the human face. Men like Floris and Impimis might find her transparent, but they could not use the fact to advantage, because she had no need to conceal a weakness.

Ansa endured the tiresome charade without difficulty. There was danger and excitement just in being near this woman. She was as famed for cruelty as for beauty, and he knew it would be fatal to underestimate her intelligence.

The other courtiers made their speeches. It was understood that the real talks would take place later, privily. The members of the Granian mission were uneasy, and Ansa could guess why. They had no lower-level courtiers here with whom to connive. The islanders had no court as these men understood such things. There were only Gasam, Larissa and their warriors. To men accustomed to the multileveled courts of the civilized lands, this was alien territory.

By the time the last of the speeches had been made, the last of the gifts examined and praised, it was time for the banquet. Slaves carried platters of food across the bridge or moved among the feasters, refilling cups from ample pitchers of wine. Most of the slaves seemed to be trained servitors, undoubtedly taken as living loot from estates of the rich. For them, the invasion was merely a change of masters.

The food was mostly wild game or domestic meats, along with some fruits. Larissa apologized for the lack of breads, pastries or delicacies.

"Some things," she said, "one learns to do without when campaigning in a hostile land. When we have broken these people to our harness, I will be able to entertain my noble guests as they deserve."

"We understand perfectly, Your Majesty," said Floris, his face a bit pale. "This is splendid, far surpassing our expectations. Even our king, on his hunting expeditions, seldom entertains this lavishly."

Losing interest, she turned to Ansa. "Is this to your liking?"

"Assuredly. We are not rich like the southerners, and our land does not support great farms and plantations. We are wealthy only in fighting men."

"That is the only sort of wealth worth having," she said. "When you are rich in warriors, the wealth of others is yours also. Do you all fight mounted, with the bow?"

"Our lands are wide," he said, "and the people are spread thinly upon them. Truly, the mounted life is the only life possible, unless you want to live in a miserable farm village. We live by herding and hunting, and in the grasslands, both predators and prey can see you from a great distance. With the cabo and the bow, we are masters of the land. For war, we also use the lance and sword."

"Queen Larissa," Impimis said, not wishing to be ignored while the queen spoke to an unimportant barbarian, "we have all heard of your glorious islanders. We see with our own eyes that they are splendid and handsome young men, but what is this quality that exalts them above other warriors?"

"It isn't something easy to describe, but perhaps we can show you a little of what they are." She turned and spoke to a guard. The man left the tent. A few minutes later a dozen young warriors filed beneath the tent's great awning. Fires now burned nearby, supplemented by the light of many torches. The warm light reflected from the oiled, glossy skins of the young men, and from their spears, ruddy on the bronze, silver on the keen steel edges.

"These are junior warriors of my bodyguards," Larissa said. "For your amusement, they will perform some of the old warrior dances of our islands."

The visitors settled expressions of polite interest upon their faces, prepared to endure whatever quaint folkways these primitive people might think to constitute suitable entertainment. The queen turned to Ansa with a conspiratorial look, as if the two of them shared a secret.

Two of the young warriors came forward, then turned to face each other. Physically, they were a perfect match, tall and long-limbed, supple as night-hunting predators. From a place near one of the fires, musicians began a rhythmic tune on flutes and tiny drums.

Holding their spears underhanded, the two men thrust at each other simultaneously. The onlookers gasped as each twisted aside and the blades lanced past, missing by a fraction of an inch. They followed through on the thrust, dancing past each other, twisting and whirling the glittering blades, one high, the other low. One man ducked the slash, the other leapt over the blade aimed at his knees. With each movement, the bands of long fur each man wore at elbows and knees swirled out, magnifying every action. The long hair of the warriors whipped from one side to the other. Never did the spears rest from their flashing, deadly motion.

Ansa leaned forward and watched, enthralled. This was not the stylized, degenerate war dance practiced by so many people. This was an exercise, an exhibition of dexterity used by warriors to demonstrate their skill. Each move was a deadly assault or a dextrous avoidance. The movements might be planned, but the slightest mistake would mean crippling injury or death to the clumsy warrior.

Now two more men stepped from the line. These, too, began a sparring dance. To the stupefied amazement of the onlookers, they passed between the other two, who did not pause in their own exercises. Then two more joined. The action was as orderly and as confusing as a number of jugglers standing in a circle, passing balls and clubs among themselves in a pattern comprehensible only to one who also possesses the skill.

Within a few minutes, all twelve were engaged in a dance that was, to all appearances, suicidal. Twelve bodies and twelve long blades were confined within an area no more than ten paces on a side. Each man was leaping, whirling, dashing about the restricted square as freely as if he were alone there, thrusting and twirling his spear for his own amusement. The only sign of the desperate danger of the environment was the occasional, faint metallic ringing when one of the weapons touched another.

"Amazing!" said Impimis. "How long can they keep this up?"

"For hours," said Larissa. "As long as I wish it."

"But surely," Floris said, "one or more must be killed before very long."

"Yes," she said, "but that would not stop the others. They live and die at our pleasure, and they ask nothing more."

She clapped her hands and the frantic action stopped. The men resumed their line while the onlookers applauded enthusiastically. Their bodies streamed with sweat and some of them were bleeding from shallow cuts, but their faces were stony and none of them breathed hard. They saluted their queen, ignoring the others.

"Dazzling!" Lord Floris exclaimed when they were gone. "Truly, these are not like ordinary men. I would not have believed that human beings could do such a thing. How is it that warriors can do things one ordinarily sees only trained dancers, tumblers and acrobats performing with such skill?"

"As Lord Ansa here could probably tell you," she favored him with another conspiratorial look, "every move you saw these men perform was a move used in actual combat. From the time they are children, our youths practice these things, first as boys with sticks, later with their spears. What you saw was an exercise in training for hand-to-hand fighting with the long spears. They also practice with the shield. They use the throwing-stick and they hurl the javelin, although these weapons are not as entertaining to watch."

"Admirable," Impimis said.

She leaned forward for emphasis. "And, they do *nothing else*. They are pure warriors. Their skill, courage and loyalty are their only meaning. They do not concern themselves with gaining power, or accumulating wealth, or any of the other things that distract most men. They apply themselves solely to waging war on behalf of their king."

"They are truly formidable," said Floris. He did not look as impressed as the others. Ansa judged that the man was used to thinking of power in other terms. Those who fought the battles, whether they be glorious warriors or ordinary soldiers, were of little account. Great lords and kings accomplished their ends in ways less crude and direct.

"Are all of your followers such men?" Impimis asked, gently probing.

"These are Shasinn," she said. "They are the greatest warriors in the world. Others of the island peoples are nearly as fine. Now we have the soldiers of many lands in our great war host. All of them are superior fighters, for my king will have no less in his army. All of them, most importantly, are absolutely loyal to their king.'' She had sidestepped the question of just how many of the islanders King Gasam had among his followers.

The diplomats seemed to wish to say more, but Queen Larissa stood. ''We shall speak more tomorrow. You have had a long journey and I know you will wish to rest. I see that your servants and soldiers have erected your tents. Please feel free to retire to them now. If you have any wish that is in my power to grant, do not hesitate to apprise me.''

Off balance once again, the Granian lords rose stiffly, their aging joints unused to this lengthy repose on the ground. They bowed and recited formalized leave-takings and left the tent. Ansa left as well, but he walked to the temporary paddock where the cabos were kept under guard. He inspected his own mount, assuring himself that all was well with the beast.

As he walked toward the soldiers' tents to seek shelter for the night, the gray-bearded man who had greeted them at the landing approached him.

''Young lord, Her Majesty requests, if you are not excessively fatigued, that you join her.''

''Gladly,'' Ansa said, with trepidation. He wondered what this might portend, but reminded himself that he was here at his own urging. He had wanted a close look at this woman, knowing how dangerous she was. He took a deep breath and followed the old man to a fire near the great tent. Queen Larissa reclined there on a long cushion, one of its ends raised on a frame to form a backrest. Her face brightened as he entered the circle of firelight.

''I am so glad you consented to join me. You have the look of a man who is accustomed to long, hard riding, and you are nowhere near as venerable as your noble companions.''

"Plague and wounds would not keep me away," he said. "I have come all this way, just for a sight of you, Your Majesty. Would I pass up a chance to have you all to myself for a while?"

"Please sit down," she said, gesturing to a pad near hers. He sank to it and accepted a goblet from a slave women. He sipped, and studied her over the rim of the cup. She rested bonelessly on her cushion, a scarlet mantle of woven quil hair drawn around her against the night's chill. One bare, bejewelled arm emerged from the cloak, her hand holding a golden cup.

"If you only knew,' she said, "how refreshing it is to speak to a prince who is not a pompous, indolent degenerate."

"I fear that I am not a prince as you understand the term . . ." he began, but she waved off his protestation.

"And I am not a queen as the southerners understand the term. I am a queen in the only meaningful sense. My husband is a conqueror, perhaps the greatest conqueror the world has ever known. You are a high-ranking warrior of a warrior people. To people such as we, what are the bloodlines, the pedigrees and families of these decadent people?"

He laughed. "Is this how you speak to your peers among the royalty of this world?"

"I have no peers among the royalty, and my king certainly has none. Oh, there are those who come close. Queen Shazad of Neva is a fine enemy. She was my slave once, briefly, and we would happily kill one another, but she is amusing. Your King Hael is a renegade Shasinn and remarkable in his own right, but he is so mad that I cannot comprehend him. As for the others, they are a poor lot."

He wanted to steer the conversation away from his father. "Do you plan to conquer the whole earth?"

"Weren't you listening tonight? Didn't you hear me pledge eternal friendship with Gran?"

"Yes. I also heard the Granian ambassadors, and I didn't believe them either."

She laughed musically. "Oh, you are so refreshing! Yes, the pleasantries traded by kings are worthless, and everyone understand it. The real talks will start later, and then we will not pledge and promise. Instead, we will bargain, each seeking advantage over the other. We will hold by these bargains as long as it seems advantageous. Did you know that this was how it is done?"

"I always suspected. By these peoples' standards we are primitive, and perhaps we are, but that doesn't mean that we are stupid. Chiefs scheme and connive, too. They make hollow promises and trade lies. Kings are just bigger chiefs, with more land and people."

"That is very true. All royal families begin with an adventurer who seizes power. Later the court flatterers make up tales about descent from the gods or divine favor or a pedigree that goes back thousands of years. The second generation is never a match for that first conqueror, and they crave respectability. Those who are ruled will believe the tales, because they refuse to believe that they have surrendered themselves to something less than godlike."

He knew that her candor was a danger signal, but he had no choice except to play by her rules. "And King Gasam is such a man?"

"Very much so. We were an obscure people living on a remote island. We were warriors and herdsmen who thought that the finest thing in life was to have lots of kagga to tend and occasionally, for fun, to raid our neighbors for their kagga. Gasam knew that there was something better."

"And he set out to seize it," Ansa commented.

"Yes. That is why I said that your statement about chiefs and kings was very true. We had lazy, indolent chiefs and elders. They had lived the longest and accumulated the most wives and kagga, so they had the highest status. They separated the young men into warrior fraternities and made them live outside the villages, in warrior camps. They were forbidden to marry or own property. Thus the elders had the pick of the young women for wives and they took all the kagga the young men earned with their blood in raids. The young warriors thought it was a fine life, just tending livestock and training for war. Men are foolish that way." Her voice hardened with contempt. "That was what our chiefs were like. They had the finest warriors in the world, and all they used them for was herdsmen."

"But Gasam learned better," Ansa said. "He must have been a remarkable young man."

"He was that," she said with pride. "He saw through their pretensions and shams. He spoke with the foreigners who came by ship and learned of kings and great nations, of priests and their gods, of armies and their conquests. He wanted those things. He wanted to lead armies and be a king and throw lesser kings into the dust before him, make them submit to him and become his vassals."

She looked directly at Ansa, steady-eyed. "Above all he wanted me. And to have me he had to overthrow the power of the chiefs. When we were little more than children, he said that he would be a king and that he would place me on the throne beside him, that together we would reign over the earth. That is exactly what he has done. He cultivated and flattered men of power to gain his ends, but to me he never spoke idle words. In all the years since, it has been the same. We have dealt with many rulers. Some he has conquered, some he had treated with for as long as it has suited him, but all are the same, and no different from the chiefs of our island."

"You speak freely, considering that I am here with the embassy from Gran," he pointed out.

She shrugged. "What is King Ach'na to you? Your land is remote from his, you are just a visitor at his court."

"That is so," he agreed.

"Tell me, are all your countrymen like you? I do not

mean necessarily as handsome, but do they resemble you in appearance?''

"I am a fair example," he said. "There are many peoples in our part of the world, and we intermarry frequently. None of us have the purebred look of you Shasinn. Tall, short, slender or stocky, blue eyes or brown and every shade of hair, we are a mixed lot."

"And yet," she persisted, "you bear a slight resemblance to the Shasinn. Your height and build, your bearing, something about the shape of your cheekbones." She studied his face and he felt a prickle of fear along his spine.

"Many people must possess these things," he said. "And, who knows but that some island people made their way into our lands long ago. People as comely as your countrymen would have been eagerly sought as mates."

"Perhaps you are right. The Asasa are an island people who resemble us much, except for their darker hair and eyes. I suppose that once there must have been many such tribes, of whom we Shasinn are the last of the pure blood."

"Undoubtedly," Ansa said, hoping to put the subject safely behind them. "How does your husband's attack upon Huato progress? On the way here, we heard many stories from Sonoans fleeing into Gran. There was a great confusion."

"It has become tedious," she said. "At first, there were some exciting battles, but now King Mana will not come out and fight. My husband has given Mana his defiance and told him to come out and settle matters in honorable combat, but he prefers to trust to his city's ability to withstand a siege."

"I know nothing of sieges," Ansa said. "Our land has no cities or forts, so it is not something we have experience with."

"We do not like them," she said. "But our army has many skilled engineers and regiments of soldiers from the lesser peoples who can be used for that sort of fighting."

"What will your islanders do in the meantime?" Ansa asked.

"I suppose my husband will save them for the final assault. As long as they can come to close quarters with the enemy, there is nothing in the world that can stand before them."

"I confess, I would not want to engage your warriors with the spear."

"It is not your weapon. I saw when you rode in that you have one of those great bows I have heard so much about. Perhaps, while you are here, you might demonstrate its use to me?"

"It would be my pleasure," Ansa told her.

"Perhaps tomorrow, then," she said, "or the day after."

"Whenever you wish," he said, rising. He recognized this as a dismissal. He bowed and took his leave.

The soldiers and other members of the embassy had bedded down for the night, the fires were low and he did not feel like poking about among the snoring men to find a tent with room for him. The night was a fine one, the stars were clear overhead and he spread his blankets on the level ground, well away from the others. Even if his mortal enemies were among those on the mission and they had henchmen by them, he doubted that a city-bred assassin could find him in this darkness.

He lay down and looked up at the stars, missing Fyana but much distracted by more immediate things. Despite her protestations, he was mystified by Queen Larissa's candor in speaking with him. Was it merely another example of her arrogance, that she truly did not care what others thought about her words? Or did she have a more nefarious plan in mind?

She had been faintly flirtatious, but he was not in the least encouraged by that. Not when she had her Shasinn guards standing a few paces away, their spears thirsting for his blood. And he was sure she could not be seriously interested in him. Although every possible crime and depravity were imputed to her, Larissa's total devotion to her husband was proverbial.

Besides, Ansa thought just before he went to sleep, he just could not feel right about an affair with a woman his father had once been in love with.

SIXTEEN

Gasam stood on the tower and watched the preparations. The men stood by their ladders, the wheeled assault towers were ready, the nusks harnessed to their pushing-poles, quietly cropping the grass at their feet. The soldiers were ranked just out of missile range from the walls. The front rank had mantlets: huge shields taller than a man and wide enough for two men to stand behind. The usual practice was for one man to handle the mantlet while another fired a bow from its protection. Moving forward in unison, the mantlets became a portable wall.

To the rear of the assault troops the Shasinn and other island warriors were massed, along with Gasam's women warriors and certain picked units from the mainland subjects. These would be committed only when a sizable breach in the wall, or a foothold atop it, made it possible to carry the city with a single, overwhelming assault.

The sapper's tunnel had been fired the night before. Great streams of smoke rushed skyward from the numerous vent-holes bored by the engineers. At the southwest angle of the wall, he could see men rushing about in confusion as the wall emitted strange creaks and rumblings. They had achieved total surprise. There had been no floodings or countermines and all had gone as planned. Now it was a matter of waiting for the wall to collapse, to see whether an exploitable breach would result. He hoped so. There was already sickness in the camp. He did not want to tarry here longer. Since receiving the news of the steel mine, his patience had shortened. He wanted to grind this place to sand under his heel.

What sort of man was Mana? How could he style himself a king and behave so cravenly? A man who wanted to maintain his reputation as a leader of men should take more pride in his warrior qualities.

A sudden crackling rumble sharpened his attention, drawing it to the southwest angle. The corner of the wall looked the same, but it was surrounded by a shimmering haze. On the wallwalk behind the ramparts, men fled the angle, the tower emptying as its garrison felt the flooring of their tower trembling beneath their feet.

Slowly, majestically, the tower and the whole corner of the city wall began to settle. The joints in the stone widened as the foundation stones beneath the tower collapsed into the mine chamber. Stones of the rampart began to topple, most of them falling outward. They struck the ground and hurtled outward, some of them striking down soldiers who stood awaiting the signal to attack, shattering mantlets and pulping flesh and bone. At the shouted orders of their officers, the soldiers in that sector turned and fell back a hundred paces. Gasam was gratified to note that there was no panic and the movement was achieved in an orderly fashion.

As the cut stone sloughed away from the wall, its rubble core came gushing out, piling and sliding into a long ramp. Above the roar of the collapsing wall he heard the loud cheers of his soldiery, elated at this reversal of the enemy's fortunes, eager to see some action at last, after the long tedium of the siege.

Quickly, Gasam descended his tower. He would have preferred to erect it nearer the undermined corner, but he had not wished to draw enemy attention to that spot. Now he ran along the front lines of his cheering troops, twirling his steel spear overhead. He halted near the southwest angle, where his soldiers were reforming their lines after the shower of stones. His highest officers joined him.

"Surely it must have made a usable breach," said Urlik.

"We will know when the dust settles," Gasam answered. The whole southwestern end of the city was enveloped in an immense, opaque cloud of choking dust. Gradually, the dust grew vaporous, revealing a gap twenty feet wide at its base. The ramp of stone and rubble sloped from the breach to the ground below. The footing was clearly treacherous, but it was usable. Gasam turned to his grinning officers.

"I am going back to my command post. Return to your places. At my signal, all subject troops are to attack. The island and other elite warriors are to remain in reserve until I take personal command of them. They will fret at being held back, but tell them that I will lead them into the city myself when I decide that the time is right."

"As our king commands!" the officers chorused.

Gasam ran back to his tower amid redoubled cheers from the soldiery. His spear was awkward to manage on the tower's ladder, so he hurled it toward the top platform, where a young warrior caught it expertly by its central grip. He flew up the ladder and took his place at the front rail. The awning had been taken off so that his followers could see him clearly. The young warrior handed him his spear.

Slowly, Gasam raised the spear overhead, its point threatening the clouds above him. Swiftly, he brought it down in a graceful quarter-circle, leveling it with its point toward the city.

With a roar like that of the falling wall, the army surged

forward. Whips and goads were applied to the nusks, and the assault towers lurched toward the wall, creaking and groaning like huge beasts in pain. The ladder teams shouldered their long scaling ladders grimly, in full knowledge that their task would be the most deadly in the opening moments of the assault.

The moment they were within range, a storm of missiles soared from the city walls. Arrows came first, soon followed by sling stones. As the army drew nearer yet, javelins and darts joined the deadly rain. When the soldiers reached the base of the wall, hand-hurled stones began to fall on the mantlets. Engines atop the wall began to throw larger stones. These were aimed at the assault towers, but they scored few hits, as Gasam had expected. Catapults had little accuracy and the few that struck bounced harmlessly from the thick timbers of the tower faces. Gasam himself had no siege artillery. His Nevan engineer had been unable to find suitable materials.

When the rolling towers reached the wall and the scaling ladders were raised, a picked force of Gasam's best infantry stormed the breach. With their long, heavy shields held rigidly before them, their spears leveled, they began a quick but careful advance up the insecure footing of the ramp. These men were the most heavily armored of his soldiers. Every man of the first five ranks had a bronze helmet, a cuirass of laced and lacquered bamboo splints, and splinted greaves covering shins and knees. Each was armed with a long spear and a bronze shortsword or battle-ax. Their officers wore cuirasses of bronze and their helmets were crested with white feathers.

Gasam watched this advance tensely. This was the assault that would carry the city. The rest was mainly for distraction. As the heavy infantry toiled up the ramp, the fine cohesion of their formation was inevitably lost. The newfallen rocks turned beneath their feet, men stumbled, and the steady advance turned into a desperate scramble. A mass of defenders emerged from the breach and threw themselves forward to delay the advancing army while men behind them worked frantically to erect a barricade across the breach. Their resistance was as futile as it was brave, for they could not amass enough force to stay the momentum of the advancing horde for long. The men fell, pierced by the long spears, and Gasam's men worked their way toward the gap in the all, a foot at a time.

While attackers and defenders struggled doggedly at the breach, Gasam scanned the desperate fighting at the wall. The teams of laddermen pushed on forked poles to force their ladders against the ramparts, while defenders pushed with similar poles to keep them away. Gradually, the ladders were forced home. Unlike the attackers, the defenders on the narrow wallwalk could not get enough men behind their poles to fend the ladders off for long. Likewise, they had no good way to stop the assault towers, save by throwing grapples onto them and trying to pull them over with ropes. The towers proved to be too heavy for this strategy, and soon their drop gates fell onto the top of the rampart, and the soldiers stormed across.

Now that it was hand-to-hand, the greater numbers of the defenders came into play. Men climbing singly up ladders, or rushing across the drop gates on a front no more than two or three men wide, were at first easily dealt with by the defenders, who were numerous and fought with great desperation. They toppled scaling ladders with their bare hands and some even left their posts on the wallwalk to leap onto the drop gates and fight the enemy on that shaky, perilous platform for the sake of keeping their enemies just a few inches farther from their city. The fighting entered a stalemate as neither offense nor defense was able to wrest an advantage from the situation. Throughout, the defenders not directly engaged with the ladders or the towers kept up their deadly sleet of missiles, now resorting to kettles of hot oil and vases filled with pitch, their open ends stoppered with flaming, oily rags. These burst upon striking ground, spraying any man nearby with a ghastly shower of clinging, flaming liquid.

Gasam found the entire spectacle deeply satisfying. It was always good to see brave men fighting, even when they were enemies. Best of all, he saw no failure in the performance of his own troops. By now, his mainland soldiery were nearly as fanatically loyal as his islanders. Once they were accustomed to the yoke of the conqueror, they were grateful to be following an ever-victorious war leader, and they showed him service of a quality their former kings had probably never seen.

He was gratified to see the excellence with which the Sonoans fought. He had not been impressed by their performance in the field, but they were as fierce as longnecks in defending their city. That meant that they, too, would become good soldiers for King Gasam once they were resigned to their fate. Already he was calculating in his mind how he would integrate his new Sonoan regiments into his army of conquest. He decided that, once he had done away with most of their leadership, he would be generous with the common soldiers. It was Mana's stubborn, cowardly intransigence that had brought this about and he would put all the blame on the king of Sono. Once they got used to the idea, the men's own pride would urge them to believe that they had been led by an inferior king and that it was their good fortune to serve the conqueror when he could have killed them all.

Gasam was not impelled by benevolence, a concept that was utterly alien to him. He was going to need a huge army for the long, arduous desert campaign ahead of him. For the first time in his career of headlong attack and conquest, he would have to provide for things such as supply lines and permanent forts. That meant garrisons, and all true warriors hated garrison duty. These Sonoans might be ideal for the task.

At the breach, his assault party had now forced the defenders back into the gap and were pressing within. Under cover of shields, some men were employed in pulling out the bodies of the slain so that those still fighting should not have to stand on corpses. The long spears thrust out, clearing defenders from the hastily erected rampart of rubble and timber. From behind the front line, the next two ranks thrust over their shoulders, spears held high to clear the shields of their comrades, helping to drive the defenders back. Those who were unable to fight picked up fragments of rubble and cast it behind them, widening and leveling the usable section of the breach. Others held their shields overhead, forming a roof against the missiles dropping from above. The roaring and screaming and cursing made a constant, maddening accompaniment to the frenzied activity of the assault.

Here and there atop the wall, the towers and the laddermen were forcing a foothold. Once two such footholds were gained, there was little difficulty in clearing the defenders from between them. Unsupported on both flanks, the Sonoans caught in that predicament had little choice except to fight to the death or risk a leap into the streets or rooftops below them.

Gasam did not wish to commit his reserves until he had a good point of vantage atop the wall where he could survey the progress of the fighting within the city. This was the frustrating stage of the battle. He was reduced to being a mere spectator, unable to affect the course of the fighting while his subordinate commanders bore the brunt of the battle.

More men were ascending and meeting less resistance. Soldiers stood in lines behind the towers to file up their stairs and across the drop gates, onto the wall. All the ladders were now in use. An officer stood atop the rampart and waved a red cloak, a signal that the wall was now secure.

With a shout, Gasam scrambled down the observation

tower and sprinted across the field toward the nearest ladder. The ground was littered with bodies and wounded men staggered back toward the camp, cradling bloody limbs, some with the snapped-off stubs of arrows protruding from their bodies.

Holding his spear carefully, Gasam made his way sure-footedly up the rungs to spring lightly atop the rampart. From behind him he heard the cheers of his Shasinn, but he ignored them. This battle was far from won and could still turn against him. He had no idea how strong Mana's force might be. If there were strong reserves within the city, the king might be holding them back for a fight on more advantageous ground, perhaps a square with limited access for the attackers or a citadel. His palace might be fortified.

A hard-faced Chiwan officer strode over to him. "We have the wall, my king, but there are many buildings within arrow range." He barked a command and two soldiers hurried up. "You are to shield the king. Be vigilant."

A broad street separated the wall from the nearest buildings. The street was covered by a virtual carpet of bodies, broken weapons and rubble. He strode southward, toward the breach. His men scrambled from his way and from time to time he heard an arrow thunk into one of the shields held by his two guards.

As he reached the breach he could see a furious combat below, as more of his men forced their way through and yet more defenders pushed in from side streets. The cramped tangle of fighting men could make little use of skill and fought on ferocity alone. It was exactly this sort of wasteful scrimmaging that he wished to spare his elite troops. In a fight where sheer weight of men was all that counted, common soldiers were quite adequate.

"Will you bring in the Shasinn, my king?" asked an officer.

"Soon," he replied. "We must clear this little plaza first. Then I will order in the elite." He scanned over the rooftops in search of anything that might be an inner citadel. He saw tall houses and some towers, but nothing that looked substantial enough to be a fortress. Some of the locals they had questioned had spoken of the king's fort or castle, his dwelling place in the city, but Gasam suspected that it was just an old word for a royal residence, probably dating from a time when the rulers of this country had lived in strongholds.

Gasam pointed across the open space to the nearest buildings, where archers and slingers were making life difficult for his soldiers.

"These men on the wall are standing around doing nothing," Gasam said. "Lead them over there and clear all those buildings. As my men make their way through the streets, I want all the rooftops in our hands as well. That is your task."

"As my king commands!" The officer shouted and waved. In moments, a stream of soldiers followed him down an access stairway and headed for the nearest buildings. Gasam leaned on his spear and enjoyed the spectacle of combat as it raged beneath him and on the rooftops beyond. Soon, the intermittent arrows ceased and his shieldmen were able to relax their wariness a little.

It seemed that light-armed soldiers were ideal for the work in buildings and on rooftops. With their small shields, wearing little or no armor, they had no difficulty in negotiating narrow hallways and stairs. On the roofs they met not soldiers with long spears and heavy weapons but rather bow-armed skirmishers and citizens desperately throwing rocks and roof tiles at the invaders below. Compared to these, even light-armed soldiery were invincible when it came to hand-blows. Gasam made a mental note of this. He never forgot the slightest stratagem of war and was always able to make use of any new observation. He had been contemplating abolishing the light-armed skirmishers, but now he saw a new use for them. He recalled his thoughts about the

Sonoan defenders and summoned the commander of the subject troops.

"My king?" said the gasping officer, his bronze armor splashed with red.

"The fighting is fierce now, but later, when the enemy see that all is lost, they will put up only token resistance. They will look for an opportunity to surrender. You are to give quarter wherever it is asked. Watch for treachery of course, and punish it by instant death, but I want these people as subject soldiers."

"As my king commands. I will pass the orders." The officer dashed down the stairs.

The defenders were now pushed into the streets emptying into the little square and Gasam's soldiers were pouring into the city. Through the breach and over the wall they came in like the tide. The battle was getting away from him again. It would be street-to-street now, with his men clearing blocks and rooftops. Unless there proved to be a central citadel, it might be an easy fight from here on, but he could not be sure of it. He gestured and one of his young Shasinn warriors sprang to his side.

"Yes, my king?"

"Go to the generals Raba and Urlik where they await with the reserve. Tell them to bring in the islanders and my women warriors. Tell them this, and tell them most carefully." He held up an admonitory finger and the youth's face sharpened with concentration. "They are to bring them in in an orderly fashion. Tell them this is not a battle in the field, but rather a bush-beating. Quarter is to be given. Even the women are to observe this. I will be obeyed."

The young warrior dashed off to seek out the commanders. They would understand what he meant by a bush-beating. In their home islands this had been their technique for clearing the forests of enemies and outlaws or predatory animals threatening their herds. Here they would conduct an organized sweep of the streets, a methodical process with none of the frenzied excitement of a real battle. They would be disappointed but their particular qualities would be wasted in this sort of street fighting. They would take many casualties without having their usual disproportionate effect on the outcome of the battle. This employment would give them a chance to vent a little of their war-lust.

Plumes of smoke began to ascend from some of the buildings nearby. Lamps, braziers, cook-fires or sacrificial fires were being upset as the buildings were stormed. If the fires spread, they could become a nuisance. The destruction was immaterial to him. Gasam had no love of cities and even their material wealth meant little to him. He did not share Larissa's fondness for these things. Wealth was important only insofar as it helped him prosecute successful wars. He could happily live his life campaigning, with only a camp but for shelter and his spear his sole personal possession. That, and his army.

As a youth, he had thought that wealth consisted of livestock. He had herded kagga for his tribe and had luxuriated in the wealth they represented. As he grew older, a discontent had developed. These animals did not belong to *him*. He set out to rectify that, and in so doing he found that true wealth lay in the ownership of living human beings. Everywhere he strode, the people acknowledged him as master, or else they died. This was the proper order of things. No human being had any right to exist save as Gasam's property. He had convinced a good part of the world of this fact, and he intended to convince the rest.

A subdued chanting woke him from his mild reverie. The islanders were at the breach. He strode to the crumbled edge of the gap and shouted down at them.

"Hold your shield-formations as you sweep the streets! I want no heroics for this fight. Fires have begun and they will come at you out of the smoke. Spear them down in an orderly fashion and don't underestimate them. They are desperate now and will throw their lives away gladly for a chance to kill one of you. When they understand that those who surrender will be spared, they will lose their fury. Give quarter, disarm them and assemble the survivors outside the city wall, under guard. Now go!''

The warriors chanted their salute and entered the city. They were not truly happy, but they were cheerful at the prospect of a little bloodshed, however constrained.

As the day progressed, Gasam grew bored. In such a fight as this, he had little to do save listen to the reports of advances made by various units. Since they were unfamiliar with the city, there was no way to conduct a systematic pacification of the place, quarter by quarter. Some officers were now in sight of the palace compound, which was fortified, but not strongly so. That was cheering news. Mana would have his best troops concentrated there, to preserve his royal hide from perforation by Shasinn spears.

Fires raged out of control in many parts of the city and Gasam gave orders for prisoners to be set to fighting the fires. It was immaterial to him if the city burned to the ground, but he wanted to reduce the confusion and prevent his own troops being killed in the fires.

In late afternoon, he was informed that the greater part of the city was secure and that the palace enclosure was surrounded. He descended from the wall and, accompanied by his women warriors, made his way toward the palace. They made frequent detours around burning buildings and heaps of rubble. The women were blood-spattered and content. Their unearthly, demonic appearance was enough to cause panic among their enemies and they had spread terror wherever they had gone that day.

The palace enclosure formed a minor city surrounded by a wall, standing in the middle of an immense plaza. The plaza itself was full of statues, ceremonial arches and free-standing pillars of unclear purpose. Just now the plaza was thronged with Gasam's soldiery, who chanted and hurled defiance at the defenders of the palace. The soldiers hailed Gasam as he joined them and strode to a knot of officers.

"Has he asked for terms yet?" Gasam demanded.

"He has sent no envoys," Raba said. "We have seen no white flags."

"Will you entertain terms from this cowardly striper, my king?" Urlik asked.

"There is no point in it," Gasam said. "His kingdom is mine now and he has nothing to bargain with. Still, it would be informative to know how desperate he is just now. Has he a strong force in there, or is it a shell?"

"One way to find out," said Raba. "Let's attack."

Gasam laughed. "I always know what your advice will be." He looked at the sun, which now touched the city wall to the west. "No, it will be dark soon. We will fight in the morning. I want an impenetrable guard around this place. There will be no escapes. Let their nerves work on them. Build big fires here in the plaza. Let the men chant, sing and celebrate all night. There is to be no drunkenness, but let them see that we are already rejoicing over their deaths."

He scanned the scene. "Find me a tent and set it up here somewhere, before the main entrance. If he sends envoys I will listen to them, if only for my amusement."

All was done as he had ordered. As the moon rose over the city, Gasam lounged beneath a quil-hair canopy, sipping at a bowl of ghul while the youngest of his women warriors performed a violently lascivious war dance to the throbbing of drums and the shrilling of pipes. The shattered city rang with the noise of the war host. The sky above it glowed with their fires. The conflagrations among the buildings had been extinguished but timber and furnishings from others fed the huge bonfires burning all over the plaza. Shops and storehouses had been looted and the men feasted, but sharp-eyed officers ensured that they did not drink too deeply. At all times one-fourth of the army stood behind their shields, alert for a sortie from the palace.

From within the palace enclosure there came no sound. A few torches burned along the rampart and shadowy forms could be seen patrolling on the wall. The gate remained shut.

Morning brought no change. There had been no offer to parley, but neither had there been any extraordinary efforts at defense. Nothing but silence came from the palace. Mystified by the lack of activity, Gasam's troops were equally quiet, standing nervously at their posts.

"I don't understand it," Luo said. "They don't want to surrender, they don't want to parley, and now it looks as if they don't want to fight, either. What *do* they want?"

"I shall find out," Gasam said. He summoned a herald and sent the man to tell Mana to open the gate or else come out and fight. The herald strode importantly to the gate and hailed the rampart above, where the night before sentries had patrolled. There was no response. He repeated his hail for several minutes, then walked back to the king.

"I see no one, my king, and I hear no one."

"Can they have escaped?" Raba exclaimed. "A tunnel?"

"Our mounted patrols are all over the countryside," Urlik said. "They would have reported any such thing."

"We will find out," said Gasam, out of patience. "Ram that gate down."

A team of soldiers advanced under the cover of mantlets, rolling a framework from which was suspended a bronze-faced log. This they pulled back and released, smashing the bronze against the heavy wooden gates. At the tenth shock the wood shattered and the double doors sagged on their hinges. The ram team shoved the gates aside and Gasam ordered the men recalled.

"Shasinn and islanders and the women in," he ordered.

"No mercy this time." He resented the game Mana had been playing with him, and he had not forgotten the terror he had felt in the tunnel.

Gasam entered the palace among his warriors. There were no sounds of battle, and there were no hordes of prisoners being led out. He pushed himself to the front of the warriors. They had halted and stood uncharacteristically subdued.

"What is it?" he demanded, then he saw. Within the wall was a courtyard surrounded by ornate buildings. In the center was a circular building of three stories, each story surrounded by a roof. Everywhere on the pavement between the buildings lay bodies amid a welter of blood. The smell of blood was sharp in the air and insects were beginning to gather over the dead. Slowly, the warriors approached the corpses. Most of them were lavishly armored and accoutred. Clearly, these were the king's elite guard.

"All dead with their throats cut," said a warrior.

"They slew each other," said Urlik.

Gasam could take no delight in the spectacle. He had not killed these.

"Where is Mana?" he demanded.

"Smoke!" cried one of the women, pointing. Tendrils of smoke were streaming from the upper windows of the circular building.

"Come!" Gasam dashed across the courtyard toward the source of the smoke. His women followed closely. Young warriors, afraid that their king might dash into danger unprepared, sprinted ahead of him and up the steps of the building.

"Stay back a while, my king," said Raba, rushing into the palace. Moments later he came back out. "All dead here, too. Come and see."

Mystified, Gasam passed within. There were bodies everywhere. Few of these were in armor, but rather had the look of servants and courtiers. Here the smell of blood was overpowering, even through the cloud of sweet-smelling smoke. In the center of the vast room was a great, inchoate heap of something, and the smoke came from its peak. Almost dreading what he would see, Gasam walked closer to the heap, braving the growing heat.

The center of the room, which rose almost for the palace's full three stories, was piled with King Mana's treasures. Furnishings and carpets and works of art, chests of jewels, flasks of perfumes and rare drugs, jars of wine, rich foodstuffs and spices, all were strewn and piled with wild profusion.

Atop the material goods lay the king's human valuables. Women and boys of every race and nation lay there, some naked, others richly robed. They were the king's wives, concubines and harem-slaves and probably, Gasam guessed, his daughters and other family members. At the crest of the pile was a great couch, around which smoke boiled, and on the couch lay a man in royal robes, wearing a high, jewelled diadem of gold. The flames were licking at the bedclothes. To Gasam's horrified astonishment, the man sat up and stared down at him. His black beard was long, curled and square-cut. Black eyes flanked a beak of a nose as he glared at Gasam with hatred and, astonishingly, triumph. The flames began to roar all around him but he managed to speak before he was consumed.

"*I win, Gasam!*" Then the flames hid him from view and hearing. Now the flames burst out everywhere, erupting in an explosion of fire and perfumed smoke as the costliest substances of the kingdom were consumed on the king's pyre.

The warriors backed away from the heat. The women laid hands on their king and tugged him from the palace, out onto its broad stair. They all stood silently, staring as the flames burst through the windows in the extravagant self-immolation of King Mana of Sono. They started at a strange, howling sound, then drew back in fear when they saw that the terrible sound came from their king. Gasam stood, his eyes rolling, flecks of foam appearing upon his lips as he moaned like a heartbroken beast. It was a long time before he could form words.

"He cheated me!" King Gasam screamed.

SEVENTEEN

Ansa was profoundly bored. If this was the way people of power exercised their authority over other men, he wanted none of it. For hours, the Granian diplomats had been wrangling with Queen Larissa. They offered treaties of friendship and mutual aid, and interspersed these with thickly veiled threats. When speaking of their admiration for King Gasam and his all-conquering armies, they reminded her of their nation's own illustrious history in the waging of wars, managing to drop into seemingly unrelated conversation the names of great kings, generals and conquerors of past generations.

The queen listened politely and, whenever she chose to speak, stressed the entirely pacific intentions of her lord toward his brother king, Ach'na of Gran.

The diplomats then spoke effusively of their king's love for her and for Gasam, whom His Majesty admired above all other men upon the earth.

"And if," Lord Impimis said at one point, "King Gasam

is having some difficulty in subduing the unfortunate King Mana, it is not entirely unthinkable that some sort of reciprocal agreement for military aid might be worked out. For, although we have been at peace with Sono for some years now, yet this was not a matter of eternal friendship, but rather was a mere cessation of hostilities after the last war."

"I am sure that my lord will bring this war to a speedy conclusion, without having to accept your generous offer," she answered. "However, I know that he would esteem a pledge of noninterference from your king. We know that the cowardly King Mana, knowing that he had overstepped the boundaries of decency and prudence, sought an alliance with King Ach'na when he realized that my husband, in just fury at his treachery, had come to exact an accounting from him."

"Truly, such an alliance was proposed," said Impimis, "but I assure you that it was not seriously entertained."

Certainly not, Ansa thought, considering that King Ach'na was flat on his back, paralyzed by poison. This was all meaningless. He wondered how the courtiers planned to approach Larissa. It would not be easy to secure a private audience on this little island. He had spoken privily with her, at her own invitation. The traitor or traitors, though, would not wish to sit openly at a fire, with guards in hearing distance. They would want to take her aside, either in the woods somewhere, or in her tent. Her guards would never allow them to take her out of their sight in the woods, so it would have to be the tent, sometime after dark. He would have to find a good place from which he could spy on them.

Surreptitiously, he slipped from the tent. The courtiers did not notice, but Larissa did. She favored him with a wry smile. He smiled back and ducked out.

Outside, the servants idled near the tents while the soldiers and Larissa's warrior guard amused themselves with arms practice, down near the river. While the soldiers gaped, the Shasinn made seemingly impossible casts with their javelins. They had set up Sonoan shields as targets and these they skewered with uncanny accuracy, the small, dense bronze heads of the short spears crunching through the hide-covered wicker with fearsome force. Ansa, who had seen his father cast the javelin many times, was not as surprised as the Granian soldiers.

The Granians, not to be outdone, hung small targets in trees and speared them with their long lances as their mounts speed by at a full gallop. The Shasinn kept their superior expressions in place. It was impossible to tell whether they were impressed by the display, but Ansa doubted it. They knew that, in battle, the real opponent would not be the man but rather his mount, and these herdsmen were not to be overawed by animals. He wondered what they would think if he were to give them a display of shooting the great bow from the saddle. He resisted the temptation. Better that, when these men should encounter the mounted archers of the plains, it should come as a complete surprise.

He walked toward the upstream end of the island. When all else failed and there was nothing to do, a man could always fish, if there was water nearby. He passed through the stand of trees, which was subdued, its animal life lying low while humans were so near. He did not blame them. Glancing back, he noticed that a pair of Shasinn strolled nonchalantly in his direction, stopping when he turned to look at them. Obviously, he was being shadowed. He thought little of it. At an event as tense as this one, it was hardly surprising that all parties concerned would watch each other closely.

The trees ended and he walked out onto the rocky, tapering end of the island. The current was swift here, and the jagged stones that gave the place its evil reputation were surrounded with foam. Among them were still pools that looked like promising fishing holes.

Ansa took a hook and line from his belt pouch and started turning over rocks. Under one he found a tiny walking-snake but quickly he found some fat, white grubs that he suspected the local fish would relish. Affixing one to a hook, he began to pick his way out among the rocks.

Sitting by a deep, narrow pool he drooped his hook into the water. He fell into a reverie about Fyana, but was shaken from it when he noticed something odd about the rocks amidst which he sat. All were of the same sort: a grayish, irregular mass with tiny stones buried amidst the gray. He knew that this was the artificial stone made by the ancients, the same stuff that his father mined for steel. He saw no great steel beams buried in this stone, but there were brown streaks on the gray. It had once held steel, but it had all rusted away in this humid climate, although men had probably broken up the stone with great labor to get at the larger pieces.

The line jerked in his hand and he gave it a tug. The fish pulled and thrashed, coming to the surface in a thrash of silvery scales. He hauled it in and stunned it against a stone, then rebaited his hook and dropped it back in. He wondered if there was more of the artificial rock nearby. What had this place been, in the old days? That had been so long ago that even the outlines of the ancient cities were lost, and only the most enduring of the ancient's works remained to give a hint of past glories. What had this mass of stone formed? The foundation of a building? Part of a bridge?

He knew that, far to the north of here on this same river, in the place called the Zone, were huge ruins strewn across a narrow canyon. Ancient legend had it that these had once formed a wall with no purpose save to hold water back, for reasons no one could now imagine. He shook his head. These were idle and futile thoughts. They distracted him from his present, precarious situation.

He caught two more fish, cleaning them and throwing the offal back into the water to feed other fish. He took his catch back to the island and built a small fire, draping the fish over green sticks and suspending them in the smoke. His two Shasinn followers stood just within the trees, wrinkling their noses in disgust. He smiled, knowing that the Shasinn abhorred the eating of fish.

"Come join me," he called innocently. "There is plenty here."

"It is forbidden," said one of the warriors, his words barely recognizable through the thick Shasinn dialect. He was tempted to banter with them, but knew better than to indulge himself so. His own people had a notoriously prickly sense of pride, and by all accounts the Shasinn far surpassed them in delicacy of honor. They might spear him if they sensed an insult. Mounted and with his full complement of weapons he would have had no fear of men such as these. Afoot, with his sword against their terrible spears, he knew better than to fancy his chances.

He thought of Fyana and wondered how she was progressing in the king's treatment. If she brought him back to health, how would he reward her? With riches, or with a strangler's noose? He had no illusions about kings. The man might resent her knowledge of his frailty. Queen Masila had treated them with great favor, but she was a desperate woman. With the king recovered, would she feel any sense of gratitude? He knew too much of such people to expect that. He wanted Fyana out of there. Right now, his only esteem for Gran was as a possible opponent for Gasam. He knew they would stand no chance against him, but they might hold him up for a while, force him to expend time and men, spread himself ever more thinly across the earth.

Surely, Ansa thought, there must be an end to the amount of land even a man like Gasam could control. His islanders were not all that numerous, his subject troops less than reliable, despite Queen Larissa's talk. How far could he extend before the great lines of communication began to break down? Before, every time he marched forth to conquer, he was forced to turn back in order to put down a rebellion in his rear?

Or was he something more than human? Perhaps he was exactly what he thought, the rightful king of the world, and there would be no stopping him. Perhaps his father's life-long work was in vain and no organization of mounted arch-ers, no regiments of soldiers armed with the revolutionary new fire-weapons would be of any use.

He shook himself. These were not the kind of thoughts to be having just now. Too much was at stake right here to be giving attention to dangers still far away. He took the skewered fish from the fire and devoured them, enjoying the appalled looks of the Shasinn guards. They appeared to be younger than he was, little more than boys, their hair dressed in the innumerable tiny plaits that he knew signified their junior status. They were no less dangerous for that.

Finished, he rose and returned to the camp. He spent the rest of the afternoon going over his weapons. These re-quired constant attention and he sharpened and oiled blades and arrowheads, checked shafts of lance and arrows for cracks or warping, smoothed feathers and made repairs to sheaths. He took out his bow and checked it over minutely, then waxed his bowstrings. By the time he was finished with these martial duties, it was time for yet another banquet.

This night was even more jovial than the night before. To judge by appearances, everlasting peace and friendship had been achieved between Gasam and Ach'na. Throughout the long evening, he studied the two high-ranking courtiers, seeking to pierce beneath their professional exteriors. He decided that Impimis was more forced in his joviality than Floris. The Senior Counselor was all too aware of the hol-lowness of Larissa's promises. Either Floris was not aware, which Ansa doubted, or he didn't care, which was very likely. It would be Floris, then, who would come to betray his king and nation.

When the banquet was ended, Ansa sought a place apart from the others to sleep, as he had the night before. This time, though, he waited until all was quiet. Then, dressed in his darkest clothing and with his face veiled by a dark cloth, he made his way toward Larissa's tent. He was wary, crawling on his belly when he made his final approach to the tent.

He knew that the Shasinn would be wary and alert, but he had been trained long and hard in this craft. War on the plains and in the hills was largely a matter of ambush, and in the hunt many beasts could be taken only by patient, lengthy stalking. The Shasinn did not hunt. They were herdsmen and despised hunters as people too poor to own livestock. He was confident in his ability to avoid them.

Scarcely breathing, he crept between the sentries surrounding the tent. They leaned on their spears and did not turn their heads as he passed. So slowly that he scarcely seemed to move at all, he reached out and placed his palms on the ground at arm's length before him and pressed down until his body raised from the ground less than a fingersbreadth. With the muscles of his arms, shoulders and back quivering with the strain, he slithered forward, bringing his feet forward alternately, placing only the sides of his soles against the ground, disturbing the grass as little as possible, trying to make no sound at all.

Every few feet, he had to lower himself to the ground and rest. He could not afford to allow his breathing to grow ragged. And there was no reason to hurry. Then there was a commotion at the entrance of the tent. Someone, it seemed, had come calling. He heard whispered voices, but he could make out no words. He scanned the base of the tent until he saw a line of light, where the cloth did not touch the ground. It would be a good place to listen and Ansa began to crawl toward it. He forced himself not to rush. It would be ultimate folly to be caught at this point because his judgment failed him.

When he reached the gap in the tent wall, he lowered himself to the ground and pressed his ear to the tiny space from which light spilled. Even before he lowered his ear to the gap, he heard voices. The first was Larissa's.

". . . since you have seen fit to call upon me this way, I take it you have things to say that are not for the ears of your compatriots?"

"These are matters of a certain delicacy," said Floris's voice. Inwardly, Ansa congratulated himself for deducing correctly. He was interested to hear what form the betrayal would take.

"Then express them how you will, but do not waste time. I am weary." The queen had dropped her diplomatic pose, demanding a display of good faith, as one conspirator to another.

"As am I, Your Highness. These proceedings are demanding to a man of my years. Are you aware that King Ach'na is not in the best of health?"

"I had not heard," she said. Ansa judged that she spoke truthfully. "Speak on."

"Some days ago, the king was stricken at a banquet. It occurred in a private passage between the banquet hall and his chambers, so knowledge of the incident remained confined to the court. Since that night he has lain paralyzed, unable to move or speak, perhaps not conscious at all."

"And the nature of this affliction?" Larissa asked. "I had not understood that he was elderly."

"No. Poison is suspected."

She cut straight to the point. "Will he recover?"

"That I cannot say. The best physicians of Gran could not help him. Then a lady of the Canyon arrived . . ."

"A Canyoner?" she interrupted.

"Yes. She arrived a few days ago in the company of that barbaric northern youth who contrived to attach himself to this mission."

"I see," she said. "Do go on."

"I take it that you find these things of interest, possibly

of great value?'' Clearly, Floris was reluctant to give up too much while receiving nothing in return.

"Of interest, surely. As to its value, I can only say when I have heard it all. How did it come about that the Canyon lady and the young prince arrived in the city just when such a person was needed?"

"That I cannot say. They arrived from the north, they became guests of a certain great lady of the city and at her house were examined by a high lord and lady of the court. The queen ordered them summoned to the palace. The Canyon woman, it seems, is an expert in medicines, but also in the properties of poisons. At the time we departed, though, she was not beyond an analysis of the poison used. The king still lay near death."

"How came she to be traveling with this plainsman?"

"To all appearances, by chance. He was passing through her land and she required an escort. He is wellborn, at least as these barbarians judge such things . . ."

"I am familiar with such people," she interrupted.

"Of course, Your Highness, I meant no . . ." Ansa could hear the embarrassment in the man's voice.

"It is nothing. So, King Ach'na lies disabled, as of a few days ago. Now, despite your most fervent protestations, I cannot believe that you bring me this information just for the love of me."

"No. As warm as are my feelings toward Your Highness, I have come to propose an agreement of far greater substance. I brought this valuable information as a gesture of the earnestness of my intentions. You understood that, should you breathe a word of what I have told you, I would be executed instantly upon my return to the capital."

"I appreciate your candor. And your proposal?"

"King Ach'na is incapacitated and his son is a child. If it comes to war between our peoples, the entire war host of Gran would be hard-pressed to hold you at our borders. That host has been summoned and even now assembles near the capital. Gran is a more populous nation than Sono, and better organized. It would not be as easy a conquest as you found on the other side of this river.''

''I take it that you know of a way to make that task easier for us?''

''My family is the controlling power in the southwestern quarter of Gran, and we provide somewhat more than one-fourth of the war host. The regional landholders of our district owe their immediate fealty to me, not to the king. Should I order them to withdraw their men from the host, they would obey.''

''And in return for this service?''

''Recognition of my family's right to our lands. A high position in your court for myself. Favorable taxation. Internal autonomy within my district.''

''In other words, the same arrangement you have had with King Ach'na.''

''But which I would be in no position to negotiate after a defeat of our forces by King Gasam. And, there are certain lands adjacent to those we now hold, lands which were once controlled by my family but which in years past were given to others by previous kings of Gran. I would like those lands restored to us, and I can guarantee their loyalty.''

''And just what makes you think,'' she said sharply, ''that we could not take it all without you?''

''I implied no such thing. I have said only that I would make the conquest far easier, far less costly. After all, King Gasam has far greater conquests in mind, and must hoard his resources. And, let us be reasonable. My lands are not such as would tempt you Shasinn. It is heavily forested, jungle, most of it, some suitable for farming and very little for grazing. What do you people want from such land save tribute, anyway? Anyone can guess that King Gasam is intent upon conquering the great plains beyond the desert. Limitless grasslands, Your Highness, where you and your herds of kagga can multiply forever. Down here, the king merely secures his southern flank against the great war to come, the war with King Hael.''

Ansa felt a shiver go through him. For once, the old man spoke the exact truth.

Queen Larissa was silent for a while. The offer had been made and now she was considering it in all its ramifications. ''You said that we would want nothing from your lands save tribute. You understand that part of that tribute must be in the form of young men of military age? As you have said, there are great wars ahead of us. These cannot be mere seasonal contributions to a war host, men who march out after planting only to return in time for harvest. They will be part of a permanent army, and they will return home only after years of campaigning, if ever.''

''I understand,'' said Floris, triumph barely veiled in his voice. He knew that his offer was accepted and now the queen was bargaining. ''Peasant lads are a valuable commodity, and to recompense their loss we must raise crop quotas for those who remain. This is difficult, but it can be managed. Perhaps a per-head payment would be in order, with an indemnity to be paid for those who do not return. This should be no burden upon King Gasam, who will hold the treasuries of many nations.''

She mused a while. ''Something could be worked out. Very well. I accept your offer. I am empowered to act for my husband in this matter. The king, of course, has control of all military matters, but I assume that the best time for you to withdraw your forces from the Granian host would be just before battle is to be joined. My people will maintain contact between us.''

''Surely not your Shasinn!'' he protested.

Ansa heard once again her musical laugh. ''No, I have men of all nations among my servants. They may approach you as merchants or as business agents. What peculiar interest have you?''

"My cabo stables are known in many nations," he said, "I trade widely for new bloodlines."

"Very well, they will be cabo traders specializing in rare breeds. To distinguish them from the real ones, each will wear a silver bracelet on his right wrist."

"I shall anticipate their arrival. I believe this concludes our work here. You have been most gracious."

Ansa backed away from the tent without waiting to hear what she said to him. He now had the important information. He knew who would betray Gran to Gasam, and he knew how it was to be done. He wondered whether Gasam would abide by the agreement. He suspected that the king would do so. He did need flunkies of other races to administer his conquests. As betrayals went, this had been a straightforward and businesslike one. Certain specified services had been offered, in return for which there would be specified payment. He did not doubt that one of Floris's ancestors had struck just such a deal with some forebearer of Ach'na's. Floris was the sort of man who would come out of any crisis well.

Crawling like a lizard, Ansa got well away from the tent without being detected. When he felt he had established enough distance between himself and the tent, he rose to a crouch and padded on soft boot-soles to a copse of bushes that stood twenty paces from his sleeping place. There he sat a while, watching his bedding and belongings, waiting for any sign that enemies lay in wait. The moon made its stately pace across the black sky, revealing nothing. Finally, an hour after he left the gap beneath Larissa's tent, he made his way wearily to his bedding and lay down. It was a tedious process, but he had a hunter's patience and knowing that his life was at stake made waiting much easier.

The next morning he woke to sounds of bustling activity. There were no more talks scheduled, and the day was to be devoted to entertainments. More delicacies and gifts had been brought in by slave-train from Sono, the pickings of looted estates. If there was further word of the siege, no-body said anything about it.

In the afternoon, Queen Larissa came to him as he was currying his cabo. She was mounted, and she wheeled her animal to a halt beside him.

"You said you would demonstrate your archery," she said. "Will you come hunting with me?"

He looked up at her, smiling but narrowing his eyes against the sunlight. "I thought you Shasinn did not hunt."

"I have learned a taste for wild game," she answered, "and I can think of no better way to see your bow at work."

"Gladly, then." He took his blanket pad and saddle from the ground and quickly prepared his mount. "Where will we ride?"

"Over there," she said, pointing to the shore. "The hunting should be good. The land is almost deserted and already the wild beasts come out to graze in the untended farms."

"It sounds good." He slid his bow from its sheath and hooked one end around his left ankle. With his right hand on its upper limb he bent it around the back of his right thigh and pushed the upper loop of the string into its notch on the tip.

"May I try it?" she asked, holding out a hand. He handed it to her and mounted. She tried to draw it, but could not bring the string back more than a few inches. "It is power-ful!"

"Among us, a boy's first toy is a little bow. As a youth you get a hunting bow, about a third the draw weight of this one. It is good for small to medium game, about the size of a curlhorn. For two years now, I have drawn a man's bow." He took it back from her and slid it into its case before his left leg. Its quiver of arrows hung opposite it.

"Then, let's ride," she said. They rode across the clear-ing and onto the wide wooden bridge. It was well built, made of heavy timbers laid over abutments of cut stone.

The stonework was very ancient, but the wood looked no more than a few years old. Ansa guessed that floods probably destroyed the wooden part with some frequency. The clop of the animals' hoofs was loud in the clear air. The queen's bodyguard fell in behind them. The men were well mounted but Ansa noted that they rode indifferently. The queen rode no better, but he found her far more pleasant to watch.

After a brief gallop that took them across grassy fields and out of sight of the island, they slowed to a walk. Soon they passed deserted farms, already showing signs of neglect. They saw hairy little domestic quil running loose, grubbing in the soil for roots and burrowing animals. Scattered bones showed that other livestock, lacking human protection, had been killed by predators. Ansa noticed that Larissa was studying him closely.

"You ride so beautifully," she said. "I can't help watching. I was a grown woman before I ever saw a cabo. But even the Nevan and Chiwan riders look clumsy compared to you. Your people are born and raised and live their lives in the saddle."

"It is very nearly like that," he agreed. "But then, we look silly on foot compared to you."

"There!" she said, pointing at something just within the treeline. The creature ambled out, standing possibly twelve feet high at its bulky shoulders. The thick, muscular neck went up another eight feet, terminating in a head the size of a cabo's, graced with spreading palmate horns. Ignoring them, it browsed daintily on the top-leaves of a tree.

"What is it?" he asked, intrigued by the magnificent beast.

"I don't know what the local people call it," she said. "I have seen four or five families of them since coming here. Will you shoot that one?"

He laughed. "That's no challenge. That would be like standing inside a house and shooting at the walls. Let's find something smaller and faster." They rode on a while, until they came to an upland valley, where the trees were small and widely separated. Ansa's experienced eye for terrain told him that this area had been burned over a few years before, and the land was not yet fully recovered. This was a good place for the smaller game animals. The grass was abundant and there was little cover for predators.

From where they halted, they could see a number of families and small herds of various species. Most were varieties of the horned grazers that abounded in every land where there was sufficient water and vegetation to support them. In the distance, up the slopes of the valley, they could see more of the towering beasts. There were no signs of big cats. Most of them preferred to attack from ambush in the wooded areas.

"This looks promising," Ansa said. He pointed. "Over there, the bachelor standing alone, with the gray and white stripes." The indicated animal stood on a slight rise of ground. He guessed it to be a close relative of the familiar branch horn, but its four slender horns swept back from its head without branchings and with only the faintest of curvature. Nearby stood a small herd of similar creatures dominated by an identical animal. The rest had far shorter horns.

"He wants those females," Larissa said. "But their lord is still too strong."

"He will be swift," Ansa said. "Come on."

He fitted an arrow to his string and advanced at a slow walk. He held his bow in his left hand and his reins he held loosely with two fingers of the same hand. As they neared the little herd, the dominant male tossed his head and bleated. All the animals began to trot away from the riders. The bachelor noticed them a moment later and began to run alongside them, but separated by at least fifty paces. Ansa began to ride faster, then urged his mount into a furious dash, placing himself between the bachelor and the herd. Instantly, the bachelor broke to the right, gaining distance in a series of graceful bounds. Ansa wheeled and went after him.

Fifty paces ahead of him, the bachelor broke to the left. Ansa had been prepared for the maneuver and halted his cabo. As the creature ran at top speed, he drew his bow, not taking his eyes from his quarry. He judged its speed, the length of his bounds and his height at the crest of each. He loosed his arrow, aiming it at the crest of the next bound.

The animal came down, its rear legs gathered beneath it. The next bound sent it soaring with forelegs outstretched. At the top of the arc, as it was gathering its rear legs beneath its haunches, the arrow struck just behind its shoulder. It landed as if nothing had happened and soared into another long, graceful leap. This time, when its forehooves struck ground, its legs collapsed and the animal went down in a heap, kicking weakly.

Ansa galloped to where the beast lay and leapt from his cabo. He jammed the butt-spike of his lance into the ground and tied his reins to it, then he knelt by the fallen animal with his knife drawn. The final mercy was not needed. The creature was dead. He cut its throat anyway, to bleed the carcass. A hundred paces away the little herd had stopped and was already placidly cropping grass.

Larissa and her guards rode up behind him. The queen was speaking quietly to the guards in the island dialect.

"That was splendid!" she said. "I've never seen such shooting."

Intent upon dressing the carcass for transport, he did not look back as they dismounted behind him. "It was easy. It fled just like the branch horns of my homeland. I hope it tastes as good. Do you like . . ." He stopped short as something touched both shoulders. The long blades of two Shasinn spears lay on his shoulders and crossed beneath his chin. He heard a faint click as a third was laid across the other two behind his neck. He held utterly still as hands plucked the knife from his hand, the sword and stone axe from his belt. His neck was enclosed in a triangle of razor-edged metal. The men had but to jerk back forcefully and he would be beheaded.

Inwardly he quaked, but he let nothing show in his face or bearing. It was his first true test as a warrior and there was absolutely nothing he could do save meet death with courage. One of the guards grasped the animal's hind legs and hauled it away. Even in his extremity, Ansa was impressed with the slender youth's strength.

"I hope you plan to eat it," he said, proud that his voice held no quaver. "I don't kill for sport."

"Straighten him," Larissa said. Gently, the warriors drew back on their spears, forcing him to kneel upright. His hands were seized and bound by the wrists behind his back. She walked around him slowly and stopped to stand before him, close enough that he had to look up to meet her eyes. She had discarded her riding cloak and almost everything else save a few ornaments and stood clothed only in her beauty. He had never seen an armed warrior who looked as terrible.

"Who betrayed me?" he demanded.

"You did. And you abused my hospitality, coming before me with an assumed identity."

"I would have been a fool to tell the truth."

"It was a brave try, I'll give you that. What is your real name?"

"Ansa is my true name."

She came closer yet and took his chin between thumb and fingers of her left hand, tilting his head up and turning it gently from side to side like someone examining a rare new jewel, admiring the play of light on its facets.

"Truthfully, there is little of the Shasinn in your looks, at least to one who is of the pure blood. You must favor your mother's people. You could have fooled anyone save me and my husband, possibly three other men with our army."

"How did you know?" he said, wanting to know this before she had him killed.

"Something you could never have guessed. Your voice. It is identical to his, twenty years ago. I recognized it the first time you spoke to me."

"You hide your feelings well," he said, meaning the compliment sincerely.

"So do you. You would have grown into a formidable man, had you lived."

"Finish it then," he said, summoning up his last reserves of defiance. "But what are you going to say to the Granian party? Everyone will know that your safe-conduct is meaningless."

"This is where your inexperience betrayed you. Did you read my safe-conduct, or hear it read?"

"I did."

"Then you should have noticed that it referred only to the island as neutral ground. Here, in my and my lord's nation of Sono, where I reign as queen, I may take as prisoner anyone I choose. The distinction will not have escaped those Granian diplomats back on the island, but none of them thought fit to warn you not to ride across the bridge with me. I think that you have few friends in Gran."

"Then kill me," he said, hopefully.

"Oh, not just yet. I love my husband too much to deprive him of this."

His heart sank, knowing that the worst had happened. Roughly, he was seized beneath the arms as the spears were withdrawn. Hauled to his feet, he was thrown into his saddle and his ankles tied together beneath the girth. He saw the beast he had killed thrown across another cabo's back.

"Oh, yes," Larissa said, "my guests will dine on it. And, truly, it was splendid shooting."

EIGHTEEN

He spent the first night under guard, at a campsite near the island, but well out of sight from it. Warriors of the guard came and went, but there were always at least ten there to watch over him. They had erected small huts to sleep in, but he was not put in one of them. Instead, he was bound to a stake driven deep into the earth. He sat on the ground with his back leaning against the stake and his wrists were tied together behind it. Even if he struggled to his feet, the top of the stake was still high over his head and he could not have slipped his hands over it.

Not that the warriors would have allowed any such action. They always stood or sat nearby, mostly talking among themselves. Once he was over his first fright and resigned to the fact that he would not be able to escape immediately, he began to take some interest in his guards. He found the study instructive and it took his mind off his likely fate.

In sharp contrast to the reserve they displayed when among strangers, here the Shasinn were animated. They talked much and laughed often, their handsome faces graced with broad smiles that made them all the more comely. Apparently, one soon-to-be-dead prisoner was not worth the usual display of arrogant reticence.

Something about them gave him an oddly poignant feeling, and he soon realized what it was when he noticed several of them standing in an odd fashion. Each man held his spear braced on the ground before him and stood on one foot, resting his other foot on the knee of the standing leg. Occasionally, through the years, he had seen his father stand thus, and no other man. Then he knew that there was much about these youths that reminded him of his father, subtle details of stance and gesture, but mostly an overall grace and nobility of bearing that made them seem something other than merely human. He did not want to admit it even to himself, but at this moment he missed his father deeply.

Only late in the evening, when he saw several of them fall to wrestling while others stood about, laughing and clapping while shouting out ribald advice, did he realize how young these warriors were. He had known that Shasinn males were sometimes made warriors as young as fourteen or fifteen, but these seemed so accomplished that he had assumed that they were older. Now, with the strangers and their queen absent, they had no one to pose for save Ansa, who counted for nothing. This gave him some encouragement. Perhaps he would have a better chance for escape when they left for King Gasam's siege. But this was accompanied by a more sobering thought: If these were boys, what must the experienced warriors be like?

At least they were not abusing him. He was forced to admit that rarely did his own people treat a prisoner so gently, even though his father had forbidden such abuse. Criminals and outlaws were not to be punished before trial and prisoners of war were to be held until they were bought or traded back to their homelands. Still, the old ways lingered and it was not uncommon for an unfortunate prisoner to come to grief in captivity.

He assumed that Queen Larissa had left orders that he was not to be touched until he was turned over to the king. Her commands were as the laws of nature to these warriors. He tried to engage them in conversation, but they ignored him. Either she had forbidden them to talk to him, or else they simply saw no point in speaking with an inferior being. He suspected the latter.

Eventually, he managed to ignore his cramped muscles and fall into a fitful sleep. He woke frequently. Each time he saw fires burned low, but always there were several Shasinn sitting near, alert and watching him. Why couldn't they fall asleep like ordinary men, he wondered. Not that it would have done him any good.

He woke tormented with hunger and thirst, unable to feel his arms. All sensation ended somewhere around his shoulders. He saw the warriors eating and drinking but he doubted that their lack of abuse extended to any real generosity. He was not disappointed in this expectation.

About noon Larissa arrived. The rest of her guards were with her and slaves led a baggage train of nusks piled with the tents and supplies of the island camp. Apparently, the ceremonies were over and it was time to return to Gasam's army. Ansa felt his heart sink even lower.

The queen dismounted and pointed to Ansa. ''Wash him,'' she commanded. His bonds were loosed and two warriors hauled him to a clear stream that flowed nearby. Efficiently stripping his clothes from him, they gave him a push and he toppled helplessly into the water.

He was unable to use his arms and for a moment almost panicked. Calming himself with the thought that the water couldn't be deep, he managed to get his legs beneath him and find the bottom with his feet. That done, he thrust his head above the surface. The water came just to his collarbones, he was relieved to note. Soon he began to regain feeling in his arms, and the sensation was agony. The Shas-inn stood on the bank laughing, and when he could stand the pain no more he ducked beneath the surface and screamed underwater, where they could take no satisfaction in it. He did this several times before the pain became bear-able. The last time he came up, he saw Larissa sitting on the bank, watching him.

"I want nothing near me that is ugly or offensive," she told him. "There is enough Shasinn in you to keep you acceptable in appearance. A daily washing will take care of the rest."

"I am to be near you?" he said.

"You will not be out of my sight until I turn you over to the king."

"Then I shall suffer in good company," he told her.

She smiled pleasantly toward him. "You are taking this well. I hope you are as spirited when you meet King Gasam."

With his hands working again, he began to scrub at him-self. Oddly, it did not occur to him to try to drown himself. In the first place, it would be futile. The Shasinn would be on him in a second and they probably swam as well as they did everything else save ride and shoot the bow. And he had not given up hope of escape. The way she spoke it was two, perhaps three days' journey to join the king. Much might be accomplished even in that short time.

When he emerged from the stream he was given his trou-sers. All else had been taken. His wrists were bound again, this time before him, and he mounted. The cabo was not his own fine, spirited beast but an elderly, gentle creature, useless for escape even from indifferent riders like the Shas-inn. He scanned the party, looking for the distinctive colors painted on his own cabo's horns. He saw that it was ridden by a scarred warrior, larger and somewhat older than the others. He was no stranger to tough fighting men, but this one looked like a daunting prospect even under favorable conditions. In his current precarious state, overcoming the man would be a futile exercise even if he could get loose from his bonds. He was confident that, once mounted on his own cabo, he could outpace the Shasinn easily.

He thought of Fyana. He had felt uneasy about leaving her alone in the palace. Now he was happy that she was not with him. Her position, uneasy though it was, seemed like paradise compared to his. What would she think when the negotiating party returned without him? What would Floris tell her? He tried to force her from his mind and concentrate on escape.

Before they had ridden far, Larissa reined in beside him. She seemed eager to talk, and considering her hatred of his father and her plans for himself, he could not understand this fascination.

"Are you well?" she asked. It seemed to him a decidedly odd question.

"Under the circumstances I am well enough," he answered. "I am not injured."

"Your bonds are not too tight? I truly do not intend to torment you as we travel."

He flexed his fingers on the pommel of his saddle. "They are not too tight. I would be even more comfortable if you would remove them."

"I cannot be that accommodating. Just remember that you cannot escape and that your fate is sealed." She was silent for a while, then said, with an effort to sound casual, "I have heard about your Canyon lady. And I know of her efforts to heal the king of Gran. How did you come to be traveling with her?"

He sensed something odd in her interest. "I was wandering south and entered Canyon territory, where I met her. She was also planning a journey southward, and she needed an escort. It was a convenient way to travel. She had medicines and healing skills to trade. It was chance that we arrived in the capital just when the king had need of a healer."

"I am prepared to believe that. As you traveled in company, did you see evidence of these healing gifts?"

"Many times," he said. "She can lay hands on a person who is ill and read what is wrong with him. Usually, there is some medicine she can prescribe."

"But she does not heal directly? That is, she cannot touch the sufferer and cure him?"

"She says that is not her gift."

"I see." She pondered a while. When she spoke, it was with uncharacteristic hesitation, as if she were choosing her words with utmost care. "It is said that the Canyoners do not . . . age, I suppose you would say, as do other people. Did you see signs of this when you were among them?"

He was mystified, but he saw no harm in answering. "Truly, it is difficult to judge age among them. The elderly resemble the young in most things save bearing."

"I had heard it was so," she almost whispered, something like eagerness coming through in her voice. "Do you think that this is a part of their healing arts, their mastery of medicines?"

"It could be," he said, as the explanation for her odd behavior began to dawn upon him. Surreptitiously, he glanced at her, looking at the queen in a different light. She had the body of a woman of twenty who had never borne children, although he knew she must be nearly twice that age. She was as well conditioned as a young racing cabo, her tanned body radiant with health. But now he noted the fine webbing of wrinkles around her eyes, the discreet lines in the corners of her mouth. There were streaks of silver in her near-white hair, and he noted that the hand gripping her reins had prominent veins between wrist and knuckles.

Now he understood. This queen, the most beautiful woman in the world, was terrified of advancing age. Legend was full of such people, rulers who were masters of everything save the common enemy of all. Each new wrinkle, each gray hair, was to her a defeat as terrible as a lost battle.

For the first time since the spears were laid upon his shoulders, he felt a glimmering of hope. At last, this fearsome woman had shown a human weakness. He had no idea how he could exploit it, but his predicament would concentrate his thoughts a thousandfold. He would find a way.

The queen dropped the subject, although he suspected that she was eager to speak further of this. The land they were passing through was disrupted, but the devastation was not what Ansa might have expected. Clearly, Gasam had sent many raiding parties through the countryside, but nowhere did he see the sort of wholesale destruction characteristic of lands where armies have fought and passed over. The raiders came here for slaves and provisions. They had not done much burning. He saw few healthy young men or women. The prime human livestock had been culled for other uses. Desperate figures sped into the woods at the approach of the Shasinn riders.

"Why do you disrupt the land so?" Ansa asked her. "Such a conquest will leave a land too poor to pay tribute and the peasants will be unable to feed even themselves."

"That is of little consequence," she said. "Inferior peoples live only at our whim and we tolerate them only so long as they serve and cause no trouble. We have wealth enough and we do not value the things prized by these people who call themselves civilized. They are worthless baubles to us."

"Then why didn't you stay in your islands?" he asked. "There you could have lived happily as warrior tribesmen without troubling people who never did anything to harm you."

She slashed him across the face with her riding whip. She did it almost absently, without malice, as if she were a mistress putting an obstreperous pet animal in its place.

"It is not for you to question the actions of your natural

king. You are his subject and his property, as are all people. It does not bother us that some people starve, because there are too many people as it is. Far more than are useful. We like wilderness better than cities and we do not like farmers.''

He knew that this was somewhat at odds with what he had heard of Larissa, for she was known to take an interest in encouraging the prosperity of their conquests. He decided that she was echoing her husband's sentiments. He felt blood trickle down his face but he knew he could not let this bother him. He was in store for far worse when he got to Gasam's headquarters.

The queen did not set an exhausting pace, so the ride was not as agonizing for Ansa as it might have been. With hands and feet tied, he felt awkward and rode his cabo more like a sack of loot than the superb rider he had been since childhood. When he thought of it, there was no reason why the queen should be eager to return to what was probably a squalid, overcrowded camp surrounding a city that would soon be a charnel house of starvation and disease. There she would have little to do save as an onlooker. That suited him well. He was in no rush to get there either.

The first night, they camped by the road in the courtyard of what had been a substantial villa, now uninhabited save for scavenging animals. The men built fires in the courtyard, using the villa's furniture for kindling. The young warriors found an unmilked she-kagga and brought it into the courtyard, where they proceeded to milk it into a broad wooden bowl. With a small, bronze knife they then nicked a vein in her neck and mingled the blood with an equal quantity of milk.

Larissa sat by a fire in a low, folding chair scavenged from the villa. She gestured for Ansa to come and sit by her. He hobbled to the fire, his steps regulated by a foot of rope between his ankle ties. Awkwardly, he sat. She passed him a skin of wine and he took it with both bound hands.

He glanced toward the young warriors and his stomach lurched when he saw them passing the bowl from one to another, each drinking deep of the mixed milk and blood. He pulled at the wineskin thirstily.

"You find milk and blood repulsive?" she asked, amused.

"It is not to my taste." He drank some more wine. "This is, though."

"We have never been able to understand how foreign people can stand to eat fish. Taste and tabu vary from nation to nation. As for milk and blood, I have never liked it myself. Back on the island, women did not drink it, only warriors, and the junior warriors consumed little else."

"No wonder they have such ferocious dispositions," said Ansa, taking another pull at the wineskin and already feeling the hardships and perils of his journey slipping away in a warm fog. "I would be as vicious if I had to live on that stuff."

"Perhaps that's our secret," she said, laughing. She took back the wineskin and pushed a bowl of food in front of him. While she drank he forced himself not to snatch at the viands. Clumsily he took a flat loaf of bread in his bound hands and wrapped it around some strips of grilled meat. He chewed and swallowed slowly. When it was gone he tried some of the fruit. She passed the wine back to him and soon his spirits were recovering.

"What is your Canyon woman like?" she asked him.

"Young. Beautiful. Her eyes are violet, with green rims."

"Do they really have blue skins? I have never seen anyone of that nation, but like everyone else I've heard rumors."

"Yes, she is blue. Not sky-blue, but the flesh of the Canyoners has a bluish tinge." He wondered whether she would steer the talk toward the subject of prolonging youth.

"Is she otherwise like normal women?"

"How do you mean?"

She gestured toward her own lithe body, sweeping her

fingertips from collarbones to toes. "Like this: breasts and hips, mound, hair, cleft and so on. There are always rumors about women of far nations who are constructed differently: six breasts arranged in rows like an animal, long tails, clefts that run sideways instead of front to back, that sort of thing."

He smiled in fond memory. "No, except for coloration, she is as other women. She has the usual number of everything, all in the usual locations."

She nodded, as if confirming something to herself. "And you say she is young. Are you sure?"

He had been thinking all day how he would respond to this. "She seems so . . ." He forced hesitation into his voice.

"How young?" she urged.

"I have always assumed about my own age, about twenty years, but . . ."

"But?" she said impatiently.

"You remember I said that the main signs of age among them were those of bearing and, I suppose you would say, attitude. Well, sometimes it seems to me that she acts more mature than her seeming age."

Now she leaned forward, her face intent. "Explain."

"She speaks with a measured seriousness I do not expect to hear from a young woman. It is more like the speech of the matrons or even the elder women of my own people. And even among strangers, she receives a deference people usually reserve for great ladies and wise women."

"You were her lover?" she demanded.

"Yes." He saw no point in lying.

"Good, then you have held her naked. Has her flesh the firmness and elasticity of youth?"

"It is smoother than still water, softer than the first down on a baby bird. She is as unlined as an infant."

The queen hissed softly, as if at the memory of something

infinitely precious, long fled. "Does her belly show the marks of childbearing?"

"None at all," he answered.

"They may be able to eradicate the marks," she muttered, as if to herself. Then, to him, "Is her sheath tight?"

For a moment he did not understand. When he did, he saw that there was no humor in her face. This was not bawdy banter. She was deadly serious and desperate to know.

"Very," he answered, truthfully.

"She is like a young virgin?"

Oddly, considering that he was trying to manipulate her, he felt the blood rush to his face. "Not exactly. I mean, she was, well, as you say, tight, but not awkward or . . ." he let it trail off.

"Do not try my patience," she snapped. "You are not speaking to one who even knows how to be embarrassed. So, she has the beauty, the firm body of a young virgin, yet she makes love with the ardency and skill of a mature woman? Surely a handsome boy like you must have experienced a few itchy widows or wives of absent husbands, unless your people are unlike any I ever encountered."

"It is as you say," he admitted. He thought he had better not overdo it, lest she suspect him. "Of course, I cannot say for certain that she is far older than she looks. It is only a matter of behavior and attitude."

She shook her head. "No, no, I think you are right," she said, as if it had been his idea in the first place. "She may well be a woman of my own years in all save looks." Abruptly, she rose, preparing to leave. Before she did, she faced him. "Perhaps, when we meet with my husband, I will ask him not to kill you immediately." She turned and walked toward the villa.

When she had gone inside, when he was alone by the fire, ignored by the warriors, he released a long-pent breath in a deep sigh. Had he prolonged his life? He hoped so. It seemed incredible to him that she could credit his words. Surely, a woman of such penetrating intelligence must know that he was only telling her what she wanted to hear, that he spoke only her own thoughts as if they had been his?

Then he remembered what Fyana had said about the desperate need of the ill to believe that someone has a cure for them and how vulnerable they could be to the manipulation of charlatans. He had sensed a weakness and had played upon it, but now he had to devise a way to use it to his advantage. The mere knowledge of the youth-prolonging capabilities of the Canyoners, false as it was, was not enough to save his neck by itself. This would bear thinking about.

Then another thought occurred to him: *Suppose it was true?*

Their first sight of Huato was from the crest of a hill, where the winding road emerged from rolling country to descend into a river valley. They had expected to find the squalor and destruction of a siege camp. Instead, they beheld something that looked more like a trade fair. Everywhere around the city were bright pavilions. In the distance, to the west, they could see long caravans approaching the city, consisting mostly of unladen nusks. Down the northern road came similar trains, these made up primarily of humpers.

"Oh, wonderful!" cried the queen. "The siege is over and my husband has taken the city!"

"Glory to our king!" shouted the guard, without much spirit. Ansa could tell that they were bitterly disappointed at missing the kill. He knew what the carnival atmosphere meant. He had never participated in a siege, but he had spoken with many warriors who had. Now that the city had fallen, the traders had arrived. They hovered around the fringes of every war like carrion bats and nothing drew them like the fall of a great city. He made a quick count of days in his mind. The queen could not have left the siege more than ten or twelve days before.

"How did so many get here so soon?" he asked. As usual, he rode beside Larissa. They had chatted of inconsequentialities for the remainder of the trip. She seemed friendly, whatever that might mean. "Some of these must have come from as far away as Neva, and I'll wager those humpers are from the Zone."

"Oh, they always come as soon as they hear Gasam has gone to war. They never wait until victory is proclaimed, since he always wins. They wait at a distance, just out of danger, then come flocking in when they hear of the kill. Some of them were here even before I left, selling provisions to the soldiers and buying prisoners. They were willing to run the risk and get favorable prices. And they always hope to be on hand when the enemy falls. Then, soldiers come running out of the city with armloads of loot, willing to sell it for a pittance and run back in to get more."

Even in his perilous situation, Ansa filed away this information. Apparently, even Gasam could not maintain tight discipline in the ecstatic aftermath of a city's fall. Their animals descended the hill and his stomach tightened. Soon he would meet Gasam, a man who had been a demon incarnate to him since earliest childhood. Growing up, it had never occurred to him that he might meet the man before his father met him in battle.

They entered what had been the siege camp, which had now been transformed into a vast market. They saw thousands of men, women and children herded into enclosures, most of them sitting on the ground with stunned faces, all of them haltered by the neck in long trains. At the entrance to each enclosure an auctioneer was taking bids. The people were not being sold individually, but in long coffles of twenty to fifty.

Everywhere, loot stood on the ground in huge piles to be examined by the buyers. It was roughly sorted, so that one heap consisted of fine fabrics, another of fine artworks, a third of perfumes, unguents and incense, and so on. They passed fields of wine jars, herds of cabos and other domestic beasts. In one field, slaves stacked slabs of colorful, beautifully polished marble. They appeared to be the facing stones of palaces or temples. There were casks of dyestuffs and bales of quil hair. The only things missing were precious metals and jewels. These, Ansa surmised, Gasam would keep for himself.

A rumbling crash drew their attention. Atop the city wall, workmen manipulated hammers and bars to topple stone to the ground. Judging by the shattered heap at its base, the wall had already been lowered by many feet.

"It looks as if the king intends to sell off and level the entire city," Ansa said. "But then, as you say, the Shasinn have little use for cities and their inhabitants." She said nothing, but she wore a worried frown. Clearly, she did not like this. They rode into the city. There had been great destruction, but wide roads had been cleared through the rubble to facilitate the systematic looting. Endless trains of prisoners carried burdens out toward the vast auction. Ansa had never heard of a great capital city being auctioned off by the piece, but that seemed to be Gasam's intent.

They found the royal tent set up in the great central plaza. A high platform had been set up before it, and atop the platform stood a simply dressed man, surveying the ongoing process of destruction. His face wore an expression of grim fury. His only mark of distinction was a long Shasinn spear, made entirely of steel. Ansa knew that this was Gasam and, to his shame, he felt his bowels quake within his belly.

When the man caught sight of the little procession making its way into the plaza, the furious expression disappeared and was replaced by a dazzling, white-toothed smile. He bounded down the steps of the platform like a boy rushing to meet his first love. He ran to the cabo and Larissa dived into his arms. He whirled her around two or three times then set her on her feet. The two kissed and embraced passionately. Ansa was astonished at this public display of affection. But then, he reflected, these two cared not at all what others thought.

On first inspection, Gasam did not appear all that fearsome. He looked much like the other Shasinn, all of whom were so similar that they might have been brothers. Since the royal couple were so occupied with each other, he examined the other warriors who lounged about, taking no part in the labor of destruction.

Most striking were the senior Shasinn warriors. They wore their long hair in a number of fashions and they had much of the same grace and comeliness displayed by the junior warriors, but their bodies were scarred and their features bore the indelible stamp of long and hard campaigns, of much slaughter and the brutality of war. The golden men were, he decided, thoroughly frightening.

Some of the others he recognized from his father's descriptions as tribesmen belonging to other island peoples. Besides these, he saw Nevans and Chiwans, plus men from a score of nations, races and peoples he had never encountered before.

At last, the king broke his embrace. "Little queen, if I could only say how I have missed you."

"As I have missed you, my love," she said, breathlessly. Then, seriously: "What do you do here? It looks as if you are destroying the city and scattering its people."

"That is exactly what I am doing." The cloud of fury came over his face once more. "The very thought of this city offends me now. The wretched Mana, whom I will not dignify with the name of king, insulted me as I have never been insulted." He proceeded to tell the tale of King Mana's funeral pyre.

"To be cheated thus of my just vengeance," he fumed, "is intolerable. Therefore, I shall obliterate the very name of this city. I will level it and have the ruins covered with soil and sown with grass. It will make an excellent pasture.''

She stroked his chest, calming him. "But, my love, Sono is now a province of your empire. It must have a capital city.''

"I'll found another. Find me a city in the north and I shall establish a provincial capital there. A city in the north will be more valuable to us anyway.''

"Yes, that is true," she said. The meaning of this exchange escaped Ansa.

The king glanced toward Ansa and his face grew puzzled. "Who is this boy?" Larissa nodded to her guards and two of them loosed his ankle ties and hauled him from his saddle. With a hand beneath each arm, they marched him before Gasam and forced him to his knees, then held him in that position with spears laid upon his shoulders. He forced himself to feel no hope. That would only make the fear worse.

"This is my present to you, my love. An absolutely unique gift. I could have searched the world without finding another such, yet it came to me as if by fate to soothe your just fury at the way this siege has disappointed you.''

"Now I am well and truly mystified," the king said. "What could give me that much joy? Is this some son of Mana's I had not heard about? He does not look like a Sonoan.''

"Far better than that. This is Ansa, eldest son of King Hael.''

Ansa awaited the deathblow, but it did not fall. Gasam made a choking sound, then repeated it. The sound became rhythmic, acquired a voice, and turned into a full-fledged, roaring laugh. Despite the spears, he raised his face to look up and meet Gasam's eyes. He had expected the eyes of a predatory beast, like a longneck, but he was wrong. It was like looking into the sky on a moonless night, a sky somehow devoid of stars. The gulfs he saw there were as black and as deep. He knew then that Gasam was not merely mad. He was something other than human.

"So this is the son of my foster-brother Hael? Greetings, boy."

"Greetings, foster-uncle," Ansa said. At this, Gasam set off on another roaring laugh.

"How shall I kill you? Surely, you shall not die as easily as falls the lot of other men."

"Best you take counsel with your queen, then," Ansa said. "Father always told me that you lacked imagination." He hoped that, if he provoked the man enough, Gasam might forget himself and strike him dead quickly. But, the king just roared with greater mirth. Nothing seemed to kill the good mood his wife's arrival had brought about.

"Spare him a while, my love," said Larissa. "I have certain plans, and, truthfully, is he not worth more to you alive? I beg you, do not kill him too quickly."

His arm around her shoulder, he smiled down upon her. "Could I ever refuse you anything, little queen? Truthfully, every minute I hold him alive will be a minute of hell for his father. If he is slain, Hael will get over it quickly. No, I shall enjoy having him among my possessions."

"I knew you would see the wisdom of it," she said. "We have much to speak of, my king."

"And much to do. But first, little queen, let me take you on a tour of my latest conquest, while some of it still exists." He turned to someone who stood behind Ansa. "Take him to our tent and guard him. He is to come to no harm, especially by his own hand."

There was a grunt of assent from behind Ansa and he was hauled to his feet. The royal couple had already turned away, absorbed in their own concerns. As he was marched toward the tent he realized, to his astonishment, that this time he was not being handled by the Shasinn warriors. His upper arms were pressed against something soft and he glanced to his right, astonished to see not the muscular chest of a warrior but a woman's breasts. He was being marched by a pair of women, and they were women of fearsome aspect. Rubies like tears of blood dangled from the pierced nipples of one, golden hoops from those of the other. They were painted and carved with ornamental scars and from them came a strange, exotic scent.

The tent was divided into several rooms and they took him to one in the rear and seated him, roughly, on a pile of carpets. Then they sat across from him and arranged their weapons across their knees. One carried a short spear, the other an axe with a slender, flexible handle, like that on his stone hatchet. He noted that both weapons were of steel. If these were elite warriors, they were the strangest he could imagine.

"I am Ansa. Who are you? Where are you from?" The two looked at him stonily, then looked at each other, then back to him. "The king did not forbid you to speak to me, did he? What harm can there be in that?" They glared at him for a while and he decided that they did not understand him. Perhaps they were mute.

"You are the king's enemy," said the one with golden rings through nipples and ears. "Why should we want to speak to you?" She spoke a heavily-accented dialect of Southern, her pronunciation blurred by the plug in her lower lip, but he could understand her.

"That's better. You should talk to me because you must be bored by each other. Now, what are your names?"

"I am Stalker," said the one with the golden rings. She nodded toward the one with the rubies. "This is Blood-Drinker."

"These are unusual names," he observed.

"We have no names until we earn them," she said. "We are the king's elite guard of women. We come from the coastal lands to the south of Chiwa, and the nearby islands." He caught a flash of metal in the woman's mouth and wondered what new strangeness this might signify.

"Who are you?" said she of the rubies. "What land do you come from?"

"I am the eldest son of the plains king, Hael. My home is far to the north and east of this place. We are a nation of riders and archers. We roam the wide grasslands as free as the winds and hunt where we please. We are a nation of equals and we acknowledge no one our master."

"Then why did you leave?" asked Stalker.

He loosed a short, bitter laugh. "I have come to regret it. Why do you follow King Gasam?"

"We were raised from childhood to follow a king, the king of Chiwa," said Blood-Drinker. "But he was a false king. Our King Gasam overthrew him and made us his slaves. He took us from the pens and made us his guard, closer to him than his own Shasinn. We learned from him that our destiny is to fight by his side as he conquers the earth."

"He is more than a king," said Stalker. "He is a god."

Ansa knew that they meant it. Their eyes had the flat, intense gleam of the fanatic when they spoke of Gasam. What sort of man, he thought, commands the love and loyalty of such as these?

"What are your special services for him?" Ansa asked. "What do you do that earn you such favor and esteem?"

"We kill!" Stalker said.

"All warriors are expected to kill. Even those Chiwan soldiers out there kill for him."

Blood-Drinker snorted, making her golden rings sway disconcertingly. "They think that is killing! Standing in lines and poking with their spears like parts of a machine. We fight with fury and style. We are overcome by the joy of battle."

"And after the battle," Stalker said, smiling dreamily, "we are given the prisoners to interrogate. They always talk."

Ansa could well believe it. Warriors trained from birth to

withstand torments inflicted by an enemy could have their spirits broken by these demonic creatures. The sheer strangeness of them would prove shattering to men accustomed to think only of other men as warriors.

"And then," Blood-Drinker said, with the same dreamy, inward-looking expression, "at the feast after the battle . . ."

"Quiet!" Stalker hissed, snapping from her own reverie. "That is for us alone, ourselves and the king."

Ansa wondered what new horror this must portend. They were interrupted when a young Shasinn warrior entered the room. He ignored Ansa as Stalker's eyes locked on his with a gleam of lust. Without a word she rose fluidly and they left the room. They did not go far. Within minutes, the sounds of furious coupling came through the walls of cloth. It seemed, Ansa thought, that these people were ferocious in everything they did.

"Perhaps," Blood-Drinker said, "the king will turn you over to us." Apparently the sounds from the next room were having their effect, for her lower body writhed slowly against the carpet. They had stimulated what, to her, were even more pleasant thoughts.

"I do not want to disappoint you," Ansa said, "but King Gasam has expressed an interest in keeping me alive."

"Alive," she purred, "is not the same thing as whole in all your parts." She slid toward him until their knees touched. "Let me see whether there is anything here you would dislike to lose." She hooked a finger behind the drawstring of his trousers and tugged forward. "Ah," she said, looking inside, "here we are." She reached inside, closing her other hand around the hilt of her knife. He was grateful that his hands had been tied before him. He fully intended to break her neck. Just a little closer . . .

"What is this?" The voice came from the room's entrance. Ansa had never thought he might be glad to see

Gasam, but he was. "My orders were to guard him, not to collect trophies from him."

Blood-Drinker blushed like a little girl caught doing something naughty. "I would not have harmed him, my king," she said. "Stalker is being pleasured, and I thought to have a little myself. I would not have drawn blood. I was just enjoying the look on his face."

The king frowned. "If you were not one of my pets, I should punish you."

She prostrated herself on the carpet before him. "Punish me, my king." She sounded as if she longed for such treatment. Ansa noted with interest that even her shapely buttocks were carved with ornamental scars.

"If I gave you all such treatment as you deserve, my whip arm would weary from the labor."

"I will be happy to perform the honors," said Larissa, speaking from behind her husband. Ansa saw a shudder pass through the groveling woman. She truly feared the queen. What could make this creature feel fear?

"No need, little queen," said Gasam. "Surely, the son of Hael needs a little wholesome fright, seeing how gentle you have been with him. He might mistake us for people who care what sort of suffering and maiming he endures."

"I would never make such a mistake," Ansa assured him. "My father has spoken a great deal about what sort of people you are."

"Spoken like a true son of Hael," Gasam said. "He was always such a dutiful boy, always anxious for the approval of the elders. I suppose that comes of being the lowest and most despised of the tribe. There was more woman than man in him. He wanted to be a spirit-speaker, not a warrior!" He laughed loudly, but the mirth seemed forced to Ansa. "How did a puny half-warrior ever become a king? Even king over a wretched band of mongrels like these plainsmen?"

"You've shown no eagerness to fight us," Ansa taunted.

"You never dared an open battle when last my father took his army into Neva to drive you out. He went into the city alone, and he defeated you in hand-to-hand combat before you dived into the bay to escape." Ansa had heard this story for so many years that he was sick of it, but now he felt great satisfaction in hurling it at Gasam. He had never gotten on well with his father, but he was proud of him now. Ansa wished there were some way he could tell him so.

"Let me cut him, my king!" hissed Blood-Drinker. "I will eat his . . ." Gently, Gasam placed the sole of a bare foot against the back of her head and forced her mouth against the carpet, silencing her.

"Quiet, little longneck. These things are for me to decide." The king stepped before Ansa and squatted until the two were at eye level. Ansa was gratified to hear the faintest of popping sounds from the king's knees. He, too, was aging. There were silver streaks in the lustrous bronze of his hair.

"You just do not understand, do you, boy? You are too young to understand what real hatred is. You certainly haven't learned how to feel true fear. I shall teach you. You have had the easy life of a petty prince. What lies between Hael and me is something beyond your experience, so do not presume to speak of it. I have determined when he is to die and how. It is just a part of my plan to bring the world beneath my heel and no action of his will make me alter my plan. He will not trick me into striking at him precipitously."

He reached forth and stroked Ansa's face softly, with the backs of his fingers, like a man gentling a prized but high-strung animal.

"You see," he went on, "there is so much hatred stored up between us that the passage of mere years affects it not at all. I will slay him with as much joy many years from now as I would have when he was seven years old. Hatred like this is not to be understood by ordinary men, and you are ordinary, though scarcely yet a man." He continued to stroke Ansa's face. "Yet you are Hael's son, and you cannot imagine what joy it gives me to have you in my hands." He rose then, and walked out to join his queen.

Blood-Drinker crawled back to her post and Ansa, despairing, rolled to his side and tried to rest. He knew that he had a terrible ordeal ahead of him. A while later, Stalker came in. She was covered with sweat and smelled strongly of her recent activities. Despite himself, Ansa felt his flesh rising and he was flooded with memories of Fyana. He pretended to sleep as the two women conversed in low voices. Eventually, he did sleep.

He woke hearing voices. They belonged to Gasam and Larissa. They spoke in conversational tones, as if they did not care who heard them. He glanced through slitted eyes at his guards. They sat as before, but their heads were sunk forward and their breathing was that of sleep. He had no doubt that they would wake instantly at any move on his part. He strained his ears to hear the conversation in the next room.

"This is a fantasy, my love," Gasam said. "I have told you before that you brood on this matter too much."

"It is no fantasy!" she insisted. "I think these Canyoners have the secret and I mean to wrest it from them."

"Is beauty so much?" the king asked. "Is power not far more wonderful?"

"Power is everything, my love, you have taught me that. But the loss of beauty is just the outer manifestation of an inner deterioration that destroys everything within us, including our grip upon power. Tell me truthfully: can you hurl the spear as far now as when you were twenty? Can you run all day without tiring, as you could then?"

"Very nearly," he said, uncomfortably.

"Well your cast will grow shorter each year from now on. And you will breathe hard when you run. All too soon, it will be as much as you can do to keep from puffing when you walk. Where will the respect of your warriors be then, when their all-conquering god-king is an old man, like other old men?''

''By the time I have reached such a pass I will be unquestioned king of the world. None will dare show me disrespect!''

''My husband,'' she said pitilessly, ''you expected to be king of the world long ere *now*. When we began, we had no idea how vast the world was. There are lands beyond Hael's kingdom, perhaps as much more as the lands we know already. How many more years to conquer them? The thought makes me weep as it is!''

''Once I have taken the plains and settled with Hael,'' the king said, ''then I can march back westward over the mountains, and Omia will fall into my hands like ripe fruit. Then I will have Neva surrounded and Neva must fall as well. I will have all the world that matters, and I will be content.''

''My love,'' she said chidingly, ''you will never be content and neither shall I and we both know it. Not as long as there breathes one human being who does not acknowledge you king and god. If there are lands beyond you must go there and break them to your yoke.''

She had stated her case baldly. Now her voice became low, intimate. ''But none of this need matter to us. The Canyoners have the secret. What care we how long the work of conquest takes if we can be young throughout life?''

''Well,'' Gasam said after a pause, ''it cannot hurt to look into the matter. After all, in the northern campaign we will pass near the Canyon. It might not be such a bad idea to secure the Canyon itself.''

Ansa failed to understand the meaning of this. Surely, their next conquest was to be Gran? Why would they march northward, into the desert?

''But there is a Canyon woman nearer than that, one skilled in their arts,'' she said. ''If she knows that we have her lover, perhaps she will come here. I will find out whatever she knows."

"But she may not come," Gasam said. "What is this boy to her? A lover? He is not of her race, and who ever heard of the Canyoners looking outside their own people for mates?"

"I will let it be known that we merely hold him as hostage," Larissa said. "And that I am ill and will reward her richly to come and treat me. Perhaps she will come here hoping to buy him from us."

Gasam yawned. "Maybe. And if not, I'll take all the Canyoners you want, possibly the lot of them, when we march north to seize the steel mine. The crater is only a few days' travel from the Canyon."

Ansa felt as if all the blood had congealed in his veins. They knew where the steel mine was! If they marched soon, there was nothing at all to prevent them from seizing it. He broke into a sweat of dread at the thought of Gasam commanding most of the world's steel. What could he do? When at length he slept, he was plunged into a sea of nightmares.

NINETEEN

Fyana waited, grim-faced. She had left the queen hours earlier, closeted with her advisers. The king was well on his way to recovery now. He was able to sit up and speak, although he tired easily. She was tired herself. She sat back in her chair and sighed. She longed to be away from this place. The queen had spoken of great rewards, but the king was not as intelligent as his wife. Fyana knew that, as soon as he had his strength back, whatever gratitude he might have felt toward her would dissolve in mortification. It would have been another matter had she just been able to administer a potion to cure him instantly and without discomfort. The treatment had been long, arduous and very undignified. She felt sorry for the stablemen who had been her assistants. He might execute them for laying profane hands upon his sacred, kingly person.

When the diplomatic party had returned, her heart had leapt with joy. When she saw that Ansa was not among them, it had plunged into despair. She had questioned members of the party about him, and had received no straight answers. She feared the worst. She would have left already to go find him, but she had promised the queen one last service. She opened her eyes as the door opened.

"Lady Fyana?" It was Lord Floris, come from the queen's council chamber.

"It is good of you to come speak with me," Fyana said. "Please be seated."

Floris took a chair. "The queen wishes me to speak with you, so I shall," he said, haughtily. "Please be brief." He winced as if at a sudden pain and his face was puzzled.

"Are you all right?" she asked. "Please take some wine."

"It is nothing," he said. He poured wine anyway. She watched him drink. "Now, what is it?"

"I want to know about Ansa. Tell me what happened to him."

"The boy left the mission," he said, impatiently. He winced again, and his hand went to his side. "He took a— a notion to go watch the siege, I suppose. He rode off with that dreadful woman." His face paled and a line of sweat-beads appeared upon his brow.

"Tell me what happened to Ansa," she said.

"I just—that is, well, he disappeared one day. Rode off to hunt with the queen. She—she, I, what have you done to me?" He glared at the wine cup. "Have you poisoned me?"

"The truth-drug does not act that fast," she told him. "I gave it to the queen and she administered it to you in the council chamber, an hour ago. Now tell me, what happened to Ansa?"

His hands formed claws on the table with his effort to resist, but he spoke. "She gulled him into riding onto the mainland with her, where her safe-conduct was not valid. There she took him prisoner. She knows who he is and took him to Gasam."

"And you could have warned him, but did not?"

"That is so. What was the boy to me?"

"What, indeed? Did you send the assassins to kill him here in the city?"

"I did."

"And would have done the same to me, except for the Bamen guards and the care I took with what I ate and drank. I did not fail to notice the poisons that appeared almost every day."

He glared hatred, but he was almost paralyzed now. "What do you want, witch?"

"I want the answer to two more questions. Did you treat treasonously with Queen Larissa?"

"We came to an understanding. I do not consider it treason to guarantee what is mine by right."

"That is one question, and you can debate the nuances of treason with your sovereigns. As for the others, did you poison the king?"

"Yes. The throne is—" He stopped when a door opened.

"That is enough," Queen Masila said. "I will continue the interrogation from here on."

Fyana rose. "He will be able to answer questions for another two hours or so. Then, if the antidote is not administered, he will die from paralysis of the lungs." She handed the queen a small vial. "This is the antidote. I would not bother if I were you, but the choice is yours."

"I cannot thank you enough," said Masila.

"Don't bother. You have given me a generous reward. Now I just want my cabo and a safe-conduct to the border. I mean to get Ansa back." She nodded toward the impotent Floris. "He may not be acting alone. It would not be good for you if I were to come to grief within your borders. King Hael would learn of it, and he would come visiting to find out what happened to his son on the Isle of Sorrow, and why I was prevented from going to him."

The queen's face was flushed, but she spoke steadily. "You shall have an escort of Bamen until you reach the Isle of Sorrow. Now, go with my blessing, before your arrogance causes me to withdraw it.''

Without bowing, Fyana turned and left the room. Then the queen turned back to Lord Floris and the old man's eyes filled with fear.

It was night when she rode within sight of the city. Many fires burned on the plain, others within the city, although these appeared to be bonfires rather than burning buildings. She had heard from fleeing refugees of the fall of the city. The last she had spoken to had related with awe a tale of King Gasam's almost whimsical behavior in showing relative mildness toward the surrendered soldiers while enslaving the noncombatants and utterly destroying the city itself. Fyana sensed that there was something more than mere insanity behind this, although she could not guess what it might be.

The sight before her caused her heart to shrink within her. Love and desperation had driven her this far, but what could she do now? Down there license and fury ruled, where men reveled in the unrestrained destructiveness of war. What chance had a lone woman of accomplishing anything? Could she even live long enough to find Ansa?

She closed her eyes and took a deep breath, forcing herself to calm, making her heart beat more slowly. Her fears, however well-founded, would do her no good now. Gasam and Larissa would want to keep Ansa close, if he were still alive. She had but to find out where the royal couple abode, and nearby she would find Ansa. She opened her eyes. There was no sense wasting time here. She nudged her cabo and it began to amble toward the fires.

A hail from an outer picket halted her as she neared the city. A soldier approached her bearing a torch. He was a short man who wore a white kilt and a cuirass of laced bone. His helmet of hardened leather bristled with stubby spikes.

"Who are you?" the soldier asked.

"Lady Fyana of the Canyon. I have come to confer with your queen." She had decided that she might as well brazen it out.

The man gaped. "The queen? Wait here." He walked back toward the picket line. She waited nervously. Everywhere she could hear disturbing sounds: sobs, wails and occasional screams. After what seemed to her an interminable wait, the guard returned with a man who wore finer armor and a bronze helmet.

"What is your business here?" the officer asked her.

"I have come to see Queen Larissa. It is on a matter about which you need not concern yourself." The man had the look of a professional soldier and she hoped a show of arrogance would be enough to overawe him. A haughty aristocrat might not buy it.

"This camp is a dangerous place at night, madame," he said, with cautious respect. "Some of the soldiers get carried away with their celebrating when their betters cannot keep an eye on them. Best you should abide here until morning. They know better than to misbehave by daylight."

"Yet I must go to the queen immediately," she said, afraid that her nerve might desert her if she waited longer and thinking: *Misbehave!* What a word for what they must be doing! "Surely, captain, you can provide me with an escort. I am certain that there will be no—*misbehavior*—near the royal quarters."

"Well," he said, "I'll see who I can round up." He spoke with the exasperation of a functionary called upon to do something beyond his customary duty. It amazed her that he did not think to challenge her right to be here. Perhaps the very mention of their queen paralyzed these men's ability to think.

A few minutes later, she was walking her cabo through the nightmarish camp. Everywhere, she encountered slave pens, which were the source of most of the sounds. She

could see bodies in convulsive movement, dimly illuminated by distant fires. Drunken soldiers wandered among
the pens. Whenever any of these strayed too close, they
were warned away by her four guards. The guards themselves were surly, probably resenting missing out on the
revelry.

They were not the only ones left out of the celebration.
As they drew nearer the walls, she saw other sentries posted
around great heaps of loot. She heard the sounds of livestock and smelled a sharp scent of blood. The fighting was
long over. She hoped that it came from animals being
slaughtered to feed the army.

They passed through walls that were little more than heaps
of rubble. Beyond lay a city in ruins. Shadowy forms lurked
among the buildings and the darkened streets. Were these
soldiers? Or were they looters who lurked in the cellars of
the ruined city and came out at night to scavenge off the
carcass of their former home? Whatever they did, they were
quiet about it. In contrast to the plain outside, the city was
cloaked in silence. For most of the trek, the torches borne
by the guards provided the only light she saw. Then they
reached the great plaza.

Several bonfires burned around the periphery of the
square, and in its center prisoners toiled by torchlight, de-
molishing a huge building. Apparently, the king deemed
this task important enough to prosecute day and night. She
was guided to a cluster of large tents on one side of the
plaza. Her escort halted before the largest. A tall Shasinn
came forward and dismissed the soldiers with a casual wave
of his hand.

"Who are you?" he asked. This was the first Shasinn she
had seen at close hand. In the ruddy light of a nearby fire
he looked like a bronze statue, his long hair tumbling unbound over his shoulders.

"I am Lady Fyana of the Canyon. I have come to see
Queen Larissa."

He eyed her sceptically. "I can promise you that she has no wish to see you at this hour. Wait here by one of the fires. The city is a bad place at night, but you will be safe here. The sun will rise soon."

"I thank you. Is there a place where I may water my cabo?" She patted the animal's neck and it made a soft grunt of contentment. The smell of blood had upset it, but now it was over the fright.

"There is a working fountain over there." He pointed to a dim area near one of the corners of the plaza. He turned and walked away without further words.

She walked the cabo to the fountain, noting that the nearby Shasinn paid her little heed. They were careful to spare no attention for their racial inferiors, a fact for which she was grateful at that moment. She realized that in the uncertain light they could not judge the color of her skin and eyes. They would have shown more interest if they had seen that she was blue.

She watered the animal and tethered it to a nearby post while she washed herself as best she could without undressing. She wanted to be as presentable as possible in the morning, when she would confront Gasam and Larissa. Her ablutions finished, she sat on the edge of the fountain and pondered her next move. Where was Ansa? The most likely place was here among the royal tents, perhaps in Gasam's own tent. But that was surrounded by alert warriors and she would have no chance to approach it. Or he might be locked in some cellar in the city. If so, she had no way to find him.

She walked the cabo to a place near one of the smaller fires and unsaddled it. The plaza around the fire was littered with sleeping forms, but a few wakeful warriors sitting near the fire blinked at her without great interest. Their features bore the stamp of exhaustion and she knew she had nothing to fear from them. They were not Shasinn, but members of some race she did not recognize. Whatever ferocity they possessed had been sated in the battle, slaughter and rapine of the preceding days.

She spread her blankets on the pavement and lay down upon them, her head pillowed on her saddle. An odd stillness reigned in this place. She heard low voices in conversation, the crackle of flames and, occasionally, the rumble of another stone tumbling from the big building. That was all. She began to compose herself for the trial ahead. Gasam and Larissa were not as other people, so she forced all preconceptions from her mind. She would accept what she saw and heard and would act only upon such direct evidence. Above all, she must be attuned to what they would want from her. She wanted Ansa free, and she had little to trade save her slight skills and whatever they *believed* she might accomplish for them. She reached far back into her reserves of knowledge and instinct, calling up every bit of training she possessed to meet this challenge. She would need each tiniest particle of her ability to read human beings, to seek out what was amiss with them, what they needed and what they wanted. Save for her ability to read the maladies of the human body by touch, she had no mystical skills, no magic. But the people of the Canyon had a reputation, and belief could be a weapon. In time, she slept.

The sounds of the stirring camp woke her in the pearly light of earliest dawn. There were smells of cooking in the air and she sat up, rubbing her eyes. In the growing light she could begin to appreciate the devastation that surrounded her. Most of the nearby buildings were little more than rubble, and it was clear that they had not been destroyed in the fighting. It was true, then, that the mad king was methodically destroying what was, after all, his own city. She rose and went to the fountain. Others were there as well, both warriors and slaves, and as she splashed her face and cleared her eyes she drew many more curious stares than she had the night before. The distinctive Canyon physiognomy was only appreciable in daylight.

When she was as presentable as she could make herself, she returned to her blankets and bundled them. She thought of saddling her cabo in case she should have to make a fast escape, but she decided not to. It would look suspicious and she had resolved to leave with Ansa, or not at all. Instead, she took a small rolled carpet from among her belongings and carried it to the royal tent. A dozen paces before the entrance of the tent, just beyond the ring of guards, she spread the carpet. It was thick, colorful and lavishly embroidered. Facing the tent's entrance, she crossed her ankles and sat, arranging her robes about her for maximum dignity. Then she folded her hands in her lap and waited.

Slaves began to file into the tent. Some carried basins of water, pitchers and towels. Others bore trays of food. The morning ritual had begun. Moving her head as little as possible, Fyana sought any evidence that might be of aid. Toward the edge of the plaza, near the line of ruinous buildings, she saw a line of tethered cabos. These, she guessed, would belong to the queen and her guard. One particular animal drew her attention. Its horns were painted in colors she knew. It was Ansa's. She quaked internally at this first evidence of his presence.

Near the entrance of the tent, under its awning, something else caught her eye. It was a pile of gear, and from it she saw protruding the upper limb of a cased bow. She recognized its deeply-curved shape. It was Ansa's great plains bow. With it she now saw his quiver and arrows and his long sword. He was here. He might even be alive.

A woman emerged from the tent. Her face wore a puzzled frown. Apparently, someone had told her that she had a visitor. Fyana began to read her as she had never read anyone in her life. She had seconds to come to a judgment she would have preferred to spend days making. She had to know how to react to this woman. As the queen's eyes widened, Fyana studied her adornment, often a simple guide to the person within. Queen Larissa, unlike her counterparts in other lands, did not dress elaborately. In fact, she barely dressed at all, save for a loincloth of beautiful fabric and some ornaments, and it was not because she was a simple savage. The woman simply did not define herself in terms of royal trappings. Instead, she was obsessed with her own beauty. And beauty, Fyana had to admit, was one thing the queen had. Even with her present look of stunned consternation, she was the most dazzling, radiant creature Fyana had ever beheld. She forced herself to look beyond the beauty.

With her specialized knowledge and skill, she made a more astute analysis than any man could have. She saw instantly the subtle signs of age. The queen was not close enough for her to discern wrinkles, but she knew they would be there. The tone of skin and muscle, the subtleties of stance and movement, the slightly dulled sheen of the hair, all these added up. Physically, the queen was superbly conditioned animal, but the animal was past its prime. The long, slow, inevitable decline had set in.

All this Fyana read before Larissa made a single step toward her. Now it was time to apply these things to the woman's inner self. Fyana was distracted by the queen's look of utter astonishment and she could not imagine what this portended. It could wait. Undoubtedly, the queen's first words would inform her.

Larissa was vain and she was famous for one other thing: her devotion to the king. If she worried about her own decline, perhaps she worried doubly about his. Their insane ambition to rule the world was a time-consuming process. She would see time as their enemy—time and age. There might be something here—something she could use to advantage. And still the woman wore that look of dismay, something almost akin to awe and fear.

Gracefully, Fyana rose from her cross-legged sitting posture. She did this as she had been trained in childhood, without using her hands and without lurching forward awkwardly. She rose with her spine straight, using only the muscles of her thighs. In her voluminous robes, she almost seemed to levitate. She saw that the queen was studying her as closely, and this simple gesture seemed to impress the woman, for whatever reason. Fyana bowed.

"Queen Larissa, I am Lady Fyana, of the Canyon."

"How did you get here so soon?" the queen asked, wide-eyed. "How could you have known? I sent the messenger only two days ago!"

Fyana's mind worked fast. The queen must mean that she had sent a messenger to summon Fyana. She attributed this sudden appearance to some uncanny precognitive ability on the Canyoner's part. That was useful. But why had she wanted to summon her? Clearly, she was not ill. Perhaps the king was.

"I needed no messenger to bring me hither," Fyana said, deliberately ambiguous. "We have things to discuss."

"Things?" Larissa said, clearly at a loss for words. From the astonished looks on the faces of all who stood around, the queen was seldom if ever so at a loss. "Yes, of course. We must talk."

"What is this?" It was a man's voice, deep and booming. Fyana glanced past Larissa and saw a tall Shasinn emerge from the tent, grasping a long spear made entirely of steel. This was Gasam, then. He was as magnificent a specimen as his queen. No wonder these two did not consider themselves to be as other people.

"This is Lady Fyana of the Canyon," Larissa said, sounding almost dazed. "I sent for her."

"So you did." The king came forward and stood by his queen, an arm draped casually over her shoulder. Plainly, the king was neither ill nor injured, not physically, at any rate. His blue eyes held great power, but little humanity. She knew that, if she was to accomplish anything here, she would have to work through the queen.

"She was quick," the king added.

"I have—ways of knowing when I am needed." The queen looked utterly convinced. The king looked sceptical. He also looked somewhat amused, but Fyana knew that people often adopted such poses to cover their confusion. The warriors who lounged about relaxed. Whatever odd mood had come over the queen, their king was not over-awed by this strange person.

"Come inside, we will talk there," Larissa said. "And welcome, Lady Fyana."

"I must see to some army matters," the king said. "Entertain our guest and I will join you later." He gave Larissa a bemused look, as if he, too, was puzzled by her strange behavior.

"Come with me," Larissa said, taking Fyana's hand. Inside the tent they sat on cushions, the queen still holding her hand. She noted that Larissa was taking surreptitious glances at its back, as if trying to read something there.

"When did you arrive?" Larissa asked.

"Last night, after dark."

"And no one came to tell me?" She glared outside, as if looking for someone to punish for this affront.

"No one here knew me, and they knew better than to wake you," she said. "You could not have left word to expect me so soon."

"Yes, but surely someone as distinguished as you . . ."

"My color is difficult to judge after dark," Fyana said.

Larissa reached out and stroked her face. "It is true. You really are blue." She almost whispered the words. Then she all but shook herself, seeking to regain her composure. "Yes. Well, so you are here. How you know to come I cannot imagine, but you Canyoners are known for mystical powers. It is for one of those that I desired consultation. I am told that you can—what is the word?—judge health by touch. Is this true?"

"The word is diagnose. Yes, I have that skill. Do you wish me to read your state of health?"

"Please."

Fyana reached forth and laid her fingertips upon Larissa's brow. The queen tensed and closed her eyes, as if expecting pain or some other unpleasant sensation.

"Just relax. Try to think of nothing." Fyana needed only a few seconds. She took her hand away. "I have seldom encountered anyone as healthy as you, certainly never anyone your age." She saw the tiniest wince in the fan of faint wrinkles around Larissa's eyes.

"And that is another thing we must speak of," said the queen. "What is your true age?"

Fyana's mind spun. Not just age, but *true* age? Then the queen thought there was some question.

"We do not count years in the Canyon." Larissa's eyes grew hooded as she regained her poise. *She thinks I am prevaricating.*

"As well you might not. Truly, it seems that your years must be of little account to you."

Fyana thought of the way Larissa had held her hand, glancing at its back. An easy way to judge the age of a woman who was otherwise youthful-looking. *She thinks I am old! She thinks this is my secret!* Fyana let out a long sigh and looked down to cover her sense of triumph. Now she knew what to do. The queen misunderstood.

"You must be fatigued after such a ride. Allow me to offer you something." She clapped her hands and slaves scurried to do her bidding. Soon they were surrounded by trays of delicacies somehow salvaged from the ruined city. Larissa observed the customs of hospitality and did not press Fyana as the Canyoner ate, slowly. She was grateful for the chance to map out her strategy. When she was finished she raised her face and looked the queen straight in the eyes.

"You want something," Fyana said, "and I want something."

"What is it you want? Name it and it is yours."

"First, let us discuss your needs." As the queen before her, now Fyana reached forth and stroked a cheek, dusted with near-invisible down, touched a shoulder. "You are the most beautiful woman I have ever seen, but we both know that beauty fades."

"It is not just beauty," Larissa said, "nor even health. It is *life*! There is never enough of it. Our great work is well commenced, but already my husband and I are showing the marks of time. Once, all of our lives stretched before us, and it seemed as if there would be plenty of time to bring about our destiny. Now, I am not so sure." She spoke the words in a rush, as if she feared that her husband would return before she could finish. As if these were words of which he would not approve.

"And with your own loss of youth and vigor," Fyana said, now confident that she knew the woman's mind, "you fear that you will lose the loyalty of your subjects. They serve so fanatically, even those that were enemies once, because they can see the two of you before them, their living god and goddess."

"Yes," Larissa almost whispered.

"Suppose I was to tell you that what you wish cannot be done, that it is a matter of blood, something that we Canyoners cannot share with strangers?"

The queen looked up, the blood coming to her face. "I would not believe you. You people of the Canyon are known for your skills with medicines, with healing. And you are the only people in the world able to combat the effects of age. It is your mastery of medicine that makes this possible, not your pedigree." She would not be gainsaid. She *needed* to believe.

"Very well," Fyana said, as if forced to admit the truth. "What if I were to tell you that it is no easy procedure, that it involves a long and arduous treatment?"

"I can endure anything!" Larissa insisted. "As can my

husband. You do not speak here to decadent, palace-bred aristocrats. The mainlanders call us barbarians and we are. We have the strength and endurance to prove it.''

''I told you that I want something from you.''

''Name it!'' Larissa said.

''I want Ansa. Give him to me.''

A look of distress crossed the beautiful face. This, Fyana thought, must be a new experience to this woman, who was so accustomed to having her way.

''There—there are other considerations. He means some- thing very special to us. Ask anything else of me.'' She sounded as if she were speaking of a beloved child.

''Ansa. There is nothing else I want from you. Where is he?''

''Anything else,'' Larissa said again.

''Then we have nothing more to discuss.'' Fyana stood, wondering if she would survive the next few seconds.

''Sit down,'' the queen said, as if granting this conces- sion caused her severe pain. She clapped her hands and called toward the back of the tent. ''Bring the prisoner.''

Two women came in, hauling Ansa between them. So intense was her relief at finding him alive that Fyana spared no attention for the women's bizarre appearance. This camp was full of strange sights. Whatever torments had been in- flicted upon him, the worst must not have been physical for he seemed healthy enough, if somewhat wan and haggard.

He managed a smile. ''I expected you yesterday.''

Larissa looked back and forth between them, as if she thought he meant it. That was all to the good as far as Fyana was concerned. She felt like slapping him for falling into a trap like this.

''I have come for you.''

He looked at Larissa. ''You would trade for so rare a prize as me?''

''That is yet to be decided,'' Larissa said. ''But it is not beyond question.''

"Yes it is." It was Gasam. He stood in the entrance of the tent, displeasure on his face. "The son of Hael is mine, and I mean to keep him."

"We do not need the boy," Larissa said. "You will kill Hael and take his kingdom at your pleasure."

"And just now it is my pleasure to have the boy with me. It will give Hael great anguish to know I have his son, and that pleases me greatly."

"There are things that would please *me* even more," said Larissa, glaring at him. He looked shocked. Fyana decided that this was the first time the queen had ever defied him.

"Do you think I would not trade this youth if I truly believed this woman could restore us to our youth?" Now he smiled at her indulgently. "You know I would never deny you that, my love. But this woman is lying. You are allowing your hope to cloud your good judgment. Think of it: If these Canyoners could truly make people young again, why are they not the richest people in the world? What aged king would not give half his treasury for such a thing? And yet her people live in the midst of a desert, in obscure and squalid villages."

"We do not value wealth," Fyana said.

"Why should people who can live forever need wealth?" Larissa asserted.

First prolonged youth, Fyana thought, and now immortality. What would this queen expect next? At least Larissa was taking her part.

"Falsehoods and mummery," Gasam insisted. "What do any of us know of the Canyon save travelers' tales and this woman's lies?"

"And if I can prove it?" Fyana said.

For a moment Gasam was nonplussed. "How would you do this?"

"I will have to leave for a while. There are things I must gather out in the countryside. I will need help, a servant who can ride."

"You will have as many as you wish," Larissa said. "And you must have an armed escort. The countryside is not yet fully pacified." She looked at her husband as if daring him to forbid this.

Gasam shrugged. "It can do no harm and should put an end to this foolishness. And, woman," he turned his fathomless gaze upon Fyana, "if after all this you disappoint my queen, you shall die."

She forced herself to show no fear. "Neither of you will be disappointed." She rose. "I will be back probably late in the afternoon." Ansa stared at her dumbfounded. At least he was keeping his mouth shut. These people seemed to have little toleration for taunting.

The queen went outside with her. She spoke brief commands, and servants and warriors scurried to do her bidding. While the preparations were made she spoke quietly to Fyana, as if the two of them were coconspirators.

"Be easy. I will calm the king's hostility. Just make this good. If you can perform as you say, I will exalt you above all others save my husband and myself. I will restore Ansa to you. He is nothing to me, and neither is Hael, for that matter. But only I can control Gasam. Remember that."

Her escort arrived, four young Shasinn on rather gentle-seeming cabos. A short, swarthy man approached the tent, leading another mount. He had the impassive face of a slave and the gnarled thighs of a lifelong rider.

"This slave was a stableman for the late king of this land," Larissa said. "He will render you any assistance you require."

"Excellent. The warriors may stay at a distance and keep watch, but the slave is to attend me closely. He must do everything I tell him to, exactly as I instruct. He must be made to understand this."

The queen turned to the slave. "If you deviate from Lady Fyana's instructions in the slightest degree, your death will not be an easy one." The slave bowed. Like her husband,

Fyana reflected, Larissa had a single answer for all questions.

"I will await your return," the queen said.

Fyana shook her head. "It will not be necessary. After I return, I will still need a few hours of preparation. I will not be ready to begin until night."

"As you will. Inform me when you are ready." The queen returned to the interior of the tent.

Fyana went to her cabo and the slave helped her saddle it. She was pleased to note that it had been given fodder. Apparently, prisoners had been detailed to feed all the animals in the square. She mounted and rode for the nearest gate, followed by her escort.

Thus far, all had gone well, better than she might have hoped. She foresaw no difficulties in the next few hours. It was the final stage of her plan that might very well prove fatal, but she could concoct no better plan, so she refused to worry about it. She would succeed or she would die, and she knew how to ensure that her death would be quick.

In the countryside, she began to gather herbs, leaves and minerals. None of them had any medicinal significance. She did not even recognize some of the plants, but she made a great and intricate ceremony of gathering each item. The guards watched with interest for a while, then they grew bored and looked elsewhere, talking among themselves in quiet voices.

The slave followed her instructions attentively, speaking only an occasional, muttered, "Yes, mistress." Clearly, he took the queen's threat very seriously. By midafternoon, Fyana was convinced that he would do exactly as she instructed from now on.

"We are finished here," she announced. With her gatherings packed up, they rode back to the city. When they were back in the square she turned to the guards. "You are dismissed." As she had hoped, they rode away. They had been assigned to escort her in the countryside, not to guard her in the city. "Come with me," she told the slave.

A hundred paces from the royal tent, she had the slave build a small fire and she began her "preparations." She clipped and chopped herbs, she pounded minerals to powder, she burned and mixed. Throughout, she kept up a meaningless chanting. Always, she kept an eye on the royal tent. Once, Gasam came out and stared at her disdainfully. Once, Larissa emerged, looking her way with hope.

Eventually, both came out together. After glancing her way, they walked away on some mission of their own. Fyana had been waiting for this. The Shasinn, like her own Canyoners, were an outdoor people who did not like to stay beneath cover for long. She would have been content to have Gasam away. The absence of both was even better. She made herself wait for several minutes. Then she rose and pointed to the basket of jumbled plant and mineral matter that lay on the pavement beside her.

"Pick that up and come with me." As the man did so she took her reins and led her cabo to the tent. She stopped in the shade of its awning.

"Put that down," she said. The man did so. She glanced around. No one was paying them any special attention. She saw Ansa's cabo still picketed with the others and she pointed at it. "You see that cabo with its horns painted green and gold? Bring it here." Without a word, the man obeyed. When he was back, she pointed to the pile of Ansa's belongings and weapons. "Saddle it and load those things on it."

When it was done she mounted her own cabo and took the reins of the other in her hand. "Very good," she told the slave, "you may go now." He walked away.

She closed her eyes and took a deep breath, then let it out slowly, trying to quiet her heart, which felt as if it were about to burst. She opened her eyes. Now she would win or die.

TWENTY

Ansa stirred uneasily. What was Fyana up to? He had tried to put on a nonchalant air, but he had been stunned when he realized that she had come for him. She must have come as soon as she knew he had not returned from the island. She had not waited for Larissa's summons. At least he had been able to eavesdrop on the talk out in the main room, before he was dragged out to confront her. He had had time to compose himself. There was still enough of the young warrior in him left to feel horror at appearing foolish before his enemies.

She actually seemed confident that she could convince Gasam of her powers, that she could truly restore youth. Not for the first time, the thought came to him: *Suppose it is true?*

Now he stretched, working the kinks out of his legs. They were unbound, for no one worried that he could outrun the Shasinn. His hands were bound before him and he flexed the fingers, keeping them from stiffening. He eyed his guards with distaste. The ones on duty now were dour-faced, older women who had no interest in speaking with him. One held a spear, the other an axe. Both were near-somnolent with boredom. Their heads jerked up at a commotion and a scream from without.

"Ansa!" The voice was, unmistakably, Fyana's.

The two women scrambled to their feet but Ansa was quicker. He snatched the axe with his bound hands and kneed the woman in the chin, knocking her back against the tent wall. Something bulky was muscling its way toward the back of the tent and the other woman cocked her arm to cast her spear. Through the opening separating his room from the main part of the tent, he was astonished to see Fyana, mounted on a cabo and leading another. With the flat of the axe, he swatted the other woman alongside the head, dropping her unconscious before she could complete her cast.

He rushed into the main room, grasped the pommel of his saddle with his bound hands and swung smoothly astride. Fyana drew a long knife and slashed his bonds.

"Ride!" she yelled at him.

He whirled the cabo neatly and bolted for the entrance, with Fyana close at his heels. He pounded for the main gate, and there he saw Gasam and Larissa, not twenty paces away. The king raised his spear and whirled it back past his shoulder for a cast, moving as fast as any man Ansa had ever seen. Ansa urged the beast forward and whipped his longsword from its sheath. He whirled the long blade in a hissing circle even as Gasam's arm rocked forward. At the last possible instant, Gasam turned the offensive hurl into a defense, twirling the great steel weapon by its hand-grip to block the descending sword. Ansa would not have believed a human wrist could be powerful enough to do such a thing.

Even so, the defense was not quite perfect. Sword rang on spear, raising sparks as it slid down the obliquely held blade to bite into Gasam's face and jaw, then down to nick the collarbone. The king fell back with a strangled cry and Larissa threw herself across him as Ansa tried for another blow.

"No time!" Fyana cried. "Ride!"

All over the square, warriors were emerging from their stunned stupor. In a moment, he would be bristling with Shasinn spears. Gracefully, Ansa leaned from the saddle and grasped Larissa's long hair, hauling her upward and screaming across his cantle. "Keep close!" he shouted to Fyana as he lunged for the gateway road leading from the square.

"No spears!" came a voice from behind him. "He has the queen!" Gasam had scrambled to his feet and stood with a hand to his bloody face. That was Ansa's last sight of the chaos in the square as he and his mount disappeared between ruined buildings, with Fyana close behind.

With one hand holding Larissa down and the other grasping his sword, he had to ride without reins. The thunder of hoofs rang from the ruined walls as people, mostly laboring prisoners, scattered from their path. They rode through the gate and out into the camp, where men goggled at them, but no one tried to stop them. The situation was too bizarre for anyone to take action. They kept galloping for two miles, during which time Ansa managed to steer his sword back into its sheath and resume control of his reins. On a hilltop overlooking the ruined city, they drew rein.

"You cannot ride double any longer," Fyana gasped. "Look!" She pointed behind them. A line of riders had passed through the army camp and galloped along their trail.

Larissa chuckled. "My husband comes for you," she said. "This time, you will not be so fortunate. He will turn you over to his women, and they will torture you and eat you. It is what they do. I have seen it." Ansa dumped her to the ground and she lay there, smiling up at him.

"I can ride no farther with you," he said, "but I can still

kill you." He drew his sword once more. Its tip bore red stains.

Fyana looked at him coolly. "Could you?"

Larissa still smiled up at him, unafraid. "Go ahead. Let this be your great warrior feat. Tell your father that you slew the woman he loved and left his mortal enemy alive."

Ansa glared at her for a while, then, slowly, he resheathed his sword. "No. I cannot kill you."

"I thought so. You have Hael's blood and you are a weakling like him."

"Don't press it," Fyana advised. "I have no warrior scruples to overcome."

"Run back to your father, boy," Larissa said. "We will come for you soon enough. And," she turned to Fyana, "we will come for *you* sooner than that. You are a remarkable person. I wish you had thrown in with us instead of with this wretched plainsman."

"I said I cannot kill you," Ansa told her, "but I can still take care of the rest of the job." He took his great bow from its case and strung it. This was an awkward task for a mounted man, but he accomplished it easily. Then he selected an arrow as he eyed the approaching riders.

"No!" Fyana said. "Let's ride now. They're getting too close."

"They are miserable riders," Ansa said, "and they can't shoot. As long as I have three cabo-lengths of lead at the start, I can outride them all day."

"You may fancy yourself the world's greatest rider," Fyana said, "but I am not. Let's go."

"Soon," he said. He rode twenty paces away, so that Larissa would have no opportunity to disturb his aim. The riders were almost within range. He began his draw. Gasam was easy to recognize. He was an even worse rider than the others, and the great splash of blood decorating him was visible even at such a distance. He was, naturally, in front, although a pair of young riders rode almost at his stirrups.

Fifty more rode behind him, and hundreds more were pouring from the camp to join in the pursuit.

Ansa nocked arrow to string and raised the bow. Slowly, he began his draw, his trained eye and mind making the lightning calculations of speed and motion, arc and trajectory, without conscious thought. The thumb of his string hand touched his ear and the string touched his mouth. He held for another two seconds, then released.

The arrow sped in an incredible, graceful arc, first upward, then descending. It was perfect, he thought. Nothing could save Gasam now.

But one of the flankers saw it coming. The youth spurred ahead, a better rider than his king and on a faster animal. He swerved in front of Gasam just in time to receive the arrow in his own chest. The young warrior reeled and fell, and the riders behind, Gasam included, had to rein in to the side to avoid a pileup.

Cursing, Ansa rode back to the woman. "Gasam! Someone else always does his dying for him. Let's go!"

Larissa smiled. "You can't kill us. We will come for you, in our own good time."

Ansa smiled back. "I spoiled his looks, though. Time will do the same for you. Farewell." They left the queen white-faced behind them.

The scarred moon was rising when they halted to rest their mounts. Pursuit was far behind them, if indeed Gasam was bothering to pursue.

"We have to ride north," Ansa said. "They—"

"A moment," she interrupted. "Are you well now? Have you recovered from being tied up and mistreated for days?"

"Yes. A little sore, but they didn't torture me except with talk."

"Good." She swung a hand behind her and brought it around, slapping him almost hard enough to topple him from his saddle.

, "What . . . ?" He was too shocked to speak further.

"That's for falling into such an obvious trap and making me come rescue you!" She gave him another slap, almost as hard. "And that's for taunting them to their faces when I most wanted you to be meek and humble, while I was gulling them! And I'd slap you again for playing warrior games back there instead of dumping that awful woman as soon as we were clear of the camp and riding like a madman, but I think I've broken my hand."

"But I'm a warrior," he said.

"That doesn't mean you *have* to be a fool! By all the spirits that live, Ansa, if I didn't love you so much I'd wish I'd left you there! I might change my mind yet."

He pulled her to him and kissed her hard enough to break teeth. "My fearless one! What need have I of wisdom when I have you?" He kissed her again, more gently but just as ardently. It was Fyana who broke away.

"Later. After we're sure we are safe."

"Nobody is safe," he pointed out. "I was about to say that we must ride north. Fyana, they know where the steel mine is! Somehow, Larissa's spies have found it!"

"I am from the Canyon, not the plains," she said. "We care nothing for your steel mine, nor for who owns it."

"You should," he insisted. "You have seen how powerful Gasam is. With the mine in his hands, he will control most of the steel in the world. He will be able to arm his entire army with steel weapons. What could stand before him then?"

"Warriors!" She snorted. "You always think that a better weapon is everything. It is not, I assure you."

"They will go to the Canyon first," he pointed out. "It is much closer than the plains, and the desert separates us from him. And, Larissa will still think that you people own the secret of eternal youth. She will not believe anything else. You yourself told me of the power of the will to believe."

She sighed. "I suppose you are right. Well, we have to pass through Canyon land anyway. I will ask our Elders what is to be done."

"And then will you ride with me, back to the plains?"

"Yes, if the Elders permit it." Then, smiling, "What's the use? Yes, I'll go with you even if they forbid it."

Now he grinned. "Then let's ride north." But before they began he turned to her once more. "Fyana, how old are you, and can you really restore youth?"

"Do you think I am going to tell you everything?" She spurred her cabo and they headed north by the light of the scarred moon.

MORE BESTSELLING
FANTASY FROM TOR